TWO WRONGS

KIMBERLY CARRILLO

Copyright © 2023 by Kimberly Carrillo

All rights reserved.

No part of this book may be reproduced or distributed in any form or by any electronic or mechanical means, including information storage and retrieval systems, without written permission from the author, except for the use of brief quotations in a book review and certain other noncommercial uses permitted by copywriter law. This is a work of fiction. Any similarities to persons living or dead are purely coincidental.

Edited by: Linnea Valle
Cover by: RECreatives, Renee Ericson

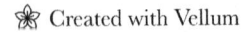

❊ Created with Vellum

This one is for my ex.
You said I dreamed too big, and thought too much of myself.
How does my dust taste?
How high can I reach?
Fucking watch me.

Special Note to Readers

This book contains some heavy topics that may be upsetting to some readers. Please be advised about the following contents of this book so you can decide whether or not to continue reading:

- Substance abuse by a loved one
- Cheating (not between the main couple)
- Emotional abuse of a spouse.
- Divorce
- Attempted suicide/self harm
- Explicit sex
- Profane language
- Smoking
- Exhibitionism
- Use of the word "daddy" by heroine to refer to the hero
- Sexual dominance/light bondage
- spanking
- Pregnancy/breeding kink

1

Wren

"It has to be perfect," I say to my best friend while I search my mother's old cookbook for ideas.

"You're going to cook? Are you sure, Wren? You know the smoke detector isn't the timer, right?" Audrey teases.

"Har dee har. I started one fire. I've been practicing since then, but I could still use some help. Please help me," I beg.

"Why are you putting so much pressure on this anniversary? You aren't pregnant are you?"

My stomach drops. I've thought about kids a lot over the last year. Liam keeps insisting we are too young, and don't have enough money to support a kid. It isn't a realistic desire, but having lost my family, I long to start one of my own. Of course, Liam is right. Now is not the best time to have a baby to look after. Kids are expensive, and he already works so hard to provide for us. My job as a receptionist doesn't help as much as I had hoped, but I can't sit at home all day doing nothing. Liam takes care of our finances, and he is even willing to work extra hours to try and make ends meet. The least I can do is stop badgering him to start a family that would only make him even more stressed out.

That's why I want everything to be perfect tonight. To show him how much I appreciate the life we've been building together for the last five years. It hasn't been easy and yet here we are, defying the odds everyone gave us when we married right after I graduated from high school.

Liam is a year older than me. He chose to go to the local community college, even though he had a full ride scholarship for football to Western State, just so he could stay close to me. At the time it seemed romantic, but I often find myself wondering if he regretted not going to school.

Sometimes I do. I got accepted into my dream university, Central Valley, and I even managed to get a scholarship. Even with tuition and books covered there were still expenses like housing and food. Still, there are loans, part-time jobs, all sorts of ways to fund an education if you're willing to work hard enough. Instead of accepting my place in the freshman class, I accepted Liam's marriage proposal. Liam thought we shouldn't start our lives out in debt, and I gave up on the idea of going away to school. I did manage to get my AA degree from the community college, and someday I'd like to continue my education.

The last six months have been the hardest. It's a rocky patch, but I know we can overcome it. That starts with the perfect anniversary dinner. All we need is a chance to reconnect. Hopefully rekindle our love life, which has been nearly non-existent except for one drunken night after one of Audrey's parties.

"I can't tonight. Really, Wren, don't you think maybe you're forcing this relationship to work? If you hadn't gotten married so young, you'd have probably broken up by now. Most people don't stay with their high school sweetheart."

Counting to ten, I force myself not to blow up at my best friend. Other than Liam, she is the only person on this planet to know pre-tragedy Wren. The carefree girl who dreamed big and lived fearlessly. I buried that girl with my parents the summer before my senior year. My mom's younger sister came and stayed with me until I turned eighteen, but it wasn't the same.

The only constants in my life are Audrey and Liam. If sometimes I have to bite my tongue to keep from lashing out when she thinks she's being helpful, it's worth it to maintain our friendship. I know she's only saying it because she cares about me. She's held my hand through every attempt I've made lately to save my marriage.

Still, I couldn't say nothing and let her think I agree my marriage isn't worth the effort. "We've talked about this. I love him."

"You shouldn't have to twist yourself into someone you aren't for him. Not even Liam is worth that."

"It isn't like cooking and cleaning fundamentally changes who I am as a person. I like taking care of him," I push back.

"If you say so. Look, I've got to go. There's a billion things I still need to do before I can close up the shop for the day," she says, and we end the call.

My kitten, a stray that had shown up on the doorstep a few weeks ago, jumps up on the table. I scratch behind her ears. "It looks like we're on our own."

It's Saturday, and the office I work at is closed. Liam and I used to spend our weekends wrapped up in each other. I guess even though we're young, the newness has worn off. Instead of spending time together, we avoid each other. Rather, Liam avoids me.

"Deep breaths, Wren. It'll be okay. Just keep breathing," I tell myself.

I throw myself into making dinner. I settle on a roast chicken, asparagus and baby potatoes. It's one of the few meals my mother taught me to make well before she died. I've avoided making it for years, because the last time she was right next to me. The night Liam came over to meet them.

What I wouldn't give to be able to turn to her now. I'd snuggle up next to her, and let her stroke my hair the way she used to do. The smells fill the kitchen, and my eyes fill with tears. "I miss you, mom," I whisper.

Silence answers me back, like it has so profoundly for the last five and a half years. Never has it been as loud as the last six months. Before that I had Liam to hold me together. He hasn't been that person for me for a while now. Now he comes home after I'm in bed, and wakes up as I'm leaving for work. When I try to call him during the day he either doesn't answer, or he is too busy to talk more than a few minutes.

I'm losing him. I know it. The sad thing is, I think he's only still here because he doesn't want to be the guy who leaves the orphan girl. It proves how little he sees me, because I'd never let him stay with me for anything less than love.

Either we find it again, hopefully tonight, or we let each other go.

THE SECOND HAND on the clock ticks loudly throughout the apartment. Each click mocks me for sitting at our table, watching wax slide down the candles that have burned down to nubs. The food sits on our plates, cooling and looking less appetizing as the night progresses.

I turn over my cell phone for the dozenth time and find the same thing I did the eleven times before, nothing.

Eight o'clock turns to nine, and nine to ten, and yet my husband doesn't bother to call or text. The candles flicker out and I give up. Dumping our dinners in the trash, I grab my purse.

Hale Automotive, my father-in-law's auto shop, is only a couple miles away from our apartment. In Harriston, everything is only a couple of miles away from everything else. The shop has been closed for five hours, and all the people are usually long gone by six. Yet, I find myself hoping for some car related emergency that has kept him for hours after closing.

Liam's flashy red Mustang is not parked in his usual spot on the side of the building. Pulling over, I slam my hand into the steering wheel over and over. My car door is wrenched open and my seat belt ripped off.

I look up into the dark eyes of my father-in-law, Griffin Hale. "What the hell are you doing throwing a fit in front of my shop this late at night? Did my son bring home the wrong kind of flowers for your anniversary?"

"What flowers?" I scoff.

He barks a short laugh. "Is that it then? He forgot the flowers. You know, being married isn't about the gifts you get, but the time you spend together."

Sitting in my seat while he leans above me makes me feel small and trapped. Okay, so I am rather on the short side. Griffin stands nearly a foot taller than me, seeing as how I'm only five-four. I climb out and duck under his arm.

"I wouldn't know. I've barely seen my husband lately. Tonight I can't seem to find him at all."

I try to move past him, but he grabs my arms and pins me against the car. "What do you mean you can't find him? What did you do?"

My nostrils flare, and I force myself not to stomp on his foot to make him let go of me. "What did *I* do? Because it had to be me, right? So what is it now? He couldn't find his favorite shirt because I didn't do his laundry? Or, how about let's tease me because at nineteen I didn't know how to cook, since my mom thought we'd have loads of time for her to teach me. Maybe you'd also like to complain that I work too much, but somehow also not enough."

Griffin steps back and I start pacing in front of my car. I can't stop ranting now even if I try. It feels too good to let all of this out.

"I know it's not that I won't have sex with him. I have been practically throwing myself at him, and he won't touch me. So what is it? Because I can't fucking figure it out!"

His fists are clenched by his sides, and I know I've pushed him too far. "I warned you that getting married too young was going to be a problem. People change the most when they're young."

"What do you want me to do about it now? Am I supposed to stop loving him because I'm only twenty-three? Are you trying to tell me he doesn't love me? Tell me, Griffin, because right now I don't have a clue what is going on."

"Calm down, okay?" He holds his hands in front of him like he's trying to ward off a wild animal. "We'll find him. I'm sure there's an explanation for everything."

He moves back to his truck. The door creaks and protests as it opens. I stand there staring at him. "What are you waiting for? Get your ass in the truck and let's find my son."

"Great. This night didn't suck enough, now I get to be stuck in a car with your grumpy ass," I grumble under my breath.

He stops and narrows his eyes. "What did you say?"

I paste on the fakest smile I'm capable of and lie through my teeth. "I said lead the way."

He grunts something about me being a smart mouthed brat, and before I can run away he barrels straight for me, throws me over his shoulder, probably exposing my scandalous underwear to God and anyone looking, before dropping my ass on the cracked bench seat of his truck.

"I suggest you cut out the attitude. My tolerance doesn't stretch far where you're concerned," he snaps at me.

"Well that's a news flash. The grouchy, asshole of a father-in-law doesn't like me," I toss back at him.

Griffin watches me out of the corner of his eye while he climbs into the cab of the truck. "What has gotten into you. You've never been this mouthy before."

"I ran out of fucks to give earlier tonight. This is who you get," I say looking out the window.

We drive through the town, passing by all of the places Liam likes to go when he's not at work. Places I didn't even know he frequented. I have a little bit of hope when we don't find his car in the parking lot of the Pretty Kitty, the one and only strip club we have in town, but the fact his father thought he might be there depresses me.

I really don't like the way Griffin is starting to look at me with pity. I much prefer it when he looks at me with disdain as he has since Liam and I eloped after I graduated high school and he convinced me to give up my scholarship.

We wind through town, and end up at the park down by the river. It's well after dark, and the park is closed, in theory, although teenagers are known to hook up in the dark corners from time to time. It's where Liam used to take me in high school when my parents were still alive.

I hold my breath. One way or another my world is about to come crashing down. I can feel it in the air, like it's charged with impending doom. Either he's here, and the reason for that can't be good, or he's been in an accident and no one has been able to let either of us know.

The headlights of the truck flash on the reflector, and my heart falls to my feet. I'd recognize that cherry red paint job anywhere. Harriston is a blue collar town. Here we drive trucks or modest sedans. Large families pile into vans. No one, except my husband, drives a sports car.

Griffin stops several feet from his car, and I throw open the passenger door and jump out. I hear him shouting for me to stop, but I can't. I won't. My feet take me to see what I know will torture me for a long time to come.

The windows are fogged up, so it's hard to see clearly. That, unfortunately, doesn't prevent me from seeing two bodies writhing in the back seat. His ass pumps as he works himself into her. Whoever she is. Likely someone I know, but she has her head tossed back in ecstasy as he works his impressive cock in and out of her. A cock I'd thought had only ever been inside of me.

We were each other's firsts, and I'd stupidly thought we'd be each other's only. I didn't feel cheated at that prospect. It was another thing about our relationship that had, until moments ago, made me feel special and cherished. When I gave myself to him, I gave him everything. He was my every fantasy, every sexual experience, and now I realize I am not his.

A tortured scream rips from my chest as I fall to my knees. Griffin runs to my side and scoops me up off the ground. The only thing I can think is, he was right. We were too young. Doomed before we started.

I look up at him, my green eyes flooding with tears. "Take me to my car, please." My voice sounds rough to my own ears, but the last person I want to be around now is the man who looks too much like my husband, and probably knew all along this was going on.

"Are you happy?" I ask him when he helps me back into his truck.

His large hands squeeze the steering wheel. "What about any of that would make me happy?"

I can't look at him anymore, and turn to glare out the window. I see Liam stumble out of the car, pulling on his pants. He sees me, and the look of horror on his face gives me no satisfaction.

"You get what you want now. Me gone," I finally answer Griffin.

"Wren, if you thought I wanted you gone, you are less perceptive than I gave you credit for."

Him thinking I'm perceptive at all brings on a fit of hysterical laughter. "I just spent my day cooking and cleaning to make a special anniversary dinner for my husband who apparently would rather be balls deep in some whore in the back of his Mustang. I think it's safe to say I'm the least perceptive person around."

2

Wren

I don't know if Liam will rush home and try to feed me some bullshit about what he was doing. I do know I don't want to be here if he decides to come home.

Pain lances my middle as I think of that word. *Home.* A word that connotes a place where you belong and feel safe. Neither of those sentiments applies to these walls anymore. Not for me.

I'm not sure where to go, or who to turn to. Grabbing my phone I try to call Audrey. It's late, but she's a bit of a night owl. She doesn't answer, so I do the only thing I can, leave a message.

"Audrey, it's me, Wren. I mean, you know that because caller ID, but—" I take a deep breath. "I need a place to stay. I'm leaving Liam. Please, call me."

Liam pays our bills, and insists I use cash for all my necessary purchases. Thankfully I never got around to cashing my most recent check. Since my boss is most decidedly living in the Stone Age, he has yet to switch to direct deposit, something I thought was annoying until just now. I open the cookie jar where I keep the household funds for groceries and such. I won't be doing the grocery shopping anymore, at least not for this apartment. I grab the measly eighty dollars inside the jar, and toss it into my purse. Next, I load my kitten into her carrier, and throw as much as I can grab into a suitcase I retrieve from the closet.

My heart pounds in my chest, as if any moment he'll come crashing through the door to stop me. Funny, all night long I'd wanted him to walk in here, and now it's the thing I dread the most.

Fifteen minutes is more time than I want to spend here, and even though I don't have everything, I have everything I can carry. It has to be enough. After all, they're only things. They can be replaced, unlike the years we've spent in this apartment. I thought we were building a life together, but I was wrong.

Never have I resented the things I gave up to be with him. He meant more than some degree, or the chance to see if my "little hobby" as he calls it could be more. No more. With that thought, I grab my laptop I use to design custom merchandise, and walk out.

Griffin has pulled up behind my car and watches as I descend the stairs and set my meager possessions down by my trunk. I ignore him until he asks, "Wren, what are you doing?"

"Nothing you need to worry about. I'm just glad right now that I never changed my last name. Liam is already living the single life, I'm going to make it easier for him and step aside."

His eyes narrow, a look I'm used to from him. "You're not going to fight for your marriage."

I laugh and hold my arms out to my sides. "I've been fighting. Every day for six months. After tonight, it's clear to me this won't work if I'm the only one who is trying. Message received. I'm gone."

"Where are you going to go?"

A sob breaks free, and I slap a hand over my mouth. My eyes sting with unshed tears, but I refuse to give a Hale man my tears. "That's not your concern. I'll be fine."

A muscle ticks in his jaw. "Of course you will, because you're coming home with me."

The need to sob once again becomes hysterical laughter. "No I'm not."

I throw my stuff in the back of my car, and gently place my kitten in the front seat. Then I wheel around and face Griffin. "Move your truck. I'm leaving."

"Do you even have any money?" He starts to grab his wallet.

"Don't insult me by trying to give me money. Liam might not let me have access to our bank accounts, but I won't take your money either."

His eyes flash, and I hold my breath. This man's mood swings make me queasy. "What do you mean he won't give you access to the bank accounts?"

"He says I'm bad with money. He takes my check and pays the bills. I use cash for groceries and such. I still have my last paycheck, so I'll make due until next payday. Now, can I please go? I don't want to be here if he decides to come home."

"You sound like you aren't sure. Where else would he go?"

I take a deep breath. Somehow it hurts worse imagining him in another woman's bed. Fucking in his car was cheap and tawdry. The kind of sex one has with a mistress, but imagining him with privacy and time to properly make love to whoever he's been seeing makes me sick. "I think you can guess that he's probably got options."

"Doubtful. There was a reason they were in the back of his car. She's probably got a boyfriend or a husband," he scoffs.

I nod. "Maybe, but that's no longer my problem. Let me go, Griffin."

His head dips to let me know he's heard the resolution in my voice. Without another word he steps back and gets back in his truck. The moment he pulls away I back out and speed out of town.

I've got two days before I'm supposed to be back at work. Two days to figure out my shit and decide what to do.

MY PHONE STARTS to ring around midnight. Even though I have no plans to answer, I look at the screen. All of my missed calls are from Griffin's number. Since I don't plan on speaking to him either, and knowing Liam has not once tried to call me, I turn off my phone.

The motel I'm staying at is clean, and out of the way. I made sure to get off the main highway to prevent either of the Hale men from looking for me, not that either cared enough to try.

By Sunday night I am still at a loss for what to do next. The only thing I do know is that I need to find a place to live, and in order to pay for that I have to go back to work.

I'm not sure why I'm surprised to see Liam standing outside of my office first thing in the morning holding two coffees. Maybe it's because it's the first time in half a year he's sought me out on purpose. I do know this time it's unappreciated.

I shoulder past him and use my keys to open the door to the office. "What do you want, Liam?"

Of course now that he's unwanted he refuses to take a hint and leave. Idly, I wonder if this is how he felt every time I threw myself at him. How stupid I must have seemed to him, begging for scraps of his attention, parading around in skimpy lingerie, all while he was getting his dick wet somewhere else.

Mercifully, there's a routine to opening the office. My boss, Carl, runs the local insurance office. Most people get their quotes and policies online now, so we don't get a lot of traffic, but there are a few technophobes such as Carl who insist on conducting business in person. I start a pot of coffee, turn on lights, and begin sorting the mail that came in over the weekend.

Liam slaps his hand down on the counter. "Would you stop ignoring me, damnit! Where have you been all weekend?"

I spin around. My long dirty blonde hair fans around me. "You lost the right to ask me that question."

"Bullshit. You're still my wife, now tell me where you were all weekend."

"Don't worry. I won't be your wife much longer. You'll be free to fuck every woman in town. Except me of course. Not anymore."

"Wren, it was one mistake. You can't throw away five years of marriage over one mistake." His tone sounds like he thinks I'm overreacting.

In the past he'd tell me not to feel how I'm feeling, and I'd question everything until even I wasn't sure how I felt. Not this time. I'm not going to let him make me feel small and stupid for being upset about this.

"It was our anniversary on Friday, did you even remember that? How much do you think I value five years of marriage after I catch my husband fucking another woman on the anniversary of the day he promised to be faithful to me?"

Liam crosses his arms, and stands in front of me, blocking my path out of the kitchen. "I want you to come home tonight. We'll talk. I'll make this up to you."

There's nothing inside of me. Anger will come again, I'm sure. There will be sadness once that fades, but right now I'm blissfully numb. "There is no making this up to me. I know when I'm not wanted. Maybe I'm a bit slow to figure it out this time, but I did."

I steel myself for the feel of his body as I slip around him. He grabs my wrist and holds on to it tight. No matter how hard I tug, he won't let go, and I don't tell him he's hurting me. "We can work through this. Please, Wren. We'll go to therapy, anything, but I won't give you a divorce."

"Why would you want me to stay? You've ignored me for six months now. And no, I don't believe this was a one time mistake. Six months."

He hangs his head. "I know I've fucked up. I took you for granted, but I don't want to lose you."

"Who is she?" I don't know why I ask him this. Harriston is a small town. We might not know every person in town, but we know most of them.

"Who isn't important. She's just a nobody," he mumbles.

Liam always mumbles when he lies. I used to think it was adorable. A sign he'd never lie to me, because he was so bad at it. I guess he's gotten better with practice, but he's thrown off by being caught.

"I don't believe you. But you're right, who she is isn't important. It wasn't her who was supposed to be faithful to me. You were my family." My voice wavers, and I clamp my mouth shut. Liam does not get my tears. He will get nothing from me ever again.

"I'm still your family, Wren."

I shake my head. "I need you to leave, Liam. I've got a life to move on with. Please let me do it."

"I'm not going to let you go."

"You didn't," I say. "You threw me away. There's a difference. I'm just choosing to stay gone."

Carl walks in, ending whatever argument Liam was going to make next. "I'll see you later," he promises and finally walks out the door.

THE DAY CRAWLS BY, as they usually do. At lunch I go and open a bank account in my own name and deposit my check. During my break I call on some ads for homes for rent and set up an appointment for after I get off work.

Dolores is an old lady who has been a customer of Carl's for decades. Her late husband invested in real estate, thinking the town would grow. It never did take off the way he hoped, but the rental properties he left her supplement her social security and provide her with a comfortable life. Her home is the largest in town, and even has a mother-in-law cottage on her property.

She offers me her elbow as we walk around her white farmhouse. In the rear, in the middle of one of the best landscaped yards in town, is a small home. There's a covered porch, shutters, and flowers planted around the foundation. The buttery yellow paint adds to the cheery appeal, and I'm instantly in love with the place. Which makes my heart sink, because on my salary there's no way I'll be able to afford to rent it.

Dolores sees the look on my face and pats my hand.

"Don't get that look on your face dear. I'm sure that husband of yours and you make enough to rent it."

The tears I've so valiantly fought for days spill over. Through hiccuping sobs I give her the abbreviated version of why I'm renting on my own.

She straightens as much as she can to her four-foot-ten inch height. "Well, we can't have you homeless or thinking of leaving town. Unless you decide to go to school. I suppose that would be okay. You're still young. That would be a choice, but if you stay, we won't let that man get you back because of not having nowhere else to go. I was friends with your grandma, and she'd whoop my fanny if I left you to fend for yourself."

"I'm confused. What are you saying?" I ask her. I never knew my grandmother, but the part of me that is tired of being alone in the world relishes discovering this thin familial connection.

"Well, dearie. I'm old, as I'm sure you've noticed. If you wouldn't mind running the occasional errand for me. Like getting my groceries when you get your own and picking up my meds I'd say I can rent the place to you for five hundred a month. Of course utilities and internet are included."

I blink. "Are you sure? This place is beautiful. You could probably ask at least twice that amount."

She nods her silvery head. "I'm positive dear. It gets lonely around here. My grandkids are grown now, and they don't come around as much as I'd like. My kids are all enjoying empty nests and traveling around the world. It would be mighty fine to have a bit of company from time to time. Not that you have to entertain me, but I certainly wouldn't be put out by it. If you'd like, I can teach you some of the recipes your grandma taught your mom. She and I used to cook together for the soldiers who were stationed in town. We had a little restaurant near the base. Of course both have long since closed up."

I smile at her as she rambles. One thing about Dolores is she takes a long path to get to her point, but her mind is still sharp. She always gets to it, and I don't mind taking the scenic route from time to time. "You don't know how much that would mean to me."

"Would you like to see the place before you decide?"

"Of course I want to see it, but I already know I'm going to take it. This feels like home, and I haven't had that in a long time now."

Her answering smile is sad. "I understand that more than you know. My Benjamin was the center of my world, and when he died this place felt so hollow. Love has a way of turning four walls into a home, and when it's gone all you're left with is a building."

Another tear slips free. "That's hauntingly beautiful."

Her gnarled hand reaches for the knob and opens the bright white door. Inside is as cheery as the outside. A cream and yellow striped couch faces the window. There's some side tables in a gray washed wood. The pine floors are a warm honey, and the rest is brightened by white walls and cabinets. The kitchen counter in the open plan room is a light gray and white granite. It's the home I'd have designed for myself when Liam and I first married. Having it alone is bittersweet, but somehow also gratifying.

She sees the look on my face and nods. "The best revenge is living well. My Ben and I had a great marriage. I won't pretend to understand what you're dealing with in that respect, but my oldest daughter Jessy went through a nasty divorce from her first husband. The family rallied around her and helped her thrive, and now I'll do it for you. You, dearie, will live well. You're a Parker. That's some strong stock if I ever met any. And when you get to feeling down, remember there are still men like your daddy around."

I look to the ceiling and blink several times. I've already cried more around her than I have since the first couple months I felt Liam pulling away from me. She pats my arm again. "I don't mean to make you cry. Let's get you settled in."

I freeze in place. In all the excitement of finding a place, I forgot one major detail. "I have a cat. A kitten actually. Is that going to be a problem?"

"What is the kitten's name?" she asks me.

"She doesn't have one. Honestly, I wasn't sure Liam was going to let me keep her."

Dolores makes a tsk sound. "Never, ever, stay with a man when you have to use the words 'let'. As my granddaughter would say, you are a grown ass woman."

I laughed for the first time in days. "How about you go grab this kitty and let's pick her out a proper name."

"She's in my car. I checked out of the motel I hid out in over the weekend."

It only took one trip to the car to grab the few things I grabbed when I left. I let the small calico cat out of her carrier and the disposable litter box I'd picked up over the weekend.

Dolores moves to the sofa and is immediately graced with feline affection. "Aren't you just a little love," she coos.

"What do you think of the name Patches?" I ask her.

She shrugs. "It doesn't matter what I think, dearie. What our friend thinks is the real question."

She turns to the kitten. "Do you like the name Patches?"

The kitten stretches out and starts making biscuits on Dolores's lap. "I think she's fond of it."

I nod. "That's settled then." I scoop up the kitty and

hold her to my cheek. "You've got a name and a forever home now girl."

"And so do you," Dolores says to me.

"Thank you," I whisper through a tight throat.

"No thanks necessary. You and I need each other, and together we'll see you through this."

3

Griffin

"Where have you been for the last couple days?"

My son jumps at the sound of my voice. "I've been thinking."

"A little late for that. Maybe you should have tried that before you fucked around on your wife."

"What do you care? You've never liked Wren anyway. You said from the beginning I was too young, that I'd regret settling down so early. Didn't you say I needed to know what was out there before I committed to one woman? Well, congratulations, dad, you were right."

"Don't lay this on me. No matter what I said to you, that doesn't excuse cheating on your wife. That isn't the kind of man I raised you to be."

He rolls his eyes. "When did you raise me? You've spent your life under the hood of a car. I raised myself."

"I've done the best I could with you, but you know what? I'm going to let you go ahead and claim responsibility for the man you have become, because I sure as shit wouldn't have raised a fucking cheater."

As for the accusation that I've never liked Wren, well, I

wish that were true. I didn't notice her much when they started dating in high school. She was a child, and I didn't expect a high school relationship to last.

When her parents were in a fatal car accident right before the beginning of her senior year, we all rallied around to help her cope. I watched my son spend more and more time with her. She seemed good for him, and I hoped he was good for her. She transformed overnight from a young girl to a woman with adult problems.

Her parents weren't wealthy people, and the mortgage on their house was too much for an eighteen year old student to maintain, so the house was sold, and the small profit from the sale let her finish school without worrying about bills. She handled every obstacle with her head held high, and she never buckled under the weight of her grief.

In truth, I've admired her for a long time. I know Liam lets on that he wanted to play college football, and probably let her think he gave it up for her. Perhaps, if she hadn't been so grief stricken, she might have noticed the fact he had no interest in sitting on the bench on a college team. In her eyes Liam was always larger than life.

I know he told her he failed his classes at the community college because of her needing him that first year. I should have stopped it then. He used her guilt to convince her to stay with him and give up her scholarship. I do believe he loves her, in his own selfish way, but if he really loved her the way she deserved, he would have convinced her to take the scholarship she earned.

Now I can see the anger I carried was directed in the wrong place. She believes I don't think she's good enough for my son, when the opposite is true. That's a hard pill to swallow, resenting your own child. Seeing what he has, and wanting it for yourself. Knowing neither of us were good for her, and still wanting to be the one to care for her.

I can't be that for her. Not that she sees me that way. I'm her asshole father-in-law and nothing more. I can't ever be anything more. Still, I couldn't help trying to push her down the path she needed to follow. Wren Parker is too good for this town, and far too good for the two of us.

If I thought my son would follow her to school, encourage her rather than hold her back, I would have celebrated their relationship. Lust and love aren't the same thing. I'm old enough to know that.

Caring about Wren doesn't mean I'm in love with her. I've gone down that road before, and I'll never be vulnerable like that again. But lust, yeah, I feel that. No heterosexual man can look at her and not want her.

She's tiny, and not just in height. I believe a better word is delicate. Her face could turn even a rugged grease monkey such as myself into a poet. I could write verses describing her expressive green eyes, high cheekbones, upturned nose, and plump bow shaped lips. The body she hides under oversized sweatshirts and cardigans is lush with tits that could fill even my giant hands, a trim waist, wide hips and a plump ass. Wren is a walking wet dream, except apparently for my dumbass son who actually has the privilege of touching her.

Even if she weren't married to my son, her age would put her firmly in the off limits category, but she is married to him. Noticing her is wrong, jerking off to thoughts of her makes me disgusting, but as long as no one knows the vile thoughts that run through my mind I can live with it. Making her think I hate her is a necessary evil.

Every time I see my words hit her I hate myself a little bit more, but it's far better she believes them than know the perverse thoughts I entertain when she's near. Regret gnaws at me now though. She's out there somewhere, trying for the first time to make it on her own. Which reminds me of something she said Friday night.

"What did Wren mean when she said you won't let her have access to your bank accounts?" I ask Liam.

I know I pay him well. I've wondered many times why they live in the worst apartments in town, and why she drives the same car her parents got her when she turned sixteen while my son drives a flashy Mustang. The signs were there from the beginning, but I stupidly let him convince me she was the one who had a spending problem.

"That's none of your business."

I grab his shoulder and force him to face me. "Please tell me you aren't using your joint money to spend on your girlfriend."

He shakes my hand free. "Stay out of it. This is between me and my wife."

"I don't think you're going to have a wife for much longer. Friday night was bad. How long have you been seeing another woman?"

Charlie, my oldest friend, and best mechanic stops near us. He slowly wipes his greasy hands off on a rag. Both of us are covered with random smears of grease and blood from the inevitable cuts we get while fixing cars. My son, on the other hand, is shower-fresh.

"It wasn't my place to say anything," Charlie begins. "The boy has been stepping out for months now. I felt bad for the girl, but I wasn't sure what to say about it."

I turn to Liam. "Months?"

He shrugs. "I got caught up in something. I didn't know how to fight it. I just needed to work it out of my system. She didn't need to find out."

"Who? Please tell me you weren't stupid enough to take up with someone from town."

Liam shakes his head. "Who doesn't matter."

I throw the first thing within reach. A wrench, unfortunately, and it crashes through the window on the back door. "It fucking does matter. People talk in small towns. How did you plan to get this out of your system and get your marriage back on track if she were to find out about this? I hope you have a plan, because she knows now, and I don't think she's going to be forgiving and forgetting."

"I managed for seven months and she didn't figure it out! Just stay out of it. I can fix this. Wren loves me."

I force a deep breath in through my nose. I've never been this angry with him before, and it feels like shit. "If you love her, let her go. Some things can be broken too much to be fixed. You should have let her go when she got that scholarship, so for once, do the right thing by that girl and let her have a life."

"She needs me. She'll see that. I'll end things with—with that woman, and we'll be fine."

"I'm not the one you need to convince, son."

WREN'S CAR is back in town. Carl has been in the shop twice this week getting his wife's brakes fixed, and he never mentioned her absence. Which tells me she's been back since Monday at least.

I haven't seen her, but that's not unusual. It's been my practice to avoid her whenever possible, but with everything going on, the need to check on her is overwhelming. I try and tell myself I only want to make sure she's okay, that she's found a place to stay, but the excuse sounds weak even in my own head. I'm the last person she'd want to see.

I look out across the shop and see my son finally getting his hands dirty and working on a farm truck brought in for a tune up. We don't get a lot of those, because most of the farmers handle a lot of their own maintenance. This customer is one of the few farms to turn a profit now, and has neither the time nor the interest to fix this old clunker.

Liam has always been gifted with machines. I'd hoped he'd channel that talent into an engineering degree, or even a vocational certification. He's been out of high school now for six years, and he hasn't really done anything more than work here. That would be great if I thought he had an interest in taking over my business or opening a second location, but he doesn't have any interest in running Hale Automotive.

Maybe he's right, and I have failed him. God knows I didn't want him to live my life. I fought him on getting married young, because that's what I did. Of course, his mom and I got married after we knew he was on the way. At least Liam and Wren still had some of the benefits of being young. I haven't been young since the pregnancy test said, "pregnant."

This town may have always been the right fit for me, but my son has chafed at the smallness of it. Like his mother, he sees the wideness of the world around us as having endless possibilities. I should have encouraged him to travel and work that wanderlust out of his system. Hell, I should have pushed him to straight up leave. I thought he would at one point. Then Wren smiled at him one day in school, and his feet grew roots. Also like his mother, love wasn't enough to keep those roots in place. Wren became another thing trapping him here, and whether he wanted to admit it or not, he resented her for it.

Mad or not, her beauty couldn't be ignored. She is a siren, calling to him to bash himself against the rocks just to stay near her. He chose the wrong way to try and save himself, but you don't blow up your life if you're happy living it.

Maybe this is all just the wishful thinking of a forty-two-year-old man who can't stop lusting after his twenty-three-year-old daughter-in-law? What I need is to go out and meet a woman. I'm not a monk, there have been a few relationships over the years. When Liam was young I avoided serious relationships because I'd just been burned by his mother. Then I had to focus on being a father and getting my business off the ground.

There's been one reason or another to stay single. When Liam was a teenager, I had an on again off again situation with a woman who came into town for business a few times a year. By design we were never going to be serious, because for most of the year we lived in different cities hours apart. She got promoted a few years back, and what we had came to a natural end.

Since then, I've had a few arrangements with women I called when I needed a release. There were no attachments, or hurt feelings. Just two people who had an itch to scratch and walked away at the end of the night not knowing if that was the last time, or if we'd be reaching out again.

Tonight I couldn't repeat that pattern. One of them would pick up if I called, and I'd show up at her house. She'd be dressed in next to nothing when she opened the door, she'd lead me to her bedroom, and I'd fuck her as hard and long as I want until the sun comes up. The problem is most of these women bear a startling resemblance to Wren, and tonight I want to forget, not play out a fantasy.

The possibility my son's marriage is ending is too tempting. Wren may soon be single, but that doesn't make her any less off limits. Not that she'd ever want me. I've spent too many years treating her like shit just to make sure she'd stay away if my resolve should ever waiver.

Charlie pokes his head under the hood of the car I've been pretending to work on for the last twenty minutes while my mind wanders. "I think we need to go get a drink tonight."

I grunt. My mind is still too cluttered to form words.

"I'm going to take that as a yes. I don't know what is going on with you, but I'm guessing your son cheating on his woman is bringing back some bad memories. You can't go and help that girl, even though I know you feel bad for her. Liam is going to need you, and he's got to be your priority."

I drop the wrench I'm holding into the tool box. "I've been doing such a bang up job with him so far. Why not support him while he screws over his wife. It's not like she's not a fucking orphan or anything."

He grabs his pack of smokes from his pocket and taps one out. "Come out and join me."

"You know I hate those fucking things," I turn him down.

"Not asking, dickhead. Get your ass outside and have a chat with me."

I kick a creeper out of my way. "Put these fucking things away before someone breaks their face. We have lifts for fuck's sake. Why is this even out?"

"Sorry boss, the lifts are still broken," my younger mechanic, Julio, says and runs to put it away. I resist throwing any more tools, and follow Charlie out back.

He lights up the second he's outside and the noxious odor fills the air. I try and wave it away, but it's no use and I reconcile with the fact I'm going to have to endure it for this little talk.

"I don't know what has crawled up your ass. You're being a miserable bastard, more than normal. Call one of your women and sort out your shit."

"I'm not in the mood," I grumble.

"Fine, then you and me are going down to Donovan's Pub right after work. We're going to drink some beers, play some pool, and hopefully find some pretty blonde for you to take home for a few hours."

"No blondes," I snap.

His eyes narrow. "I'm trying really hard not to pick up on things I've seen over the years. Your son isn't the only one I see right through, ya know?"

I nod a slight tip of my head. "It's nothing."

He points at me with his lit cigarette between two of his fingers. "Keep it that way. Shit like that will blow up in your face. No matter how you try and argue something, it will never be right. Feel me?"

4

Wren

"You already work so much, dearie," Dolores argues as I get ready for my new part-time job.

I look myself over in the mirror. Tight black pants, ripped up and exposing a lot more skin than I'd normally show, and a tiny white t-shirt showing a sliver of my stomach make up the uniform for Donovan's Pub. It's somewhat seedy, and not in the best part of town, but it draws a larger crowd than the only other bar in town that tries to cater to the high class crowd not present in Harriston. While I might not have to show as much skin at The Garden Club, I wouldn't earn as many tips either. Plus, Donovan's was hiring, so it was a no brainer.

"It's like you said last night, the best thing I can do now is stay busy."

"I meant you should learn to knit or something," she mutters.

I turn around and give her my best deadpan look. "I might have been married for the last five years, but I'm still young. I think I need to remember that. Also, I want to earn extra money. I think it's time for me to go back to school."

Dolores claps her hands. "Oh, that makes me so happy to hear. Do you know what you want to study?"

"Maybe graphic design? I think I might like to run my own business though, so maybe I'll study business and design. I like making logos and websites, but it's just a hobby for now." There were a lot of choices for me to make now that my future was solely in my hands.

The end of my marriage still stings like a bitch, but I realized over the weekend I could either roll over and let the pain consume me, or I could roll with it and change my stars. Losing my parents like I did taught me that life goes on even when you don't want it to. There's nothing to be done about it except get on with it.

I grab my phone and my purse and start for the door. "Don't wait up for me. I'll be fine, I promise."

"I'm old. I'm sure I'll be up several times over the night. Just turn your porch light off and I'll know you made it home safely. Then I won't be one of those overbearing grandmas and come knocking in the wee hours."

I smile at her. "Sure thing."

"I'LL SHOW you to the break room so you can put your things in a locker," Donovan says as I clock in for my shift.

"Bess will be in soon and she'll show you the ropes. She can be a little crass, but you'll get used to her. She's no worse than our customers. You let me know if anyone gets out of line. I won't stand for them playing grab ass with the waitresses," he continues as we wander through the bar.

The night starts out slow. Bess comes in closer to Happy Hour, and I shadow her in taking orders and pouring drinks. Donovan is the main bartender, but both of us grab bottles of beer and pour drafts while he handles the mixed drinks. This crowd is more of a beer crowd though, so aside from the occasional whiskey and coke, there's not much demand for any fancy cocktails.

I get light-headed when I see Liam walk in the door. We haven't spoken in over a week. The last time wasn't even the morning I caught him cheating. I try to wrack my brain, but I honestly can't remember the last real conversation I had with my husband. I know it's unlikely I can escape my farce of a marriage without ever speaking to him again, but I am not going to seek him out.

I told Dolores a small white lie earlier. I'm not ready to admit that a major reason for me to get this second job was because I need extra money to pay the lawyer I found earlier this week. There's no point in waiting to file for divorce. There's no amount of counseling that will erase the image of his naked ass flexing on top of some random slut.

Once I've filed, I do plan to sign up for college. Maybe I'll even apply at Central Valley again. I doubt I can get another full scholarship, but perhaps I can still end up where I obviously should have gone in the first place.

I grab Bess's arm and pull her around the corner, out of sight of Liam. "I know you have to go over and serve those tables, but that's my soon-to-be ex-husband, and I really don't want to see him."

She pops her gum. She's a few years older than me, but dresses like a teenager. Instead of pants she chose a black pleated skirt with a neon plaid pattern that makes her look like a goth Catholic school girl. It actually works for her, but I don't think I could do it even for better tips.

"Did he cheat?" she asks.

"Yeah," I croak. "I caught him last weekend, but I think he's been cheating for a while."

She nods, her expression serious. "I'll take it tonight, but this is a small town. Everyone pretty much comes through here except for that uptight Lady's Auxiliary group. Eventually you're going to have to face him."

"I plan to get the hell out of this town as soon as the ink is dry on my divorce papers," I tell her.

"So did I, doll. Hell, maybe you'll do it. Okay, I'll take their order."

I work diligently behind the bar for nearly thirty minutes. We're slammed with customers and I fill beer after beer while I continue to watch Liam's table from the corner of my eye. I think I'm going to get away with avoiding him until there's a knock on the bar in front of me."

"Wren, what the fuck are you doing working behind the bar?"

I look up and try not to melt. His face is so familiar that for a split second I want to leap over the bar and burrow into his arms. Then I remember it. Every vivid detail flashes in front of me, and I can't make it stop.

"You don't have the right to judge me. Not anymore," I say quietly.

I hate that my voice wavers, that there's a part of me that wants to cower and hide in the break room until he's gone. It takes all the strength I have to lift my head and face him directly.

Liam throws some bills down on the bar. I look at them confused. His wallet is filled with cash. "Get your things. We are going home to talk."

I can't stop staring at the money. "I thought we were broke. How do you have so much money?"

"That's what you want to talk about? You don't need to

worry about money. I handle that stuff so you don't have to think about it. I know it stresses you out."

"But I did worry. You never let me spend a dime. I didn't even have access to our accounts, but you're out living it up with a wad of cash."

He holds out his hand. "Come home and we can talk about all of this. I know I messed up, but we can fix this. Things can go back to the way they were."

I laugh, and move to the other end of the bar. This is not the place to start screaming at him. Talk? Like I could have a civil conversation with him. I feel so stupid. It took him cheating on me to open my eyes to all the other things that were wrong about my marriage.

Liam doesn't drop it and follows me down the bar. He always was a stubborn ass. "Wren, get your things," he says through clenched teeth. He's on the verge of losing it, but this time I won't cater to his mood.

Donovan comes over and slips his hand onto my waist. It doesn't feel sexual, but it doesn't look good either. There's a very petty part of me that relishes how this must look to Liam.

"Is there a problem here?" He jerks his chin in Liam's direction.

"Just my soon-to-be ex-husband trying to tell me I can't work here," I tell him honestly.

"I'll be the one to decide that," he says. He turns his attention to Liam. "If you want to go back to your table and drink your beer, that's fine. Wren has made it clear she doesn't want to talk to you. Bess is your server, so there's no need for her to. If you can't leave her be, then you're going to have to leave."

"Get your hand off my wife," Liam demands. He's ignored everything Donovan said to him. I've seen him get like this before, and I know this night might be the shortest employment on my record.

Donovan waves at someone back at the table. I'd been so focused on Liam I hadn't noticed who else was at his table. That is made clear when Donovan shouts, "Griff, come get your boy before I have him thrown out."

The crowd parts as the towering mass of muscle that is Griffin Hale stalks toward the bar. He moves with determination and grace no mortal man should possess. I snap out of it once he turns to look at me. The scowl he reserves for me is firmly in place, and I see the muscle in his jaw clench when he too notices Donovan's arm around my side.

He drops a large hand on Liam's shoulder. "Now's not the time to beg for her forgiveness, son."

Liam tosses the hand off his shoulder. He grabs the cash off the bar and shoves it in his pocket. "Drinks are on you dad." He leans in closer to him, but his whisper carries over to me. "Get her out of here."

The door slams shut behind him, and I fidget realizing all eyes in the bar are focused on my drama. I have never liked being the center of attention, and find I like it even less now.

Griffin's eyes narrow on Donovan's hand. "I can't make her leave, but you should probably get your hand off my daughter-in-law."

"You're not her father, Griff."

Donovan looks at me with sympathy, and my stomach drops. I take a step and his hand falls. "You knew why I wanted a job here. I didn't think anything of you not asking me any questions, but it was because you knew, didn't you?"

He nods. "Liam isn't always careful when he gets a few drinks in him. I've noticed he was paying attention to a woman that wasn't you for a few months now."

"Do you know who?" I ask him.

He opens his mouth, but Griffin slams his hand on the bar. "I think that is part of the discussion Liam needs to have with her, don't you? Let him at least have the chance to salvage his marriage."

I lean over the counter, feeling bolder than I have in years. I'm not sure where this strength is coming from, but it feels good. "Listen here. There's not a damn thing he can do to make me stay married to him. There's a part of me that is sad about that, but not a single part of me is sad that you and I won't have to pretend to be family anymore. The moment I sign those divorce papers I'm putting you and your son in my rearview mirror and I'm going to throw a fucking party that I never have to look at your judgmental face again."

His nostrils flare, and I think he's going to grab me and pull me the rest of the way over the counter, but then he steps back. His expression becomes neutral, and he nods. "You should do that. Leave this town Wren, and never come back."

I swallow. I knew he hated me. It wasn't like he ever hid it, but I didn't realize how much.

"What did I ever do to you?" My voice is small, and I hate how weak I sound now after feeling so strong moments ago. Horrible or not, he and Liam were the only family I had up until Friday.

He looks me up and down, and if he feels bad I can't tell. "You exist."

A tear slips down my face, and I don't bother to try and hide it. I refuse to be ashamed of my emotions. They exist, and I'm determined to stop walking through my life numb. It's all I've known in one way or another since my parents died.

With a shaking hand, I wipe the errant tear away.

"Yeah, that's about all I've been doing. Existing. But that's going to end soon."

I'm going to finally live. I don't bother to tell him that though. What's the point? He doesn't care, and like Dolores said, the best revenge is to live well. Clearly, not something Griffin Hale will care about either way, but he's no longer my problem.

5

Griffin

"That's it," Donovan rounds the bar and shoves me back toward the door. "I want you and your son out of here. Regular customers or not, if my waitstaff can't work without being disturbed I won't have anyone working here."

I toss my hands up in surrender. "We're going."

Casting a look back over my shoulder I see Wren trying hard to compose herself. I can't get her words out of my head. *"Yeah, that's about all I've been doing. Existing. But that's going to end soon."*

I can't leave, not until I talk to her. I'll wait all night in the parking lot for her if I have to, but I have to make sure she isn't a threat to herself. Better yet, I should go back in and talk to Donovan. Maybe I can convince him to give her the rest of the night off and make sure she's okay.

Mind made up, I turn to go back inside. Charlie intercepts me before I make it to the door. "No you don't."

Liam heads toward his car. "How much have you had?" he asks my son, acting more like a father than I am.

"One beer. I'm fine," Liam snaps.

Charlie points his finger in my son's face. "Get your ass home and stay there. If you should happen to talk to your side piece, man up and fucking end that shit. If you can't do that, let Wren go."

Liam gets into Charlie's face. "You don't get to judge me old man. You've never even been married. You don't know how hard it is to be with one woman forever."

"Then you're in luck. You don't have that problem anymore," Wren says, surprising us all.

"No," Liam tries to move around Charlie. "That's not what I meant."

Charlie holds on to him to keep him from getting to Wren. "Boy, get your ass in your car and go home before you make this worse."

He thrashes against Charlie's hold. "Let me go. I need to talk to my wife."

"You need to leave her alone. Give her time to think," Charlie advises.

"I can't leave her alone. She's my wife."

"Why not? You've left me alone for six months. What's a little bit longer?" she taunts him.

Liam lunges for her, and Charlie struggles to hold on to him. I toss my keys to Charlie, who manages to catch them while trying to hold on to Liam. "Take him home. We'll get his car tomorrow."

I grab Wren's elbow. "You and I are going to have a chat." I hold out my free hand for her keys.

She clutches them tighter in her hand. "Go home, Griffin. I don't want to talk to you or your son."

"Too damn bad, baby bird." I rip the keys from her hand and drag her to her car. "Get in the car," I bark, holding her passenger door open for her.

"You're not driving my car," she argues, and drags her feet.

I laugh. "You're a fraction of my size. Either get in on your own, or I'm going to pick you up and drop your ass in there."

She assesses me. Her plump lips slip into a pout, and I know I'm about to be graced with a dose of sass. "Are you trying to fix our relationship too? Did we miss out on special daddy-daughter time? Am I being bad, daddy?"

She blinks her large kewpie doll eyes at me, no idea what effect her words are having on me. I press her against the side of her car. My body burns everywhere it touches hers. I hate her for making me feel this yearning I can never indulge. Most of all I hate her for marrying my son, because knowing she belongs to him makes me hate him a little too.

"You want me to act like your daddy, little girl?" My brain short circuits, which is my only explanation for leaning forward and whispering in her ear. "If I were your daddy, I'd spank your ass red and put you to bed for sassing me."

A throat clears behind us, and I jump back from her. My heart pounds as I turn around. "Donovan," I say, relieved. "I was just leaving. I'm making sure Wren gets home without my son bothering her anymore."

"Looks to me like the one she needs to be protected from is you." He looks at Wren, and I notice she's trembling slightly.

"I'm fine. It's like you told me inside when you said I should try my first night again tomorrow. I'm shaken up seeing Liam." She slaps my chest harder than necessary. "Griffin, is a pain in my ass, but he is just trying to make sure I'm okay."

He nods his head over and over as he's working

through whether he believes what she's saying. "Okay, take care of yourself and I'll see you tomorrow."

"We'll see about that," I mutter under my breath.

Her face screws up in confusion. "What did you say?"

"Get in the car, Wren. We're going to chat."

WREN TWISTS around in her seat after I drive away from the bar. "Where are you going? This isn't the way to my new place."

"Kinda hard to take you to your place when I don't know where it is," I point out. "Also, did you expect me to drop you off and take your car?"

"So, you're taking me to your place?" she asks in a shaking voice.

"Does that scare you, baby bird?"

"Why do you keep calling me that?"

I don't have an explanation for her, at least not one I want to give voice to. I reach out and crank up the stereo instead.

My house is a modest three bedroom, ranch style on a wooded lot just on the edge of town. I got it a few years after Melinda left. Sometimes I wonder what it would have been like if she could have held on a few years longer. Past the years we lived in a cramped one bedroom apartment in the same complex Liam and Wren rent. If she could have had faith that my job fixing cars would grow to become a stable business, would it have made a difference?

I've spent too many years being bitter. Raising a kid alone is hard, especially when you're practically a child yourself. At twenty, I was too tired from chasing a two-year-old to do much more than survive. Somehow I seem to have been frozen in that state.

That's why what Wren said struck me so deeply. I knew what she meant when she said all she's been doing is existing. I want to find out how she's going to do more than that. She's never struck me as suicidal. She fought too hard to build a life after her parents died to believe she'd try and end it just because my son made a stupid mistake. Maybe she could teach me how to leave the past behind and do more than exist as well.

I pull in my driveway and turn off the engine. My hands squeeze the steering wheel, because I know the second I get out of the car she's going to bolt. Still, I have to try. "Wren, please come in for a few minutes. I'd really like to talk to you."

She stares straight out the windshield. "Do you really think that's a good idea?" Slowly, she turns to face me, and there's a wariness in her eyes I've never seen from her before.

Disdain and hurt I've seen, but this is different. "What happened back at the bar? You've never been like that before."

I huff and stare deep into her eyes. For the first time I let her see it all. She'll be out of our lives soon, and I can't seem to hold it back from her. If she's leaving, and I pray she is, I have to give her this. To let her leave knowing I didn't hate her. She's been hurt enough by my son, it's time I stop adding to it.

She scoots away from me, as far as she can inside the car. "I don't understand what's going on."

And she wouldn't. Not completely. I would never reveal to her the depths of my depravity, but I could let her know she never did anything wrong. "Let's talk inside. I only need a few minutes, then you can be on your way."

I hold my breath while I wait for her to answer. Finally, she nods. "Okay, let's get this over with."

Yes, that is what we need to do. End this. The torment of seeing her, wanting her, and having to deny myself. Adding to it that I know she'll never be happy with my son. I can't have her here. Wren needs to spread her wings and fly far from this town.

SHE WALKS around my living room like she's never been in here before. "I know it's been a while," I say as she starts to randomly pick up some of the pictures I've got set around the room.

"I've always thought it was sweet how you have pictures of Liam all over." She looks at me, and the sadness on her face nearly brings me to my knees.

"I am sorry for what he did, but he's still my son."

She smiles, but it looks like she could just as easily cry. "I'm glad he'll have you." She pauses in front of another photo, and traces his face with her finger. "I think I'll always love him, but he doesn't love me the way I need him to."

"Are you going to be okay? What you said at the bar, about your existing ending soon, it worried me."

Wren turns to face me. "I'm going to live. If there's one good thing that will come from all this shit, it's that I'm not going to sacrifice for anyone anymore."

I walk up behind her. It's a compulsion since I know this will be the last time I'm this close to her. "You will someday," I whisper. "And you'll love every minute of it. When you hold your child in your arms, you'll gladly give everything to give them the life you didn't have."

"Maybe," she concedes. "Someday, far in the future. Once I can forget what this feels like. I don't know that I'll ever be able to trust someone again with my heart. It hurts too much when they aren't careful with it."

I nod, knowing exactly what she means. "It really fucking does."

She turns around to face me. "Did you ever get over it? Liam's mom leaving, I mean."

I shrug. It's always been there, this emptiness, but for a long time it hasn't been Melinda's face I've pictured when I close my eyes. I don't know when it happened, but it isn't her I miss. "I've gotten over her, but the anger held on longer than the love did."

"Yeah, I can see that." She finally stops moving and sits down on the sofa. I take the love seat facing her. "Is this what you wanted to talk about? My anger?" she asks.

"I just wanted to check on you. Make sure where your head was at," I say.

She rolls her eyes, and my palm tingles to warm her ass. Not an appropriate response considering I need to encourage her to leave, not play house with me.

"You just wanted to make sure I wasn't planning on hurting myself, or worse," she says, interrupting my dirty thoughts.

"Basically," I admit.

"I'm not going to start telling you all my plans, since they include divorcing your son, but you can rest easy. I'm not going to try to end my life."

I rest my arms on my legs so I can be closer to her eye level. "You need to get out of this town."

"Congratulations," she says and stands from the couch. "You're finally going to get what you want."

"Wren, that's not what I meant. I don't want you to leave here thinking you aren't wanted."

She laughs and shakes her head. "My husband has ignored me for months. He's been sleeping with another woman. I've thrown myself at him over and over again. Then there's you. Almost from the moment Liam and I got married you have treated me like the worst thing that's ever happened to him. You've never been hesitant to try and convince him to leave me. Now, you'll both get what you want, a life without me."

My jaw clenches hearing her say she's been throwing herself at him. In many ways, Liam is still a child in my mind, but I know he's not. My jealousy over hearing that has nothing to do with my fatherly feelings for my child, and everything to do with a misplaced feeling of possessiveness for this woman. It's fucked up and I need her to leave so I can let go of this sick infatuation I can't shake.

"That's not what I meant. You need to go for you. This town, my son, it's bad for you. And I was pissed off when you guys got married. He wasn't mature enough to be a husband, and you gave up too much to be his wife. He never should have asked you to give up your scholarship." That all sounds good, and it's mostly the truth. The best thing for her is to leave.

"I'll be out of here soon enough. Until then, can you keep Liam out of Donovan's? I just need some time to get some things in order."

I'm nodding before she's even finished speaking. "It's the least he can do."

"And you?"

"I'll try, baby bird."

She walks backwards toward the door. "You're confusing the hell out of me, Griffin."

I stalk her, until her back is pressed against the wood. "I know, and believe it or not, I am sorry."

"You don't like me," she says, her voice weak and unsure.

Getting close to her ear I inhale the tropical scent of

her shampoo. "Maybe I just don't like how much I like you. Fly away, baby bird. You're not safe here."

Reaching behind her I open the door and turn my back to her. She wastes no time in fleeing down the porch steps. Her car cranks on, and sprays rocks as she speeds away from my house.

6

Wren

I yawn as I walk into Dolores's house. It's been a quiet week since the night the Hale men turned up at the bar. Not that my anxiety lets me enjoy the relative peace. Every time the door opened at the bar I tensed up. My body is now a patchwork of knots and tight muscles.

There's a clock counting down now though. I stopped by my lawyer's after work at the insurance office yesterday and signed my divorce papers. Sometime Monday Liam will be served, and hopefully he'll sign the papers and we can both move on with our lives.

He can date anyone he wants, out in the open, and even fuck them in his own bed. I can stop asking myself what I've done wrong while I sit at home alone night after night. Now, being alone is my choice, and not because my husband gave some lame excuse about working late.

"There's fresh coffee in the pot, dearie," Dolores says as she enters the room.

"This late? You usually have your coffee at the crack of dawn, and it's—"

She raises one gray eyebrow. "The crack of noon? I

heard your alarm going off a few times this morning, and when it stopped I knew you'd be heading over."

Another yawn forces its way out. "You can hear that from here?"

She moves to wash her hands at the sink, and that's when I notice all the dirt. "Of course not dear. I needed to winterize my roses, and plant a few bulbs for the spring."

I pour a huge cup of coffee. I don't actually like coffee, but working as much as I have been, I'm practically living off of it now. Of course, I have to doctor it with plenty of cream and sugar.

"You're working too much. I know I told you to stay busy, but you could hang out with a friend or something. It doesn't all have to be work," she advises.

"Lawyers aren't cheap," I tell her and drink a large gulp of coffee.

"You work until close, and then get up at seven to be at the office by eight. There's no way you're getting enough sleep."

"Trust me, I wouldn't be sleeping much either way," I tell her. "I can't get the image of Liam with that woman out of my head."

"Donovan can give you a few nights off. Go to a movie with a friend. Be young. You've got the rest of your life to work too much."

"I asked him for the hours. I've tried calling my best friend, Audrey, but she's been too busy. I think I've only talked to her for about five minutes combined. The rest of my friends all moved away after graduation," I admit.

She pushes my phone toward me. "Can't hurt to try again."

Maybe she's right. There were many times I was too busy when she wanted to do something. Nights when I was still wrapped up with Liam and didn't want to let anyone else into our bubble.

"I'll try," I promise and take my phone and coffee to go, before I remember what I came in here for. "Still need me to go to the pharmacy for you?"

"Oh, can you? I asked my grandson, but he's showing a house today, and I really need my blood pressure medicine."

I smile at her. "It's no problem. I'll go get ready and get them for you."

THE PHONE RINGS several times as I try Audrey again on the short walk through the back yard. I'm about to hang up when she answers the phone out of breath. "Hello?"

"Hey, Audrey. Is this a bad time?"

"Uh, hey, Wren."

My eyebrows crunch together. The way she said my name seemed a bit off. Her breathing increased, and it sounded like there were some grunts in the background.

"Oh, ew. Did you answer the phone while you're having sex?"

"I'm waiting for an important call," she dismisses.

"And you think it's a good idea to answer it while getting railed?"

"We're not all old married people. It's not like it's a job, I'm waiting to hear about a house I'm trying to rent."

"Well, I won't hold up the line then." I hang up before she can throw another barb my way. I really need to talk to my best friend, but more and more that person seems to be an octogenarian who likes to garden.

"And this is why I work a lot," I mutter to myself.

The sucky thing is, Donovan didn't need me tonight,

and since it's Saturday I don't even have work at the office to distract me. Dolores is right, I do need a hobby.

I put more effort into getting ready. It became a habit over the last several months, thinking if I were more attractive, Liam would pay attention to me. Now I just want him to eat his heart out. There's also a bit of curiosity at the way Griffin seems to react to me now, and I guess I like poking the bear.

Standing in front of the mirror after my shower I lift a lock of my dirty blonde hair. My style can best be described as long. That's it, just long. Audrey once told me I looked religious, which I'm pretty sure was an insult.

What did I want? For so long I've approached my personal grooming thinking about what Liam would like. Do I like the clothes I usually wear, or do I wear them because I thought he preferred them? Suddenly, it isn't enough to walk away from my marriage, I need to say goodbye to the girl I was, so I can become the woman I'm meant to be.

"HEY MR. PALMER," I greet the pharmacist. He's been the pharmacist here my entire life, and probably when my parents were young as well.

Palmer Drugs is one place to go to learn all the town gossip. That's why most of the teenagers drive out of town to a large chain store to get contraceptives. The few who didn't plan and came here ended up having a serious talk with their parents when he *let it slip* what they were buying in the store.

"Hello, Wren. Lovely to see you. I'm so sorry to hear about your divorce. Can't say I'm surprised, though. Couple been married as long as you and Liam are usually trying for a family by now, and that boy has been buying condoms in bulk for months. I'd hoped you were both considering college. Damn shame."

My smile is brittle, and I feel all eyes in the store staring at me. Like I said, if you want the town gossip, hang around the pharmacy. Anyone who hadn't figured out Liam has been cheating on me knows now. By this evening we'll be the talk at every dinner table.

"You really should try shutting the fuck up every once in a while. You'd lose less business if you did," a gruff voice growls behind me.

I don't have to turn around to know it's Griffin Hale. My spine straightens and I hold my breath. I haven't seen him once since the awkward exchange a week ago.

"I guess I really shouldn't be surprised your son turned out to be such a lousy husband, with you being his father and all," Mr. Palmer grumbles.

"Just fill her order and let's move it along. Those of us not hanging around here for the gossip have places to be," Griffin barks.

Stupidly, I turn around and see him carrying a giant size box of condoms. Really, who needs to buy condoms in bulk? "Magnums? That's a stretch," I scoff.

I feel his hot breath blow across my ear before he whispers, "The only stretching will be her pussy as she takes my giant cock."

Making a gagging sound, I step to the side to give myself some room. "What is wrong with you? I think I preferred it when you acted like you hated me."

The expression on his face turns glacial. "I still hate you, just not for the reasons you think."

Mr. Palmer shoves a white paper bag at me with Dolores's meds. "Wren, why don't you go on home and give these to Mrs. Howell. She really should have her pills before it gets too late."

"Good idea. How much do I owe you?" I reach into my purse for the cash she gave me to get her medicine, but Mr. Palmer waves me off.

"I think it's best if I send her a bill this time. Go on home now," he instructs like I'm still the thirteen-year-old girl he ran off when he thought I was buying too much candy.

I shiver as I walk out to my car. How did I miss how sexy my father-in-law is? Griffin's words should disgust me as I told him they did, but I can't stop replaying those images in my head and wondering what it would be like to be used in the way he described. I've fantasized about it before but never felt comfortable mentioning it to Liam. Now I can't stop wondering what it would be like to catch Griffin's attention instead of his anger.

AFTER I DROP OFF DOLORES' meds I decide to do something for me. All the extra hours I've been working are supposed to go to paying off my lawyer and getting me the hell out of this town. But, that was before my lawyer refused to take my money beyond the costs he incurred to file for my divorce.

I run into Bess while I'm mindlessly walking around what passes for a mall in town. She hooks her arm through mine. "Girl, why are you looking around like you don't know how to shop?"

"I know how to shop, but I don't know what I want to buy." I pull at the sweatshirt I threw on when I left the house earlier. "I'm not really sure what my style is."

She claps her hands together. "Please say I can give you a makeover," she begs.

"Uhm," I pause to think if I want to be made over by a punk school girl. I'll hand it to her, she has flair, and she does seem to know herself pretty well. I had thought that the Catholic school girl thing was her take on the uniform, but she's wearing something similar today, except in lime green with hot pink accessories.

"I see that look you're giving me. Don't worry, I'm not going to turn you into my clone. Not just anyone can pull this look off."

"We can look, but I think I know myself well enough at least to know what I don't want," I finally agree.

Bess smiles. "See, that's something. If you don't know what you want, knowing what you don't want is a good place to start."

"I don't want to be Liam's Wren anymore," I say quietly.

She bumps me with her shoulder. "And so you won't be."

Taking my hand, Bess drags me as she skips through the mall. "Let's go find the new Wren Parker. And then tonight you and I are going out."

I pull against her hand. "I'm not sure I'm up for that."

Bess spins around in a rainbow of colors. Despite her perpetually peppy personality, the look she gives me is serious. "I know people are talking. I've lived through my fair share of this town feeling like they are owed every morsel of your personal business too. I also know you're planning on getting out of this place as soon as you can. But, until you do, you need to toughen that exterior of yours. Roll your shoulders back, keep your head high, and tell them to kiss your ass."

I smile at her and hope some of her bravado wears off

on me. "If I'm going into battle, let's find me the right armor."

Her fingers lift a lock of my hair. "How do you feel about color?"

"I've always wanted highlights," I admit.

She mock gasps, and puts her hand over her heart. Her dramatics are amusing. "Wild woman."

I roll my eyes. "I'm a work in progress."

"Aren't we all."

7

Griffin

I throw the bag from the drug store down on my desk. Getting a rise out of Wren was entertaining, and more satisfying than I care to admit. Charlie has been on my ass to find a woman to hook up with, as if I haven't been doing just that over the years. If it hasn't worked by now, I'm not sure what he expects is suddenly going to change.

Not that he knows how long I've been hiding my feelings for my daughter-in-law. Neither of us have said the words out loud now, but judging by the way he's being such a pain in the ass right now, he certainly suspects something is going on. At least on my end.

"All stocked up for the night?" Charlie asks, and jerks his chin at the bag.

"You certainly are invested in me banging some random chick tonight. Maybe you're the one that needs to get laid," I snap.

He doesn't take my bait and yell back at me. "Nah, I'm just trying to keep you from playing house with your pretty little daughter-in-law."

I start to argue with him, but he gives me his *don't bullshit me* look. "I've seen the way you look at her when Liam isn't around, and I've noticed he's not been around a lot lately. Thank fuck you didn't notice, or you might have gone and fucked up your relationship with your son by now."

My eyes narrow. "Listen here, asshole, I'm capable of not fucking a woman."

He nods. "Yeah, your self control is infamous. It's not like you regularly skipped class in high school to bend Melinda over under the bleachers. And I'm certain you haven't made sure that Wren hates your guts because you've got such stellar skills at keeping your dick dry."

My fists clench. "I've never done anything to betray my son. I fucking hate cheaters and liars, and I will not become one. I don't care how beautiful the woman is."

He points his finger at me. "Ha! I knew you thought she was beautiful."

"You dumb fuck, I have eyes. Are you telling me you don't think she's beautiful?"

And I see the answer before he speaks. He doesn't see her like I do. "She's a kid, Griff. I've helped you raise Liam, for what good it did, and we've both watched that girl grow up. Hell, I played softball with her dad. Her mom used to bring her to the games. I can't see her and not see the gangly nine year old in overalls. So if you're asking me if I see her the same way you do, the answer is no."

I'm relieved by what he says, and disturbed by the fact I'm relieved.

"You're in danger here. Find a woman, work this out of your system," he says for the hundredth time.

Slamming my hand down on my desk, I shout, "I've fucking tried. She needs to go. For her sake, mine, and my son's, she needs to leave town."

"They could reconcile," he says.

I flop back in my chair. That's not a scenario I can wrap my brain around. I know Wren loves my son. I've seen the way she looks at him, or rather looked at him before that night. But, I think I might be the only person who sees the strength inside of her. There's no way she will forgive Liam. Or if she does, she won't take him back.

"Can we talk about something else?" I would control myself if I ran into her again. No more whispering in her ear, or making suggestive comments to see her skin flush. I'd certainly make a better effort to stop imagining making her blush in other more satisfying ways for both of us than pissing her off.

"Believe it or not, I didn't come into your office to bust your balls about your kinky daddy fantasies." He steps in and closes the door.

"We've had three vehicles we worked on in the past month come back in today because the parts we installed failed. There's been a spike in this happening for months, but Julio was the one who looked at most of the others, and the kid is good with motors, but—"

I nod. "Yeah, he's not much of an independent thinker."

"So what is going on?" I ask, although I've had my own misgivings lately. I've ignored them, because what I'm afraid is going on will change something fundamental inside of me.

"I think, for now, you should take back being the one to order our parts. We don't have to read into this. Maybe Liam thought he could increase profits by ordering cheaper parts," Charlie excuses.

Several months ago, Liam came to me and asked for more responsibility. He said it was time he started taking his life more seriously, and I agreed with him. Truthfully, I was relieved. Him doing the ordering and helping with the billing freed up more of my time to do what I actually liked to do, work on cars. Gradually, he started taking on more and more responsibility, and now he handles ordering, billing and our accounting.

Liam and I don't share a love of mechanics. He's got a high aptitude for it, he did grow up running around an auto shop after all, but he doesn't love it like I do. Liam doesn't really like getting dirty. Still, I fostered hopes that someday he'd want to expand, or take over this shop.

"I'm going to look over the books," I say, mostly to myself.

Charlie nods. He said it was probably a mistake, but we both know he doesn't believe that. "In that case, you should check the bills that we sent out."

He sets a stack of letters in front of me. "Maybe compare our records to some of these. I have been meaning to do it myself, but I wasn't really sure how to go about it."

This brings out a laugh from me. "It's a computer Charlie, you really should learn how to use one."

He waves me off. "It's a fad. It'll be gone in no time."

"You said that when I sent you to school to learn the new diagnostic tools too," I remind him.

"I'm old and set in my ways. I'm okay not being on the net, and I don't think any of the chat rooms are missing anything with me not being in there," he grumbles.

"Your lack of knowledge about modern technology frightens and fascinates me," I comment.

He doesn't reply. Not verbally at least. He flips me the bird on his way out of my office.

I take a deep breath and open the first envelope. Twenty minutes later I've gone through a stack of invoices, clearly our header, and I recall the jobs and customers these invoices came from, but the markup is higher than what is listed in our accounting software. The discrepancies are alarming, and combined with the fact the wrong part numbers, manufacturers and costs are listed I can only come to one conclusion. Someone is skimming off the profits, and that someone can only be my son.

There's an ache in my chest as that realization sets in. Part of me wonders if this is how Wren felt when she saw him fucking in the back seat of his car. The betrayal is enormous.

Charlie's urging for me to go out and find a distraction, take on a new purpose. I am not going to go in order to forget Wren though, I'm going to try to forget that my son has been screwing me over for months.

CHARLIE KNOCKS on my office door around quitting time. "Hey bossman, wrap it up. Let's get some beers in you, and you inside a woman."

"You're creepily invested in my sex life, you know that right?"

"Move your ass. Sitting there staring at that computer isn't going to change anything. You need to regroup so you can figure out what to do next."

I take a deep breath in through my nose. "I want to know why. If he needed money I would have helped him."

Charlie looks like he's aged in the last few hours. We've been best friends since middle school. He was my best man when Melinda and I got married, and helped me take care of Liam in the days right after she left. I know he loves Liam almost as much as I do, and this betrayal cuts him too.

"Liam is the only one who can answer that question,

and he hasn't been in all day. There's nothing you can do about it right now, and you can't undo what he's already done. So, grab your shit and let's get out of here."

I reach for my keys, and he snatches them away from me. "You know what, let's have the kid drive it to your house. He only lives a few blocks away."

Following him out into the shop, he tosses my truck keys to Julio. "We're shutting down for the day. Do me a favor and take Griff's truck to his house. Leave the keys in the mailbox."

We decide to walk the couple blocks down to Donovan's. I pause before we go in. "Maybe this is a bad idea." If the goal is to avoid Wren, going to where she works is not how to do that.

He gives me the side eye. "Do I look like an amateur? I called Donovan. She's got the night off."

"I didn't mean—"

He holds up his hand stopping me. "Let's not lie to each other. You've got some kind of sick fascination with your daughter-in-law. If she was just some other young woman I'd tell you to bang it out of your system, but you can't do that. You need to shove that shit deep down with the rest of your feelings and embrace the denial you have mastered since Melinda left."

The bar is crawling with people when we enter. The town never really recovered after the last recession, and there aren't many things to do in Harriston on a Saturday night. There is a dollar theater, a bowling alley, and Donovan's. There's also The Garden Club, but honestly I don't know how they stay in business. Most of the people in town don't have the money for ten dollar cocktails and thirty dollar dinners.

The vibe at Donovan's fits much better with most of

the people in Harriston. There's a jukebox in the corner that is loaded with classic rock up through the nineties grunge hits. Both pool tables have a line waiting to use them, and the waitresses flit around in tight uniforms. My teeth clench remembering Wren in those jeans she had on seemed to be painted on and ripped practically up to her pussy.

"I need a drink," I growl.

"I'll grab a pitcher," Charlie offers.

We settle in the corner, and one pitcher becomes two, and then three. Soon we're joined by a couple of women. They're in their mid thirties, much more age appropriate, and I couldn't be less interested. Charlie is close to sealing the deal with one of them, so I stay long past when I'm ready to go home to entertain her friend.

I let Brandi hang on me. She leans forward to show off her rack and the lacy edge of her bra. When my eyes dip down, because of course they're drawn to tits, she slowly traces the edge with her finger. I contemplate taking her home. I know she wants to. There's nothing wrong with two consenting adults enjoying each other. I let the evening play out in my head.

We would take an Uber back to her place, as was my habit since Liam was little. Clothes would start to come off the moment we walk through the door. I'd get a front row viewing of the tits she's waving in my face. We'd proceed to fuck on every available surface in her house, except for a bed. Beds were for lovers, and we were both seeking quick and dirty satisfaction. I didn't need to worry about her forming an attachment to me, or getting pissed when I hit and quit. She is out to use me as much as I am her.

It would be something I've done dozens of times over the years. Like all the times before it would be gratifying in the moment, and after I'd be left feeling empty. There are things you can do with a partner you trust, sides of myself I can only show when there's familiarity. I've had a few arrangements over the years with women who enjoy rougher sex. Women who like to be dominated in bed. Something tells me Brandi would run if I pushed her to her knees and demanded she gag on my cock. And just like that the semi that started to form while I imagined the things I could do to her deflates.

Not that I can tell her we're not going back to her place. Charlie needs a release as badly as I do, and I can't cockblock him just because I'm still fantasizing about a woman I can't have. So I let Brandi continue to flirt and toss her hair while I down more beer than before. Maybe I'll be lucky and she'll believe I've got whiskey dick. Is beer dick a thing? Of course I'll promise to reschedule. Either way, I'd be lying to her, but it is one that will hopefully let her save her ego.

Charlie and his girl are getting bolder the longer we sit at the table. Hands are roaming, and he's too busy sucking her face off to carry on a conversation. When he finally comes up for air he gives me the look. The one we've perfected over the years. Without words he manages to let me know he's leaving. I tip my head to let him know I'm fine.

He stands up and throws some bills on the table. It's probably too much, but it's a flashy move that impresses the kinds of girls he pursues. I'll sort it out after they leave and give him back the extra on Monday.

They leave quickly, and I'm left to figure out how to extricate myself from Brandi.

"What do you think, big guy? Want to go to my place?" She trails her finger around the rim of her glass while giving me her best seductive look.

I'll give her credit, it almost works. A month ago, hell a couple of weeks ago, I'd be chasing her out of the bar. That was before my son fucked up his marriage.

The door opens, and it is like thinking about her conjured her out of thin air. At least I think that's her. Her long hair, that she usually wears in a messy bun on top of her head, falls down her back in loose waves. It's highlighted a lot blonder than when I saw her earlier today. She's wearing heavier makeup with dark eyeshadow and blood red lipstick. If that isn't bad enough she's wearing a micro sized skirt with fuck me heels and a tiny tank top showing off a lot of her cleavage.

Immediately two guys approach her and Bess. I'd only ever seen her hang out with that girl, Audrey, and I'm not sure I approve of this new development. Wren is a good girl, quiet and studious. Bess is loud and vulgar, but I guess I can see why she'd bond with her now. Being a good girl didn't keep her husband from straying. Bess is the type of woman who eats men alive. No one fucks that girl over.

Wren leans over the bar and fixes herself and Bess a couple of shots. Her skirt teases me by showing the bottom of her round ass. She tosses back the shot and makes a face as the burn travels down her throat.

Donovan is watching her, and I recognize the hunger in his gaze. I thought he was trying to protect her last week, but I'm starting to think he's really trying to keep her to himself. He's not the only one with eyes on her, and the girls are quickly surrounded by men their age. I don't recognize any of them, which means they are probably college kids from a couple towns over who like to come and slum it here on the weekends.

She laughs at something one of them says and I see red. Brandi chooses this moment to remind me she'd asked me a question. "Well? Are we going?"

"No," I bark. She pouts and sits back in her chair. I don't really care what she does, as long as she lets me keep an eye on Wren.

Of course, this is when she looks over and sees me sitting in the corner. The game we're playing increases stakes as she whispers something in one of the guy's ear. He puts his arm around her and they head to one of the pool tables. It seems one of his friends had the next game, and they seize the opportunity to teach the girls how to play pool.

I happen to know she already knows how to play like a shark. Liam taught her back in high school when they used to sneak out. Her guardian didn't keep a close eye on her, and my son took full advantage of his access to her in those days. Since he'd already graduated from high school I didn't try to stop him.

Still, she plays along and pretends not to know how to line up her shot. He slides his hand down her arm in the guise of helping her get into the right position. He stands close behind her, his groin lined up with her plump ass. I'm about to go and rip him away when she looks at me over her shoulder.

She's toying with me. For the first time tonight I'm excited. More than I felt with Brandi throwing herself at me. But the game has begun, and I aim to win. I turn to Brandi and soothe her hurt feelings when I said we weren't leaving.

"I just want another drink. Are you okay to stay a bit longer?"

She smiles at me and presses her breasts against my arm. "Another beer sounds fine. We would have more fun at my house."

I raise an eyebrow at her. "Anticipation increases the experience."

Brandi practically purrs, and I go back to ignoring her to watch Wren. When she leans over to take another shot, the guy who's salivating over her slips his hand up her thigh toward the hem of her skirt.

I don't think. My chair falls back as I jump up and it clatters to the ground. "You're going to need to find a ride. That girl over there is family, and I need to stop her from doing something stupid."

Brandi grabs for my arm, but I shake her off. She's incredulous, and sputters, "You're going to pass up a sure thing to take care of a kid?"

My jaw clenches and I say through clenched teeth, "She's not a kid."

I walk away from her. I guess I managed to piss her off anyway, but I can't be bothered to care. Stomping off toward Wren, I grab the guy by the shirt and shove him away from her.

He puffs up his chest and starts to get in my face. "What's your problem, man?"

"Back off junior," I snap. "This doesn't concern you. Find someone else to play with."

I grab her arm and pull her through the bar. "Let go of me," she hisses quietly.

Down the hallway I toss open the door clearly marked *Employees Only*, and shove her into the storeroom. There's a lock on the door, and I turn it to keep us from being interrupted.

"What the fuck has gotten into you?" I yell at her.

"I'm not your problem anymore, Griffin."

"Oh, baby bird, you're in so much trouble."

She pops out a hip, and props her hand on it. "What are you going to do? Spank me?"

I move closer to her, so that she has to crane her neck to look up at me. "I think you want me to. I bet your panties are soaked right now hoping I'll force you to your knees and make you mine."

Her big green eyes blink, but she doesn't speak. My hand slips around her throat so I can feel her pulse. It races like the beating of a hummingbird's wings. "When I ask you a question, you will answer me." I need to see how she'll respond to an order.

"Seriously, Griffin. You aren't my father. I'm divorcing your son. Leave me alone."

A dark chuckle slips free, and she starts to back away from me.

I should stop at being reminded about her relationship with my son and the reminder why she's off limits. Instead, the anger I felt earlier rises to the surface. Everything I've worked my entire life for is at risk because my son is selfish.

"What kind of daddy would I be if I didn't punish you for being a bad girl? You want me to spank your ass. Admit it. I need you to say it, and I'll do to you everything I described at the pharmacy. I saw the look on your face. You want to submit and stop thinking for a while. To accept whatever pleasure I want to give you, and I will if you admit it."

Her chest heaves and I can see she's fighting with herself. She just needs a little push to give in.

"That's why you came in here, dressed like a slut. You want an escape from your marriage. You want a man who burns for you. Is that how you want me to treat you? I think you want it to be me. To get back at him for ignoring you. How better than to let me control you for a while. And you know what? He's taken enough from me. I've wanted you for years, and I'm tired of sacrificing for him when he doesn't appreciate it. So tell me, do you want to be daddy's whore?"

I pull her hair back, and force her to look up at me. "Say it."

Her voice is quiet when she answers me. "I've been bad, daddy. I don't want to think anymore tonight."

"Turn around and put your hands on the door. Daddy is going to spank your ass for being a bad girl, and for making me want you so fucking bad, then I'm going to treat you like the slut you so badly want to be."

She spins around and places her palms flat on the door. I put my hand on her back and force her down lower so her ass sticks out. I flip up her skirt revealing the full globes of her ass.

I'm not surprised she gives in so easily. I've suspected for a while she's naturally submissive and longs for the freedom and peace found in handing over control to someone else. What a treasure a woman like her is to a man like me.

The tension melts off of her as I take control. Her worries are temporarily gone, left in my hands to take care of. I might not be the answer to all her problems. Hell, this probably causes new ones, but this is a chance for her to gain some of her dignity back. It might sound odd to find dignity in degradation, but this is her choice. Not only that, it's her chance to dip into all the dark urges I've realized she and I share.

Rubbing my hand against her smooth skin she presses back against my touch. I raise my hand and give her a quick slap. The sound echoes through the storeroom, and I rub away the sting.

My handprint pinks her ass, and I alternate swats until her bottom is a nice rosy pink. "Your ass looks so pretty with my mark on it."

"Tell me you're sorry," I demand.

"I'm sorry," she blurts out.

I smack her again. "Try again, baby bird."

"I'm sorry, daddy," she corrects.

"If you want to be treated like a whore, you don't need to come to a bar. All you need is to come to me and beg."

"Please, daddy," she says immediately.

"Please what, baby bird?" I ask.

"Let me be your slut," she pants.

I undo my belt and jeans. I rip her tiny panties off of her. "I'm going to fuck you now, and it's going to be rough."

"Yes, daddy."

"That's a good, slut. You're being so good for daddy."

I slam my cock deep in her tight pussy. All thought flees my head except for how good she feels squeezing my cock. I squeeze her hips and take her hard. The door slams rhythmically against the jam, and she groans every time I slam my large cock inside of her.

I start pulling her back to meet each one of my thrusts. "Does that feel good, baby bird?"

She nods. "More."

My mind flees. Everything about this is wrong, but it feels like the most right thing ever. "You're going to be daddy's perfect slut. I'm going to take you home and make you gag on my cock, and you're going to love it, aren't you?"

"Yes," she moans.

I slap her ass, hard, and I feel it vibrate around my cock. "Yes, what," I demand.

"Yes, daddy."

I need to come. The fire races up my spine, and as loud as we're being it won't be long before someone interrupts us. I can't let go until she gives it to me.

I reach around and start rubbing her clit hard and fast.

I know it's too fast a build up, and she's going to scream, but I can't be bothered to care.

"Come for daddy. Be a good whore and soak my cock." As I thought, my dirty words send her over the edge. She screams, and as her walls clench around my dick I come. It's only then that I realize I forgot to use a condom.

8

Wren

For a moment there's nothing but the sound of our breathing, then suddenly all the sounds of the bar flood my consciousness. Feelings of elation give way to horror and embarrassment.

I work here. How the fuck could I let him, my father-in-law of all people, do that to me in the storeroom closet? Maybe I am a slut. I know those words were used in a way they were supposed to be sexy, and they were, until now.

My skirt is still up around my waist, and I flip it back down to cover my smarting ass. Another thing that was hot, in the moment, but now the only hot part is the stinging of my flesh.

How was it Liam was able to do this? Did he feel this dirty every time he met up with his mystery woman in secret? Did he also feel like he'd trampled on something that was supposed to be sacred, something meant only for us?

I sneak a look at Griffin and he looks as horrified as I am. He refuses to meet my eyes as he tucks himself back in his boxers and refastens his jeans and belt.

Shame can safely be added to the mix of emotions I'm feeling. While I might have technically cheated on my husband, since we are still legally married, Griffin betrayed his son. A son I know he loves deeply.

I flip the lock on the door, straighten my spine, and prepare myself to walk through the bar with everyone's eyes on me. It won't be the first time I've had the attention of everyone around me. I prefer to blend in rather than stand out, but there are times life doesn't give you that option. Like when I became the poor orphan girl everyone watched to see if I was going to fall apart. I hadn't recognized the attention the last few months, but looking back I can see clearly some people already knew Liam was having an affair. Charlie in particular watched me with more sympathy, and a wariness I'm only starting to figure out had to do with Griffin.

At least when they watch me now I'll own my shit. This time I won't be the poor put upon wife sitting at home waiting for a husband who's balls deep in some skank. No, this time it'll be him who's pitied because his wife screwed his father in the bar store room.

I guess I am a slut. But, I'll be leaving this town soon, and in Centralia, assuming I'm lucky enough to get into Central Valley again, no one will care about any of this.

For a moment I expect Griffin to stop me, say something, anything, before I walk out of here, but he stays silent. Sometimes silence says everything.

THE BAR IS CLOSED on Sunday thanks to some archaic law that says liquor can't be sold on a Sunday. Like they expect the people who would usually be nursing last night's hangover with the hair of the dog to suddenly wake up, become church goers, and be sitting in a pew listening to a minister rebuking all the sins they so gleefully engage in the other six days a week. But, I do appreciate the day off, so when the sun starts to slip into my room, I pull the covers over my head and go back to sleep.

It's around noon when I finally crawl from my duvet cave. I'm disoriented, and a little freaked out that Dolores hasn't barged in with her usual grandmotherly concern. Sometimes she claims to have heard a noise, other times she brings me baked goods, but every time I see through her and know she is only making sure I'm not crying myself puffy into a pint of ice cream.

One time that happened. Okay, two. Maybe three, but some things need tears and Cherry Garcia in order to recover.

I really should go and check on her. In the back of my mind I wonder if this is another ninja grandma tactic to pull me out of my den of sadness as she calls it. If it is, she's an evil genius because I rush through a shower to go over and make sure she's fine.

It's only ever the two of us here, her family keeps in touch, but they don't live in the area so their visits aren't a usual occurrence, except for her grandson who lives only one town over. He works a lot as a realtor in a much wealthier community, so again, we almost never see him.

In my hurry to go and check on her, I throw on a simple ribbed tank top and a pair of boyfriend jeans. My hair goes up into my usual messy bun, and once I slip my feet into a pair of flip flops I race across the lawn.

Bursting through the door to the kitchen, I freeze when I see the reason Dolores hasn't come around to do her usual check on me. At the table, as if he visited her weekly, sits Griffin Fucking Hale.

"Close your mouth, baby bird." His eyes dance with amusement seeing my shock.

I recover quickly, and send him a glare. I'm acting like a bratty teenager, and a dark place in the back of my mind wonders if I can get him to spank me again. Thankfully, those are not the words that leave my mouth. I sound much more like normal, sane Wren Parker when I finally find my words. "What are you doing here?"

"Wren," Dolores flutters. "Is that any way to speak to our guest?"

I give her a warning look as well. Really, the way she's carrying on you'd think she was any other horny twenty something in this town rather than an eighty-two-year-old great-grandma.

"Don't tell me he shows up with his," I flap my hand in his general area, "Griffinness, and you simper like all the other women in this town."

The dimple in his cheek becomes more pronounced with his growing amusement. Enough so that I can see it through the heavy stubble on his face. "Does that include you, baby bird?"

The urge to growl almost won, but him acting like an animal doesn't mean I need to reciprocate. Instead, I choose the much more evolved route and ignore him. Okay, so maybe it's not evolved so much as juvenile, but at least I'm not grunting and growling at him like he does to everyone alive.

Griffin stands, and puts his hand on my back. "It was nice to visit with you, Mrs. Howell."

Damn her, she is actually blushing. She and I would be having a talk about this later.

"Oh, you too, Griffin. Please, do stop by again. I'll make you that apple cobbler I remember you liking."

He gave her the first genuine smile I think I've ever

seen him give anyone who isn't Liam. The woman is talented in making the hardest and saddest hearts smile, I'll give her that. The sight of it almost brings me to my knees, and not in an awe kind of way, but in a way that I shouldn't be thinking in front of my elderly landlady.

"I'd love to. It's been too long, I won't go as far between visits," he promises.

Then he puts pressure on my back guiding me back out of the house. "You and I need to talk."

Gone is the lighthearted, albeit dirty, teasing from moments ago. In its place is the Griffin I'm used to. The one who seems to hate the fact I exist, and would love nothing more than to never see me again.

He starts to direct me back to my cottage, but I halt mid step, causing him to almost trip over me.

"What the hell, Wren. You know how to walk, right?" he growls.

"I don't want you inside my house." It's harsh, and if I knew he was coming, I'd have explained. My space needs to be free of any reminder of Liam.

His arm slips around my middle, and he pulls me flush against his front. His warm breath fans across my neck as he bends down to whisper, "I was inside of *you* last night, I think you can stand to have me in your house for a few minutes."

The swaying of the curtains in the window indicates we have an audience. "Fine, but only because Dolores is a terrible spy, and I don't like the idea of her standing on a chair trying to see out the window."

"How did you know where I live anyway?" I ask as I open the door and let us into my tiny living room.

"You said you were picking up Mrs. Howell's meds at the pharmacy yesterday. When my ex wife first left, Dolores babysat for me until I could get Liam into daycare.

She has talked me off the ledge many times. I'm glad you're here with her."

My mouth fell open. "You're giving me whiplash, you know? First you hate me, then you want to fuck me, and now you're actually being nice. What do you want? If you came here to say that we made a mistake and we can't do it again, save it okay?"

Griffin comes up behind me and tucks some of my hair behind my ear. His fingers trail down my neck, and my skin breaks out in chills. "First, I never hated you."

I scoff. "Come on. You have glared at me, snapped, growled, and ridiculed me for the last five years."

"I'll admit, I hate that you were married to my son. I do think you were both too young. Clearly, Liam wasn't mature enough to make that kind of commitment to you for forever. That never had anything to do with you, and everything to do with me knowing my son. Then, over time I started to admit you weren't a child and when I started seeing you as a woman, for the first time, I was jealous of my son. Then I think I did hate you a little."

"What's second? You said first, so what is second?" I try not to tremble as he continues his hypnotic touches. One stroke down my neck, another brush of my hair, his finger trails the shell of my ear and I'm about to melt into a puddle at his feet.

He chuckles seeing my reaction and leans closer to say the next part closer to my ear. "Second there's never been a time since I started seeing you as a woman that I didn't want to fuck you. You can't imagine the many different ways I've imagined using this little body for my own satisfaction."

"That's all nice to hear," I begin.

"Nice? It's nice to hear I want to tie you up, gag you and use you however I want. That I want you to be bad so

I have an excuse to warm your ass again? Does that sound nice to you?" he snaps.

"That's more like it," I mutter to myself.

"What? You expect me to say perverted shit to you?" he snaps, and I giggle.

"No, I expect you to lose your temper and yell at me," I answer honestly. "What I mean is, thank you for telling me how you feel, but we both know what happened last night can't happen again."

Griffin threads his fingers together behind his head and paces the room. It's something I've seen him do when he's trying to work out a difficult problem. Also, makes it very hard not to ogle the bulging biceps and triceps the way they are flexed. Not that I try this time.

"Look, I know you're right. I'm dealing with my own Liam shitstorm at the moment, so maybe it's temporary insanity, but right now I don't particularly give a shit how this would make him feel."

"So, whatever this thing is between us, is that revenge?" I'm a little hurt by this, and surprised that I feel that way.

He smiles, but instead of the wholesome smile of a long friendship he gave Dolores, this smile is a little wicked, and a lot suggestive. "No. This is me rationalizing the fact I want to fuck you more than I care to take my next breath, and if I don't get inside of you soon, I'm going to lose my mind."

I swallow, hard. "You're not going to feel that way whenever you get a chance to talk to Liam. I can't be another man's mistake."

He forces me to turn around and tips up my chin. "Wren, you are not the mistake. Liam's side piece is the mistake. Losing you will be his mistake. And I'm a big boy. If I mess up my relationship with my son, such as it is, that will be my fault."

"What are you talking about? You and Liam are so close." They talk every day, work together, and even socialize together. I'd say Griffin is Liam's best friend at this point in his life. If that isn't true, then I know less about Liam than I thought.

"I thought we were too," Griffin says, but doesn't elaborate.

Whatever drove a wedge between them, I have a feeling it is much worse than broken marriage vows.

9

Griffin

"I'll tell you, but first I'm going to need you to put on a bra. I can't think with your tits playing peekaboo in that white tank top."

She looks down at herself and realizes I can see most of her nipples through her shirt. She throws her arm over her chest and runs back into her bedroom. A few minutes later she comes back out wearing an old hoodie.

"There she is," I whisper and touch the side of her face.

She puts her hand over mine. "Stop. You can't be sweet one minute and mean the next. It's too big of a mindfuck, and I can't take any more. Not now."

Guilt is a bitch. This girl, woman, has been through so much in her twenty-three years. Losing her parents, then her marriage, and all the while I've made her feel unwelcome because of my own hang ups about marriage. That and my attraction to her.

I still want her to leave. Need her to, and not just for me. I know I can't have an honest relationship with my son while I am chasing after her. Even if they get divorced, she'll always have been his wife.

Besides, there's so much more out there for her than she can find in this town. Now that they are getting divorced, there's nothing here for her anymore except for two dead end jobs and Dolores. I still need to convince her to leave, but I have to find a different way to do it. I never enjoyed hurting her, I guess I didn't realize how much of an effect I had.

Outside there's a rustling of the plants too focused in one spot to be the wind. I peek out the window and see the fluffy silver head of Dolores pretending to poke around in one of her many flowerbeds. When she sees me looking, she quickly focuses on her task, trying to look like she's not spying on us.

"You're right, she's a horrible spy." I dig my keys out of my pocket. "Take a drive with me. Let's go some place we can talk."

"Not your place," she blurts out, and then blushes.

"I said some place to talk, not some place I can fuck you. I don't think either of us can behave if we're left alone."

"Okay, let's go," she agrees.

I drive us out of town, about an hour beyond places most of the townies frequent. There is a state park deep in the forest with a winding road that goes up into the hills. At the crest there is a wide vista that overlooks the tops of the trees and the rivers beyond. It's peaceful here, which will hopefully help the conversation we need to have.

After I turn off the car, I take a deep breath. "Charlie came to me yesterday. Some of our customers have had problems with the parts we installed during repairs. I guess Julio dealt with the ones that came in before, so we didn't catch it earlier. When Charlie got under the hood of a few of the ones brought in, he noticed we didn't use parts from our usual manufacturer. These were cheaper, and lower quality. He had also spoken to some of our customers who had questions about their bills, and noticed the same parts were charged at the rate of the previous ones we used, except the bills were changed in our system for the lower amounts."

Her hands start to shake, and her lip quivers. "What are you saying?"

My head drops down. I can't look at her when I say this. "I think Liam has been stealing from the shop."

"Is that why—" she starts to ask.

"Why I gave in to what I've wanted?" I finish her sentence.

Wren nods.

A strand of hair has fallen loose from her messy bun, and I tuck it behind her ear. "Because we are both feeling betrayed and hurt. Both of us have sacrificed a lot for his happiness, and I feel so angry with him. I hate that feeling. The disappointment is crushing me. Then all of a sudden there you were. I know this is wrong, that what we did, what I'd like to do can cause so much more damage, but I'm drowning in this feeling. That's new for me. I'm a simple man, Wren. I don't want what I can't have, before you that is. And for him I was willing to overlook that. But then I found out what he did, and I started to wonder why we both had to hurt because he chose himself over the people who love him."

She looks away, but I catch a tear trailing down her cheek. I reach out and squeeze her hand. "Don't do that. Don't hide."

"Why did he do this?" she asks.

"I wish I knew."

She wipes the tears from her face. "What are you

wanting me to do?"

"We can't be together, not long term, but we can be there for each other now."

"How would that work?" she asks me.

"Did you think about Liam last night? Did it hurt as bad?" I think I know the answer, but I can't be sure until she says the words.

"No, and I don't know how I feel about that. I think I'm numb," she admits.

I can see it, the weight resting on her. I feel it too. "Come stay with me."

She shakes her head. "How would that even work? We both have work tomorrow. Liam is going to be there, and when you see him again you're going to regret this. I know what I get out of this. An escape, and even if he never finds out, a little bit of revenge. I know you don't want to hear that, but what he did cut me deep. I can't use you like that. I'd be no better than him if I did."

For years I've treated her like she was too young and immature to have gotten married. I blamed her for my son's choices, because I saw he was stalled in life. Maybe if he hadn't married right out of high school, I thought, he might have found a path and made something more out of his life than I had mine.

The truth is, she is more emotionally mature than me, and I'm nineteen years older than she is. And now I have to admit Liam's problems weren't that he committed to her too young, but that he never fully committed to her at all. If he loved her completely, the way I fear I would if we had the freedom to fall, then he'd move mountains to please her.

"You're right," I agree. "I'll admit, I'm disappointed, but also relieved because you're making the choice I'm not strong enough to make. Promise me, when the divorce is final and all the strings to Harriston are cut, you'll leave. You can't become the person you're meant to be stuck here in the past."

"Is that why you've always been mean? You made it clear you wanted me to leave Liam."

I shake my head, and realize I'm sending mixed signals. "It wasn't really about Liam. I love my son, but I hated watching you throw away your future. I've been mad at him for pushing you to do that. If he loved you, he'd have gone with you."

A single tear slips down her cheek, and she scrubs it away with the back of her hand. "I think it's pretty safe to say he didn't really love me."

CHARLIE SPENDS the morning watching me. I know he suspects something happened between Wren and I over the weekend, because he hasn't once asked me about Brandi. That's not normal for him. Charlie's never been one to respect my privacy.

He grows more suspicious as the morning passes and Liam still hasn't shown up for work. We're both stomping around each other. Tensions are high, and when lunch time rolls around he snaps. "Have you even gone and checked on him, or have you been too busy chasing after his wife?"

I throw the wrench in my hand, and it bashes into the tool box denting it. "What crawled up your ass?"

"How did things go Saturday night with Brandi?" he asks.

"I think you already know, don't you?"

"God fucking dammit, Griff! We talked about this. All you had to do was go home with the age appropriate woman who wasn't your daughter-in-law, not fuck Wren in the storage closet."

My teeth clench hard and grind against each other. "Is everyone in town talking about it?" I don't give a shit what they said about me, but Wren doesn't deserve to be gossiped about behind her back. It's bad enough people have started talking about Liam's affair. She doesn't need this too.

"Let me ask you a question, did you make sure Brandi left before you dragged Wren off like a caveman?"

I remember throwing money for a cab on the table in front of her. Then the only thing I saw was that frat boy pawing at Wren. Jealousy, like I'd never experienced before washed over me, and I couldn't think beyond getting her alone.

"I'll take your silence to mean that you left a horny, pissed off woman at the table."

I nod. "I was a little distracted."

"Too distracted to notice she didn't leave. She followed you both down the hallway, and heard the door rattling, and all the grunts and groans coming from inside. She called Laura, the woman I was with in case you forgot," he explains.

"I didn't forget, I never cared to get her name in the first place," I admit.

"Well, she called, bitching up a storm, so thanks a lot for cock blocking me. What the fuck were you thinking?"

"I wasn't thinking, is that what you want to hear? It was all too much. Liam's betrayal, my feelings for—"

"His wife," Charlie chimes in.

I suppress a growl at hearing her called that. Ever since the moment I took her into the storage room I've struggled to see her as anything except mine.

"I've tried to fight this," I say.

"It sounds like you've given up."

"Charlie, I did that years ago."

He gets in my face. "Snap out of it. This thing you have for Wren will go away. What's important is that you sort Liam out. He cannot find out about this."

Charlie grabs my shoulder and gives me a little shake. "He's the priority. Go find him."

I grab my keys and head out to my truck. The drive to his apartment is quick since it's only a couple miles away. His car is in the parking lot. I rush up the stairs and start pounding on the door.

"I'm coming," he slurs on the other side of the door.

I push past him when he opens the door. There's take out containers strewn about, and a smell I can't tell whether it's from him or the rotting food. I pull my shirt over my nose, and start opening windows.

"Go take a shower. I'll clean up a little, then we've got to talk."

"Just go, I don't need you here," he slurs.

"Are you drunk?" I look around for empty bottles, and find several scattered around mixed in with the rest of the trash.

"My wife left me, so what if I am?" He stumbles toward the fridge, and pulls out another beer.

I rip it from his hand, and pour it down the sink. "Shower, now." I shove him toward the bathroom.

Before she left, they argued over chores. Liam always made it sound like Wren didn't pull her fair share. Stupidly, I believed him. It was one of the many excuses I used to justify my treatment of her, rather than look deep and admit the reason I resented her being in his life was because she couldn't be mine. It seems without her, my son is falling apart.

I find cleaning supplies and trash bags under the sink.

Since the apartment is small I'm able to have the majority of the mess cleared away before he emerges from the bathroom.

"Why are you here?" he asks, already a bit more sober from the shower.

"It's Monday." I wait for recognition, but he continues to give me the same annoyed stare. "Work, Liam. You work during the week."

"I'm nursing my wounds," he grumbles, and drops onto the couch.

"They're self-inflicted, so don't think you're going to get a lot of sympathy."

"I never meant for her to leave. I love her. I know it doesn't seem like it. After my accident, I've just felt like I was missing out on being young."

"You make it sound like you almost died. It was a fender bender."

"I had a concussion and whiplash."

"And Wren babied you for a month. Why would you repay her for that by cheating on her?" It makes no sense. It's like his entire personality has changed.

"I don't expect you to understand. Not everyone is willing to spend decades mourning for a lost relationship. I wanted to see what was out there while I'm still young."

Staying calm takes effort. My job is to support him. Like Charlie said, Liam is my priority, but listening to him makes me see red. "And Wren? Was she supposed to just wait around while you figured it out?"

"Yes! Why do you care? Isn't this what you wanted? You always wanted her to leave. Well, looks like you got your wish." He reaches out to the coffee table and throws a manilla envelope at me."

Inside are the divorce papers I already knew she had

prepared. I'm not supposed to know, of course, and I can't let my son find out.

"She filed for divorce. Can you really be surprised?"

His hands shake, and his brow is breaking out in sweat.

"Can you go? I want to be alone," he insists.

Something feels off, and deep down, I know if I leave I'll regret it.

"Go," he shouts.

"Liam, what's going on?" There is more here than the breakdown of his marriage. I've dropped the ball as his dad, and went and made it worse by sleeping with his wife.

Guilt eventually wins, and I leave to let him lick his wounds. It's the least I can do.

10

Wren

An out of town number comes across my cell phone. Usually, I reject numbers I don't recognize. I figure if it's really important they'll leave me a voicemail, and I've avoided talking to someone about some extended car warranty on my bucket of rust and bolts. But, I'm waiting to hear from the process server to tell me my divorce papers have been signed.

"Hello, is this Mrs. Hale?" the caller asks.

"For now," I mumble.

"I'm sorry, we must have a bad connection, I'm looking for Mrs. Wren Hale, wife of Liam Hale. Do I have the correct number?"

I groan away from the phone. "This is she. How can I help you?"

"I'm calling from Wood River Medicine. There's an issue with your husband's prescription. We need to have the doctor resend it, but we don't seem to have contact information for them on file. That's very unusual, but can happen. However, before we can fill a prescription for a schedule II drug, we have to verify it with the doctor."

"A *what* kind of drug? What is the prescription for?" Liam has always been a little weird about taking medication. The man won't even take ibuprofen for a headache, so for him to actually fill a prescription without being pestered by me is pretty remarkable. He almost ended up in the hospital a few years ago when he refused to take antibiotics for strep throat.

I hear papers shuffling on the other end of the phone. "I'm not sure what the inciting event was, but the prescription is for pain management."

"Uhm, can I ask why you are calling me instead of him?" I ask.

"We've been unable to reach Mr. Hale, and while we can't give out private medical information, we do have you listed as an approved medical contact. Considering this is for pain management, we wanted to make sure Mr. Hale gets his medication approved in a timely manner so he can rest."

"Thank you for letting me know. I'll see what I can do." I don't wait for them to respond, and hang up the phone. After searching the internet for the type of prescription drug the technician mentioned, I'm concerned to find that Liam is trying to get opioids.

Before things in our marriage turned bad, he was in a minor car accident. Even a minor accident can leave some lingering issues. His airbag went off when the car behind him pushed him into the car in front of him. He had a concussion and whiplash. Neither condition had long term effects, but he was in a lot of pain in the short term, and the doctor gave him pain meds to manage it. It was the one time I didn't have to push him to take his meds, and the one time I wish I'd stopped him.

His personality changed on painkillers. He started to withdraw, was quick to anger, and he rarely slept. At the time, I worried his concussion was worse than they first thought. His doctor tried to reassure me it wasn't, but I didn't believe him. It's possible the concussion was never the problem, and his use of prescription pain meds was.

It looks like that confrontation I've been wanting to avoid is going to happen after all. I grab my keys, and drive across town to go to our old apartment. As much as I don't want to see him, I need to. I can't work up enough anger to want something bad to happen to him. Maybe that makes me weak, or just maybe it means I'm stronger than I ever thought.

KNOCKING on the door to the apartment I shared with my husband until a couple of weeks ago is strange, but I've already caught him having sex once and that was enough.

"Liam, it's Wren. Open the door."

I switch to banging on the door with the side of my hand, but there's still no answer. "I'm coming in Liam," I announce as I use my key to open the door.

I'm surprised to see the place is relatively clean. I expected to find take out containers covering every surface. Liam doesn't do a good job taking care of himself. If his choices are to cook or starve, I fully expect him to starve. I'm not even sure he knows where the dumpster is for the complex.

It's odd to admit all of that to myself. For so long I've made excuses for the imbalances in our relationship. None of the things I told myself make sense to me now. I told myself he worked hard and needed to relax when we were at home. The truth I hid from myself was that I also worked hard, then came home and continued to work.

Even when our sex life started to dwindle I blamed

myself. I thought he wasn't attracted to me anymore because there was something wrong with me. I started dieting and exercising. I hate exercising, but I did it religiously for months. More of my time was spent grooming, cooking, cleaning, and basically trying to be a traditional house wife, all with the added responsibility of being the other wage earner of our household.

As wrong as what Griffin and I did the other night is, I think it might also be responsible for saving my sanity. The fact that he wanted me so badly that he'd risk everything important to him filled the dark spaces inside of me. When he took control, I didn't feel weak, it made me feel free in a way I've never felt before. Turning him down yesterday was one of the hardest things I've ever done, but I couldn't be selfish with him. The best I can hope for is to hold on to the memory of that night for as long as I can, and find someone, someday who makes me feel that way again.

I shake myself out of my reverie as I enter the apartment. The last thing I need to be doing is fantasizing about Liam's father as I go to check on him.

"Liam," I call out. There's not a lot of places to go in this tiny apartment. I think my six-hundred-square foot cottage is larger than this place.

Looking around, I spot his car keys sitting in their usual place on the coffee table. Since he always insists on driving himself, I suspect he's somewhere in the apartment.

Inside the bedroom the bedding is rumpled, and there's a stale odor of sweat in the room. She's probably been here since I've been gone. Whoever she is. I try not to let my mind wander down that rabbit hole, because this is a small town. It's probably someone I know, and I'm not ready to face who that could be yet. Once I find out, it'll be hard for me not to compare myself to her. Whatever she has that I don't, clearly interests him more than me. Enough to throw away our years together.

"Please don't let me find them in the shower together," I whisper to myself. I can hear water running, but it doesn't sound like the shower. "Or a bath," I beg to whatever deity that might be listening to me.

I bang on the door, but there's no answer. Taking a deep breath, I twist the knob, but there's something keeping it from opening all the way. Something is wrong, I can feel it. I shove harder, and manage to open the door enough to squeeze myself through the crack.

Liam is sprawled on the floor, his feet pressing against the door keeps it from opening. Then I notice the blood trickling from a gash on the side of his head.

"Oh god! Liam." He doesn't respond to my voice, and I fight to compose myself enough so I can do what I can to help him. His pulse feels strong, but what do I know? I'm pleased to know he has one.

It feels like I'm watching someone else from that moment on. I call 911, wait for the ambulance, then hop in with him on the way to the hospital.

"Is your husband on any medication?" the EMT asks. "Mrs. Hale?"

I blink and try to focus. "Sorry, I, uh, I'm not sure. We're separated. I did get a call from a pharmacy in Pine Bluff. I think she said she was calling from Wood River Medicine. She was trying to get information for the doctor that prescribed him a schedule II pain killer."

"We've got a possible overdose," he says to his partner. The other EMT quickly prepares a syringe and plunges it into his thigh through his jeans.

I zone out again and the next time I snap back to the present, Griffin is shaking me.

"Wren, what happened?" He's looking at me like I'm the one that's injured, and I look down at myself.

There's dried smears of blood on my hands and clothes. "I'm covered in blood."

My chest feels tight, and spots dance in my vision. The world tilts sideways, and it feels hard to breathe.

"Nurse," he shouts.

Everything goes black. My last thought is, "Griffin is here, he'll fix everything." Then I let oblivion take me away from all the things I can't deal with.

A BRIGHT LIGHT assaults my eyes, and I turn away from the stinging intrusion. "Mrs. Hale is waking up," I hear a voice say.

"That's not my name," I croak. My mouth feels stuffed with cotton, and I feel like I'm swimming through mud trying to get to the surface.

"I'm sorry. Wren is it?" the voice asks.

I nod, and try to get away from the light.

"You fainted in the waiting room. It seems you've had quite the stressful day."

Everything starts to flood back, and I feel my body start to shake. A rough hand takes mine, and instantly I feel calmer. "How's Liam?" I ask. The hand in mine squeezes, and we hold on to each other. I chance a peek at him, and Griffin tips his head to me.

This is right. No matter what happened between us the other night, we are family. For now at least. It makes sense someone would have called him. I'm glad he's here, because Liam is going to need him.

"Your husband overdosed on prescription pain medicine. He was under the influence of the drugs which led him to fall and hit his head on the side of the tub. He's got a concussion, but it appears you got to him in time for us to pump the drugs out of his system and administer treatment to counteract what he took."

My head drops. If I'd known, I'd have found a better way to serve him with divorce papers. "Did he try to kill himself? I didn't even know he had any of his prescription left."

"Oh, he's way beyond his original prescription. Liam has been on the list of drug seekers for a few months."

"What are you saying, doctor?" Griffin asks.

"Liam is addicted to opioids. It's going to make treatment for his head injury challenging, as it will be harder to manage his pain during recovery. He's going to go through withdrawal, which needs to be medically supervised. My recommendation is to place him in a rehabilitation facility so he can get the help he needs."

Griffin is nodding the entire time the doctor is speaking. "Does he have to agree?"

The doctor grabs either end of his stethoscope. This part of the job must be so difficult to bear. We all know Liam needs this treatment if what the doctor says is true, and we all know he's going to refuse.

"Unfortunately, since he didn't intend to die, I can't list him as a self harm risk. He's going to have to willingly agree to go to treatment."

"Wren." Griffin swallows hard and I am fascinated by the way his Adam's apple bobs up and down. I know he's going to ask me to do something I won't like.

"You want me to talk to him," I say when he doesn't continue.

"I want you to do whatever it takes to get him to go to rehab."

We both know the price I'm going to have to pay. Liam

has called and left countless messages on my phone asking me to come back, and now it seems he's found the leverage to make me.

11

Wren

Griffin and I sit in silence in the waiting room for a couple of hours while we wait for Liam to wake up. Me being here doesn't make sense. Liam is going to have to come to terms with life without me in it and what better time than while surrounded by medical professionals.

"Wren," Griffin begins.

I hold up my hand. "Just don't. I already know you've been sitting over there trying to figure out how to convince me to stay. How long am I supposed to put up with the farce?"

"He needs you," he argues.

I nod. My mind slips back to a conversation from the past.

"DID YOU HEAR ME? I said I got a full ride to Central Valley. I know that will make things hard for us, but we can do it." I try not to bounce with excitement. He put off college to be with me, and over the last year I've watched him flounder with what to do.

I thought he'd go back to school, maybe even come with me. I don't want to push that on him, but I know he doesn't really like working for his dad.

Not that I can blame him. Griffin Hale is the surliest asshole in Harriston. Old ladies cross the street when they see him, and babies cry at the sound of his voice.

Liam and I have been dating for almost two years, and in that time I think he's said one thing to me. "Wren isn't a name, it's a damn bird."

It really didn't matter in the long run. I love Liam, but who stays with their high school boyfriend? Not that I have plans to end it. Going away to school is a risk. He's a good looking guy, and when I'm gone I know there will be a line of girls vying for his attention.

He loves me, I believe that, but I also see a weakness in him when it comes to self control. He's spontaneous and always looking for a good time. Being with him is thrilling, but it's also exhausting. I never know what the next day will bring, and he's always surprising me.

The problem is, I've had enough surprises to last a lifetime and most of them have been bad. The last year in particular has me longing for some peace and stability. The death of my parents in a car accident turned my world upside down.

For a while, I loved the distraction Liam provided me. His zest for life can be infectious, and I felt like I was doing what my parents would have wanted by living every moment to the fullest. Really, I was just shoving down my grief and ignoring my pain. At night, when Liam would drop me off, I'd come home to an empty house. The quiet was the loudest sound I'd ever heard. My mom's laughter no longer rings through the house, and I'll never hear my father's booming voice yelling at his favorite sports teams again.

I miss them. Every day the reality that they are never coming back sinks in a bit more. I've been on my own since I turned eighteen. My mom's younger sister stayed with me for a few months, but the moment I was legally an adult she went back to her normal life. Since she left, I managed the loneliness by clinging to Liam, but I couldn't use him to fix my life.

"Liam?" I ask again.

"I heard you," he snaps. "So is that it? Are you breaking up with me?"

"What? No! I said it would be hard, but we can make it work. Or, I don't know—"

"I could come with you? Is that what you were going to say? I should abandon my dad and go to college with you. What am I supposed to do when I get there?"

This conversation is not going the way I thought it would. "I know you put off going to school when everything happened." I gulp, saying this is still so hard. "When my parents died. You can go now."

He sneers. "Thanks so much for your permission. I gave up my football scholarship for you, remember? I can't just get that back."

I shake my head. "I never asked you to do that. I never would have asked you to do that."

"You didn't have to. You and I are meant to be together. I don't need to waste time and money getting some fancy degree so I can take over my dad's business when it's time. What is a degree going to do for you?"

"Don't you want more? I don't want to struggle like my parents did," I tell him.

"You never learned how to appreciate what really matters. Your parents loved each other, and they had enough to support a family. Why can't you learn to be happy here?"

"I can. It isn't that you're not enough for me. Please don't take it that way." A panic like I only experienced the night the police showed up at my front door slams into me.

"I want to marry you now, not in four years. Haven't you learned how short life is? Let me be your family, be mine, and show me that I made the right decision staying here for you."

———

I LOVED LIAM. In my head I spun that moment until the story I told myself was the most romantic thing I could have ever imagined. Five years later I see some things more clearly than I did at eighteen. I loved him, but it was my fear of being alone and losing him that drove me to say yes. Not only that, but Liam's issues with his mother leaving is probably what made him ask me in the first place.

Right after my graduation, while my classmates were surrounded by their families, I stood in the crowd alone. The plan was to get into Liam's old clunker, and drive a couple of miles away to Grant Fork, the nearest decent sized city, and elope. We were checking into a hotel and going to the court house first thing in the morning. After Liam proposed, I'd had some second thoughts. Going to college and growing up were normal things I needed to do.

Yet, the loneliness I felt in the middle of the crowd shook me. It sunk so deep I feared I'd carry it around with me forever. Then I saw him standing off to the side holding a bouquet of yellow and white roses. "I know these are supposed to mean friendship, but they're your favorite, so I didn't want to bring you red ones," he said sheepishly.

Suddenly I didn't feel alone anymore. I took his hand, and tried not to look back. Maybe we were doomed from the beginning.

"Wren, are you listening to me?" Griffin breaks through my walk down memory lane.

"I'll stay, for now. I'll help you convince him to go to treatment, but that's it. I've given up everything for him once. I can't do it again. I know he turned down his scholarship for me, and I've tried everyday to make sure he didn't regret that decision. But I've sacrificed for him too, and he broke me."

I turn to walk away but look over my shoulder before I leave the room. "I'll help you as much as I can. There's a part of me that will always love him, but I have to try and love myself more. Once you get him into the facility, I'm gone. You Hale men might be the worst thing to ever happen to me."

12

Griffin

A doctor comes into the waiting room, and looks around. He's probably looking for Wren, but she stepped out about twenty minutes ago. I'm not even sure she's coming back, and I honestly can't blame her.

The doctor leads me through a maze of hallways, all heavily scented with antiseptic. He knocks on a door halfway down the hall and opens without waiting for a response. Liam is propped up in the bed, wires crisscross his body and a steady pattern of beeps from the heart monitor. I stand out of the way while the doctor completes his examination.

He doesn't say much, just writes some things down on his tablet, and tells both of us to push the button if we need a nurse.

"Great bedside manner," I mutter to myself.

"I can't wait to get out of here," Liam says.

I pull up the chair near the bed and settle in next to him. "I'm afraid that's not going to be for a while."

He starts to struggle with his blanket like he's going to get out of bed. "I'm not going to rehab."

"The fuck you're not. You almost died. If Wren hadn't found you on the floor of the bathroom you'd be dead right now. Tell me, how long did you wait for me to leave to get high?"

"Where is she? I got her papers, so is that it? She did her duty, and left?" There are bags under his eyes, and his skin is pale. He tries to look angry, but he's too weak to pull off more than irritation.

"Can you blame her?" I ask. We've both done a lot of damage to her, not that he knows the extent of it.

Liam rolls his head to the side. "Can you just go?"

I lean back and prop my feet on the bed, and settle in for a long stay. "I'm afraid I've left you alone a bit too much. Maybe if I'd paid more attention it wouldn't have gotten this bad."

He turns back to glare at me. "You sound like the doctors. I'm not an addict. I just get pain sometimes, and I accidentally took too much. Sorry I missed work, but I was tuning up my car and tweaked my back. It happens sometimes since the accident, and I thought the alcohol was out of my system. It was a mistake, but I don't need to go to rehab. I just need to actually take care of my back."

I drop my feet off the bed. "I'm glad to hear that. You had me worried. You can stick to the office tasks while we find you a doctor who can really take care of your pain so this doesn't happen again."

"You don't really believe that load of bullshit, do you?" Wren asks from the doorway.

My mouth falls open. As far as excuses go, this one is believable. He's shown no signs of addiction.

"I can see that you do. But, answer this for me, if this was a one time thing, what has been going on with him for the last six months? He's barely been sleeping, irritable, hiding things. If he's not using, why did he steal from you?" she argues.

Liam takes a deep breath, and his shoulders slump. I'm not sure if it's guilt, or resignation because he's been caught. "She's right. I want to believe you, but there's a lot that doesn't add up," I finally admit.

My son has a petty streak, a bit of my spite I'm not proud to have passed on to him, and I can see him preparing to unleash it. "We couldn't have just had problems? Maybe my dad was right, we got married too young, and I got bored. I know I handled it wrong, but you're not blameless here. You stopped paying attention to me."

"Enough, you're not going to blame this on her. I didn't raise you like that," I rush to defend her.

His eyes narrow on me, and I worry he knows. "You're defending her now? I thought this was what you wanted? She's leaving me. I screwed up, and she's bailing without a fight. You said we didn't have what it took to make a marriage work, and I guess you were right."

"Isn't he?" he speaks to Wren. "There's nothing I can say or do to make you stay."

Her eyes find mine, and I know she's about to sacrifice herself. I'm not sure how I know other than that's how she is. Wren always puts others ahead of herself. She breaks the connection and focuses back on Liam. "If I said there was, would you get help? There's no chance for us if you're using drugs."

Liam plucks at the blanket, avoiding looking at either of us. "If you stay, I'll go to rehab."

Wren nods. "It's not fixed. We will deal with your cheating, but if you want a chance this is the only one I'm going to give you."

He exhales, and relaxes back against the bed. "I'll fix everything, baby, I promise."

I clench my teeth. Helping my son is all that matters, but them being together is going to be hell to watch.

"WREN WAIT UP," I shout after her when she walks out of his room. I feel like a piece of shit making an excuse to my son so I can go chase after his wife, but I owe her something.

Her steps speed up, and she hurries out the door. I grab her arm, and spin her around. "Where are you going? You rode here in the ambulance."

She jerks her arm out of my hold. "I'm perfectly capable of walking."

"Five miles? Don't be ridiculous, baby bird."

Wren whirls around and points her finger at me. "Don't you dare call me that! I did what you wanted. I'm getting him into rehab. I get what happened between us, what *you* initiated, was a mistake, but you don't get to pass me off to your son one minute and chase me down the next."

Her words hit a wound, and I lash out like I always seem to with her. "He's your husband, and you took vows. Those should mean something."

"They really should have. It would have been nice if they'd kept my husband from fucking some random woman on our anniversary." She's screaming at me, but I can handle it better than her tears.

"Shit," I mutter to myself. "I'm sorry. I'm worried about him, and I forgot to think about you."

She shrugs and sniffs, trying to fight off tears. "Well, so did he."

"You can't walk home, though. I know I'm an asshole.

This isn't easy on me either, but please let me drive you home."

Wren shakes her head. "Take me to my car. It's closer, and I want to go through the apartment and find his stash."

"I'm parked over here," I point to my truck, "that's not something you should have to do alone."

Thankfully the drive to the apartment is short, because once again she's taken to ignoring me.

Something tells me to get to the door of the apartment before her. I hold it open while she glares at me. "Planned on shutting it in my face, huh?"

She rolls her eyes. If things were different this whole argument would be handled with her bent over my knee and my palm warming her ass. That's not in the cards for us, no matter how badly I want it to be. My son needs her more, and we can't pass her back and forth. It isn't fair to either of them, and frankly I'm not sure I could handle it either. As it is now, I've got a lot of work to do so I don't constantly feel jealous of my own son.

"Did you mean it?" I need to know, and she's offering no details.

She's searching through the freezer, not a place I would ever have thought to look. My search through the couch cushions yields nothing except some spare change and a couple stale French fries.

"Wren, would you stop fucking ignoring me?"

She pulls her head out of the freezer, and blinks her large green eyes at me. "Did I mean what, daddy?"

My next breath stutters out of my chest. "Don't," I warn her.

She smirks. "Whatever you say, daddy. I don't want to be a bad girl."

Blame stress, jealousy, or her bratty mouth, but the

logical side of my brain shuts off. I drop the cushion I'm holding, and stride toward her. She squeaks when she realizes I'm coming for her, and tries to run away from me. I catch her easily, and swing her over my shoulder.

"First I'm going to spank this juicy ass for being a brat. Then I'm going to force my fat cock in that smart mouth so you can't give me any more sass."

That's the only warning I'm giving her, and my hand comes down with a crack on her denim clad ass. The way her flesh feels under my palm makes my cock swell to bursting. I let her slide down my body, and guide her until she's on her knees.

She looks up at me, all large eyes and bee stung lips. She's like a wet dream, and right now she's all mine. I undo my jeans to relieve my painfully large erection. "Let's see if we can find a better use of that mouth."

She licks her lips and I almost come. I make quick work of the zipper and drop my pants enough to free my cock.

"Look at my baby bird so hungry for my cock." I fist her hair in my hand and tap the head against her lips.

"Be a good slut and open your mouth for daddy."

Her hands go to rest against my thighs, and she opens obediently. I pet the top of her head.

"My girl knows when she's been bad, and how to make it up to daddy, doesn't she."

Wren nods her head. It isn't enough though, and I pull her hair back. "I want the words."

"Yes daddy. I've been bad."

I thrust into her mouth and hit the back of her throat. "I'm going to fuck your mouth now. Be a good little slut and open your throat."

She gags the first time I push back, but soon she's sucking and letting me deep into her throat. Filthy words tumble from my lips as she enthusiastically swallows my length. Tears run down her face from the effort, but she doesn't stop working my dick.

"Is your pussy getting wet while you suck my cock?"

She hums, and the vibration sends a tingle through my balls.

I groan. "Keep doing that for daddy. You'll be a good slut and swallow when I come, won't you?"

She groans, and her hand slips from my thigh toward her pussy. I pull her hair again. "That's my pussy. You aren't allowed to touch it. No one else is allowed to touch it," I growl, and hate myself for meaning it.

The sounds are obscene as I slip in and out of her mouth. Her teeth lightly graze my shaft, and I explode. I hold myself deep inside her throat as I spill everything I have, and she slurps it down like I told her to.

"Strip your clothes off," I demand, not nearly done with her. If we're going to fuck up, we might as well enjoy it.

I pull out one of the chairs at their tiny kitchen table. Furniture she picked out with my son. Shoving that image out of my mind I give her the look. The one that says she's going to get spanked if she doesn't do as she's told.

She has my full attention as she peels off her sweatshirt, pushes down her jeans, and slips out of her bra and underwear.

I grunt. "I can't believe I fucked you without seeing the magnificence of your naked body. I am going to enjoy feasting on you. Now come here, daddy's hungry."

She's much more timid naked. "Don't hide from me now," I tell her as she fidgets trying to cover herself with her arms.

I pat the edge of the table. "Come sit that sweet ass right here in front of me."

Wren hesitates, and I lift her up and set her down on the spot in front of my chair. "Open your legs," I order.

When she doesn't do it, I force her legs open, and slap her pussy. "Don't hide what's mine."

She groans and writhes on the table. I hum. "Daddy's little slut likes it rough, does she?"

I spank her mound a few more times, paying attention to hitting directly on her clit. The tight bundle of nerves swells and reddens from my swats and her excitement.

"You don't know how badly I want to fuck you right now," I groan.

"Please, Griff. I want you to," she begs.

"Not yet, baby bird." I sit back down in the chair and drape her legs over my shoulders. This might be the last time I get to have her this way, and this time I'm going to savor it.

I bury my face in her pussy and swipe my tongue up her slit, flicking her swollen clit with each pass. My cock stands at full attention, and the tip weeps to slip inside the tight heaven of her cunt. I won't be able to hold back much longer, so I fuck her with my tongue the way I will shortly be fucking her with my cock.

She grunts and groans and presses harder against my mouth. I add two fingers, curling them ruthlessly against her g-spot and she detonates, flooding my mouth with her release. I make a show of wiping her juices from my chin, and she blushes.

I start to work my pants back down, but she pushes me back with her foot in the middle of my chest. "I want to see all of you."

"What my baby bird wants, she gets," I agree and shed all of my clothes.

Her eyes fixate on my chest and stomach. "Like what you see?"

"Very much," she says in a husky voice.

"Me too," I match her tone and lean forward to suck one of her nipples into my mouth. Giving the other one equal attention, she squirms underneath me.

I line my cock up with her opening, and she freezes. "Condom," she says.

Sliding the head up and down her slit, I push the tip inside, ignoring her demands. "No, I'm going to fuck you raw. I'm going to paint your tight cunt with my cum, and you're going to let me like a good little slut. Do you know why?"

"Why, daddy?" she asks in a meek tone.

"Because this is my pussy, and I'm going to claim it."

I slam so hard inside of her the table scoots across the floor and my balls slap against her ass. My fingers dig into her hips hard enough to leave bruises, and in this state I hope they do. I want my marks on her body just like I want my cum in her pussy. Pulling her back to meet each of my thrusts we slam together over and over.

Each thrust sends my body soaring, and my heart pounding against my chest. How am I supposed to walk away from her? To watch her reconcile with my son?

I already know I can't. When Liam is better, either I'll have to encourage them to leave, or I will. Knowing my time with her is coming to a close, I bring us both to climax, claiming the one woman that can never really be mine.

13

Wren

We're quiet after we get dressed. Instead of me ignoring him, like earlier, there's a cloud of melancholy hanging over us. At least for me, there's a sense of loss I can't shake, like I found a missing piece of myself, but I can't hold on to it.

I knew it before I pushed his buttons. I'm tired of being rejected by these men, and I wanted to walk away on my own terms. No matter what I told Liam back at the hospital, I still plan to leave. I'm a forgiving person, but I can't forgive his betrayal.

I go back to searching the freezer. It's one of Liam's favorite hiding spots for money, so it seems a safe bet if he has any drugs, this is where he'd keep them.

"Why are you looking in there?" he asks, while he puts the couch back together.

In the back of the freezer I find a box of Girl Scout cookies. Considering I haven't bought any of them for at least a couple years, I pull it out. Opening the end, I find a large storage baggie filled with round, white pills.

I hold it up. "This is why."

"Son of a bitch," Griffin shouts and kicks the table, busting one of the legs.

"We're not done yet." I move through a few other places I know he likes to hide things, including the vent in the bedroom, and the false bottom of one of his dresser drawers.

After we've torn apart the entire apartment, we've got several dozen pills, and a wad of cash.

"You were right," Griffin admits. I jump as he comes up behind me. "I'm not sure I even know who my son is anymore."

"That makes two of us," I agree.

He puts his hand on my shoulder. "Thank you for helping me get him help. You never answered my question earlier, by the way."

"Yes I did," I say, and point to one of the bags. "I know he needs help, but he's been lying to me for half a year, cheating on me, and treating me like shit. I care about him enough to get him help, but I can't be with him anymore."

He squeezes my shoulder. "You should go on home. It's getting late, and Liam is my mess to clean up from now on."

I nod and head to the door. Turning in the doorway, I pause and look at him. He holds my gaze and gives me a sad smile. We both know whatever is happening between us needs to end. No matter what Liam did to me, two wrongs don't make a right.

"OKAY, bitch, spill. Why do you look both satisfied and sad at the same time?" Bess hops up on the bar and swings her legs back and forth while I put bottles of beer into the coolers under the bar.

"Can you make yourself useful and get some ice?" I complain.

"Fine, don't tell me, but you obviously got some bow chicka bow wow today. Was it bad? Did you have to lay there and think of England or something?" she continues to carry on her ridiculous conversation without my input.

"Shit," she whispers dramatically. Her head swivels around scoping out all the exits. "It wasn't Donovan, right? You aren't supposed to shit where you eat, which is a really gross way of saying, don't fuck the boss, if you ask me."

I flap my arms at her. "No, it wasn't Donovan. Can we drop this please?"

She claps her hands. "But it was somebody." She does a wiggle on top of the bar. "Wren got her pipes cleaned," she starts to sing before I slap my hand over her mouth.

"Fuck, you're extra today. I'll talk to you if you keep your voice down," I hiss.

Bess does a little shimmy and hops down from the bar. "You know, in the future, it would be a lot less painful for you if you'd just give in to me from the beginning. These are things you should know if you're going to be my BFF."

I can't help but smile at her. "Just like that? We go on one shopping spree and to the salon and now we're best friends?"

"Need me to make you a bracelet? My macrame skills are a little rusty, but I'll hit the craft store tomorrow and whip you up a friendship bracelet." She nods like this is the best idea she's had in a while, and I'm pretty sure she's already picking out colors to use on what I would bet will be matching bracelets.

"You're a little bent, you know that right?" I ask her.

She shrugs. "Life is more fun this way. Better to be bent than boring."

Truthfully, I am in the market for a best friend. Audrey

has been increasingly absent for the last few months. So much so, I've stopped reaching out. It's at the point now that I have to assume we have the relationship she wants.

"Ugh," I groan. "I might have, kinda, hooked up with my father-in-law." The last words I rush out and purposely say a bit garbled.

Her mouth falls open, and she hops up and down. "You are my hero. No, not *he-ro*. We can't let men get the credit for this. You, my dear, are my *she-ro*."

She waggles her eyebrows. "You slut, I absolutely worship the skanky ground you walk on. That man is a meal."

I blush, remembering Griffin call me that, then school my features. "I don't think slut is supposed to be a compliment."

Bess shrugs a shoulder. "I'm reclaiming it. In my book slut and bitch are both aspirational goals. I'm going to throw my kitty wherever I want to and I'm not going to take any shit while I do it."

"Huh," I say. "Maybe you're my shero."

"I bet he's a kinky fuck, amirite?" she asks.

I laugh. "My lips are sealed."

"Hopefully not for daddy Hale," she says while doing a dance.

My eyes widen and my mouth falls open.

She looks at me, and a smile slowly spreads across her face. "Oh my god! I was joking, but do you...oh you kinky bitch. Real talk," her joking demeanor turns serious, "your husband did a number on you. Even if this thing with his dad is just good sex and revenge, I'm one hundred percent behind you. Whatever you need to do to get a piece of your power back, you do it, and don't you feel any guilt for how that douchebag ex of yours feels about it."

"Well, whatever it was, it's over. Nothing happened

between us while I still lived with Liam, but no matter what, that's his dad. So, I might not have anything to feel guilty about, I can't put Griffin in that position."

We got pretty busy considering it is Monday. There's not a lot to do in this town, and there's a lot of reasons people want to forget everything, even for a little while. So Bess and I hustle serving drinks for the next few hours. It's around midnight by the time the bar starts to clear out. I don't envy the shift managers in the morning when they're trying to get a day's work out of a hung over crew.

I yawn, and Donovan guides me to sit on one of the stools. "You can't keep burning the candle at both ends. You work at the insurance agency tomorrow, right?"

I bob my head. The emotional toil followed by working two jobs is starting to drag me down. I long for my bed, and at least six hours of unconscious peace.

"Go on and take off. Bess will stay and help me clean up. Won't you Bessie?" he shouts across the bar.

"Would you quit calling me Bessie, for fuck's sake? That's the name of a cow, or like a grandma."

"A really hot grandma," he says and alternates waggling his eyebrows.

My attention bounces back and forth between them. "Are the two of you? Uhm, is there a thing here?" Then my brow furrows in confusion. "But you asked me if he and I?"

Donovan props his elbows on the bar, and rests his head in his hands. "Please, continue. I'd love to hear how Bess asked you if we were doing the horizontal tango."

She pops a hip and puts her hand on it. A sure sign something sassy is about to come out of her mouth. "No one talks like that."

I raise my hand. My sleep deprived state making me punchy. "You pretty much always talk like that."

"I might say boinking, porking, aggressive cuddling, boning, bumping uglies, feeding the kitty, humping, laying pipe, nailing—" I put my hand over her mouth.

"We get it, Bess. Why did you ask me if Donovan and I were," I flap my free hand around, "doing any of that?"

She mutters against my hand, and I drop it so she can actually answer me. "Because, sometimes, when neither of us are seeing anyone, Donovan asks me if I want to stay late to help clean up. Really, it's just code for asking to bend me over the bar."

"To be fair, I also want you to help me clean up," he adds unhelpfully.

"What about don't shit where you eat?" I ask.

"That advice is for nice girls like you. I rather enjoy ending the night with a bonus from the boss," she winks.

"I would actually like to see you outside of the bar," he says and rolls his eyes.

"And you will," she begins, and he leans forward, excited. "When you walk me to my car," she finishes.

"You're a wicked woman," he grumbles.

"A very bendy one," she quips.

I toss my bar rag on the counter. "On that note, I'm going to leave."

"I'll walk you to your car," he offers. I take him up on it because even Harriston can be sketchy after dark.

Bess wiggles her fingers at me. "Sleep well my little Wrenegade!"

I shake my head. "Now that's a good one."

Donovan holds the back door open for me and walks me to my car. He lingers a bit while I open the door and toss my bag inside. I can tell he wants to ask me a question away from my newly minted BFF. He leans against the side, and fidgets. It's kind of adorable.

I like the two of them together. She's a punk princess

with platinum hair, and he's got this whole golden boy with a naughty streak thing going for him.

"Did she really ask you if you and I had hooked up?" he finally musters the courage to ask.

I nod. "But I think she's trying to feel out if you two are more than," I look back at the bar, "whatever happens when you turn on the closed sign. Despite her calling me her BFF, she and I are just getting to know each other."

He draws lines in the gravel with the toe of his boot. "So you don't have any advice for me?"

"Don't give up?" That should have sounded like a statement. "Don't give up," I try again.

"You sound really sure about that," he mutters.

"Okay, you go in there and rock her world. Make her see entire constellations, then when she's still riding that high, ask her out," I advise.

"So sex her into a date?"

I shrug. "If she keeps coming back you're obviously giving her what she wants. Step it up a notch then go in for the kill." I slap him on the back. "You can do it, Tiger!"

He narrows his eyes. "I'm not sure she's the best influence on you."

Going for gold, I shoot him with a finger gun. "Agree to disagree, champ."

"I think I preferred Tiger," he grumbles.

I shake my head. "Nah, I'm going to keep searching. Have to find the right one for my GBF."

He rolls his eyes. "I can see it now, what she likes about you. You're both nuts. I'm not gay, by the way. Not that it matters, but you might not want to go around calling me your GBF."

I scrunch up my face. "So that doesn't mean guy best friend?"

He ruffles my hair. "Nope, little Wrenegade, it does not."

Shrugging my shoulders, I say, "Okay, well I'll find something for that too. Now go rock her world and put a label on it."

He walks toward the back door and salutes me. Only once I'm in my car does he go inside. My heart swells. I really needed the reminder that not all guys were cheating assholes, or their father. Maybe someday I can find myself an adorkable guy of my own.

14

Griffin

I usually like going into the shop early in the morning before Charlie gets in. I find it peaceful when it's just me and the cars. At least usually. This morning I can't stop replaying the little scene I witnessed outside Donovan's last night.

It occurred to me after Wren left the apartment yesterday, that she still had a shift at the bar. At least I assumed she did since she seems determined to work herself to death. I didn't think it was too creepy of me to drive by and make sure she made it home okay.

What we're doing is wrong. Liam has to be my priority, but she's also worked her way under my skin in a way I don't think I can dig out. Wanting her, worrying about her is an infliction I fear I'll be living with for a long time to come. After what I saw though, I think I'm alone in feeling that way.

The first time I saw Donovan with her, I knew he wanted her. Why wouldn't he? She's beautiful, vibrant, caring, smart and funny.

Normally I wouldn't be jealous of Donovan Miller. We're both business owners. Compared to a lot of others in town, we're both doing pretty well financially. In Harriston that means we can pay our bills, and own our own home. But, Donovan is ten years younger than me and not Liam's father.

Those things play in his favor, but he's too much of a golden retriever for Wren. She might not admit it about herself, but she's got a kinky side to match mine. She likes my dirty words, the sting of my hand on her ass, and when I fuck her hard. I might be able to tolerate seeing her with my son, maybe, but no one else is going to have her. She's a Hale, whether she took the name or not.

The booming bass of my music cuts off suddenly. I pull my head out from under the hood and see Charlie standing by the sound system with a look of pity and judgment on his face.

"Whatever you're going to say, save it," I bark.

Of course, he ignores me. He's the only one who's truly immune to my perpetually gloomy demeanor. "How's Liam?"

"Alive and pretty damn lucky. You didn't know he was abusing drugs, did you?" I ask.

"Do you really think I'd keep something like that from you?" He shoots back.

"You didn't tell me my son was cheating on his wife," I point out.

His eyes narrow. "I saw what you weren't willing to admit to yourself. You want Wren for yourself."

I squeeze the wrench in my hand so hard my knuckles turn white, then force myself to put it into the toolbox. There's already been one broken window this week due to my temper. "I never acted on it until she left him."

"Do you think that will hurt him less? He still loves her. She's his wife," Charlie yells.

"What about her? He's fucking lied to her for years. She thinks he gave up a scholarship for her. He's been screwing some woman for months behind her back. He's been doing fucking drugs," I shout back.

"All of that is really shitty. I wouldn't blame her for being with someone else, as long as it isn't you," he says in a more normal tone.

"I get it, okay?"

He shakes his head. "I really don't think you do. Liam isn't the only addict in the family. Wren is your drug."

When Julio arrives, I retreat into my office. It isn't Charlie's scowls that send me away, but the words he shot my way. Wren is under my skin, in my brain, and I could imagine she could be the fucking air I breathe if I let her. Is that an addiction?

It's true that my feelings for her haven't made me the best person. I've treated her like a nuisance, when in reality seeing her is always the best part of my day. It's also the worst knowing the damage it would cause if Liam ever figured out how I really feel.

But, to label these feelings as an addiction is also wrong. Falling for her might be a curse, but it's not a disease. My wanting her isn't selfish, because I still intend to convince her to leave town. Even if we were different people, free to love and be loved without someone else getting hurt, I'm still too old for her. She deserves this time to be young, to figure out who she is, and to fall in love with someone without all the baggage someone nearly twice her age brings.

There's a knock on my office door, but it's just a courtesy as it swings open without me saying a word. Charlie stands in the doorway when he'd usually stroll in and make himself at home. He doesn't speak, and I don't try to end the awkward tension by asking him what he wants.

Finally he breaks, and speaks first. "You're thinking awfully hard in here."

I grunt. He's not willing to listen, and I'm not even sure how I feel about the things I've done over the last couple of weeks. How far I've fallen as a father, and how quickly I'd do it all over again.

He comes all the way in and sets the cordless phone down on my desk. "You left this in the shop. The doctor called. Liam is getting moved to rehab tomorrow as long as his vitals stay stable."

I nod. "Yeah, his liver enzymes were elevated and they wanted to make sure there wasn't more extensive damage to his internal organs."

Just saying those words churn my stomach. Not only had I missed all the signs, but now my child, the one person I am actually responsible for in this world, is in the hospital being monitored for an overdose.

"Did he say when I'll get to see him?" I ask.

"I asked, but he said you'll find out when they call you from rehab, but expect it to be at least a week after he gets there," he relays.

I actually already knew this. I've Googled the facility, and they have a section for frequently asked questions. What I don't understand is why Charlie is still looking at me like my world is about to fall apart.

"What aren't you telling me Charlie?"

He takes a deep breath, and I know it's going to be bad. My apprehension grows when he closes the door and sits down in front of my desk. "You actually missed two calls. I was coming back to tell you about the first, but you were talking to the supplier Liam had canceled. Then the doctor called."

"Fucking spit it out, man. We're getting old, and I'm not sure how much more stress my ticker can take," I gripe.

He rolls his eyes. "It didn't give out when you were boning a twenty-three-year-old, so I think you'll be fine."

Something in me snaps. I stand up so fast my chair clatters to the ground. I've got his shirt in my fist before he even registers that I've come around my desk, and I'm leaning him back over his chair. "Do not fucking talk about Wren like she's some slut I picked up in a bar."

He knocks my hand away, and gives me a shove back. "Get a grip, Griff. You're falling for her, and you can't let that happen."

I force myself to go back a few steps and lean against the filing cabinet. "How many times are you going to lecture me on what this will do to my son? I fucking get it okay? Do you want me to admit I'm falling for her? We both know I am. Hell, I think you've known it for longer than I have. But, do not question what I'm willing to give up for my son. If I have to cut out my heart to keep him safe, I'll fucking do it."

Charlie shakes his head. "Do you hear yourself? She's your heart now?"

My teeth grind and ache with how hard I clench my jaw. "It doesn't matter. She needs to get out of this town. I won't hold her here like Liam did."

"What are you talking about? They fell in love and got married. I don't think she should have given up her scholarship just because he lost his, but that was her choice."

"Bullshit. She wasn't given a choice, not a real one." I force myself to take a breath and shove down the anger bubbling up.

"I'd never heard the story from her perspective before. Seems my son has lied to her for longer than the last six months. He told her he put off his scholarship to stay with her, because he didn't want her to be alone after she lost her parents. Then when it was time to go to school he wouldn't go with her."

Charlie's shoulders slump. "I didn't know."

"What difference would it have made if either of us had known?" I ask.

"I doubt you would have spent the last five years treating her like shit if you'd known. I don't know if I'd have kept the boy's secret about his cheating. She could have had an entirely different life, Griff. Liam is your boy, hell he feels like mine too, but Wren is part of this family. We both watched her change from a teenager to an adult. I was friends with her dad, so I've known her a lot longer."

"The truth is, I'm not sure I would have done anything different. If I thought it would make her leave, I'd treat her the same way I did," I admit.

"It was never about Liam, was it?"

I shake my head. "She's always been meant for more than the life she can have in this town."

Turning the chair I knocked over back upright, I sit back down. "That isn't the bad news you are struggling to figure out how to tell me."

"Our insurance won't cover the costs of the rehab."

It's a good thing I'm sitting or I'd fall over. "How much?"

"Fifteen thousand, and they need half up front," he says.

"We're running in the negative here at the shop thanks to Liam's creative accounting practices. Reordering all those parts at our expense, and refunding the overcharged customers is more than we had on hand. I had to take out a line of credit against the business to cover it. And in order to pay that back, I had to cancel the new equipment we ordered."

Charlie looks over his shoulder, out the window of the door. "We're going to have to lay off the kid, aren't we?"

I nod. "We're basically fucked. I am taking a pay cut to try and prevent letting Julio go, but that means—"

"You don't have the money," Charlie concludes. He pinches the bridge of his nose. "Shit."

"You just realized I need to go talk to Wren, didn't you?" I ask.

"Just don't slip and let your dick fall into her," he jokes.

"I make no promises. The way my kid keeps fucking up my life, she's the only person keeping me sane."

He holds his hands up in surrender. "I don't like it, but I do understand. But, forget what I said about hurting Liam, don't hurt Wren. She's been through enough."

I HURRY over to the insurance office to catch Wren as she's closing the office for lunch. Before she moved out, she used to head home to make herself something to save money. I don't know what she's been doing the last couple of weeks since Dolores lives a bit farther away from the office. Not that Harriston is a booming metropolis, but we've definitely mastered the art of suburban sprawl. People here like their space. It's one of the few luxuries most of us enjoy.

She steps out of the office at exactly twelve o'clock, and is so focused on locking the door she doesn't see me leaning against my truck. I wait for her to look over, but she's totally oblivious.

"I know it's pretty safe here, but you should still be

more aware of your surroundings," I say, alerting her to my presence.

Wren jumps and turns around. With her hand over her heart, she leans forward to catch her breath. "Damnit! You scared the shit out of me. I swear, I see you more now than when I was actually part of the family."

"It's a bit different now," I grumble.

She crosses the sidewalk to stand in front of me. "What's up?"

I cross one foot over my ankle. "Couldn't I just have wanted to see you?"

One eyebrow curves up, and she purses her lips, but otherwise says nothing.

"Alright, I need you to go to the bank and get access to your bank accounts," I tell her.

She crosses her arms. "Why?"

I exhale a puff of air. "Because I found out today that the health insurance I got to cover the shop's employees won't cover Liam's rehab. It's going to be at least fifteen thousand dollars. I'd take out a loan to cover the costs, but—"

She nods her head over and over. "Let me guess, because he cheated some of the customers you're in the hole, because of course you're replacing parts and refunding the customers."

"How did you know?" I was under the belief Wren thought I was pretty much the devil.

"Because, while you may be really grouchy, pretty much all the time, you're a good man," she says softly.

I fight the urge to grab her, and pin my hands under my arm pits. "You still believe that?"

She nods. "Despite what Liam did, your first instinct was to take all the burden on to yourself. I'm not sure he deserves you as a father, but I am glad he has you."

I look away. "I'm not sure about that. A good father doesn't fuck his son's wife."

"Why are we going to the bank?" she asks, and I know she's going to do it no matter my explanation. I'm not sure I've earned this level of loyalty, but I'm determined not to betray it.

"I'm hoping he's got some of the money he took from the shop. It's a long shot, but I'm not sure what else to do."

She takes a deep breath. "I do. Let's go and check the accounts, because I want to know what's in them too, but if there's nothing, there's still one thing we can do."

I stand straighter, a kernel of hope blooming in my chest.

Her head drops down. "My parents had a life insurance policy. It doesn't make sense to me now, but last year, Liam convinced me to use it to buy him the Mustang. I insisted the car be put in my name if we were using my money."

"He took your savings to buy himself a car, and you aren't even allowed access to your own money?" I ask. I'm aware my voice has dropped to a growl.

Her green eyes turn glassy, and she looks away from me. "You don't have to point out how stupid I've been. Believe me, I know. I keep getting the feeling there's going to be a lot more before I know the full extent of how much Liam betrayed me."

I can't resist anymore. I take one step and wrap my arms around her, tucking her against my chest. "I promise you that I'll make this right. As much as I can, you will not live with this forever."

She shakes her head. "I appreciate that you want to fix this, but some things once broken can never be put back together."

"When do you have to be back?" I ask, knowing she's still got work today.

"I actually have the rest of the day off. Carl had a family thing come up, and will be out of the office for the rest of the day. He thinks it's dangerous for me to be here alone since people know he takes cash payments."

"He's right. Okay, let's go to the bank, and then I'll get you lunch."

15

Wren

Harriston Savings and Loan is the only bank in town, but even in a town as small as this one, most people do their banking online. In order to stay in business, they are one of the few businesses in town that has stayed current with technology. They have an app for smart phones, and the ability to deposit cash at the ATM.

I'd love not to have to face a person and admit my husband wouldn't let me have access to our accounts, but that's one thing the internet services can't help me with. Instead I stand in line, with Griffin, in a bank I'd recently opened my own account in only a couple weeks ago. If the town isn't already talking about me, they would be by the end of the day. Arlene, the bank teller, is almost as bad of a gossip as the pharmacist.

There's a couple people in line ahead of me, and my anxiety increases the closer I get to her window. When it's my turn, I'm digging my nails into the flesh of my palm to keep from hyperventilating.

Arlene practically bounces in place as my turn comes

around. "Hey there, Wren! So nice to see a young person actually use the lobby. What can I do for you?"

I force a smile. It's not her fault this makes me uncomfortable. It's probably why, even though I didn't like that Liam kept me from the bank accounts, I didn't force the issue. I'm not the best at confronting people.

"I need access to my joint accounts with Liam," I say, faking as much confidence as I can muster.

She looks at me sadly. "Honey, you don't have any joint accounts."

I feel a dark cloud brewing. Specifically, a six-foot-three-inch storm of pissed off standing right behind me. He presses up close to me, and leans against the counter. "What do you mean she doesn't have joint accounts with Liam?"

Arlene blinks rapidly. Griffin has that effect on women. Even when he's pissed off, he's stunning. "I'm sorry, Mr. Hale. Liam never put Wren's name on the accounts."

"Were her checks ever deposited into those accounts?" he pushes.

She nods. "Yes sir. Twice every month for the last four and a half years I believe."

Griffin raps his knuckles on the counter. "Then why can't you show her what was being done with her money?"

She trembles slightly, and part of me feels bad for her. I know what it's like to be the focus of his ire. Arlene looks to me for help, but Griffin and I are on the same side for once.

"I'm sorry, really. I can't disclose private financial information. I can show her the lines of credit she has open," she offers.

My jaw drops. "The what? I didn't open any lines of credit."

Two Wrongs

Now she really starts to shake. "Oh, my." She puts her hands on either side of her face, and she pales.

"I think I better go grab Greg." Before we can say anything, she runs off to the back office.

Greg Johnson, the bank manager, comes out wringing his hands after fifteen of the longest minutes of my life. "Wren, can you come back to my office?"

I start to follow him, and realize Griffin is right behind me. For a second I think to make him wait in the lobby, because it has to be about something Liam has done. Griffin has already dealt with enough disappointment where his son is concerned. I can't lean on him to get through this. It's not fair to him, and will only make it harder on me when I have to cut both of them out of my life.

Then he slips his hand into mine and squeezes, lending me the strength I wouldn't have asked for. The thing is, he'll find out about this whether I take him into that room with me or not, and maybe he needs my support too.

Greg waits for us by the door to his office, and once we enter he closes the door and takes a seat behind his desk. He steeples his fingers and takes a deep breath, which makes me hold mine while waiting for him to speak.

"Wren, I'm not sure how to tell you this. Apparently, Arlene assisted your husband several months ago in opening a few lines of credit in your name. I can't tell you why she did this as it's against policy, but if you like I can help you start the process of disputing them. I can see that you've never had access to the bank accounts, but since this is a community property state, and I see your checks have been deposited, I'm going to grant you access to those."

Words won't come out of my mouth. I sit there staring, my mouth opening and closing. Griffin puts his hand on the back of my neck, and squeezes. The move grounds me. "Greg, can you give us a couple of minutes?" Griffin asks.

"Of course," he says. He stands up and pauses before he opens the door. "I'm terribly sorry for the role the bank has played in this. If you'd like I can go pull a credit report and see if there are any other accounts opened in your name."

I nod, still unable to speak.

Once we are alone, Griffin turns my chair to face his. "Breathe, Wren."

His demand is enough to make me suck in a lungful of air. "Slower," he orders, and I instantly obey. Later, I'll reflect on why I am so eager to follow his instructions, but right now I need him to get me through this. So much for my decision not to lean on him.

"Okay, now that I'm not worried you're going to hyperventilate and pass out, let's sort through this," he says.

"How? We don't even know the extent of what it is, other than Liam opened accounts in my name. I don't know if he's made payments on them, or what they were used for," I point out.

"What if—" he starts, but I cut him off by holding up my hand.

"I'm usually the one getting ahead of myself. Let's just get Greg back in here and find out what we're dealing with," I suggest. I'm surprised at how calm I'm able to appear when inside I'm falling apart. All my plans, leaving town and going to school, seem to be evaporating right before my eyes.

Griffin nods. "Let me go get Greg."

He opens the door, and waves him down. Greg rushes back in with papers clutched in his hand. The look on his face is all the confirmation I need that this is exactly as bad as I fear.

He takes forever to get situated. The entire time he fidgets with the papers, I clutch the arms of the chair. Thankfully, Griffin hasn't given up being an asshole completely. "For fuck's sake, will you tell her what you found already?"

This only serves to fluster the bank manager even more. I try a more gentle approach. "Greg, Mr. Johnson, the sooner I know what I'm dealing with, the sooner I can do something about it. I know this is unpleasant." I have to swallow the urge to yell at him as well. Being considerate of the feelings of others is second nature to me, and I'm getting fucking sick of it.

My words have the desired effect though, and he composes himself. He extends his hand with the report. "I can't read it," I say, panicking. "The paper won't stop shaking." The pain in my chest is sudden, and once again I find it hard to breathe.

Griffin takes the papers from me. "The paper isn't shaking. You are." He flips through the two page report, and I watch it start to crumple in his hand.

"There's three lines of credit." He turns his pissed off gaze toward Greg. "All opened at this bank. He took out a total of ten thousand dollars and has made only sporadic payments."

Greg cringes. "Actually, several hundred of that amount is from late fees and interest."

"How does she go about getting rid of the negative reports and this debt?" Griff asks the question I need to know, but am too afraid to ask.

Greg looks down at the table, afraid to meet Griffin's eyes. "She'll have to file a police report for fraud, and then we'll go through the steps to clear her credit report of the charges."

I stand up, not wanting to face this yet. Being cheated

on was bad, but in a way I don't think Liam was trying to hurt me. Sure, being ignored for six months while he ran around with another woman behind my back didn't feel good, but he did try to keep me from finding out. This feels worse. Taking out money in my name, and not paying it back was always going to have a negative impact on my life.

My car is back at the insurance office, but that doesn't matter right now. I rush through the bank, aware Griffin is yelling after me. Every eye in the bank turns my way, and I know this will get added to what they're already whispering about me all over town. Right now I don't care. I can't listen to Griffin try and talk me out of doing what I have to do. Liam has taken away too much. I can't let him take the dream of a future from me too.

"Wren," he shouts outside of the bank.

My brain must have vacated my body, and I attempt to run in my pencil skirt and heels.

He could easily chase me down, but we're on the main road through town, and there's a few people out who would no doubt be alarmed at a grown man chasing down a woman and manhandling her into his vehicle.

I didn't factor in the fact that Griffin Hale doesn't give a shit what anyone thinks of him. His footsteps thunder on the concrete behind me. I risk a look back, and one of my heels gets stuck in the seam of the sidewalk. It's enough to throw off my balance. I have just enough time to tuck my arms around my head, and brace myself.

Before I hit the ground his arms catch my middle, and I'm tossed over his shoulder. I hear the crack of his hand hitting my bottom before I feel the sting. Even though he's just punished me in broad daylight, our previous interactions of this nature have conditioned me for pleasure, and I start to squirm, but not to get put down.

He strides back to his truck and drops me into the passenger seat. Reaching across me, he buckles my seatbelt in. "We are going to deal with you running from me later, but first we've got some things to sort out."

"THIS ISN'T the way to the office," I say when he passes the turn.

Griffin squeezes the steering wheel and slowly exhales. "We're not going back to your car. If we do, you'll run off. I told you, we need to talk."

After a couple of minutes, he pulls into his driveway. I start to open my door, and he growls. "Will you just fucking sit tight and wait for me to get a god damn door? I know my son forgot everything I taught him about how to treat a lady, but I sure as hell didn't."

I raise one eyebrow. Surely he hears himself. He must, right? "Where in the gentlemen's guides does it say you're supposed to yell at a lady?"

"Page eight, smart ass, just above where it says if your woman is acting like a brat you're supposed to take her over your knee and redden her ass," he says back without missing a beat.

I'll give the man one thing, he gives good banter. Then all of his words play in my head. "Your woman?"

His Adam's apple bobs in his throat, but he doesn't answer. He just jumps out and storms around the front of his truck. The door groans as he opens it. It might be rust and metal, but I think even inanimate objects can feel when he's annoyed.

Griffin paces in the path in front of the house. I can feel his frustration crackling in the air from where I stand by his truck. I don't know if it's what I said or the whole situation with Liam, but there's a war raging inside of him. One that seems to come to a conclusion as he stops pacing and focuses on me with a sort of laser precision.

Griffin's long legs eat up the space between us. One hand slips into my hair while the other presses into the window next to my head. He pulls my hair, forcing me to look up at him. "It's not forever. We can never be forever, but for now you're mine."

"For now," I agree.

16

Griffin

I push away from Wren before I take her on the front lawn of my house. I keep telling myself we can't be together, then some other truth wiggles up to the surface about what my son has done, and I care less and less how Liam might feel about it. Maybe that makes me a shitty father, but he's not being a great son either.

"Let's go in," I grumble. I take her hand and drag her behind me.

A nervous energy fills me up, and I fight the urge to start pacing again. I know a sure fire way to work out all of this anxiety, but before anything physical happens between Wren and I again we need to talk. I could be delusional, but I'd like to think we could help each other through this. Hell, if she's the only one of us who benefits from this arrangement I plan to propose, then that'll be enough.

While I'm trying to sort through all the things I need to say to her, she sighs. "Can you sit? All your fidgeting is making me nervous."

I make sure to sit as far away from her as I can to keep from giving in to the urge to touch her.

"Thanks," she mumbles. "I don't know what to do. If I file a police report Liam is going to get in a lot of trouble, but if I don't my life is fucked."

I nod. Of course I want to tell her not to file a report. Despite everything he's done, he's still my son, and I want to protect him. But, she's right. Her life will be harder to start out six thousand dollars in debt, with a negative payment history. There will be enough trauma starting over as a divorced twenty-three-year-old woman.

Her eyes narrow, and I can tell she's getting pissed off. "Don't just sit there and agree with me."

"What do you want me to do, baby bird? I want to protect my son, but you don't owe him shit after the things he's done to you."

She deflates, and folds in on herself. I rush to her side. I've never been good at watching a woman cry, that's even more true when it's Wren. I thought it was hard to see her happy with someone else, my own son at that, but I was wrong. Seeing her misery is worse.

I wrap my arms around her and hold her against my chest. I don't tell her everything is okay, or to stop crying. She deserves to shed every tear she needs to. This entire situation is shit and it's better to get it all out. Eventually her breathing evens out, and she falls asleep in my arms.

Our discussion can wait. The shit storm we're in isn't going anywhere, and for a few minutes her mind is at ease. I scoop her up in my arms and make a decision I may end up regretting.

Bypassing my guest room, I take her straight to my bed and tuck her in. I brush her hair from her face and kiss her forehead. "Sleep now, baby bird."

I HAVE hours alone to sit and look at the life I've built. My business and home were things I didn't believe were possible when I was a child. Growing up with alcoholics for parents, I thought I was doing well not to spend my days at the bottom of a bottle. Then Liam came into my life much too soon, and everything changed. I had someone else to think about, and all the negative voices in my head weren't enough to stop me from trying.

When Liam was eleven, I managed to buy this house. It was a foreclosure, and in rough shape. I remodeled it one project at a time. Those days were filled with watching lots of how to videos and teaching myself all the things I should have been taught how to do by my dad. It was an eyesore straight from the seventies, shag carpet and all. All of the rooms were separate, giving the house a boxy closed in feel. I knocked down some walls, removed the wood paneling, new counters, appliances, and wood floors and it became an entirely different house.

I'm proud of it, not only because I did all the work myself, but because I was able to give my son a stable home. After his mother left we bounced around to different rentals in town. Once I started Hale Automotive and saved some money, I was able to really give him the kind of life I'd always dreamed of as a kid.

I guess I thought he'd end up better than me if I could give him more. Unfortunately, along with things, it seems I also gave him my parents' tendency for addiction. I've failed at a lot of things in my forty-two years, but none of them felt as heavy as failing as a parent. Logically I know his actions aren't my responsibility, but knowing I raised a man who'd cheat on his wife, steal from her, and from me makes me wonder if there was something I should have done differently.

Wren strolls out of my room looking rumpled. She

yawns and looks around confused. There's a crease on her cheek from the pillow, and her newly dyed blonde hair is mussed.

"Hey, you slept a long time. I hope you're hungry, dinner's almost ready," I say.

It's clear she's still coming out of a deep sleep. The kind where you wake up not remembering falling asleep. It probably doesn't help that she woke up in a different spot than where she fell asleep.

"You cook?" she asks in a husky voice.

We weren't the kind of extended family that did holidays together. The few occasions we were all together Charlie's mom was the chef for the holiday dinner. Liam and I had a few traditions as he was growing up, but the way I treated Wren after they got married drove him away a little, at least when it came to trying to make us all one big happy family. They both thought it was because I didn't like her. For many years I tried to believe that as well, but I've fantasized about her too many times to really accept the lie as fact.

"You don't?" I'd known her parents a little, and I'm surprised her mother didn't pass along that talent.

People tend to marry young in this community. When you don't go off to college, real life starts almost immediately. There's little reason to put off marriage when two incomes can mean the difference between having a place to live and food to eat. Then there's way too many people like me who find themselves parents before their age loses the word teen.

Elisa and Martin Parker were a couple of years ahead of me in school, but this is a small town. I knew they got married after Martin got his AA degree and started working as a radiology technician. He made enough money for Elisa to stay home and they had Wren a year after Liam was born. Charlie and Martin had played basketball together in high school and stayed friends so I saw him every once in a while.

I knew that Elisa practically ran the parents group at the school, and her cupcakes funded most of the sports equipment they managed to purchase while she was alive. They had the kind of family I'd wished Melinda and I had. We never did. Instead our marriage looked more like the one my parents had, minus the booze.

"My mom always said she would teach me later. Funny thing about later is that it doesn't always come."

Her words hang heavy between us. There are so many things I'd like to do with her. I keep telling myself we can't, but when I look at it through the lens of never having another chance with her, some of my reasons seem inconsequential. Even my son's feelings might not be enough to keep me from taking what I want.

"Go sit at the table. We'll talk over dinner," I tell her.

She obeys without arguing, and I'd be lying if I said it didn't arouse me. There was a twisted side of me that liked it when she submitted to my demands.

I set the pan of lasagne I made on a hot pad in the middle of the table and go about serving her food first. Once we've both got food on our plates, I start talking. I've had hours to think while she slept and even had a chance to talk to a lawyer I'd helped rebuild an engine for last year.

"I spoke to a lawyer earlier," I begin.

Her mouth falls open, and her eyes spark with anger. Before she gets a chance to argue, I hold up my hand. "Let me explain, and if you still want to yell at me, go for it."

Wren closes her mouth and nods.

When I'm sure she's listening, I continue. "He thinks we can cut a deal with the prosecutor. He'll go with us to help file the charges. It will go on record that Liam committed fraud, but he'll get probation as long as he completes rehab and pays you restitution. I even had a chance to speak to Greg Johnson again. He said if we were able to pay off the debt, they'd report it to the credit bureaus as fraud without waiting for a court decision, and remove the negative marks on your credit."

She shakes her head, and I brace myself for her to turn down everything I've managed to arrange. As usual she surprises me. "How would I do that? I don't have any money. You can't pay it, because you need to pay for Liam's rehab."

I smile at her. Of course she'd be worried about me. I don't think Wren knows how to be concerned about herself.

"You don't have any idea how much Liam's car is worth, do you?" I ask.

She shakes her head. "I know he's put a lot of work into it. There was some body work, and I honestly didn't understand all the stuff he said he did to it."

"Charlie took a look at it earlier. He did good work. How much did you give him for it?" I ask.

"I had ten thousand from my parents after we moved into our apartment. I wanted to save it for college, but I felt bad about that after he gave up his chance to go for me."

I wince. "Wren, he never gave up anything for you. I never knew until the other day that you thought he had a scholarship. There were some scouts interested in signing him his senior year, but he didn't have the grades. I offered to get him a tutor, but he was lucky to graduate at all."

She clenches her fork in her hand. "What?"

A laugh bursts past her lips. "Why am I surprised? Was anything about my marriage true?"

I shrug. "I wish I could answer that for you. I'm afraid

we're kind of in this together. Nothing I've been learning about my son gives me the warm and fuzzies. And I've been on your side of things when his mom ran off with another man. Be happy you're not pregnant on top of everything else."

Just thinking of her carrying someone else's child causes a surge of anger to burn in my chest.

She laughs again, this time it carries an edge of hysteria. "If I was, it would be yours."

I shake my head. "You can't know that."

Her green eyes rise to meet mine. "Oh, I can. I haven't had sex with Liam in five months."

"How is that possible?" I wonder out loud.

She shrugs. "He didn't want me. Hasn't for months. The last time we were intimate was after a party and we'd both had a lot to drink. Now, looking back, I'm not even sure it was me he was with. Not in his mind at least."

Clearing her throat she brings the conversation back on track. "You were telling me about Liam's car."

I smile at her, grateful. "The work he did brought value back to the car. It's worth about twenty thousand dollars. Charlie confirmed it's in your name. If you sell it there'll be almost enough to cover the cost of rehab and pay off all the money he took out in your name. Especially if I apply a bit of pressure to Greg and get him to remove interest and late fees from the total. If he won't, I can figure out how to come up with one thousand dollars much easier than twenty-one thousand."

Wren stands from the table and carries her plate to the kitchen. She's barely eaten, so I take it from her. "I'll wrap this up. I don't have much of an appetite right now either."

She stops in front of the window and stares out. Her arms are wrapped around her middle, as if she's trying to comfort herself. I wonder how many times over the last several months she's stood like this waiting for him to throw her some small morsel of attention.

I'm done fighting this, whatever this is. She's hurting so much, and I know that I can hold her together for now. I hug her from behind, and she shudders in my arms. "We've got one other thing to discuss tonight," I whisper.

"What's that?" she asks. There's a weariness in her tone that makes her sound closer to my age than her own.

"Us. I told you earlier that for now, you're mine. It's time we went over what that means."

She turns in my arms, and for the first time, she kisses me rather than waiting for my move. I lift her in my arms and carry her back to my bedroom.

17

Wren

A bad pattern is developing between us. Every time I learn something new about Liam, I turn to Griffin like he's the only person who can help hold me together. I did the same thing to Liam when my parents died. It's not a healthy habit.

Still, I can't seem to stop. This time I can't even say it's Griffin who's taking things too far. It's my hands in his hair holding his mouth pressed against mine. I need him in this moment more than the oxygen in my lungs, or the blood racing through my body.

We kiss frantically, perhaps because we know there's a giant clock ticking down the seconds that we can get away with this. Each second is one less I can turn to him to hold me. Every minute is one closer to me walking away from him forever.

There was a time when that would have been something to celebrate, but in the here and now, it feels like a curse. In a matter of only a couple weeks, the person who had been the biggest bane of my existence is now vital to keeping my sanity.

This time he's not demanding. There's no dirty words, no rough touch. Griff is almost tender, and it's making my head spin. After a moment he pulls back, and looks at me. There's a lot unspoken between us, but I'm afraid he's about to burst this bubble. I need him right now, in whatever way I can have him.

His eyes hold mine as his fingers slip under the hem of my shirt. There's a silent question as he slowly raises the fabric up my stomach. I nod, granting him permission. Our eyes only part as my shirt comes over my head.

Griffin guides me up to the middle of the bed and urges me onto my back. Not a word is spoken, but this is part of the conversation we need to have. This is the part we can't admit out loud. I'm telling him I need him, and he's telling me he wants me. There's the physical side, but it's deeper than that. I need him to argue with me, to joke with me, I just need him. When his body tells me he wants me, I know it's for more than an orgasm. He wants my voice to fill the silence he lives in and my eyes to see him like no one else does.

I lift his shirt the way he did mine, and he sits up to take it off the rest of the way. A sigh slips from my lips seeing him. He might like to be called daddy, but Griffin definitely doesn't have a dad bod. He's ripped, which is probably due to the physical nature of his job and the home gym he made out of the converted garage. There's a light dusting of hair on his pecs and then a thin trail that dips under the waist of his jeans.

The corner of his plump lips curves up as he watches me take him in. I don't turn my head, but stare enraptured while he unbuttons his pants and lowers them showing me he goes commando under his worn denim. I lick my lips, wanting a taste of him. I wonder how far he'll let me take this.

Both times we've had sex have been controlled by Griffin, and I don't think he's used to being passive during sex. But, while he's being so amenable, I want to see what I can get away with.

I sit up and slide down to my knees. His eyes heat while he watches me position myself between his legs. His hand slips into my hair, pulling a little, but this time he doesn't guide my head.

My lips slip over the head of his cock, and I swirl my tongue across the top to gather the drop of pre cum beading at the slit. The salty taste makes me ravenous for him, and I hollow out my cheeks as I pull his length to the back of my mouth. I fight the urge to gag like I did before and take him deep into my throat. It's not a comfortable feeling, but the groan I hear rumble in his chest spurs me on. Making him come, to be the one giving him pleasure, fills me with a sense of joy I've never experienced before.

His grip in my hair tightens, and I think he's about to take over, but he pulls me off of him. I blink up at him confused. His cock is harder than when I started, and he's panting hard. I know he was close to coming, so I don't understand why he stopped me.

He lets go of my hair and pulls me up by my arms. Griffin's hands shake a little while he strips the rest of my clothes off. Still, neither of us say a word.

When he's positioned me back in the middle of the bed he sheds the rest of his clothes and climbs up the length of my body. I let my legs fall open as his hands slide up the outside of my thighs. Our eyes lock as he sinks inside of me.

My head falls back at the feeling of his cock stretching and filling me, but he grabs my chin and brings my eyes back to his. Slowly he works himself in and out of my pussy, never once looking away. The connection feels so much deeper than he's buried inside of me. Our breathing turns choppy. I can't take it any more. Words I'll later regret are threatening to trip off my tongue.

He must feel the same way, because he takes away the risk one of us will ruin this moment by speaking a truth we should keep inside. He kisses me, but it's almost worse than speaking the words out loud. I feel loved in this moment, and my eyes well with tears.

Our kiss becomes wild matching the tempo of his thrusts. His hands hold mine above my head, and we abandon the slow lovemaking. In and out, his cock slides past every sensitive nerve ending sending bolts of electricity racing through my body. His hands slip from mine and he grabs the headboard for more leverage.

Each hard thrust drives my body higher on the bed. I hold on to him tight, vaguely aware that my nails rake hard against his corded flesh. We're no longer quiet, and in this moment the primal grunts he makes sound like music to me.

I loved the slow and tender side of him, but I'd be lying if I said I didn't prefer this rough and savage side of him. I want my body marked by his touch. I want to feel the throbbing deep in my pussy hours after he's taken me. It makes me feel owned by him, and Griffin always protects what's his.

His movements become more erratic, and I know he's on the edge. I've been holding back my orgasm as long as I could, but when he starts grinding his pelvis against my clit I lose the battle. I come so hard I can feel my walls squeezing his dick hard. He groans loud, and holds himself deep as his hot release fills me.

I expect him to pull out and for the bubble we're in to shatter, but instead he practically collapses on top of me. The weight of him feels safe, but he only lets us rest like this for a moment before he rolls us onto our sides. He doesn't pull out though. I press my face against his chest and kiss him right over his heart.

We stay wrapped up in each other for several minutes before all the unsaid words press down on us again. Griffin slips out of me and takes my hand. "Let's go clean up, then we'll talk."

He gives me a minute alone in the bathroom to pee. I wrap a towel around myself before I open the door.

His eyes narrow on the offending material, and he rips it away. "Don't hide from me."

Griffin slips past me and turns on his amazing shower. There's a waterfall shower head, gorgeous tile work all enclosed by a large glass with an opening near a wooden bench.

I stare at him with a raised eyebrow. "This shower is big enough for two."

"Three actually, but it's been a while since I tested it."

I shake my head. "I don't want to hear about that." Jealousy is a bitter feeling. It burns, and I have no right to be upset if he has a past. I am a moment in his life. A man as sexy as Griffin Hale won't stay alone.

He smirks at me. "I think I like it when you get jealous."

I stick out my tongue. "Well, I don't," I complain.

Griffin's nostrils flare, and his eyes narrow. "You ran from me earlier, you've talked back to me, and now you're sticking out your tongue?" he tsks. "Baby bird, do you need to be punished?"

Instinctually I take a couple steps back. I'm not actually afraid of him, but I can't help reacting as if I am.

"This will be much better if you take your punishment like a good girl." His voice is low and has a dangerous edge.

"Bend over and hold on to the bench, baby bird," he demands.

My body shivers as I immediately obey. I bend over and grab hold of one of the slats in the bench. The steam swirls around me, but even though I'm not cold, my body erupts with goose bumps. His hand cracks against my ass, bringing a little extra sting from the moisture gathering on my flesh.

"Should you have run from me?" he asks.

He slaps the other side, when I don't answer right away. I know what he's looking for, but I'm starting to crave this side of him. I don't know how I'll ever give this up. "No," I answer, withholding what he wants to hear.

His hand lands across both cheeks and my pussy making me shiver again. "No, daddy, I shouldn't have run." I answer.

"Should you talk back to me?" He doesn't wait to spank me again, this time hitting my clit.

I groan instead of answering him, and he swats me again like I'd hoped he would. "No, daddy," I reply.

His hand fists in my hair and he pulls, and my pussy contracts at the slight sting. He catches my eyes, and the heat in his makes my clit pulse uncomfortably even though I've just come less than thirty minutes ago.

"The only time I want to see your tongue is when I'm feeding you my cock."

I only nod since he didn't ask me a question. I loved experiencing the gentle side of him, but I need this part of him too. It speaks to something in me I didn't know was missing.

One hand squeezes my hip while the other drags his cock up and down my slit. "I'm going to fuck you now. Hard. This is for me, because bad girls don't get to come.

If you take your punishment like a good girl, then you'll be rewarded. Do you understand?"

I nod, but I'm not sure he can see it the way I'm still bent over. His fingers dig into my flesh. "Words, Wren. Do. You. Understand?"

"Yes, daddy, I'm not allowed to come."

He thrusts inside of me in one hard stroke. I bite my lip to stifle a groan. I have no idea how I'll keep from coming. The feel of him inside of me, especially when I anticipate getting fucked hard almost makes me come instantly.

I squeeze the bench hard enough to pinch against my fingers. Both of his hands are on my hips and he proceeds to take me hard. It's glorious and frustrating because I've never wanted to come so much in my life. He sounds like an untamed beast behind me grunting and groaning with each stroke of his cock.

I turn my head and see his reflection in the glass. His muscles strain and bulge. I have to bite the inside of my cheek again to force my orgasm back. I might cry with the effort not to come.

"Your cunt is so tight. I feel it start to flutter, but you are holding back. You know why you don't get to come this time, right?"

"Yes, daddy," I pant. It's getting harder to hold back.

His large hands pull me back onto his cock as hard as he's thrusting his hips. Our wet flesh slaps together, and my eyes roll back into my head. I'm not going to survive this. I'm going to die of a denied orgasm.

"This is lesson number one. I told you earlier that you're mine, and you didn't believe me. I showed you in my bed that I'm yours, but you still aren't accepting this. So now, I'm going to prove to you who owns this pussy by using it for my pleasure, and not letting you come."

One hand slips around to rub my clit, and tears start to

roll down my face with the effort I'm exerting not to come. I start to think he wants me to lose, but before I am forced over that cliff, he stops. As soon as my pussy isn't pulsing like it was, he repeats stroking my clit. I'm grunting in time with his thrusts, but somehow I manage not to come when I feel his hot release spill inside of me.

I'm shaking, and tears are slipping down my face when he pulls out and turns me around, but I'm also proud of myself because I did what he told me to do.

He smiles at me, and I feel like I could fly. "Good girl," he coos, and strokes his hand through my hair. Griffin guides my shaking body to turn around and sit on the bench. "I did promise you'd be rewarded if you did as you were told."

I have no idea what he has in mind. His dick hangs heavy and spent between his powerful thighs. He's got stamina, but even he needs some time to recover. I can't wait that long. My skin tingles, and I feel like I'm hot all over.

Griff kneels between my thighs and pushes his shoulders under my knees. His mouth latches on to my clit, which is swollen and overly sensitive from being teased over and over again. Two of his large fingers plunge inside of me, and he fucks me as ruthlessly with his hand as he did his cock. When he adds a third finger and sucks hard on my bundle of nerves my entire body starts to shake. I can't hold back much longer. He pulls his mouth away. "You're allowed to come now, baby bird."

His words release the strangle hold I'm exercising over my body, and I tremble harder. When his tongue starts flicking hard against my clit I get so close I'm dizzy. Then his fingers curl and stroke my G-spot and a guttural scream rips from my throat and everything goes black.

18

Griffin

"Wake up sleepy head," I coax Wren awake the next morning with a mug of coffee.

She rolls away from me and pulls the pillow over her head. I rip it away from her. "Five more minutes," she begs and reaches for my pillow.

"You're going to be late for work," I tell her and she bolts up straight.

The sheet slips revealing her full tits. I have to force my eyes not to look down. If I do, she'll definitely be late for work. I set the coffee on the nightstand and start to back out of the room. "I'll, uh, go make breakfast."

I've got pancakes on the griddle when she comes out of my room wearing one of my shirts and nothing else. The spatula slips out of my hand and clatters against the floor. "Baby bird, we need to have that talk now, because if you think I'm going to let you out of my sight wearing nothing except for my shirt, I'm going to have to clarify what it means to be mine."

"You keep saying that, but we both know I can't be

yours." Her voice sounds melancholy, and I wish I could reassure her.

I'm so absorbed by her I forget all about the pancakes until the smell of them burning fills the kitchen. "Shit, so much for making you breakfast."

I kiss the top of her head. "Let's talk after you get off work. If we hurry we can swing through a drive through before I take you to your house to change and drop you off at your car."

"We don't have to go through a drive through," she says.

"You have to eat," I demand. "We burned a lot of calories yesterday, and then you passed out."

Wren laughs. "You're taking this daddy thing a bit far. We don't have to go through a drive through because Dolores is going to swing by with something the second she sees your truck pull in so she can snoop."

I laugh. "Yeah, that sounds like her. She really is a horrible spy."

Wren pulls at the hem of my shirt she's wearing. "Do you have some pants or something I can put on with this?"

I pull her to me and kiss her until she's melting in my arms. It takes effort to stop, but we both have jobs we need to get to. "I've got just the thing."

As much as I like seeing her in nothing but my shirt, I go to my dresser and dig out a pair of sweatpants and a sweatshirt that will have her drowning in fabric.

She laughs when I hand them to her. "I'm starting to get the idea you're a bit possessive."

"Wren," I pull the sweatshirt over her head, "I'm a *lot* possessive."

Her purse is sitting on the bench seat of my truck when we go to leave. She digs inside and pulls out her phone. "Huh, I usually have this thing glued to my hand, and I haven't reached for it once." She drops it back inside without checking her messages.

It makes me wonder what her life is like. My son has neglected her for months. She doesn't really have any family. The aunt who stayed with her for a few months before she turned eighteen hasn't been back in town since. Honestly, I was surprised Hattie came back at all. I'd gone to school with her like I had Wren's mom. She never fit in here, but at least she came back when Wren needed her.

"I'm surprised someone of your generation isn't rushing to check her messages. Surely your friends must be wondering where you are," I say, fishing for more information.

Wren chews on her bottom lip and looks out the window. I haven't started the truck yet, so I wait for her to gather herself. When she looks back, there's a sadness in her eyes. "There might be something there from Bess."

"What about Audrey?" They have always been attached at the hip. Personally I find her immature and loud, but Wren holds on tight to the people she cares about, even when she should let them go.

She shrugs one shoulder. "I've stopped calling her. Every time I do she blows me off. I don't know what I did."

"I can't imagine you did anything," I say.

"It must be something. We were fine, then a few months ago, she started avoiding me," she says, turning back to the window.

I start the truck and leave her alone to her thoughts.

Dolores lives on the other side of Harriston, which only means it takes me ten minutes of driving through town to reach Wren's small cottage. There's no driveway direct to her place, and when I pull into the spot Dolores hasn't used since her license was taken by the state, I notice the curtain swing in the front window.

"Worst spy ever," Wren mutters.

I take her hand, because Dolores has already seen her wearing my clothes, and walk her around the house towards her cottage. While Wren searches for the keys in her purse, the curtain on this side of the house moves and I see a fluffy mass of silvery white hair peeking through the crack.

I predict she'll be at Wren's front door in the next five minutes. When she gets the door open I hurry her inside. "Go on and change, and I'll get you to work."

She fidgets with the strings on the sweatshirt. "You don't have to wait for me. I know you need to get to work too."

I sit down on her small sofa and make myself comfortable. "One of the perks of owning your own business, making your own hours. Go, I can wait for you."

"If you insist." She turns around and goes into her room to change.

Just as I thought, Dolores is standing at the front door the moment Wren steps into her room. I head her off by stepping out onto the front porch. "Morning, Dolores," I greet her.

"Come chat with me in my kitchen for a bit," she says, and turns around expecting me to follow her.

She's not even five feet tall, but there are few people I look up to as much as I do this woman. Whatever she wants to say to me, I owe her the time to hear her out. It doesn't take long for me to catch up to her, and I beat her to the door so I can hold it open for her the way she taught me when I was a kid.

Dolores goes about making two cups of coffee. She knows I take mine black and places a mug in front of me. I wrap my hands around it to keep them from shaking and prepare to face the scorn of the one person who seems to care about Wren like family should.

"What are you doing with her, Griffin? She's your son's wife."

I nod my head. "I know, but I can't help myself."

Her blue eyes aren't as bright as I remember them, but they still pierce right through me. "Can't or won't?" she asks.

I set my cup down. "Do you think I'd risk my relationship with my son if I could stop this?"

She nods as if my words answered a different question. "You love her."

My mouth falls open, to what, argue with her? Dolores raises one gnarled hand. "I'm going to stop you there. You aren't ready to admit it, but I see it."

She looks off over my shoulder, lost in a memory from her eighty-two years on the planet. Her smile is sad, when she turns back to me. "Remember, sometimes love isn't enough."

"You don't have to worry about Wren. I won't hurt her," I promise.

Dolores pats my hand. "She's not the one I'm worried about."

Wren chooses this moment to rush into the kitchen. Her hair is still a mess, but a more controlled mess than this morning. It's windblown, and somehow sexier than when she's styled it. I like seeing her wild and free.

Wren has her cell phone in her hand. "My phone is finally charged. Carl left several messages, apparently he's going out of town for longer than he expected. His mother is in the hospital. I just called him, and he said he's thinking about shutting it down for good. He's, uh, transferring his clients to another broker."

"Oh dear, that must be why he called and left a

message on my machine. You must be so upset, Wren, but you shouldn't worry. Everything will be alright, I promise." Dolores stands and starts fixing her a plate of fruit and yogurt. I swear she believes every problem in life can be solved if the right meal is provided.

Wren's breathing turns shallow. Her green eyes search for mine, and I can see fear and desperation shining back at me. "What am I going to do, Griff?"

I jump up and pull her into my arms. I run my fingers through her hair. "The first thing you're going to do is breathe."

She fights to take several slow deep breaths. After a minute I feel her chest expand fully, and it doesn't feel like she's vibrating in my arms.

"Okay, now that I know you're not going to pass out, let's go grab some breakfast and talk," I suggest. She nods against my chest.

Dolores watches us with a mischievous fascination. "Wren, darling, I hate to pile more on you. My son came by yesterday, and he thinks the house has termites. Personally, I think he's overreacting, but he called in an exterminator to have the house fumigated."

"What does this mean?" Wren asks.

I step back and take her hand. "I think she's saying you need to find a place to stay for a few days."

"Oh," Wren says and chews her lip.

Giving her hand a tug, I guide her toward the door. "Let's go back to your place and pack some of your clothes. You can stay with me for a few days."

"What about my kitten?" Wren asks.

I roll my eyes. "The kitten too."

Before I make it out the door Dolores winks at me. I don't believe for a second she's having this place fumigated. Whatever she saw after Wren came inside changed her mind about me being with Wren. I'd love to know what it was, because I can't see a future where I don't have to encourage her to leave.

———

THERE'S a diner one town over. I hate that I feel the need to avoid being seen with her in town, but no matter how right it feels when I'm with her, what we're doing is wrong. We also need to talk someplace with people. Every conversation we attempted yesterday ended with an orgasm and no resolution of the issues.

Wren picks at her hash browns. "This is all wrong. We have to go to a different town in order to have breakfast together. You're missing work. Griff, what are we doing?"

"We're surviving. Our worlds were both turned upside down by one of the people we trusted the most. No one else understands what we're feeling."

She looks down at her plate and plays with her food. "Is that all this is? We're using each other to cope?"

I take a deep breath. "No. I wish I could say that it was. That I haven't been fighting an attraction to you for longer than I was willing to admit to myself. I really wish I could say that those feelings haven't grown to more than the desire to fuck you, but I'm done lying to myself. I've held all of this back, from you, Liam and even myself, but his betrayal made me weak."

Wren laughs lightly and shakes her head. "Never in my wildest imagination would I have guessed that was why you were always such an asshole to me. I loved Liam, and I'm not going to tell you I've thought about you like that before that horrible night. Sure, I saw you. Audrey and I used to joke about my hot father-in-law, but when I looked at you I imagined what Liam would look like in the next twenty years."

She sets her fork down, and looks directly at me. "He broke me that night. No," she pauses and gives a slight shake of her head, "he had been breaking me for months. Tiny little cracks at first, each time he worked late and forgot to call. When he started to avoid being in the same room with me those cracks grew. That night I shattered. You were there holding me together. I didn't see Liam in you after that. At least I didn't see who he'd be in twenty years, I saw the man he should have been. Everything is so mixed up in my head." She licks her lips and whispers, "I'm afraid."

"Of what?" I ask her. Inside I'm shaking, because I realize I do want this to work with her. It can't. I know that much at least. There's no scenario where Liam would ever accept her and I together, but I can't stop wishing it could.

"I'm afraid I'm using you. The only time I don't feel like glass is when I'm with you. There's been so much weighing me down, but when I'm with you I feel free. But I think I get more out of this arrangement than you do. If Liam finds out you could lose him, whereas he's already lost me. You're the only thing I will lose, and that scares me more than it should."

"Why?" I'm a masochist for even asking the question, but I need her to tell me. Maybe she'll say something that will help me end this obsession I have for her.

"Because I think it'll hurt more to leave you than the end of my marriage did."

I reach across the table, palm up. She doesn't even hesitate to slide her hand over mine. "Is this my fault? Did I do something to make him turn to drugs?"

My hand tightens around hers. "Fuck no. Why would you think that?"

She chews on her bottom lip, a sure sign she's nervous to tell me something. "Liam never told you I wanted kids, I take it?"

An image pops in my head uninvited. Wren pregnant, smiling, and cradling her swollen belly. I can't imagine how hard it would have been to witness her pregnant with another man's child. My grandchild no less. I'm speechless, because the jealousy coursing through me burns. I'd have had to see it every day. Eventually, at least I hope, I'd have been able to be genuinely happy for them. I'm sure I'd have loved that child, but I wonder if a part of me would have always wished it was mine.

Wren mistakes my silence, and pulls her hand away. "I did, didn't I? I put too much pressure on him. This is all my fault."

The waitress chooses the worst timing possible and swings by to check on us. We've barely eaten, but I've lost my appetite. "How is everything tasting, folks?" she chirps.

I glare at her. "Just give me the check," I snap.

"Griffin," Wren hisses. "She's just doing her job."

The waitress stands by with her mouth opening and closing. I pull out my wallet and throw some bills on the table. It's too much, and I've probably tipped at least fifty percent of the bill, but that's for the best. I do know when I'm being an asshole, I just don't usually care enough to stop doing it.

Like, now. I know Wren thinks I'm pissed at her. I'm being abrupt and irritable, but I need a minute to get my thoughts straight in my head. I grab her arm and pull her out of the booth when she doesn't move fast enough.

Outside in the parking lot, I pin her against the passenger door of my truck. I grab her chin so she can't hide her face from me like she's got a bad habit of doing. "I don't ever want to hear you take the blame for the way

Liam treated you. He chose to ignore you, to cheat on you. He is the one who took drugs, which was not your fault. If anyone is to blame for that, it's those damn doctors for giving him narcotics for a minor concussion."

She tries to dip her head, but I force her to continue looking at me. "I know I seem angry, but it's not because I think you wanting a baby drove him to drugs. I think he was damn lucky he had someone like you wanting to build a family with him. I'm pissed because I'm jealous."

Her eyes flutter. "Why?"

I laugh in frustration, and drop my forehead to rest against hers. "You just refuse to see it. I want you. I'd love for it to be my babies growing inside of you. I hate myself for being jealous of my own son, but I am. I'm fucking green over the fact he had that possibility with you and I only get a few weeks."

I lift my head so I can look her in the eyes. Just as I fear, they're filling with tears. "So that's it then? That's all we get?" she asks.

Wiping an errant tear away, I try to smile at her. "I don't see how we could have more. But, please don't worry about that now. I promise, when it's time for you to go it'll be so you can have a better life."

"And what about you?" Wren whispers.

Unable to stop myself, I kiss her softly. "I'll have my memories of you, and that is more than I ever could have hoped for."

19

Wren

"I don't think this is a great idea. I can go ask Donovan for more hours at the bar," I argue with him as he pulls me through the doors of his garage.

"You will not turn to that overgrown frat boy for help," he growls.

Now that I know how possessive he can be over me I let his attitude toward Donovan slide. A little. "It's my job. I want to ask him for more hours to cover what I'm losing from the insurance agency, not asking him to let me stay with him while my place is getting fumigated."

Griffin growls, which would have had me running a few weeks ago. "He wants you. I saw how he was looking at you the other night."

My forehead creases as I try and think of what he might be talking about. "What are you talking about?" I ask when I draw a blank.

"He walked you to your car, and lingered a while," Griffin accuses.

I start to laugh, finally remembering what night he is referring to. "You mean the night he sent me home early instead of me staying to help close so he could have the bar alone with Bess?"

He rubs his hand against his cheek, and his callouses scratch against his always present stubble. "Him and Bess?"

I shrug. Truthfully, I was shocked to learn those two were hooking up as well, but I'm not going to let Griffin know that I'd also thought Donovan was flirting with me a couple times. Donovan is just a natural flirt. I don't think he's even aware he's doing it.

"That discussion you witnessed, that was me giving him some advice on how to move things along with Bess."

He raises an eyebrow. "This I've got to hear. What advice did you give him?"

My face heats. My advice that night was mostly based on how easily Griffin had me under his spell.

"Why are you blushing?" Griffin confused is adorable.

"I told him to sex her into agreeing to go out on a real date," I mutter.

Griffin puts his hand behind his ear. "What was that? You have to speak up, I'm not as young as you, remember?"

I slap his chest. I like playful Griffin much more than the asshole version. "You heard me fine."

"So the waitress and the bartender are banging after hours. That sounds like a porn I watched once," he says laughing.

"With Bess, anything is possible." I roll my eyes, and make a mental note to call her.

"I didn't see you becoming friends with her. She's such a ball buster, and you're—"

"A doormat?" I cut in.

"Sweet," he contradicts.

"Stop distracting me with your crazy. I really don't

think it's a good idea for me to work in your shop. What am I even going to do?" What I knew about cars couldn't fill a paragraph.

"The shop is hemorrhaging money after what Liam did. The first thing I need is to sort out the books once and for all. Then I need to audit my suppliers and orders for the last year and see if there are alternatives with equal or better quality. Liam was on to something by buying cheaper parts, unfortunately they were not even worth what he paid for them. If we can't bring in money that way we'll need to look at other shops around the area and see what they're charging. I like to come in less than they do, but that might not be possible to maintain anymore," he explains.

I wish I had a notebook so I could write it all down, but I would remember. I've always been good at remembering what I heard almost word for word. It's part of how I managed to snag a full-ride scholarship to Central Valley University.

"I'm certified on accounting software, and I got my Associates degree in accounting. I can handle all of that, as long as you don't expect me to do anything with the cars," I say.

Griffin laughs as he holds open the door to his office. "No, I actually want to keep my business."

The phone starts to ring, and he starts to dig through piles of paperwork to find it. I can hear noise coming through the phone, but I wouldn't have been able to understand even half of the conversation since Griffin does little more than grunt his replies. Whatever is asked, he scribbles the information down on a random scrap of paper, which immediately gets lost in the piles once he sets it down.

"You know, I think part of the reason you're losing money is all of this," I say and gesture to the chaos inside.

I shoo him out of the office. "I'm going to spend some time making sense of this mess and getting it organized, then I'll dig into the finances."

The phone rings again, and I rip it out of his hand. "Hale Automotive," I greet the customer.

"Hello. Do you guys tow cars?" an older man asks.

I put my hand over the receiver. "Do you tow cars?" I ask Griffin.

He nods, so I take my hand off the phone and continue. "Yes sir."

"Oh heavens, thank you. My engine overheated and my roadside assistance says there's no providers in the area."

I continue gathering his information and write it down on an actual clean sheet of paper before I hand it over to Griffin. He strolls to the door and shouts out into the shop, "Julio you've got a pick up at the Qwick Stop on highway seventeen."

"Why isn't your towing services listed with the roadside assistance providers?" I ask.

Griffin scratches his stubble and shrugs. "Everyone in town just kinda knows we do it."

"You don't have a website either, do you?" I can tell he doesn't just by the look he's giving me.

"Wow, okay. I've got a lot of work to do. Go fix something, and I'm going to fix all of this."

I WORK THROUGH LUNCH, trying to find Griffin's desk under all the random pieces of paper. There are appointments, reminders to order supplies, and notes for customers scribbled on any available scrap of paper. I'm so focused on the database I'm building to log every note, I don't hear the door opening.

"Do you know what you're doing?" I look up and see Charlie standing in the doorway.

"Building a database? Sure, I've made a lot of them." I put the papers I've entered into a file box I found in the supply closet.

He comes into the office and closes the door. "Not here at work. Here, with Griffin. Have you thought about how this is going to impact Liam? Are you ready to deal with that?"

I fight the urge to laugh. "All I thought about for months was Liam. Where is he? What is he doing? Why doesn't he want me? I made myself sick over it. Literally."

I grab my purse and dump it onto the desk. I find a prescription bottle and throw it at him. "This one is for anxiety attacks." I reach for another one and launch it at him too. "This one is for depression." The last bottle rolls across the desk, and I toss that one at him as well. "That one is so that I can sleep. I developed a nice case of insomnia always waiting up for Liam on the nights he didn't come home."

Charlie just stands there, not speaking. Even that is pissing me off. "What? Nothing more to say? Tell me, how much more am I supposed to give him?"

The door bursts open and slams into the wall with a bang. "What the fuck is goin on in here? I can hear Wren shouting from the auto bay over Julio's horrible rap music."

I quickly shove my things back into my bag and pull the strap over my shoulder. "Ask Charlie. It's late, and I've got to go talk to Donovan. The system I've set up is pretty self explanatory, I'm sure you guys can figure it out, because this isn't going to work."

I'm not sure what I expect when I rush out the door, but I didn't think I'd just leave without having to explain myself to Griffin. After all the talk about me being his, I guess I thought maybe he cared a little.

After I walk to the insurance office and grab my car, I head straight to the bar. Happy hour is in full swing when I arrive, and it'll be a couple hours before business is slow enough to be able to talk to Donovan about getting more hours.

He examines me when I walk in, two hours before my shift is supposed to start, and gestures to the end of the bar with a jerk of his head. I go over to wait for him to finish up with the customers he's serving.

"I've got some spare shirts in my office. I heard Carl shut down the insurance agency. You'll need some more hours I'm guessing?"

I nod. I should have factored in the town's propensity for gossip before I worried about having to start this conversation with him.

"Go change. You can help me behind the bar. They've got me running more than a toddler hopped up on sugar."

I find a small t-shirt, and tie the corner to show off a little skin. I'm usually fully covered and buttoned up, but my talk with Charlie has me wanting to be anyone other than myself. I'd changed into a tight pair of ripped jeans when I got the news of my office being shut down, so I am not otherwise overdressed to start working now.

Donovan and I develop a rhythm pretty quickly. I like how busy it is. There's not any time to think, let alone answer any questions about my personal life. People are laughing and joking with friends, and it helps soothe some of the loneliness I'm feeling.

Bess comes in after about an hour of me working behind the bar. I give her a look, silently asking her how the other night went. She winks at me and ties her apron around her waist. Donovan cranks up the music, and even though it's the beginning of most people's work week, it's a party inside the bar.

When the crowd finally starts to thin out, we're exhausted, but I've got a wad of tips in my apron pocket that should help me makeup for what I'm losing at the office.

Donovan stops wiping down the bar and leans in front of me. "I figure I owe you, so if you need more hours, they're yours. I'll even teach you to tend bar if you like, that can give me some time to do the admin crap I hate so I don't have to come in so early."

I look over at Bess. "I don't want to take away any hours from anyone else."

She waves me off. "Please, I'm finishing up my AA degree online. I could use a little extra time to study. I've been working so much because he refused to hire extra help."

Then Donovan's words sink in. "What do you mean, you owe me?" I ask him.

He starts concentrating hard on wiping a non-existent spot off the bar. "Donovan," I shout.

Taking a deep breath, he looks up at me. "Liam wasn't all that sneaky. He came in here a few times and left with different women. It's only the last few months that he stopped. I assumed the two of you made up."

My legs buckle, and if not for Bess guiding me to a barstool I'd have fallen on my ass. "Different women, so not a singular affair then," I mutter to myself.

Bess wraps one skinny, bracelet-laden arm around my back and leans her head on my shoulder. The silent support says a lot that words can't seem to accomplish.

Donovan looks at me with pity. "Please don't look at me like that," I whisper to him.

He nods. "I'm sorry I haven't said anything to you. We didn't really know each other well, and if I went around telling all the things I've seen in here, I'd never have any customers. But, let me ask you this, whether it was one woman or a dozen, does that really make the betrayal any less?"

Does it? I sit with that for a moment. "I think it does. As much as an emotional relationship hurts, I think I like the idea that his feelings got the best of him better than he just wanted any warm body as long as it wasn't mine."

"If Bess won't hit me for saying this, he's a fucking idiot. You're hot," Donovan says.

Bess rolls her eyes. "You're supposed to wait for me to say go ahead, dumbass." She looks at me and smirks. "But he's not wrong. You're hot as fuck. I'd do you if I didn't have this idiot and if you were into girls."

"I've never really thought about if I'm into women or not," I muse.

Bess laughs. "Trust me, if you haven't had it cross your mind, then you're not."

There's one self-discovery item I can cross off. "I take it the two of you sorted everything out the other night?"

She drops her arm from my back, and props her elbows on the bar with her head cradled in her hands. "Oh boy did we. He did this thing with—"

Donovan puts his hand over her mouth. "I don't think our little Wrenegade is looking for details."

"I'm really not," I confirm.

"You're both boring," Bess complains.

Donovan pours each of us a beer. I take a big drink of mine, and wipe the foam away from my mouth. "So this is what it's like. Meeting friends at the bar, talking about anything and everything."

Bess mumbles into her drink, "Not everything. You won't let me tell you about the thing he did with a bottle."

I choke on the beer I'd just drank, then start laughing. "What would I have done without the two of you."

"Probably had more time to bang your father-in-law," Bess says.

Donovan spits his drink across the bar. "It all makes so much more sense now! That's why he's been acting so pissy with me. He knows that you and I aren't anything, right?"

My mouth hangs open for a second. "That's it? Bess," I glare at her, "let's it slip that I'm having an affair with Griffin, and that's all you want to know?"

Donovan shrugs. "I can't really think of a better form of revenge. Liam fucked around for months, so you do his dad. It's brilliant. I can't think of anything better."

I down the rest of my beer. "Yeah? Well, I'm going to sell his car too."

Donovan starts laughing so hard he has to clutch his stomach. Bess looks at me with pride. "I fucking love you, girl."

"Don't get too excited. He stole money from his dad and opened lines of credit in my name. The car is in my name, so I'm selling it to fix the shit storm he left behind," I explain.

"Doesn't matter," Donovan starts, "he's still going to be pissed, and I fucking love this for him."

Yeah, I kind of did too. I know Charlie is worried about Liam, but I don't think it's my place to care anymore.

20

Griffin

"Charlie, you're my best friend, but I'm only going to say this once. Leave Wren alone." I fight the urge to hit him. Never in the decades of our friendship have we ever fought out of anger, but that could change depending on how he chooses to treat her after this.

"You know what people are going to say. How this is going to look. They're going to say that you're more concerned with that girl than your own son."

"People, or you?" I ask.

I pick up the prescription bottles she threw at him and look at them. The dates on them are recent, and I don't know if these are a recent prescription or something she's been taking for a long time. I know her parents' deaths hit her hard, but Liam never said anything about her taking medication. Back then he used to share a lot more with me, at least I thought he did. Maybe he didn't know.

"Put yourself in her shoes. She's lost her family, and her husband has betrayed her in pretty much every way possible. He stole from her too, Charlie."

I press on, because he needs to hear this. He can judge

me all he wants, but he will leave her the the fuck alone. "Today she got a message from Carl. He's had a family emergency and has decided to shut down the insurance agency. So, I thought since she needs a job, and we need help, she could come work here."

Charlie steps close and gets in my face. "That's not all she's doing though. You don't think I understand why she'd want to get some of her own back? Screwing her husband's father ought to teach him a lesson for cheating."

My anger bubbles over. I explode and shove him against the wall. Before he has a chance to react I press my forearm against his throat. He gurgles when I push down a bit harder. "Say what you want about me, but you will keep your fucking mouth shut about her."

I shove myself away from him, and he doubles over to catch his breath. "At least you're man enough to defend her. I'll ask you the same question I asked her. Are you going to be able to handle Liam's reaction? He could cut you out of his life. Is she worth that?"

My eyes narrow and I take a step toward him. He raises his hands and holds me off. "Chill the fuck out and listen to what I'm actually saying, will you? I'm not judging you, I'm asking you if you are going to be able to handle what Liam and others are going to say. Yeah, I took a cheap shot saying she was screwing you for revenge, because that's what others are going to say too. You need to be ready to deal with it."

It's like letting the air out of a balloon. For a moment I was all puffed up and ready to burst. He relaxes when he sees I'm listening to him. "Don't get me wrong, I care about Liam. I practically helped you raise him, but he has you. Her father is gone, and he was a good man. I urge you to drop this and let her be. She's going to have too much thrown her way when the rest of the town figures out what is going on with you two."

"I wish I could. I can't even explain what is going on, except she's vital to me," I explain.

"How are you ever going to let her go? She can't stay here, not once this all comes out," he pushes.

I nod. "I honestly don't know, but I will. You're right. She can't stay here, this town has nothing left for her."

"She would have you," he offers.

"No." I shake my head. "I'm not enough, and I won't ask her to sacrifice like my son has."

Charlie looks around the office. "I hope you can get her to come back to work tomorrow. Did you know there was a desk under all that paper?"

I give him a light-hearted shove. "Like you're any better with all this office shit."

"No, I'm absolutely garbage at all of this. That's why I write my notes down on whatever is around and let you deal with it," he replies.

I pick up a piece of paper off of the few remaining stacks of paper. "Which I clearly haven't been doing."

Charlie slaps me on the back. "I've got your back. You better go and convince Wren to come back tomorrow. I really should have thought about how to start that conversation with her. I didn't mean to drive her away. I only wanted to prepare her for what would come your way once everyone finds out. I'll apologize to her, just get her to come back."

"I've got some groveling to do, no thanks to you," I grumble.

Like the jackass he is, he tries to shoo me out the door. "Better get on with it then. I doubt she's getting any less pissed off since you didn't chase after her."

I flip him off. "Sometimes I forget why we're best friends."

He shrugs. "I picked you first for kickball and you shared your fruit snacks with me."

"It might be time to re-evaluate how I make my life choices," I mumble to myself.

"If that is what makes you realize that, and not starting an affair with your son's wife, I think you have bigger problems than how you and I came to be friends," he yells after me.

I SLIP into the bar without Wren noticing me and watch her interact with Bess and Donovan. More importantly, I watch how Bess and Donovan behave around each other. She was right, there is definitely something going on with the two of them. I'm not thrilled that she's developed a close friendship with one of the more eligible men in town. He's ten years younger than me, and although still nine years older than Wren, that's much more appropriate than dating someone nineteen years older.

When he reaches over and ruffles her hair I have to force myself to stay in my seat. It's a big brotherly show of affection, but it still makes me want to rip his arm off and beat him with it for touching her. I can't do that though. Wren's world has been very small for too long.

I didn't help that with the way I treated her. If I'd been a better man, less envious of my son, perhaps she'd have had Charlie looking after her. She could have come to me with her struggles. Maybe we could have figured out that Liam had a drug problem before it got to the point he was stealing from us. We'll never know, because I am a jealous asshole.

Happy hour is almost over by the time I show up, not that the bar completely clears out. I'm seated off in the corner in a spot not readily visible from the bar. It's a pretty serious design flaw if you ask me, because I can see them while they'd have to know I was here and search me out. Naturally, this table isn't the most popular one, because as one would imagine, it's not the best to get the attention of a server. It's great for spying though.

They sit at the bar drinking a beer when the demand slows down. I debate letting her finish her shift and approaching her in the parking lot, but there would be nothing stopping her from driving off and staying somewhere else. She might be speaking to Donovan and Bess now about crashing at either of their places. I can't let that happen. My time with her is already painfully limited. I won't give up any of it over a misunderstanding.

"Can I talk to you?" I ask, walking up behind her.

She jumps when she hears my voice. "Have you been standing there long?" she asks.

Her eyes shift attention to the side and Bess fights a bout of giggles. "Am I missing something?" I ask them.

They look at each other and reply in unison, "No!"

Donovan rolls his eyes and hands me a bottle of my favorite beer. "Ignore them. Neither of them can drink for shit, and they're a bit giddy after all the running around for the last couple hours."

"I mean it, we need to talk," I say again.

"Go ahead and use the supply closet," Donovan offers looking right at me, "I believe you are familiar with it."

Wren's face turns a bright red, and suddenly I'm aware of what they were talking about. She lets me take her hand and pull her into the closet. I take several steps away from her so we don't have a repeat of the last time we were in here. There's not nearly enough noise in the rest of the bar for something like that.

"I'm sorry I didn't come straight after you. I wanted to confront Charlie without you around so you didn't have to overhear anything else that might hurt you," I explain.

Her arms wrap around herself protectively, and she waits for me to tell her how it went. The pain I can see in her large green eyes makes me want to punch him, even though we already worked out what he was trying to do.

"I choked him a little if that makes you feel better." The corner of her lip twitches as if this does make her feel somewhat better. "It was a huge misunderstanding. Charlie, being an enormous dumbass, thought he was helping prepare you for what is going to happen once people find out."

She licks her lips. "So he wasn't asking me about Liam because he thought I should be more concerned about how my actions were going to impact him, but— No, I've got nothing. Explain it to me."

"He said he wanted you to think about how you were going to handle his reaction. He wants you to think about how you are going to handle when other people find out, to prepare yourself for the fallout," I tell her.

She looks down at her feet. "I don't plan on sticking around to deal with it. I guess that's unfair of me to leave you with the consequences. Charlie was right to worry, but asking about Liam was the wrong string to pull. He should have asked me how I'd deal with you possibly losing your son."

When she looks up at me her eyes glimmer. It's amazing how something so sad, like her eyes filled with unshed tears, could be so pretty. "We have to stop this. Too many people have already found out, and if one of them lets it slip to Liam, he might not ever forgive you."

I cradle her face in my hands and kiss her softly. It should be a kiss goodbye, but I can't seem to end this. "I can't walk away from you. I know I should. Everything you said is right, but I can't do it."

She gives me a fake smile. "Then let me do it. I'll do it for both of us."

It occurs to me if she can walk away at all then Charlie's right and I'm risking everything for no good reason. "Can you walk away, just like that?"

She bites her lower lip. And after a second, she shakes her head. "I know I should. If this was just sex, as good as it is, I'd walk away, easy."

I can't hold back any longer, and I kiss her. If the next words out of her mouth end this for good, I have to have one more taste of her. A real goodbye kiss. It isn't a frenzied tangling of lips and tongues like before, but it lingers. When it ends, I feel the loss. "This was never about sex. It only seemed that way. I could have fought my lust for you, but not this."

Wren looks at me for answers with an innocence that reminds me she's only twenty-three. "What is this, Griffin?"

Warmth spreads through my chest, but I don't have words for how I feel. "I've never felt like this before, so I don't know, but being with you feels necessary. I'm not sure I can breathe anymore without you."

She nods. "Me either. But where does that leave us? Eventually Liam is going to come home. We both deserve more than a life lived sneaking around."

I kiss her again. A quick brush of my lips on hers. "I know. I won't ask you to stay here and live half a life. You've given up too much already. Caring about you the way I do means I want the best for you, even if it hurts to watch you go."

"Is it just me, or have we talked ourselves back to the beginning?" she asks.

"You want to know what we're going to do?" I ask.

Wren nods.

"We're going to live a lifetime in the next few weeks. Let's make them count. Some people aren't lucky enough to get forever together, and I'm desperate enough to take even just an hour with you if it's all I ever get."

Her eyes narrow. "When did you get so romantic?"

A rare smile curves my lips. "I'm sure it was a fluke. I wouldn't expect too much of it."

Wren wraps her arms around my middle, and presses her head against my heart. Without thinking I wrap my arms around her in return. We stand together, holding each other, or rather holding on to each other. I thought I'd be happy knowing I get time with her, but holding her like this, I know even forever wouldn't be enough time.

I press my lips against her hair and breathe in her shampoo. "How am I ever going to let you go?"

"When the time comes, you'll have to choose, and we both know how that has to go." I hear the sadness in her voice, the surety I will choose my relationship with him over her. That is the way it should be. He's my son, but I think Wren might be my heart.

21

Wren

Griffin and Donovan chat for a long time at the end of the bar. I can't tell if they're talking about me, or whatever sport is currently in season.

Bess strolls over and sighs dramatically. "It is so dead in here tonight. I wish Donovan would just close down early. I've got a test to study for, and I'd like to have an orgasm before I go to sleep."

I look off to the side at her and raise both my eyebrows. "You can do that last one even if he doesn't close down early, you know."

She bumps her shoulder into mine. "Not if I don't want to give one to myself. The man has plenty of stamina, but he falls asleep fast after working all day."

The guys continue to talk with their heads bent together. Bess gets the bright idea to start doing the end of the night cleaning to signal Donovan to shut down early. She makes a production out of putting the chairs on top of the table, banging them around. At one point the few customers we have think she's trying to signal them to leave, and they immediately ask for their check.

Finally, Donovan and Griffin pull out of their huddle to see what is going on. "Elizabeth, what in the hell are you doing? You just ran off the few customers we had left tonight," Donovan barks.

Her chin lifts defiantly. "Those lumps of flesh were sitting there for the last hour, nursing one glass of beer. They were fine to drive, and I'm sure their wives wanted them to go home. It was a service to the community. Now you've got two choices. You can stay open to an empty bar, and I'll help you close. Then I'm going home to study for my Econ midterm. Or you can close early, bend me over your desk, and we can have some fun before I go home and study."

Donovan throws his rag down on the bar. "Bar is closed. Go on home Wrenegade, I'll see you tomorrow."

Griffin raises an eyebrow. "Renegade?"

I roll my eyes. "Bess started it."

Donovan hands him my bag, and I give him a glare. He holds his hands up in surrender. "You know you're going home with him, so save that fire for home. I'm still working on pinning Bess down on our relationship status, and I can't do that with you here."

"Start by pinning me down on your desk and we'll talk," she yells as she walks backwards toward his office.

"Liar! You'll be racing out of here before I can even get my pants up," he shouts back.

"Well, that was too much information. I'll, uh, lock the door behind me," I say, not sure either of them are listening.

"Miller," Griffin calls out Donovan's last name. "If you want her to hear you out, tie her up first."

"You're a genius," Donovan exclaims and runs after Bess.

Griffin hurries me out of the bar, and grabs my waist as I try to head to my car.

"What are you doing?" I wiggle to try and get free, but he dumps me in the passenger side of his truck. He's got a mischievous grin on his face as he buckles me.

I shake my head. "No."

It's a half-hearted protest. I've enjoyed all of his kinky ideas so far, but that's a level of control I've never handed over before. I'm intrigued, but nervous.

"WHAT ABOUT MY CAR?" I ask as he peels out of the parking lot.

His thumbs tap against the steering wheel and I can feel the anxious energy building in him. "You won't need it for the next few days. Donovan said you can leave it there tonight. I'll send Julio to get it tomorrow."

"I can drive it back myself," I argue.

With his head focused on the road, he turns just his eyes on me. He's able to broadcast exasperation and a bit of annoyance in that one look.

I sink back into the seat. Fighting Griffin is pointless. He's a force of nature, and no matter what I try to do, in the end he's going to get his way.

Griffin's house is close to the bar, which is a blessing since the tension in the truck is thick. He explained what happened back at the shop, but that doesn't mean the problems are solved. Charlie was right. When people find out about Griffin and me, they're going to judge us. Even though I'm leaving, I don't know that I'm ready to hear everyone's opinions on how I live my life. Worse, I don't think I want to see what being with me will do to Griffin.

I'm leaving town as soon as I can arrange everything,

but his entire life is here. Am I selfish enough to destroy everything he's built just because he makes this horrible time less awful? He's not planning to leave Harriston, but if people find out his business and his relationship with his son could be ruined.

This entire situation blows. When he came into the bar earlier I was ready to walk away from him. Then he said a few sweet words, and I softened. The doubt won't leave though. As much as I'd like to hide out in this for a few weeks, I don't know if I will survive when it ends.

He parks in his driveway and goes around to lift me out of his truck. I'm so much shorter than him that it's hard for me to get in and out of it on my own. I savor the feeling of being in his arms. When he holds me I feel like I'm home. It's something I haven't felt in so long and forgot how much I craved it. Griffin makes me feel both safe and alive, and I don't know if I can feel like this for a few weeks and walk away from him when it's time.

"You're thinking awfully hard," he says as he lets me slide down his body.

I try and summon the words we both need me to say, but my throat is too thick.

Griffin shakes his head. "No. I know you're trying to find the courage to end this, but I won't let you."

I can't say this and look at him, so I let my head drop and stare at my shoes. "This can't end well. Even if we get away with it, I don't think I can handle walking away from this if we spend more time together. I'm not as strong as you are."

His finger slides under my chin, and he tips my face up so he can look me in the eyes. "You're stronger than me, baby bird. You can walk away now, but I can't. It's too late for me. Whether you walk away now, or a couple weeks from now this is going to hurt. But, if we're going to live with the pain, shouldn't we get the memories to hold on to?"

I feel the first trickle of tears rolling down my face. I can't hold them back as the deep well inside of me spills over and every hurt comes pouring out. "I thought Liam was going to be the one to destroy me with his indifference, but I'm afraid loving you might be what wrecks me."

GRIFFIN TURNS and heads into the house. Part of me wants to kick myself for taking away any of the time I get to spend with him, but I fear a person can only be so damaged before they're unable to splice themselves back together.

I can't leave though. Not only do I not have my car, but I remember I don't have anywhere else to go. Damn Dolores and her fictional termites. I saw the wink she gave Griffin. I don't know what he said to her to win her over, but I doubt there are many women who can resist the honeyed words he spouts so easily. She probably did have the house fumigated just to make sure I didn't come back and check.

I also can't shake the sense that Griffin is right. I know it will hurt when the time comes for this to be over. That's true now or two weeks from now. What I don't think I can live with is the regret of giving up the weeks we might have together. I have a sense that whatever life I scrape together for myself after Griffin will be a pale comparison to what I have with him. Isn't it better to have this feeling for however long it lasts than to never experience it at all?

I go inside and find Griff sitting on the couch with his head in his hands. "I don't want to break you," he says when he hears me come in.

I join him on the couch. "And I don't want to be the reason you lose Liam."

His head lifts, and he looks at me. "Whatever happens between Liam and I will not be your fault. I don't want you to think about him anymore."

A shaky breath puffs past my lips. "Logically, I know all of this happened because of his addiction. Knowing doesn't take away the pain or feeling like I failed."

Griffin's dark eyes, usually a warm chocolatey brown, cool as he narrows them on me. "That's not why."

He takes a deep breath, and his hands tighten into fists on the top of his thighs. The tendons strain over bones and his knuckles turn white. "I don't want you thinking of another man when you're with me. I need to consume you, be your everything."

This truth is hard to part with. Every fiber of my being is screaming at me to keep this locked deep, but the rawness in his gaze rips it from me. "You already are," I whisper.

"I don't need another reason to be angry at my son. He stole from me, lied to me, but what feels like the biggest offense isn't even something I am allowed to be angry about."

My pulse pounds and my hands go clammy. I don't know how many more hits I can take when it comes to Liam, and I'm afraid to hear what Griffin is going to say. "I don't want to know." I look up at him, and see a pained look on his face.

He rubs one of his fists hard against the center of his chest. "Yeah, well I don't want to feel this, but here we are. I don't like being pissed at my son because the woman I'm falling in love with misses him."

"What?" I ask. His words hang around me like a fog,

muddling my thoughts and turning everything I thought I knew upside down.

Griffin gets up and starts to pace around the living room. "You heard me. I don't want you thinking about Liam, because I don't want you to think about any other men. Not even if one of them is my own son. My business is falling apart, my son is in rehab, and all I can think about is when I'm going to get to see you, and how many more times I'll get to be with you before this all blows up in our faces."

"Oh," I sigh.

My reaction seems to make him more agitated. "Oh? That's it? I basically tell you I'm obsessed with you, and all you say is 'Oh'?"

I shrug. "I thought you were going to tell me he's done something else. I can't imagine what more he could have done that would be worse than everything he's already done, but I didn't want to find out."

He turns his back to me. "I am so fucked."

Without thinking, I go to him. Every muscle in his body is coiled tight, and I want to soothe him in any way I can. He shakes when I wrap my arms around him, and lets me hold him for a minute before he turns around in my arms. He doesn't say anything, just holds me to him.

"I'm not in love with Liam," I admit. My chest expands with the release of those words.

"But you were so upset." His forehead rumples as he tries to suss out what I'm thinking.

He leads me back to the couch and waits for me to compose myself. "I think I need you to explain that," he says.

A laugh escapes me, and I cover my mouth. "Yeah," I say after I regain composure. "I think I might need someone to explain it to me too. I only just realized it now as the words came out of my mouth. I don't know when it happened. Was it over the six months I sat alone wondering where he was and what was happening to my marriage? Was it when I saw him fucking some random woman in the back of the car I bought him? Or was it the first time you touched me? I don't know, and honestly it's freaking me out a little."

Griffin brushes my hair away from my face. "I'm sorry I wasn't paying attention to what you were going through. All that time you spent alone, ignored, and I didn't even know you were suffering."

No one was paying attention. My mind whirls to the place I swore I'd never go back to. Absent-mindedly, I rub my thumb across my left wrist. His eyes drop to my hand, and I quickly drop it.

He reaches out and grabs my arm. I try and yank free, but he digs his fingers in to keep hold of my wrist. His thumb traces across the same spot mine did, and I know he feels it. Two raised lines. A reminder of the worst night of my life.

"Wren, tell me this isn't what I think it is," he demands.

"I can't," I mutter.

He doesn't say anything, just turns and walks out of the room. I hear something shatter from the other side of the house.

Shame is heavy. It's hard for me to face myself, let alone someone else, especially Griffin. No one outside of my doctor knows about that night. I'd have kept it that way if I could have.

22

Griffin

Hot, consuming rage swells up inside of me at myself, Liam and even Wren. Mostly at myself though. Fear follows closely behind. The kind that claws at your insides and makes it feel like you can't take a deep enough breath. Which only makes me more angry for feeling so out of control.

It's not a feeling I'm well equipped to handle. I hurry out of the room before I say something to make everything worse. Being away from her isn't enough to calm the storm brewing inside of me. I grab a lamp off the nightstand in my room, rip the chord from the wall, and throw it across the room.

The ceramic base shatters against the wall, but it doesn't help alleviate the tight ball constricting my chest. Wren bursts into my room and freezes in the doorway. Her eyes search desperately until she finds me sitting on the floor by my bed trying to control my breathing.

She rushes to my side and drops down next to me. "Are you okay? Did you get hurt?"

I take her hand in mine, and rub my thumb across the

scars I'd found earlier. Wren flinches and tries to pull her arm away. I hold on tighter. "Me? How long did you suffer alone before it was too much?"

She sighs, and quits trying to pull away. I touch the two raised lines, evidence I almost lost her before we got to really know each other. More than the superficial relationship I allowed for the last five years. I tried in the beginning. I'd married young, and just because it didn't work out for Melinda and I didn't mean Liam and Wren couldn't make it work.

The problem was that the more time I spent with them, with her, the less I saw them as kids. It should have helped me believe they could beat the odds. Instead I started seeing Wren as a woman. A smart, funny, beautiful woman who fascinated me completely. From that moment on I pushed her away. I made sure she felt unwanted, unwelcome, and unloved by me when the truth was she was very much wanted and, I was afraid, easy to love.

"I need you to tell me about these." I stroke the raised skin again to make sure there is no confusion about what I want her to talk about.

"I don't know where to start. It doesn't make sense to me now, knowing I could do something like that. It seems like forever ago, but—"

"When did you do it?" I ask.

Pulling her arm up so I could get a better look at it, I notice the skin is still a bit pink. "How did I not notice this? It looks freshly healed."

She gives me a sideways glance. "Really? How did you not notice this? It isn't like you've paid a lot of attention to me over the years."

"For a smart woman, you're pretty unobservant. All I've done is pay attention to you, why do you think I tried so hard to push you away?"

She shakes her head. "Well, you missed this," she mutters.

I nod. She's right after all. I missed her crying out in pain. Hell, I contributed to it, and it nearly cost me the one person I wasn't sure I'd ever recover from losing. Yes, I am going to have to let her go. It's what is best for her, but at least I'll live knowing she's out there somewhere. If she'd died, there'd be a void in my life I'd never come back from.

"I did, and I'm so sorry for pushing you away. I thought I had to. Self preservation is a strong instinct, and I did everything wrong," I apologize.

"Four months ago," she whispers.

The urge to break things comes over me again, but I shove it down. I try to remember what was going on four months ago. I'm ashamed to realize I have no idea what was happening in her life then. "I'm sorry I wasn't there for you, but I'm here now. Please talk to me."

She takes a deep breath. "Liam had been pulling away from me for a while. Really, it had been more than the last six months, but he'd shake out of it. But six months ago whatever would bring him back before, just disappeared. He started staying out late, sleeping on the couch, and he barely talked to me when he was around."

She looks up from the spot she's staring at on the floor. "I really don't think you want to hear all of this," she warns.

She's right, I don't, especially if this is heading where I think it is. I don't have some fantasy about her being an innocent virgin, but that doesn't mean I want to hear about her sex life with my son. But, I don't want her to think that there's things she can't talk about with me.

"I can handle it," I promise her, and I steel myself to mean it.

"There was a party at my best friend Audrey's house.

She wanted to introduce me to the guy she was seeing and invited a few other people we hung out with in high school. I know there were some guys there that Liam had been on the football team with, and they were showing off a little. They'd all gone away to school and had just started their careers. I know he felt left behind and started drinking a lot heavier that night."

Her brow furrows. "Maybe that was it. Now I wonder if he hadn't drank that much because he was already an addict."

She gives a little shake of her head and continues. "I drank quite a bit that night, not as much as he did, but I was pretty tipsy by the time we got home. All our inhibitions disappeared. We went at each other like when we first got married, it was—"

I jump to my feet and start pacing. "You know, maybe I don't need every detail."

Wren's shoulders slump, and I return to her side. "I'm sorry."

She purses her lips and nods. "I don't think I could take hearing about you and any of your many women, either."

"I wouldn't say there's been many women," I scoff.

Her eyebrow curves up. "Is it more than two?"

"What kind of question is that? Of course it's more than two. Like you haven't—" I stop mid sentence when she levels her gaze at me.

"Liam and I have been together since I was sixteen. Unlike my husband, I didn't cheat, so you do the math. And before you say anything about what you and I are doing, I left him. As far as I'm concerned, the state of my marriage is a technicality. One I intend on formalizing the moment I can get him to sign the damn papers."

My head falls back to rest on the edge of my bed and I

stare at the ceiling. "Sometimes I forget how much older I am than you, but right now, I feel every one of those nineteen years."

"I thought you liked the age difference. Isn't that the fantasy of most men in their forties, to have a young girlfriend?" She says and rolls her eyes.

"I'm not having a mid-life crisis, if that's what you're suggesting." I ignore the girlfriend part of her comment, because that leads to believing we could be a normal couple in the light of day. That's not possible for us.

"Really, daddy?" she teases.

"I think you just really want to distract me so you don't have to tell me what happened. For the record though, your age isn't what attracts me to you. If anything, other than the fact you're married to my son, it's part of the reason I worked so hard to avoid you. I won't lie and say I don't love dominating you, but the daddy thing is mostly because I like taking care of you."

Wren clutches her wrist in her hand, and I know her mind is going back to that night. I remain silent and let her finish telling me what happened in her own time. "Yeah, okay. No more distracting. That night was the first time in two months he slept in the same bed as me. Despite my pounding head, when I first woke up, I snuggled up to him like I used to. He smiled, held me tighter and mumbled something about loving waking up with me."

She pulls her knees up to her chest, and it's like she's folding in on herself. "For a few seconds I felt like everything was going to be okay again. Whatever was going on was over. I told myself it had nothing to do with me, and we'd be fine. Then he opened his eyes, and the smile slipped off his face. He shoved me away and jumped in the shower."

She starts to rock herself, and my heart is breaking for

her. "A switch flipped alright, but not in the way I'd hoped. When he came out of the shower he was pissed off. He picked a fight about how clean the apartment was, my inability to cook, and said I spent too much money on useless shit. He even said that was why he wouldn't *let* me have access to our bank account. I told him the apartment was only a mess because we were a bit wild, and pointed at the trail of our clothes leading through the apartment."

Wren turns her face away, but not before I see a tear slide down her cheek. "He accused me of seducing him. Asked me if I was even still taking my birth control, and implied I was trying to trap him. He said that I couldn't take care of him, so why would he want to have a kid with me. Then he stormed out."

My fists clench, but by some miracle I manage to stay quiet. A breath shudders out of her mouth. "I cleaned the apartment and waited. He didn't come back. So I sent him messages, begging him to come home. He texted me back and told me to stop being pathetic. I waited for two days and he didn't come back. I think it was the hope I entertained for a few minutes. Losing it made everything feel so much more desolate."

She takes a deep breath and holds it before forcing it out. "I spiraled. Started looking at old pictures of my family. I wondered what was wrong with me that I was always alone. I didn't sleep the entire time, and I just wanted it to stop."

More tears fall down her face, which seems to agitate her. She scrubs at them. "I got pissed off at myself for cleaning up everything thinking it was going to bring him back. I was mad at myself for being so weak. For being so afraid to be alone that I stayed with someone I wasn't sure I even liked anymore. In that moment, I hated myself more than I hated him though. So, I trashed the place.

Then I broke a mirror. The fragments felt so poetic. All their broken and jagged pieces would never go back together again, not and function the way they were supposed to. The picture it presented would always be a little bit skewed."

My chest squeezes knowing we've arrived at the part of the story I asked to hear, and yet I didn't want her to speak the words.

She blinks up at me. "I can stop."

"No," I croak. "You've carried this alone for too long. I wasn't there for you then, let me be here with you now."

She nods. "I wasn't thinking about life and death. There was no plan. There was just one moment where everything was too much, and I gave in."

Her finger traces one of the lines. "I don't know why I cut myself the first time. I think maybe I just wanted to feel something different than everything inside of my head. I chickened out after it started to bleed. But a little while later I did it again. I panicked after I realized I'd cut deeper than the first time."

"What happened then?" I manage to ask.

"I thought if I wrapped it the bleeding would stop. I started picking up everything I wrecked. The activity and my shitty attempt at a bandage made me lose a bit more blood than I thought. I blacked out for a bit. It was only a few minutes, but when I came to, I drove myself to the hospital."

"What?" I shout the question. "You fainted then thought it was a great idea to drive yourself to the hospital? If you thought I was overbearing before, then you're really going to hate how I'm going to be now."

She rolls her eyes at me again, and I refrain from giving her the spanking she's clearly begging me for. "I think we can agree I wasn't in the best frame of mind that day," she comments.

"Okay, so you drove yourself to the hospital, what happened then?" I concede.

"I was rushed back to a room, where I got several stitches. They had to give me blood because I'd lost a little bit too much. I tried to tell them it was an accident, but they didn't believe me. I stayed at the hospital for a few days on a psychiatric hold."

"How did I never hear about this? Liam never said a word," I say.

She shrugs. "I didn't go to the med clinic here. I drove to Galesburg. They asked for my next of kin, and I told them I didn't have any family, which I think was accurate. That they believed. It was good that they kept me though. They had me meet with a therapist, and I've been going a couple times a month since."

"Where did Liam think you were?" I ask.

Her eyes open wide and fill with tears, which she furiously blinks away. She might not love him anymore, but the hurt hasn't gone away. "I don't think he ever realized I was gone. He didn't ask when I finally got home, and I never told him."

"Why were you with him for four more months?" I don't want to say that it sounded like he was trying to leave her then. He's fighting the divorce now, so I really want to know what changed if he was still seeing someone else.

Wren shrugs. "I should have left. I told him I was going to leave. We fought, and it wasn't like I came out of the hospital cured. He started by promising me we'd go to counseling. That lasted a week before he denied he said it. He convinced me I couldn't make it on my own. He said I couldn't handle our money, I don't make enough to live on my own, and I never would. I was afraid he was right, because I only have a high school diploma, basically I needed him. I didn't have anyone else, and that feeling I had sitting alone for two days terrified me."

"You're one of the most capable women I know. Why would you believe him?" I didn't think it was possible to be angrier at him than I was. Cheating on her was bad, stealing from me was a horrible betrayal, but this is disgustingly abusive.

There's so much sadness and shame reflecting in her eyes when she looks at me. "Because not long ago I was telling myself the same thing to the point I convinced myself, even if just for a little while, that I shouldn't even be alive. Believing I couldn't live without him wasn't a huge stretch."

23

Wren

Talking over my darkest moment leaves me shaking. I feel like I'm on the verge of another breakdown. I never should have let those memories bubble back up. Even with my therapist we haven't gone that deep into that night. There was still so much for me to face, and four months later, I'm still not ready.

My skin feels tight and stretched uncomfortably over my bones. That feeling of needing out, needing an escape climbs up my throat, and I find it hard to breathe. The urge to shut down and flee chokes me. I grab it, hoping I can ease the tightness, and take a full breath.

Griffin pries my fingers off. "Wren, baby girl, what's happening?"

I can hear the fear in his voice, but it doesn't touch how scared I am in this moment. No wonder people find being vulnerable so terrifying. I can't say I've ever actually allowed myself to be this open before now.

My eyes finally land on him, but I can barely see him through the tears filling them. "Griffin, how do I make this stop? This pain and fear feels like it will never end."

It feels cruel for me to lean on him after what I just told him. I hate that when he looks at me now he's going to see me through the lens of my worst moment. It's too much. My head is swimming, so I shift to my knees and use the bed to pull myself up. Watching Liam pull away from me, seeing myself as a burden through his eyes was tough, but if I see Griffin look at me the same way it will shatter me. I'll be no more than that mirror, shards of glittering pieces.

"Where are you going?" he asks, panicked.

I freeze. Where am I going? A fresh new wave of anxiety washes over me. I don't have anywhere to go. Bess is a new friend, and Audrey has pretty much abandoned me. My aunt Hattie would let me come stay with her, which might work if she didn't live in Florida. We aren't really close either, even though she did drop everything to come stay with me after my parents died.

Then it occurs to me, when Liam gets out of rehab, which will happen faster than I'm ready, I'll have to move on. The plan was to stay in Harriston until I saved enough money and move to Centralia to attend Central Valley University. That would have taken months, not weeks, but I know there's no way I can stay here and pretend there's nothing between Griffin and I.

I might have fought my way out of that darkness, but it's looming just on the edge and I don't know if I can escape it a second time. Of course, I don't tell him this. My mental health is my burden to carry. Making it his problem might make me feel better in the short term, but I've learned the hard way that I can't rely on anyone except myself.

I might not know where I'm going, but I know I need to leave. Griffin was right, self preservation is instinctual. "I've got to go."

My bag sits by the door of his bedroom. I move toward

it, but before I can grab it, Griffin wraps his arms around my middle and lifts me off my feet.

"There's no way in hell I'm going to let you walk out the door when you are so clearly agitated, especially after everything you've just told me," he seethes between his teeth.

He drops me down on the bed, and I curl into a ball. "I need it to stop. All the hurt inside of me, I need it to quiet down for a little while."

The bed dips down as he climbs up behind me. He tucks me tight against his chest. "I shouldn't have pushed you to talk. You weren't ready. This is my fault. I didn't think about what bringing all of that up would carry with it. Tell me what I can do to help."

Being in his arms helps, but I don't think I can admit that. "There's nothing you can do. I have to learn how to stand on my own, to get used to being alone. Soon I'm going to have to leave here and start over. I don't have any family, I won't have a husband, and—" I bite my tongue so I won't say the rest.

Griffin turns me in his arms, our legs tangle together, and he gently tucks my hair behind my ear. There's so much tenderness in the way he looks at me right now. It's hard to remember the asshole he was just a few weeks ago. It's odd that this version of him shares space with the more dominant part of his personality, but I'm learning Griffin Hale is a lot more complicated than I ever gave him credit for.

But I don't want his tenderness right now. What I'm feeling from him feels a lot like love, and it's freaking me the fuck out. Those emotions are warm and make me feel like I'm home. That's the last thing I need, because I'm not staying here.

"What else won't you have, baby bird," Griffin whispers.

"You," I whisper back.

He rolls onto his back, and I feel the loss of his touch instantly. "I wish it didn't have to be this way. That we could lock ourselves away and keep the world out. I promise you, when it is time for you to go, it will be to have a much better life than anything you can have here. You won't miss me, not for long."

A tear drips down onto my lips and I lick it off. "You can't promise that. I've lost so many people in my life, and nothing is ever better. I don't want to keep losing people."

"What can I do?" he asks in a pleading tone.

"Make me forget. Make all the doubt and pain go away, even for a little while. I can't breathe, Griff. And I feel like if I don't make it stop I'm going to disappear into a dark void I can't crawl out from."

"I shouldn't. This isn't the best way to cope. At least not how I hope you'll deal with these feelings in the future."

My pride is gone, ego shredded, and I do the one thing I told myself I'd never do. Not after that night. I beg. "Please, just make me forget."

He inhales deeply and reaches across me to the nightstand. "I can't refuse you."

In his hands is a length of silky looking black rope. He pulls it through one hand, and my stomach drops, but this time not in shame or fear. Anticipation floods my body, and I am humming with sudden, painful need. "Yes," I sigh. This is exactly the distraction I need to shove all the bullshit in my head out.

Griffin hovers above me. The tender look on his face morphs into a more serious expression. "Any time you want to stop you tell me."

A devilish smirk spreads across his full mouth. "Actually, if you really want to stop, use the word red. You might be begging me a lot before tonight is over."

I nod my head. "Red, I got it."

His eyes heat and slowly slide over the length of my body. I feel them as they go. His gaze feels like a feather light touch, and my pulse migrates to my clit. My legs press together as I seek some relief, but it only increases the ache.

"If we're going to get you out of your head, you need to get out of your clothes first. Be a good little slut and strip for daddy."

My eyes close, and I gasp. His words always sink into my body in ways I don't think he's aware. My flesh buzzes with an electrical current, and I'm compelled to follow his directions. Climbing off the bed, I stand in front of him.

There's no sexy way to take off shoes, with the exception of heels, but I make quick work of my socks and shoes. The rest of my clothes I take off slowly, and what I hope is a sexy strip tease. When his tongue swipes across the crease in his bottom lip, I'm fairly sure I've succeeded.

He rises off the bed, and when he's next to me I have to tip my head back to look up at him. His stance is wide, and his entire body radiates authority. Griffin puts one of his large hands in the dip in my waist. Lazily, he strokes his thumb across the lower part of my rib cage.

"Get on the bed, baby bird."

I obey immediately and scoot to the middle waiting for him to give me my next direction. He nods when he sees I've listened. "Good girl, now put your arms above your head."

When I put both my arms over the pillow, he picks up the rope again. Griffin moves to straddle me. The denim from his pants rubs against the outside of my thighs. His spicy cologne fills my nose as he leans over to fasten my wrists together.

He studies the binding, and cocks his head to the side. "I'm not sure that will be enough." Rooting around in the drawer once more, he retrieves another piece of rope. Looping it between my wrists, he ties a knot there and another one to a ring hidden in his headboard.

I can't help myself and pull against my restraint to see if they'll hold. "I don't remember you having this nifty set up before," I say and give another tug, rattling the ring.

The corner of his mouth curves up, making him look like the bad boy I'm sure he once was. "You were preoccupied before."

A hot rush of jealousy fills my belly, and my eyes narrow. "Is this your normal thing? Do you bring women back here and tie them up?" I turn my head, not really wanting an answer to my question.

Griffin grabs my chin, and forces me to look back at him. "We both know I'm not a saint, but I haven't had any other women in this bed. I always went back to their place because this—"

"Was your home with your son," I finish.

He nods. "He doesn't belong in here with us either. Not right now. Tonight, we're shutting out the world. Yes, I've done this before. I've had a few subs over the years, and I know what I'm doing. You are safe with me, but I think what you need to know is that they weren't you. I cared about them, of course, but I think we both know what is happening between us is more than that. Even if neither of us is willing to say it."

Love. He's right. That's possibly what this is. Probably even. I realize I haven't felt those feelings in a long time, and I'm ashamed to admit it never felt like this. Terrifying, captivating, invigorating, and freeing. As right as that label feels, I won't admit it aloud. Maybe, if we keep it to ourselves it will save us even a little pain when this has to end.

He leans down and whispers in my ear, "I bolted the rings in the bed frame after our encounter at the bar. I told myself it couldn't happen again, but I wanted it to. The ropes are new too. Everything I've got in that drawer is new and was bought with you in mind."

While those words sink in, and my arousal comes back stronger than before, he gets off of me and strips down until he's only in his jeans.

My fingers flex and curl with the need to touch him. I want to run my fingers through the light dusting of hair on his chest and feel the ridged muscles of his stomach. Griffin takes his time taking something else out of the drawer. I realize what it is when a buzzing sound fills the room.

He holds up a small bullet shaped vibrator. "You'll be a good little slut and let me play with you, won't you, baby bird?"

I nod.

"I want to hear the words."

I know what he wants to hear, but I'm learning I enjoy being a bit of a brat. "Yes," I answer.

"Wren," he growls, and the buzzing cuts off. "You know that's not what I was asking for."

I say nothing, which elicits a dark chuckle from him. "Oh, so my baby bird really wants to play."

There's just enough slack in the rope for him to flip me onto my stomach. "Pull your knees underneath you."

Now we're getting closer to what I want, so I immediately follow his demand.

He runs his hand down my back. "Open them wide and lean forward so your juicy ass is in the air."

Griff uses the hand on my back to press my chest down further so I'm propped up and exposed to him. Without warning his other hand comes down with a loud crack against my butt. I wriggle, the pain only lasts a second before it moves to increasing the ache between my legs. He alternates swats until I'm a writhing bundle of pure need.

The buzzing comes back, and while I'm focusing on what he's going to do with the toy he lands another smack, this time directly on my pussy. I cry out, but not in pain. Every sensation has me on edge, and I feel like if he doesn't touch me soon I'll combust.

"Please," I beg.

"Please what, baby bird?"

"Touch me," I demand.

This time he spanks right in the middle, hitting both cheeks and my clit. I groan and start to slip into a space where nothing exists except for how he makes me feel.

Before the feeling starts to lessen, he places the vibrator against my clit. I'm overly sensitive, and the pleasure is almost painful. I'm mindless, and I pull on my bindings, push against his touch, anything to find relief. He holds the toy in place while I groan and sigh wordless pleas.

My eyes start to roll back into my head, and then suddenly the buzzing stops. He pulls away from me, and the orgasm that was starting to build disappears. I whimper.

"Do bad girls get to come?" he asks.

"No," I reply. I'm not ready to give in to him yet, and as frustrated as I am, I want to see where this game is headed.

He reaches back into the drawer and I hear a cap flip open. I feel a slippery liquid slide down the crack of my ass, and I try to pull away. When his finger starts to circle my nether regions, I clench tight. His other hand holds me in place. "You're mine. My toy to play with how ever I want. I'm not going to fuck your ass tonight, but there isn't a part of you that isn't mine."

I shiver and wonder how something I'd never wanted to do sounded so evocative. When I don't move, he goes back to working the lubricant into my ass. At first it feels like an invasion, and I wonder how anyone could ever find this pleasurable, but then he adds a second finger and manages to stroke something inside of me that causes tingles to spread through my entire body.

I whimper when he pulls out his fingers, but before I can miss them too much, I feel a cool metallic object pushing past that bundle of nerves. "How does that feel?" he asks, and I can hear the desire in the roughness of his voice. Knowing he's getting turned on by me, increases my arousal exponentially.

My voice is husky when I say, "Full."

He swats my ass again, causing the plug in my ass to rub against my channel. "I know you want to get fucked. I'm going to take you hard after I drive you out of your mind. You can stop playing this game and give me what I want."

I lick my lips. "Yes, daddy."

"Mmm," he hums. He presses something blunt against my pussy.

I hear a quiet click, and a different sounding buzz kicks on. "This is a much bigger vibrator. I'm going to fuck you with it, but you are not allowed to come. If you do I'll fuck your mouth and leave this tight cunt missing my cock. Do you understand?"

"Yes, daddy, I won't come," I promise and hope I can do it.

It slips inside using some of the lube he drizzled on me earlier. Griffin doesn't waste any time thrusting the toy deep, hard, and fast into me. The buzzing, and the fullness from the plug, bring me to the edge fast. When he starts to rub my clit with vigorous strokes I scream, "Stop!"

I whimper as the orgasm I felt coming slips away.

"Good girl," he murmurs.

The bed dips as he gets off. I hear the whoosh of his zipper being lowered. His hands grip my hips, and he flips me back over onto my back. "I want to see your face as I drive my cock into your tight cunt. Watch your eyes glaze over as I use your body to get off. I want to see your tits bounce every time I bottom out inside of you."

He pulls me to the edge of the bed and drapes my legs over his arms to rest in the crook of his elbows while his fingers dig into the flesh of my hips. His eyes focus in on my pussy, and he watches intently as he lines his dick up with my opening. Despite promising me hard and fast, he slowly pushes into me.

"Uhh," I groan. I thought the feeling of the combination of the vibrator and the plug made me feel full, but it was nothing compared to this.

Griffin slowly pulls out and repeats the pattern over and over. The build this time is slow, but intense. My nails dig into my palms as I try and prolong the feeling as long as possible.

He bends forward and sucks one of my nipples into his mouth. His pelvis grinds against mine, and tiny sparks shoot behind my closed lids.

"Are you trying not to come?" he asks me.

"You didn't tell me I was allowed to," I rasp.

That evil smirk reappears. "Go ahead and try not to."

"What will happen if I can't?" I ask.

"Nothing, but I want you to try. You won't be able to," he challenges.

He knows enough about me to know that I can't resist a challenge. "I'll try," I say.

"I'm going to fuck you now."

My legs are trapped against his torso with the way they're caged against his sides. He pounds into me hard and fast like I craved. Each thrust drives me farther up the bed and slams the headboard against the wall since I'm laying at a diagonal.

His eyes find mine, and the distance we'd established in this scene evaporates. I see all the words we refuse to voice. His mouth slams into mine, and his kiss is angry and loving. It's full of longing and yes, love. There's nothing left to say that his kiss doesn't express.

I know instantly, beyond a shadow of a doubt, that I love Griffin Hale. I also know it won't make a damn bit of difference. We both come together, but the release is less satisfying as my heart starts the long process of breaking.

24

Griffin

"Where the fuck is Julio?" I shout to Charlie as I roll out from under a truck I've jacked up to check the brake line.

We've been running on fumes and prayers for over a year since my lift broke. Charlie and I have been assigning all undercarriage work to Julio since we're both over six feet tall, and bulky, while Julio is around five-ten with his shoes on and reed thin. One of us still has to roll under on a creeper to sign off on his work, but that's a less back-breaking chore than trying to maneuver around under the limited space the jacks provide.

"Fucking, Liam, " I mutter. Charlie and I have been researching several upgrades the shop desperately needs, and now they're all on an indefinite hold until I can get the finances out of the red.

"Wren has him cleaning out that little room by the front door," Charlie answers.

"The storage closet?" I ask while I try to wipe the grease from my hands with a rag.

Charlie shrugs. "She says storage closets don't have a door to the outside."

"That's because they don't. It was supposed to be your lobby. Anyway, I've found all the stuff you need to furnish it, but you've got a lot of junk in there. I'm going to make a run to the thrift store to drop off what isn't worth selling and post pictures of the bigger stuff to sell it on-line. I'm also making a coffee run, can I get anyone anything?" Wren rambles.

I'm wondering how long it will take her to remember we left her car at the bar. She makes it halfway to the door, before she turns around. By the time she comes back to me with her hand out I've already fished the keys from my pocket and am dangling them for her.

"Black coffee, one sugar," Charlie hollers across the bay.

Julio shakes his head. I open my mouth to tell her what I want, but she waves me off. "I know, black coffee," she says as she rushes out the door.

"Hey kid," Charlie shouts to Julio, "go wash the tow truck."

He grabs the bucket, sponge, and soap and hurries out back. Charlie watches him go and moves closer to me as soon as the back door clicks shut. "Now that the kids are gone, we can chat."

I raise my eyebrows. "Are we going to gossip like the old folks that hang around the pharmacy to hear the news?"

"Shut up, jackass. I took a call this morning while you were under the truck, and thankfully, Wren was busy with her project this morning."

My eyes close, and I take a deep breath. I don't need him to say it to know this is about Liam. Good or bad news I don't know, but constantly waiting for any news is wearing me down.

"I'll take your silence to mean you're ready for the

message. The center called. Liam's first week is coming to an end in a couple of days. He wants to set up family therapy a couple times a week, starting next week," he says.

"I expected there to be some kind of counseling involved."

Charlie continues to stare at me like he's trying to send me a telepathic message. "What?" I snap.

"With the entire family, Griff."

I exhale. There it is, the bad news. "I see. So, uh, they want Wren to come along? Did you tell them they're separated?"

"It didn't come up. I wasn't exactly worried about the state of their relationship so much as the state of yours. I can't even be in the room with the two of you without picking up on the sexual tension crackling between you. I thought the goal was to keep Liam from finding out about your affair?" Charlie asks.

My jaw clenches. "They're separated. What she does is none of my son's fucking business."

Charlie levels me with a look. "Do you really think Liam is going to make that distinction when he finds out what's going on between you?"

"We can control ourselves. I'm more worried about what it would do to her to be forced to talk to him before she's ready," I admit.

"I thought this was what you wanted. Didn't his doctor say it would help him work through his issues?" Charlie presses.

I nod. "Yeah, but it isn't just about him. I know addiction is a disease, but I don't think that it absolves his other choices while he's been using. Cheating on his wife is not the same thing as a cough. She should get a choice."

"What are you going to do? He only went to rehab because she told him she'd try," Charlie reminds me.

"I'm going to ask her. No matter what Liam decides, he's not her problem anymore."

"Are you saying that because you are worried about her, or because you're a possessive caveman who doesn't want to see her with another man?" he asks me.

I give him an exasperated look. "Why can't it be both?"

"DID you still want to learn how to cook?" I ask Wren on our way home from work.

"Yes, but can I have a raincheck? I've got to change and get over to the bar."

"Didn't Donovan tell you that you've got the next couple nights off?" I ask. After I saw him with Bess, my jealousy decreased considerably. Enough that I felt comfortable asking for a favor.

"Why would he just give me a couple nights off?" she asks, and I can tell by her tone she knows I interfered.

"Because the bar has been dead, and he said you work too much. If money is a problem, I'll make sure you get what you need. I can pay you a bonus for creating the lobby."

"You can't do that. You're having money problems too for the same reason I am. That reminds me, have you put Liam's Mustang up for sale yet?"

"Charlie did this afternoon. He picked it up and looked it over so we could get the most money for it. I actually need to talk to you about Liam anyway."

Her shoulders tense. "What did he do now?"

"I just want you to know that you can refuse," I try to prepare her.

Her arms wrap around herself, and I wish her first instinct wasn't to turn to herself for comfort. "Rip the band aid off, Griff."

"His therapist called and left a message with Charlie. They want to set up family therapy with us," I say all in a rush.

"Us, as in both of us at the same time?" she squeaks.

I shove my hand through my hair. This is hard for me to say, so I buy time by turning off the truck, and going around to help her down. "Yeah. Like I said, you can say no. You don't owe him anything."

She's quiet for a little bit. "I said I'd go if he went to rehab."

"Actually, you said you'd give him a chance if he went to rehab. That's not going to happen," I growl.

Wren drops her arms and steps close to me. She nuzzles close to my chest. "I should be bothered when you get all growly, but I find it kind of hot."

I hold her tighter. "Lucky for you I seem to speak mostly in grunts and growls."

She takes a deep breath, holds, then exhales slowly. "When is this therapy session?"

"Next week. I haven't talked to the doctor yet."

"Maybe you can still catch them. Call, and we can talk about it while you teach me to cook," she offers.

I take my phone out of my pocket and find the text I had Charlie send me with the phone number. When it starts to ring, I put it on speaker. If she's going to be a part of this, then I want her to be involved.

I'm about to hang up when I hear someone answer the phone. "Dr. Taylor," he answers.

"This is Griffin Hale and Wren Parker returning your call."

"Oh, I didn't realize you'd be on with Mrs. Hale. Liam made it sound like the two of you don't get along."

Wren winces. "Griffin told me he was going to try and call you back, and thought I should be here for the call so we could schedule this easier."

"Of course, that makes sense," Dr. Taylor agrees. "He's done well here for the first week. He's mostly through detox, and once the physical symptoms subside we can schedule a group session."

"Detox? I didn't realize he was that bad, or that his symptoms would last over a week," I say.

The doctor makes a noise, and I can hear papers flipping on the other end of the line. "I see he did sign a disclosure form for both of you. Liam was abusing both drugs and alcohol for several months. While that usually wouldn't be too long for someone to quit without medical intervention, the amount and combinations he was using have made it necessary to be handled by trained medical professionals. That's why I'm reaching out to schedule therapy. Liam is very lucky he got help when he did. He was very lucky he didn't overdose with how much he's been taking. It's imperative we all work together to help him work through the issues that prompted him to use and start to address those things while he's still under supervised care."

"When are you thinking about having the therapy session?" Wren asks.

"Let's set it for next Thursday. He should be over the physical side effects by then," Dr. Taylor says.

Wren nods, even though the doctor can't see her, and walks out of the room. "We'll be there," I answer for both of us, then go after her. I'm always either running from her or chasing after her.

I find her sitting on the back porch looking out into the

back yard. This is my favorite spot in the world. The edge of my property is wooded and gives it a secluded feeling. Wren stares straight ahead, her knees pressed against her chest with her arms wrapped around them. I kneel in front of her and push her hair back from her face.

"Baby bird, what's wrong?"

She blinks, and the blank look in her eyes fades. She tries to smile, but it's weak. "I'm just not ready for this to be over."

My chest tightens. Funny, in all the talk over meeting with the therapist, I forgot there was a clock hanging over our heads, ticking down to the moment where she'd leave and I'd be here picking up the pieces. Somewhere in this mess I guess I started to think we'd somehow find a solution where we could stay together and keep Liam from getting hurt. That's pretty naive thinking for a man my age.

I take her hands and help her to her feet. "It's not over tonight. I'm not ready either, so for tonight, let's just be us."

She exhales, and her smile becomes more natural. "Okay," she says softly.

"Ready for that cooking lesson?" I ask.

"Whatever you want, daddy," she teases.

"In that case—" I lift her and toss her over my shoulder. "I think I need to work up an appetite first."

25

Wren

Griffin's hand covers mine, stopping me. "I said dice, not destroy."

I let go of the knife, so I don't get angry and stab him with it. Through my teeth I say, "I told you I don't know how to cook."

He takes the knife and shows me how to cut the onions into really small pieces, rather than hack at them like I was doing. "I didn't realize we'd have to start with the very basics."

I scowl at him. "You're usually in a much better mood after you come. What the hell is wrong with you?"

The muscle in the corner of his jaw twitched. "Maybe I didn't find everything I was looking for."

Without meaning to, I gasp. Then I back away to go find my pants. Suddenly standing in nothing but his shirt makes me feel too vulnerable. Every time Liam rejected me, criticized me, all of it ran through my head.

It took me a few months to realize he picked fights with me and then used them to keep a barrier between us. In about a week, I'd have to sit in a room with him, the man

I'm sleeping with, and a therapist and start to confront these issues. Running away sounds better and better every day.

All of these thoughts fly through my head as I'm shoving my things into my duffle bag. I thought it was so sweet that Griffin cleared out a drawer for me to use, but now I wish all of my things were still in my bag.

"What are you doing?" Griffin asks from the doorway to his room.

I ignore him, unconcerned with pissing him off. It's pretty clear what I'm doing, and I don't feel like talking to him. I've already put up with as much shit from a Hale man as I'm ever going to deal with.

Griffin steps into the room and between me and the dresser I'm removing my clothes from. "Wren, I asked you a question."

"And I'm choosing not to answer you. Now, please move aside, I need the rest of my stuff."

"Wren," he says in a tone that sounds like a warning.

I spin around. My hair whips around me, and I point my finger in Griffin's face. "Don't *Wren* me. I thought you were done acting like an asshole. If you didn't 'find what you were looking for' I'll move along so you can continue the search."

Screw the rest of my things. It isn't like I had designer clothes. I grab my bag with what I'd already been able to shove inside, and push past him to the front door. My keys are sitting on the counter, and for once my car isn't left at some other location.

Griffin rushes around me, and closes the front door as I start to pull it open. "Would you just wait a minute? You're right, I'm being an asshole, but before you run away again, let me at least explain what I meant. I guarantee it's not how you're taking it."

"Five minutes, and then you won't try and stop me from leaving?" I hedge. My body language is still confrontational, but inside I'm practically begging him to have an explanation.

"Come sit with me," he says and takes my hand. Together we move into the living room and sit on the sofa.

Griffin takes a deep breath, but doesn't look at me. "I don't want you to go to the therapy session."

That takes me by surprise. I thought he wanted to do practically anything to make sure Liam finished rehab. I know a lot has changed between us since then, but I didn't think it had changed that much. Just a week ago he stood by and let me tell Liam there was a chance to save our marriage if he went to rehab.

"I'm so confused. I thought you wanted me to do whatever was necessary to make sure Liam followed this program," I say. I can feel the tension gathering the muscles in my forehead.

Slowly he lifts his face and I can see a war brewing inside of him. "I love my son."

"I know you do," I interrupt. My heart is breaking for being one of the reasons he feels he needs to even assert that. His entire adult life he's focused on Liam's well being.

His hands shake, and I know what he's about to admit is hard for him. "I also resent him," he says in a whisper. "I put up with his mother so he could have a shot at a normal family. Then I raised him alone when she cut and run. Never did I think twice about myself, or what I wanted. Everything I did was to make sure he had what he needed and most of what he wanted. I didn't date, because it felt like too big of an upheaval for Liam if it didn't work out. I stayed in too much anyway because there was always a practice or game we needed to run out to. Not once did I get frustrated with him over any of that, because he didn't ask for irresponsible teenagers as parents. Then he married you—"

I nod. "I screwed everything up. I know he gave up too much for me, and now he resents me for it. Maybe if I hadn't encouraged him to stay, although I don't really remember doing that, he'd have gone off to school, and not been in such a dark place that he ended up stealing from you. I know you said he didn't have a scholarship, but maybe he would have gone to community college and played there."

Griffin is shaking his head. "Of course you wouldn't have discouraged him from going to school. I have no doubt you'd have waited for him that first year, and moved mountains to join him. The only one who got manipulated out of pursuing an education was you."

My heart starts to pound too fast and it's echoing in my ears. "No," I argue, but I'm not sure why. It makes sense actually. "He said he wanted to go." I'm finding it hard to pull in a deep breath. "I know you already told me this, but I guess I had hoped maybe you were wrong. And even if you were right, it was easier to believe he had planned to go."

He looks at me with a combination of sympathy and pity, and frankly it's pissing me off all over again. I might have been a fool, but I don't want anyone's pity. "Have I just been a joke to all of you? This whole time while you were making sure I didn't feel like I was good enough, have you, Liam, and Charlie just been laughing at me behind my back?"

Hysterical laughter bubbles up. I can't sit here facing him anymore, and I start pacing the room. "Did you know he was cheating on me too? Poor, stupid Wren. Why did he even marry me? Was it all about my parents' insurance money?"

I hold the wrist with the scars with my hand. Sometimes, when emotion gets too high, I can almost feel the sting and burn of the cuts. My doctor said it is phantom pain, but I think it's fear that I could get that low again. Holding it tight in my hand, I feel like I can hold in the feelings that brought me the scars in the first place.

Griffin doesn't miss the movement. He stalks across the room and puts his hands on either side of my face. "You need to listen. I didn't know he lied to you about having a scholarship, nor did I know you gave one up to stay with him. I wondered why you didn't go off to school, but I believed you loved my son that much."

"I did," I whisper. It's awkward telling the man you're currently sleeping with that you were madly in love with another man, especially his son, but I don't have the mental capacity for bullshit at the moment.

He winces and nods. "I know. There turns out to be a lot I didn't know though. I did not know he was cheating on you. I don't actually go out that much. I guess I can now, but I probably only make it out a couple of times a month, and only when Charlie drags me out. I'll be honest though, Charlie admitted to me the other day that he did know."

"That answers that question," I mutter.

"What's that?" Griffin asks.

I shrug. "I've just wondered if Charlie felt any loyalty to my father. He's been rather cold to me the last few years, but when I was a kid, I just remember him being fun and nice."

He tips my chin up so he can look into my eyes. "Don't hold Charlie being a dumb ass against me. I'm afraid I've got enough stuff of my own to apologize for, and if you add his to my score, I'll never get right with you."

Griffin is being adorable, and I want to laugh and live

in this lighter-hearted moment with him, but it's time to stop deluding myself. "What are we doing? This is so much more than sex, and it's getting really complicated considering there's an obvious end date to what we're doing."

"Logically I know that. But then I get all pissed off at the prospect of you even being in the same room as my son, and I know that I can't walk away from you. When it's time you're going to have to go."

I gesture to my bag sitting on the floor by the front door. "I was doing just that."

"Not like this. I want to know you'll be okay. I can't have you out there thinking I didn't want you, that I used you. That's what you thought I meant by what I said earlier, isn't it? You know what I didn't find that pissed me off?" he asks me.

I'm afraid to hear the answer, but I need to. "What?" I mouth.

"A reason I could keep you. A way that I don't have to sit by and watch as you convince my son there's a chance to salvage your marriage if he gets help. I want him to get that help, badly, but I don't want to sacrifice you for him to do it."

Lying to Liam never set well with me. If he is only going through the motions to keep me, then he's going to relapse the moment I leave. I feel like I'm going to end up being held emotionally hostage in a marriage I no longer want.

"I don't plan on lying to him. I can't tell him we have a chance. If he's only getting better for me, it won't last. I'm hoping we can talk to him and help him decide to stay for himself," I tell him.

Griffin pulls me into his arms, and I melt. This is becoming my favorite place in the world, and I already miss him, even though he's right here. There's so many reasons I should go grab my bag and walk out the door, but there's a big reason why I won't.

I love him. I shouldn't, and I doubt I'll ever tell him. Hell, maybe it's some kind of trauma bond, but right now, right here, my entire body and soul belongs to Griffin Hale.

Basically, we're fucked. He says he will need me to walk away in the end, and I'm not sure I will ever find the strength to do that.

26

Griffin

"C'mon," I tug on her hand, "I still want to teach you how to cook."

I can't really blame her for the skeptical look she shoots my way. "Really? Look, I forgive you for being an ass earlier. It is after all one of your core personality traits, but it kinda makes you a shitty teacher," she scoffs.

Closing in behind her, I wrap my arms around her stomach, and lift her up. "I wasn't asking. I need to know you can take care of yourself."

She squirms in my arms, but I don't put her down until we're back in the kitchen. "You mean when I'm out in the world, on my own, no family, and no friends for the first time in my life? Yeah, I guess the main priority would be whether or not I could make," she picks up the can of tomatoes, "what the hell are we making anyway?"

I take the can and put it back with the other ingredients in the order they'd be used. "Lasagne," I answer her after everything is back where it belongs.

Wren looks closely at all the ingredients I've lined up for us. Her eyes flick back to mine, and she bites her bottom lip. "How annoyed would you get if I just mixed this all around?"

"Very," I grunt.

She smirks at me. "So, just your normal, everyday self then?"

I pull her against me. Her plump ass rubs against my hardening cock. "Don't you know it turns me on when you act up?"

Her back arches, shoving that firm ass harder against my aching dick. "Also your normal, horny self."

"Behave," I warn her. Somehow I summon the willpower not to fuck her on the countertop. We can save that for when the food is in the oven.

Wren blinks, and her face transforms into the innocent mask that haunts my dreams. The wet ones at least. "Yes, daddy," she says, but the husky rasp in her voice lets me know I'm not the only one on edge.

She refocuses her attention on my obsessively organized ingredients. "Where's the marinara sauce?"

I grab the tomatoes, garlic, onions, oregano, and basil and push them towards her.

"We're making the sauce too? Do you make your own noodles?" she asks as she grabs the ingredients to look at them.

"Not for lasagne. I've tried it before, but dried ones work just as well. Better for some recipes, like this one."

Her face is flushed and her pupils dilated as she stands there and looks at me. "I don't think I've ever been this turned on."

I nervously shove my hand through my hair, probably making a mess of it. "If this turns you on, wait until you see my garden in the spring."

Immediately I realize that was the wrong thing to say. Her head falls forward, and she wraps her hands around her stomach. Once again the elephant in the room has made its presence known again. She doesn't need to say the words, we both know she won't be here when spring rolls around.

Wren clears her throat. "You'll have to send me some pictures. I'm sure it's lovely."

With my hands on her hips I turn her around. She's pinned between me and the counter. Her hands rest on my biceps, and we just stand together. Looking at her hurts, but I know that all too soon I'll miss this pain. "If there was one thing in this world I could have just for me, it would be you."

Her fingers tighten where they rest on my arms. "Maybe someday we won't have to sacrifice our happiness for everyone else."

Letting go of her waist, I lift one hand to cup her face. My thumb traces her cheek bone, helping me memorize the delicate structure of her face. I want to burn every part of her into my brain, because I know I'll never get over her. I won't tell her that, because, while I know my life has fundamentally changed, I love her enough to hope there'll be more for her after me.

"I'm not going to learn how to cook like this," she says, lightening the heaviness between us.

I take a step back and let her turn around. She follows my example as we chop, dice, and sauté ingredients side by side. When it's time to shove our masterpiece in the oven she asks, "Where did you learn how to cook?"

Of course she knows at least some of my history with my parents. Liam grew up not knowing his grandparents on either side, and I imagine he's told her about them at some point in the seven years they've been together. If he hasn't, she could have heard it from town gossip. My parents were notorious drunks. Their shouting matches, when they were both drunk, had the cops out at least once a month when I was growing up.

"Dolores taught me," I finally answer her. "She said that I needed to step up and give Liam the home I didn't have, and she'd show me how. By the time he was in high school he was usually too busy for dinners at home, but when he was younger I was quite the homemaker."

Wren looks down at her clothes, which are splattered with sauce, and there's even a streak on her cheek. "Meanwhile I look like I tried to bathe in pasta sauce. I'm going to go clean up before it's ready."

"Good idea. I'll set the table." I wipe the sauce from her face, and stick my finger in my mouth. "Tastes good," I hum.

I shove my hand down the front of her pants, and seek out her clit, rubbing it until I feel the bundle of nerves swell under my touch. She's already wet, so I'm able to thrust two fingers deep in her cunt and give her a preview of how hard I plan to fuck her after dinner. I take her right to the edge and pull my fingers free. Slipping my fingers into my mouth, I lick them clean. "But, you taste better."

She lets out a low groan, which makes me want to tease her more. I lean down next to her ear. "I plan to eat you for dessert. I'm going to bring you to the edge over and over again, until you beg me to let you come."

Wren shivers. "How do you know I won't just go take care of myself in the shower?"

I grip her chin in my hand. "If you touch what belongs to me without my permission I'm going to spank your plump ass, and you won't get to come at all."

She pouts, and I can't resist the urge to kiss her full lips. "Be a good girl and I'll make you feel so good tonight no one will ever live up to what I can do to you."

She stretches up on her toes and kisses my cheek.

"You've already done that," she whispers before she runs from the room.

THE SHOWER KICKS ON, and I hurry to create a romantic atmosphere for the two of us. I'd avoided doing things like this because I was afraid it would make it harder to let her leave when it was time. Her whispered words let me know it's already too late. If this ends, when it ends I correct myself, it's going to hurt like a bitch. It doesn't matter if that's tonight or in two weeks. Nothing I can do will lessen the blow.

So instead, I decide to live without regrets. Not showing her how I feel isn't going to save either one of us the heartbreak we both know is coming. My only hope now is that the memories we make now will last the rest of my life.

I can easily say this is the first time in my life I am upset with myself for not caring about things like dishes and place settings. My cabinet has an assortment of mismatched dishes I've purchased as needed from a local thrift store, and unfortunately my silverware is the same. I'm able to find two plates that are close to the same color, forks of a similar size, and some tea lights I don't even remember buying. Using my phone, I find a playlist with some rock ballads and hook it up to my bluetooth speakers. It might not be as romantic as classical, but at least it won't put me to sleep. Sleeping during a date is not most women's definition of romance.

Maybe the next guy she is in a relationship with will have his shit together and be able to make her a romantic dinner without starting a fight because he's afraid to lose her. Even simply letting that thought enter my mind has my fists clenching. Every instinct wants to scream that she's mine and make sure every man around knows it. The worst part is, a dark part of me wants Liam to find out, if for no other reason than to end any thought he has of getting her back.

The timer dings at the same time the blow dryer kicks on. I figure I have enough time to make a salad before she's done. I'm digging through the refrigerator for ingredients for the salad when there's banging on the front door.

As Wren has pointed out many times I'm a grouchy asshole. I've got one real friend, and I don't bring women back to my home. I have no idea who could think pounding their way through my door is a good life choice, but I'm going to correct them quickly and go back to spending time with my woman.

I rip open the front door, ready to rip someone a new asshole, only to find Wren's best friend, Audrey, standing on my porch. My forehead scrunches in confusion. I thought Wren said they hadn't spoken much for a while. I'll have to talk to her about not sharing details of our relationship together to people who could talk to Liam. It is bad enough Bess and Donovan know, but I feel fairly sure they'll keep our secret.

Something feels off about her showing up at my house, so I stop myself from asking her if she's looking for Wren. My eyes slip down her body, and a sick feeling fills my stomach. She looks nothing like the primped party girl I'd seen hanging around Wren for the last several years. Her hair is piled in a messy knot on top of her head, and not in an adorable way like when Wren does it. There are bags under her eyes, and she's practically swimming in fabric when I've only ever seen her parading around town in tight tops and pants. She's trying to hide something, and I pray I'm wrong.

The thing is, when I was a senior in high school, and Melinda found out she was pregnant, she was so exhausted the first few months she looked a lot like what Audrey does right now. Right down to the super baggy clothes she thought would hide her growing belly.

"Where's Liam?" she asks in a rush. The way she looks around her, it's obvious she doesn't want to be here, but her need to find my son made her brave enough to come to my house.

With one hand on the door frame and the other on the door, my body language screams she's not getting let into the house. "Why are you looking for my son? Aren't you Wren's best friend?"

Her lip curls for a second, then she tries to make her expression more neutral. "We're friends," she says, noticeably dropping the *best* label.

This time it's my turn to give her a look. Except, I make no effort to remove the condescension on my face. "Is that so?" I make a show of looking her up and down. "Because my guess is you were the one Wren and I caught Liam fucking in the backseat of his car. Now you're here at my house, dressed like a bag lady, probably thinking no one will realize you're knocked up by the husband of your best friend. So, how did you see this going? You were going to show up here, and I was going to help you?"

Audrey glares at me. Her hands fall to her belly, and when they stretch the fabric, there's an obvious bulge in her midsection. "Yeah, I did. This is your grandchild. Liam is leaving Wren, and he wants to be with me."

"Then why did he beg me to stay with him?" Wren's voice startles me, and I jump.

Gone is the woman who pretended to be Wren's friend. Her hatred is written all over her face. "There's no way. He told me he'd help me with the baby. He's leaving you to be with me."

"When did he tell you this?" I ask, trying hard to keep from scaring her, at least until she confirms my suspicions.

Audrey fidgets. "Well, he didn't say it exactly, but I know that he's a good man. He'll take care of us."

Wren starts laughing. "He's going to take care of you? With what? He has no money, and I sure as hell am not going to give him anymore. He doesn't even have a car. Shit, he'll be lucky to stay out of jail."

Audrey's sallow face twists up into a sneer. "What would you know about how much money he has? He told me you don't want anything to do with the finances, and he made sure you don't have access to it. He's been hiding money from you for almost a year."

Wren nods. "That's probably true. After all, he did commit identity theft and fraud. Hiding money is the least horrible thing he's done lately, and that includes screwing your skanky ass in the back seat of the car I bought him with my parents' insurance money. So go ahead, take my husband. I don't want him anymore. Good luck getting him to be on board with the whole baby thing, Liam doesn't want kids."

Audrey starts to tap her foot. She ignores Wren and addresses me, "Just tell me where he is. I lost my job because I'm too sick to work. I need his help."

"We're going to see him later next week. I'll tell him you are needing to talk to him, and that's all I can do," I tell her. If it's true, he does have a responsibility to his child. Whether he wanted children or not, he probably has one on the way.

Her attention swings back to Wren, and I tense knowing she's starting to realize it's not normal in our relationship for us to be hanging out. "Why are you here?"

I expect Wren to slip up and give us away, but I didn't realize how good of a front she can put up. "I really don't think it's any of your business why I'm spending time with the only family I've got."

Audrey makes a big show of putting her hand on her swollen stomach. "It's your family for now. Don't get too comfortable."

There's one more thing I need her to tell me. "When did you tell Liam about the baby?"

"A few weeks ago," she answers.

"Was that the last time you spoke to him?" I ask.

She bites her lip and nods.

"That's very enlightening. Now get the fuck off my porch. If he wants to speak to you he'll call. I'll make sure to let him know you filled his wife in on all the dirty details," I say and slam the door in her face.

I expect Wren to crumble. Hearing another woman is going to have the one thing I know she's wanted for the last couple years has to be like rubbing salt on an open wound. But she doesn't appear to be feeling anything, and that scares me more than her tears.

27

Wren

My hands start shaking the moment Griffin closes the door. I need to try and hold it together, because the rage building up inside of me is the kind that destroys. "I need a minute," I say to him and rush out of the room before he has a chance to respond.

By the time I make it to his room I'm breathing hard through my nose. I'm surprised by the level of calm control I'm able to exercise as I slowly close his door, because I really want to slam it. I grab the pillow I've been using, bury my face into the fluff, and scream.

It's the cleansing kind of scream that releases all of my anger, frustration, and intense disappointment. I pull it away to suck in a breath, then repeat until the razor sharp edge of my fury has dulled. My kitten, Patches, deciding the danger has passed, crawls out from under the bed and hops into my lap. I haven't spent as much time with her since I've been either working, or with Griffin.

She bumps her head into my arm to get me to pet her. I scratch the top of her head, letting the pillow fall back onto the bed. Her purr soothes the rest of my jagged corners, and I'm able to slow the painful racing of my heart.

"A baby." I shake my head and make a sound that is a mixture between a laugh and a sob. Patches purrs louder trying to comfort me. "He wouldn't touch me for half a year, but his stupid ass will knock up his mistress."

"Would you rather be the one carrying his child right now?"

I jump, having not heard Griffin's loud steps come down the hallway, or him opening the door. I drop my hand to my stomach. Did I want that?

I take a deep breath. "I want a baby. Someone in this world I'm connected to besides my aunt whom I rarely speak to. I want a family again. I know those aren't great reasons to have a baby. They're selfish, but not having that connection hurts deep into my soul. But, do I wish I were having Liam's baby?"

Griffin's fingers grip the door frame as he waits for me to answer him.

"No, but somehow I'm sad he didn't want to be with me. It doesn't make sense, but even though I'm ending it, I'm still pissed off that his mistress is getting the baby he wouldn't give me."

He lets go of the door, and sits next to me on the bed. Without looking at me, he reaches over and takes my hand. "He won't stay with her. Liam might have gotten her pregnant, but I don't think you can say he's having a baby with her. She's probably going to raise that baby alone."

I turn to look at him. "I really don't want to have *his* baby." What I can say is that I wish our stars were different, that there could be a future for the two of us.

"You'll have it someday. The family you want." What he doesn't say, but I can see in his expression, is that he wishes it could be with him.

Two Wrongs

So do I, but I won't say it either.

"SHUT UP! That cow pretended to be your best friend and was sleeping with your husband? I'm totally your real best friend, right?" Bess says in a rush.

I load my tray up with beers for the back table of frat guys while she keeps talking. "I'm totally the best choice. I promise I won't sleep with daddy Hale."

Donovan walks past and slaps her ass. "You better not. I don't share my woman."

Cocking my eyebrow I stare at her until she squirms. "So, you're his woman now?"

Bess shrugs one shoulder. "He kept pestering me until I agreed. It's not like there's a lot of choices in this town."

I roll my eyes. "He's hot, sweet, and into you. Why can't you just admit you like him for more than his dick?"

She looks around us to make sure he isn't listening again. "Fine, you hooker, I kinda, sorta, maybe love the big doofus."

Donovan shaves about five years off both of our lives when he jumps up from behind the bar. He points his finger in her face. "I knew it! We're getting married."

"Were you hiding behind the bar eavesdropping on our conversation?" she accuses, totally trying to distract him from his declaration they were going to be married.

"How did the two of you miss the fact I walked past you carrying a case of beer? It's not my fault you're so absorbed with your drama that you didn't realize I needed to stock the coolers behind the bar. Back to the point, we're getting married," he says, oozing confidence.

"That is a shit proposal," she replies.

"It really kinda was. You're going to have to try again."

I hoist the heavy tray and carefully make my way to serve my tables. After dropping off the rounds of beer to the surprisingly polite college guys, I make a loop around my section and see if anyone needs a refill.

I freeze behind a table filled with some women I know Audrey hangs out with. It used to be only when I was busy with Liam, but my guess is they've seen her more than I have. "Can you believe she actually went to his dad's house?" one of them, Tina I think, says.

The other three lean forward, completely engaged in gossip as though my pain is thrilling for them. Or maybe, they're not real friends to Audrey, and it's her pain they're enjoying so much. "I know!" another woman squeals. I can't remember if she's Heather or Heidi. Doesn't really matter. None of this will matter to me when I leave this town.

Heather or Heidi continues, "Did she tell you that Wren was there?"

The other three nod. I wonder why, if they all know the story, they feel the need to discuss it in detail, but Harriston is a small, boring-ass town. "And she told her she's having Liam's baby! Ugh, poor Wren."

That is surprising. Not that I really care to have their pity, but not having their scorn is kind of refreshing. It doesn't last though.

"Hardly, Audrey says he's been trying to leave her for years. That he wished he never married her, but he felt so bad for her since she's an orphan and all," a third woman adds. I stop trying to remember what their names are after that. I'm just calling this one cuntasaurus. I think it fits.

My head tips up, and I see the multicolored bundle of chaos that is my newly-appointed best friend approach their table. She must have been checking on a table close by.

Bess pretends to trip, and my mouth falls open watching in fascination as an entire pitcher of beer lands on cuntasaurus. "Oh my," Bess says dramatically, and if I'm not mistaken, using a fake southern drawl. "Well, bless your heart, I suppose you'll be needin' your check so you can go clean up." Definitely a fake southern accent.

"Donovan!" the woman screeches.

He rushes over and takes in the woman who reeks of cheap beer. Her friends weren't completely safe so close to the splash zone, and all of them resemble contestants in a wet t-shirt contest.

"Bess?" he asks, trying not to get angry at her. After all, that would seriously hurt his chances of her accepting his declaration they were getting married.

Bess blinks her eyes, failing miserably at looking innocent. "Yes, fiancé?"

A dopey grin spreads across his face, and I believe she could get away with just about anything with him. He returns his focus to the women, and tries to soothe things over. "I'm sorry ladies, your tab is on the house tonight."

Cuntasaurus, being true to her species, blusters. "I want her fired! Don't you know who I am?"

I raise my hand, not sure what has come over me. "I have no idea who you are, but you seem to know everything about me. Except for the part where Liam convinced me not to take my full ride scholarship so I would stay here with him, and how he was begging me a couple weeks ago to forgive him." I gave her a thumbs up. "But you totally nailed the part where my parents were killed in a car accident. Good job, you!"

Donovan's face hardens. "Hmm, well. I suggest you get the fuck out of my bar, and mayor's daughter or not, don't come back."

Her mouth opens and closes several times. Clearly,

she's not used to anyone calling her on her shit. "I'm going to tell my daddy!"

"No need," Donovan waves her off. "I see him once a week when he comes in here after your weekly dinners. I'm sure he'll believe me when I tell him you were being a bitch and my fiancée poured a pitcher of beer on your head. He'll probably be surprised this is the first time it's happened."

The three of us turn as a unit and leave them to flounce out of the bar. When we are far enough away, Donovan points at me. "You're supposed to be a good influence on her. You better do a good job as maid of honor. No strippers for her bachelorette party."

He doesn't stay long enough for Bess to come up with a retort, both of us too stunned to speak. The slam of his office door snaps her out of her shock, and she slaps me on the arm. "I'm totally going to have to marry him, and I think it might be your fault."

"Ow!" For a tiny woman, smaller than even me, she can hit. "How the hell is this my fault?"

"You're the one who told him to rock my world. Well, he did. He rode me so good my vagina is confused. It only wants his cock now, and I'm going to have to marry him so no one else can have it," she complains.

"You two are really weird. And for the record I told him to sex you into a date, not marriage," I reply.

She shrugs. "He's an overachiever."

"He does know that you get to pick your own maid of honor, right?"

She playfully bumps into me. "Like I'd pick anyone else." Bess fidgets, and looks back to Donovan's office. "Do you think he's serious?"

Before I have a chance to answer her Donovan comes out from his office and slaps a small box in her hands. "You said you hate, 'that mushy, romantic shit.' So, I won't piss you off by getting on one knee. If you agree to be my wife, I promise to do that thing with my tongue whenever you want. I'll pull your hair and fuck you hard every day, making sure you come before I do."

His proposal is oddly perfect for Bess. Over the years with Liam I gave up on the notion that there was another person who was made just for you. I thought you were supposed to find someone who you hopefully loved who wanted similar things out of life.

Bess is vibrant, from the colors she wears to the way she talks. Some men would try and dim her shine. Not Donovan. In fact, he celebrates her. I envy them for the ease of their relationship. They can declare their love, even in their oddball way, and plan a future. They can do all of these things in public without worrying about what other people will think, or who might find out.

I watch as Bess flips open the box and squeals. She pulls out a black ring with a brightly colored purple stone and slips it on her finger. Her smile is contagious, and in seconds the two of us are hopping around, celebrating.

Bess stops jumping around and stares at the door. She leans close and whispers in my ear. "If I wasn't so happy right now I'd be so jealous. The way daddy Hale is looking at you, I'm not the only one who will be getting fucked hard tonight."

My head swivels to the door, and I watch him look for me. The bar has a decent sized crowd tonight, all stumbling about getting drinks, flirting, and avoiding reality for a few hours. He not only stands above them, since he's nearly a head taller than almost everyone in the room, except for maybe Donovan, but he's got a magnetic pull that is purely Griffin.

I take in his wide stance that screams confidence and

power. Doesn't hurt that it perfectly displays his strong thighs encased in perfectly worn denim. A gray Henley stretches across his wide chest, and showcases his trim waist.

His nostrils flare, and my stomach clenches. Griffin doesn't look like he's here to drag me into the storage closet for fun. No, he looks like he's pissed off and looking for heads to bust. I don't know what it says about me, but I get wet anyway.

The moment he spots me his long legs eat up the distance between us. He grabs my elbow and starts to move me toward the back of the bar. I guess we're going to the storage closet after all.

Donovan waves his bar rag at us. "It's fine, not like she's on the clock or anything."

"I'm not in the mood, Miller," Griffin snarls.

"Ooh, whipping out last names now. Okay, Hale, I'm in too good of a mood to let your grumpy ass bring me down. Go have your chat, but tone down the giant dick energy," Donovan snaps back.

"It's big dick energy, baby," Bess whispers to him.

"I know it is, but he's acting like a giant dick not a guy swinging around a big member," Donovan matches her whisper.

Griffin abandons the conversation to drag me into the storage room. "Are they for real?" he asks as soon as he closes and locks the door.

I nod. "Oh, that is only a small fragment of what they've been like tonight."

He takes a breath and seems to calm down. "What were you and Bess jumping around for?"

"Donovan told her they were getting married and shoved a ring box in her hands. Then told her he promises to pull her hair and fuck her hard every night. Super romantic." I roll my eyes on the last part.

I'm confused at the turn in his mood, but I know if I push him for answers he's not going to budge. Unless he wants to that is. Patience is a hard skill, and one I've yet to master. "Griff, why are you here tonight?"

"I take it you didn't see Charlie in the bar earlier, did you?"

"No, is there a problem with him being here? He comes in a lot to pick up women," I reply.

"The problem is when someone gives you a hard time, and you don't turn to me. Why did I hear from him that Audrey's minions were in here giving you shit?"

I raise my eyebrows. "Do you really expect me to run to my daddy when some girls are being mean to me? I can assure you, they were handled."

His eyes narrow, and some of the tension is back in his body. "Not by me."

"There's going to be a lot of fallout from what Liam has done. You're not going to be able to protect me from all of it. Especially not in public, not in this town."

Griffin's hand slips into my hair, and pulls my head back. "Yes, I fucking can. I'm going to prove it to you. We're going out on your next night off."

28

Griffin

I swing by Dolores' house while Wren is dress shopping with Bess. Donovan isn't letting her sit and think too much about getting married. I admire that about him. He's making sure he gets to claim his woman in front of everyone he feels is important. If I were in his place I'd have my ring on Wren's finger and be working on putting my baby in her belly already.

Hearing her talk about wanting a child left me with fantasies about being the one to give her one. When Melinda told me she was pregnant all I felt was fear. I'm ashamed to admit that, even just to myself. I mourned the future I might have had if I had gotten to leave this town.

When the time came, I stepped up, and I was the best father I could have been at eighteen. I made mistakes, but show me a parent who can say they did the perfect job raising their kid. But, it was never something I planned. Doesn't mean I love my son any less, but I do wonder what it would be like to anticipate becoming a father with joy instead of fear.

I thought spending this time with Wren would let us both live without regrets. I see now you can never escape that completely, it's just a matter of choosing which ones you can most easily live with. The more time I spend with her, the less sure I am that I'm making the right choice. Choosing a son who steals from me over a woman who is probably the other half of my soul might not be the best one.

Dolores is sitting in a rocking chair on her front porch when I pull into her driveway. I stop in front of her and lean against one of the posts. "I see the house has survived. What was it, termites?"

She laughs mischievously. "Worked, didn't it? Now, you owe me a favor."

I roll my eyes. She never changes. "What is it now? You need your gutters cleaned out? A new garden tilled?"

Her watery blue eyes sparkle with amusement. "If you're offering, sure. But you'll have to plant that new garden as well." She looks down at her hands, covered in spots and gnarled with time. "I'm afraid these old bones don't work as well as they used to. My current flowerbeds are about all I can handle anymore."

I cross one ankle over the other and prop my hip on the porch rail, settling in for a longer conversation. She'll make her point when she's ready to and not a moment before. If anything, she's gotten more stubborn with age, not less. She did summon me here this morning, so I know there's something she wants to tell me.

"What are you planning on doing with Wren?" And there it is.

"Are you asking me what my intentions are?" It's an uncomfortable question, but I'm glad there's another person who cares enough to ask about Wren's welfare.

She narrows her eyes at me. "I think she's been jerked around enough by your son. For that matter, so have you. What I want to know is, do you have the stones to be happy? Mark my words boy, if you let her go, you'll regret it for the rest of your life. Have I ever lied to you?"

Leave it to Dolores to strike right to the heart of what's bothering me. "How do I know the right thing to do?"

"Some things are cliché for a reason. Follow your heart, it already knows what to do," she answers me.

"That worked so well for my son," I mumble under my breath.

Dolores might have a hard time getting around and takes a handful of pills daily, but her hearing is still sharp as ever. She shakes her head. "Liam didn't follow his heart, he followed his wiener. There's a big difference."

"How do you know that's not what I'm doing?" I'm trying to ignore the fact I'm having a sex talk with an octogenarian, who frankly scares me a little. Also, I'm planning to scrub the fact she said "wiener" out of my brain the first chance I get.

"I hope you aren't. I might have cataracts, but I'm not blind. I know she's a pretty girl, but I also know you. There's no way you'd risk your relationship with your son just to get fresh with his wife."

Hard to argue with her logic. As much as I'd like to tell myself what Wren and I have is just physical, I know she's right. "That's the problem though. You say to follow my heart, but what do I do if it's tearing me in two different directions?"

"Considering what Liam has done to both of you, he should know he has no right to assert any kind of claim on Wren. And if he loves you, he'd want you to be happy. Love forgives. Answer me this, if you choose him, will Wren forgive you?"

"Of course. Wren is the most selfless woman I've ever met."

Dolores rocks the chair until she's able to hoist her tiny body out of it. She shuffles over and pats my arm. "Perhaps the one who will let you walk away without anger is the one you should hold on to. I suspect you'll get a lot wrong before you get it right. You always have. Just remember forgiveness is given not earned, but a good grovel goes a long way to hurry it along."

She turns to head back into the house, no doubt to do a never ending list of chores that keeps her busy. "You let me know if you need another bug infestation to buy you more time with her."

I chuckle. The woman hasn't changed in the thirty years I've known her. I hope I won't have to take her up on her offer though. I want Wren to stay with me because she wants to, not because I've manipulated her into it.

MY PHONE BUZZES in the center console just as I pull in front of my house. Wren's car is already in the driveway, so I sit in my car to answer it, already suspecting who the call is from based on the unknown caller ID.

I answer and immediately hear Liam's voice. "Can you bring me some cigarettes when you come up?"

A sharp pain starts to pulse behind my left eye. "Since when do you smoke?"

He huffs. "Considering you didn't know I was washing down pills with whiskey, does that really matter?"

God this kid. Maybe I did fuck up too much having him so young. I shake that thought out of my head. I can't take the blame for all of his mistakes. I sure as hell own all of mine. My parents were class-A dickbags, and I never once blamed them for me becoming a teenage father.

"Is that really something they allow there?" I ask.

"Everyone here smokes like a chimney. It helps with the shakes and shit. I know it's replacing one addiction for another, but pick your poison."

"Smoking will kill you," I say, and I realize I sound exactly like a lecturing father.

"So will pills, old man. At least I'll have years to quit smoking," he shoots back.

I grunt. "Fine, as long as they let you have them I'll bring some."

He's quiet for a moment, and I know where the conversation is heading. "Is Wren coming with you?"

"She said she would. Although, it would serve you right if she backs out. Did you really have to fuck around with her best friend?"

I hear him suck in a breath. "How do you know that?"

"Because that bitch showed up here while Wren and I were talking about this visit, and she made sure to tell Wren she's carrying your baby."

Something crashes on his end of the phone. "That fucking bitch! She was supposed to let me tell her."

Not for the first time I am engulfed in a wave of sadness and disappointment. "How exactly did you think that was going to go over? From what it sounds like you've been checked out of your marriage for months, arguing over whether or not to have kids, and her best friend shows up with the one thing she wants most?"

He's breathing hard now, and I fear I've said too much. Shown him a bit more of my feelings than I wanted to. "How close have you gotten to my wife?"

"She's all alone, Liam. You made her family. Am I

supposed to ignore her and leave her to deal with this by herself?"

"You always have before," he states.

"That was before you screwed us both and left us to pick up the pieces," I snap. I hate this feeling, wanting to end this conversation. I miss the time when everything he did was a marvel to me, and filled me with pride.

"Just make sure she shows up tomorrow. She's still my wife, and she promised she'd give therapy a chance if I came here. I'm going to hold her to that."

My jaw is clenched so tight the muscles in my face ache. I know he's going to use every tool he's got to try and keep her. I know why I want her, but I can't figure out why he does. He doesn't seem to even like her, not if he could betray her the way he has. Going by what Wren has told me of the last year, I don't think he's going to be very nice about how he goes about trying to make her stay either.

"Look, I'll do what I can. I also promised Audrey to tell you she stopped by. So besides bringing you cigarettes, is there anything else you need?" My tone is short, but the words are genuine. Pissed off as I am, if he needs me, I'll still move mountains for him.

Dolores is right, love forgives, whether the other person deserves it or not.

"Just be here for the therapy session at three," he says in a clipped tone and hangs up.

For a moment I sit alone in the car and try to let the anger dissipate. Somehow I'm going to have to figure out how to protect Wren from him. I'd like to convince her not to go, but sure as shit Liam will sign himself out of the program if she doesn't come with me. The rate he's going, I honestly don't know how long my son will live if he doesn't stay.

Hatred fills me, for my son, but also for myself. If I

loved her more, I'd make her go, damn whatever he chooses to do. She's more hurt than she lets on, and I don't know how much more emotional abuse she can take from him. Worse though, I'm afraid he'll manage to convince her to stay. Darkness swells inside of me, and even though I have no right to claim her, I can't seem to stop myself.

I guess we're going out after all. At least for tonight, I'm going to show Wren who owns her, body and soul.

29

Griffin

"I didn't take you for a club kind of person," Wren shouts over the heavy bass of the music.

Bodies writhe against each other under the flashing lights of Club Bacchanalia. It's a couple hours away in Centralia, closer to the rehab facility where we're seeing Liam tomorrow. Also, it has the convenience of being away from the prying eyes of Harriston.

"I'm not really." I have to lean down and yell next to her ear for her to hear me. "I just wanted to do something different with you."

She turns and gives me a shy smile. She would probably run away if she had any idea what my idea of different is. I want her, in public, to let other men see her, and see me with her. I want to show her off to strangers who won't bat an eye wondering what we're doing together other than the fact I'm nearly twice her age. But if I were in a different income bracket, that wouldn't be all that uncommon either.

"Let's get a drink," I suggest and thread our fingers together.

Wren starts to slip her hand from mine, then seems to remember no one here knows us. This awards me with a bigger one of her smiles, and she stops trying to pull away.

At the bar I order us a couple of beers. Something stronger might be better to calm her nerves when she realizes what my plan is, but I don't want her to have alcohol to excuse either of our actions tonight.

Drinks in hand, I lead her out onto the dance floor, and we dance to the music. Most of my friends back in high school stood around and watched the girls all dance in a cluster. I believed they were missing prime chances to feel up chicks, so I taught myself to dance. Turns out Wren isn't immune to my dance moves.

I don't know any of the songs, preferring classic rock to newer more synthesized stuff, but I'm able to find the beat. That's all I need. Dancing is a lot like fucking. With a good partner, it's all about finding the rhythm and anticipating your partner. Then you bend and twist their body until you're both breathing heavy and riding an endorphin high.

Wren follows my lead perfectly. Even here she naturally submits her body to me, and it's a heady feeling. All around us men watch her hungrily, but as usual she doesn't see their interest. Her eyes never stray from me, and the anticipation is making my blood sing.

After our drinks are gone and a few songs have passed, I get to the real reason I wanted to come to this club, all of the dark corners. This place isn't called Bacchanalia just because the alcohol flows freely. It's known for all sorts of debauchery, and I'm ready to join the revelry. I take her hand and lead her to the second level where there's more seating and a place you can stand along a half wall to watch people dance down below.

Clusters of tables are interspersed along the floor. If you look too long you might see a hand slide up a skirt, or into a waistband. Wren is right, I'm not really into clubs, but Charlie is. He dragged me out here several months ago when he was trying to hook up with a woman who would only go out with him if her friend could come along.

Dumb fucker forced me to go along only to find out both women were interested in him. It wasn't a horrible evening for me though. The friend was annoying as hell, and I was already having a hard time ignoring my attraction to Wren. Besides, I get off on watching all the dark deeds people think no one can see.

I kept picturing Wren pushed up against the railing, trying hard to be quiet, and working to make sure she failed. Now I get to see if the real thing lives up to the fantasy.

Leading her over to the iron rail, I place both of her hands on it. With my front pressed against her back, I lean forward and whisper in her ear, "Don't move your hands or I'll punish you."

Being the brat she is, she immediately drops a hand and turns around with a questioning look on her face. That won't do at all. I grip the back of her neck and turn her back to look out at the crowd. Pinning her in place by pushing my hips against hers, she sucks in a breath when she feels my erection dig into her hip.

I move my hand to wrap around her throat and trace my nose up the side of her neck. "You want to be a good girl for daddy, don't you?"

She trembles in my hold. "Yes," she says in a shaky voice.

Increasing my hold just enough to get her attention, I ask her, "What was that?"

"Yes daddy," she says softly.

My free hand slides over the round globe of her ass,

and her fingers clench tighter on the rail while she tries to remain still.

"Mmm, good girl," I praise as my fingers flirt with the hem of her skirt. "Are you wet for daddy?"

"Why don't you see for yourself?" she taunts.

I give her ass a smack, and feel her flesh jiggle. "I'm going to and you're going to be quiet, aren't you?"

Moving my hand under the skirt of her dress again, I brush my fingers against the smooth skin of her thigh, and move up to the heat of her pussy. I find the naked skin of her ass. Surely she didn't come out without underwear. Moving forward, I find the tiniest scrap of material nestled between her cheeks.

Pulling her thong to the side, I lightly stroke the lips of her pussy, and find soft skin. "Did you wax for me, baby bird?" I murmur against her skin.

"Yes, daddy, do you like it?" She presses her ass back against my dick, moving my fingers through her slit.

"I told you to be still," I chastise her. With my foot between hers, I move her legs shoulder width apart. Once she's positioned the way I want her, I slap her wet cunt.

She inhales loudly, but bites her lip to keep from making more noise. Since I know she likes my rough treatment, I slap her pussy again, right over her clit. Her head rolls back to rest on my shoulder, and her knuckles go white with how hard she's clutching the railing.

"Do you want to know what tonight is for?" I ask her.

"Yes, please tell me," she begs.

I pinch her clit, and she shudders in my arms. "Why haven't you taken off your wedding ring?" I ask her.

She rubs the offending metal against the iron bar. "I don't know." Her forehead crumples in a scowl, and I can see that she hadn't considered it.

The need to mark her overcomes me, and I bite the

spot where her neck and shoulder meet, then suck hard. "All those men were watching what's mine while you were dancing. They're going to go home and stroke their cocks with thoughts of you playing in their head. My son has his ring on your finger. Tomorrow I'm going to have to sit there and watch the two of you talk about your marriage and maybe even lose you if he convinces you to give him another chance. But tonight, you're mine. And even while you sit there tomorrow, you won't be able to forget tonight. I'm going to fuck you so hard you'll feel me for days."

"Here?" she squeaks.

"Mmm. We're going to start here. Every man around will know I'm the one who owns this pussy, who gets to stroke it, lick it and fuck it when I please. Then we're going to go to the hotel where I'm going to take you over and over again until exhaustion won't let me move." I don't tell her that I'm claiming her heart too, because I can see by the way she looks at me that it's already mine. Hopefully, she knows mine will always be hers as well, but if I say it out loud, she'll be mine forever. That's who she is. I can't ask her to give me forever, because Liam will always be between us.

"You're going to be a good girl for daddy, and let me finger your tight cunt. And once I know you're nice and wet for me, I'm going to fuck you. Right here, where anyone can look up and see. This will be good practice for you when you're sitting across from my son and trying to pretend your cunt isn't throbbing from being fucked all night."

"Now, please," she begs again.

Instead of punishing her for speaking again, without calling me daddy, I decide she's been patient long enough. I shove two fingers inside of her, and build her up fast. Without any pressure on her clit she squirms getting just enough friction to want more, but not enough to come. I add a third finger to stretch her knowing it'll still burn when I force my large cock into her tiny body.

Out of the corner of my eye I can see we've caught the attention of a couple that were kissing when we first came up here. "We're being watched," I tell her, and turn her head so she can see.

Wren gasps, but I don't let her go. My hand on her throat trails down her chest, where I squeeze her breast through the satiny material of her dress. "How about we give them a show?"

Free to move her head, she looks me in the eye. I can see a hint of fear, but also intrigue and lust. "Is that what you want?"

"I get off on being watched. I'll never share you, but to know that someone wants what is mine, and knows he can't have you? Yeah, it gets me off, hard."

"Then, like you said. I'm yours. Use me how you want, daddy."

I groan hearing her complete surrender to my will. "Very good girl."

My hand moves back up her chest, and slips one of the thin straps of her dress off her shoulder. Just as I suspected when I laid the slinky number out for her, she'd wear it without a bra. Her breast is exposed to anyone who cares to look at us. We are standing in a shadow, so it is possible they won't see us well enough if they are on the dance floor, but the couple watching from the table can see the creamy swell of her tit and the way her nipple tightens to a point as I pluck the tender bud.

Taking my hand from between her legs, I unbuckle my belt and lower my zipper. I give my cock a few hard pulls before I line it up with her opening and bottom out inside of her with one hard thrust. I move my hand around her front and work her clit as I drill my cock into her wet heat. The act lifts her skirt, further exposing her to anyone who cares to look.

I glance back at the couple and see the woman has slipped under the table and has taken her lover's cock deep into her throat. He watches us with a heated gaze as he holds her head down as she bobs up and down on his dick.

"He wants you," I tell her, and push her other strap off her shoulder. With one hand vigorously rubbing her clit I alternate pinching her nipples until they're both hard as rocks.

"Watch how he uses her mouth because I'm the one who gets to fuck your pussy," I demand.

I'm painfully hard, and I slam into her over and over trying to relieve the ache taking root in my balls. I use my hold on her to lift and lower her on my cock in time with my thrusts so that the sound of our skin slapping together can be heard up on this level even over the volume of the music.

"When we get back to the room I'm going to clean you with my tongue and suck these tight nipples until you come from just me playing with your tits."

She tries to fight it, but a groan escapes her mouth. I need to feel the flutters of her pussy as her walls squeeze my cock. I don't think I can come without the vise grip of her inner muscles milking me.

I look over across the opening, and see another man watching from the balcony across the building. "You've got more admirers, baby bird."

Pulling her hips back, I tell her, "Hold on tight. I need to fuck you harder."

"Oh, god, yes. Fuck me daddy," she groans.

She was told to be quiet, so I slap her pussy, and feel the vibrations on my cock. Holding on to her hips, I chase my orgasm. A few people watching is good, but too many could lead to consequences I don't want, like someone recording us.

This new angle tips her forward so her back is level with the rail, and her tits sway freely in front of her. I start to fuck her harder than I ever have. The new voyeur is squeezing the railing as he watches me take her. The man in the corner is grunting as he comes in his woman's mouth. My balls pull up close to my body, and with a few more hard thrusts I feel her walls clamp down on my dick, prompting me to let go and come inside of her.

I pull out of her body and fix her dress. Placing a soft kiss against her mouth, I take her hand and lead her away from our audience. The rest of tonight is for our eyes only.

30

Wren

My lids feel like sandpaper rubbing over my eyes when the blaring alarm on Griffin's phone forces me to open them. Taking a page out of his book, I grunt at him. The short guttural sound is meant to say, "Turn it off, dammit!"

He made good on his promise, or perhaps it was a threat, when we made it back to the hotel last night. He took me over and over. On the dresser, in the shower, bent over the table, and finally in the bed. I even woke up at one point in the middle of a massive orgasm and Griffin once again buried deep inside of me. He finally showed signs of being human around five in the morning and fell asleep.

"You're cranky in the morning," he chirps. Fucking chipper as a bird.

I crack open a single eye and give him the best glare I'm capable of after three hours sleep, and with only one eye. "Someone didn't let me sleep last night."

"You'd think with the number of times I made you come you'd be in a better mood. I know I am." He smiles easily, and it does go a long way to brightening my mood.

He so often carries the weight of the world, and I hate seeing how it pushes him down.

I roll toward him and snuggle against his chest, placing a small kiss between his pecs. The light dusting of hair tickles my face.

"Why are we up already? I thought check out wasn't until noon?" I mumble against his skin.

"Don't you want to get breakfast? They stop serving at ten," he reminds me.

"No, I want to sleep. I don't care about food."

Griffin combs his fingers through my hair. "You say that now, but when you wake up again you're going to be hangry, and I don't think I want to experience two cranky moods from you in one day."

"Just wait until after we're done at the rehab facility, I'm sure I'll be in a pissy mood then too," I grumble.

His hand reflexively tightens in my hair at the mention of where we're going later. "I don't like this," he says quietly, and he forces his hand to release my hair.

I give myself just a moment to soak in the heat of his body and hope today isn't the day this blows up in our faces.

I count to ten in my head. "Fine, but there better be coffee." I make myself climb out of bed and into the shower.

The heat and steam of the shower went a long way into tricking my body that I got more than three hours of sleep. I wrap a towel around my body and use a hand towel to wipe the foggy mirror.

It takes several seconds for my eyes to recognize what I'm looking at. The moment it clicks, I scream, "Griffin!"

He bursts into the bathroom, ready to defend me from danger. Instead he finds me in the middle of an anxiety attack, one hand clasping my neck, the other trying to hold up the tiny hotel towel.

A deep furrow forms between his eyes as he assesses me, trying to figure out what is wrong. He finally notices my hand on my neck, and his eyes flash with desire. His tongue sweeps across his lower lip, and I can tell he's fighting the urge to smirk.

I shake my head. "Are you proud of yourself? I'm hiding a hickey like I'm a teenager again. What was the point of this?" I drop my hand and point at my neck. "It's not like he'll even see it."

The muscle in his jaw twitches. "It's not for him. It's to remind you that no matter what is said in there—" his eyes slip down to my ring, "you remember who you belong to."

I twist the plain gold band around my finger and slip it off. "I belong to me, because I can't belong to you."

Looking at him hurts sometimes, and I let my eyes fall to my feet. I admit, quietly, "I would be yours, completely, if that was possible."

He clears his throat. "There's a store down the block. Finish getting ready, and I'll go buy you a scarf."

———

THE DRIVE to the facility is quiet. Griffin doesn't even turn on the radio. Still, somehow the silence is loud. All of my apprehensions yell inside of my head. Each one tries to be heard over the others. There's so many things for me to worry about. Like if the therapist wants to dig into our relationship rather than Liam's addiction.

I'm not sure I want to examine the why and how of the deterioration of my marriage. Talking through it can't save it any more than an autopsy can heal a patient. My marriage is dead, and I'm ready to bury it.

"You're thinking awfully hard over there," he says as we turn onto a long dirt road leading to Hidden Lakes Health Center.

My thumb brushes over my scar. "I don't like therapy."

He drops his hand over mine, holding over my wrist for a moment, then continuing on to lace our fingers together. "I've never been. Probably should have, but it seemed like something only people with disposable income could afford."

"Or when you're deemed a risk to yourself," I mumble.

"I guess Liam falls under that category," he says.

"That's the thing though. When you first start therapy under those circumstances it feels like an intrusion. Maybe it does the rest of the time too, but when you don't have a choice, it makes you feel backed into a corner."

He turns his eyes on me for a second before looking back at the road. "And you did all that alone?"

I nod. "But I wouldn't have wanted to bring him in when I was already so raw and vulnerable. There was only so much I was ready to face, and the deterioration of my marriage wasn't on the roster."

"Wasn't that the entire reason you were there?" he asks.

The simple answer would be yes, but it wouldn't be the most honest answer. "It might have been a catalyst that made what was inside of me feel so much bigger than I could handle. Yeah, as my husband, it would have been great if he'd have been around to see that I was struggling. Maybe, if he'd been around I'd have been able to keep ignoring how I felt about myself and life in general, but Liam isn't responsible for my mental health."

Griffin shakes his head. "That seems like you're letting him off the hook."

I purse my lips, thinking about how to best explain this.

"He didn't help what was going on with me. And yeah, his treatment of me made it worse, but I'm responsible for my feelings. No one else should get to dictate how I think and feel about myself. I didn't get help after the death of my parents, and it left a chasm inside of me, that for a while Liam was able to fill. When he stopped showing up for me, that wound was exposed again."

"I still say he should have noticed how bad it had gotten for you." His eyes drop pointedly at my wrist.

I shrug. "I could have reached out for help."

"To whom? Your best friend that he was fucking? Me, when I made sure you felt isolated and alone? Charlie, after he made sure you knew he was on Liam's side? Fuck that. He made sure you were wholly dependent on him, then left you to drown in the loneliness. You might not be willing to blame him, but I sure as hell can," he snaps.

Moments like this I feel like I could lose myself in this thing growing between us. Then I remember what it feels like to be lost, and I pull back. "I learned a valuable lesson," I mutter to myself.

"I'm afraid to ask what you learned. It's going to be some bullshit about not letting anyone help you, isn't it?"

I take a deep breath in through my nose. "I learned not to depend on anyone else but me."

"That's a shit way to live," he grumbles.

I narrow my eyes. "It's my way to stay alive."

Mercifully, we pull up in front of the main building. The tension between us is thick enough without being locked in the car together for several more minutes. To think, I was nervous we'd be too affectionate and Liam would see through us. At least we are acting more like what he'd think is normal.

The front desk agent shows us to a pretty standard waiting room. The kind with hard furniture, complete with wooden armrests, a television playing a game show on silent, and dated reading material spread out on the coffee table. The wait feels long, because we're each locked in our own heads.

Finally, an older gentleman enters, ending the pain of anticipating the session. He extends his hand to me. "You must be Mrs. Hale."

I shake it, and reply, "It's Parker, actually."

Griffin grunts, and I shoot him a warning look. Now is not the time for him to show signs of jealousy. He steps in front of me and catches the man's attention. "Griffin Hale," he greets, squeezing the man's hand a little too hard. "I'm guessing by that white coat you're Dr. Taylor?"

He nods and shakes out his hand. "I am. If you'll both follow me to one of our meeting rooms we'll start the session."

My knee jerk reaction is to reach for Griffin's hand. Despite the tension between us, I know there's comfort in his touch. I manage to catch myself in time and wrap my arms around my middle. The desire to be anywhere other than here is so strong I almost turn around to run out the door.

Liam is waiting for us in another blandly decorated room. He's wearing scrubs and looks more haggard than I've ever seen him. His hair isn't styled the way he usually wears it, and there are large bags under his eyes.

Griffin steps up to him, and they do that manly half hug, backslap routine so many guys do. He passes over a bag of clothes he got together for him, all without drug or alcohol references, drawstrings, buttons or zippers. Liam immediately pulls out the slip on boat shoes and puts them on. I hadn't realized until then he's only wearing socks.

Liam finally looks over at me and smiles. He heads my way, and I can see he's coming in for a hug. I try and stop it, but my entire body recoils, and I step back to avoid his touch. Now that I know who he was cheating on me with, and that they're having a baby, I feel physically ill at the thought of his hands on me.

His face falls, and he lets his arms fall to his sides.

Dr. Taylor steps in to smooth things over. "Let's all have a seat, shall we?"

At least this room has comfortable looking arm chairs. I guess forcing someone to sit on a hard wooden chair doesn't exactly entice someone into emptying out their psyche. Griffin jumps ahead of me so that he is sitting between Liam and I. He's struggling with the need to stake a claim on me, even here. While it appeases a primal side of me, I hope no one else catches on to what he's doing.

"You don't have to protect her from me," Liam grumbles.

Griffin's mouth opens, but I give him a subtle shake of my head. The last thing we need is for the two of them to get into a pissing match over me. That will lead to questions, and unlike my husband, I'm a shit liar.

"Maybe it's you he's trying to protect," I spit out. I'm not exactly sure why that's the first thing that comes to mind, but I decide to run with it. "I wasn't exactly excited to come here."

"Let's start there," Dr. Taylor interrupts. "Why were you hesitant to be here today, Mrs. Hale?"

"For fuck's sake, she already told you her last name is Parker," Griffin snaps.

The doctor looks at my left hand, then flips through the papers in his file. "I'm so sorry. I was under the understanding that Wren and Liam are married."

"We are," Liam asserts. "She chose to keep her name for some asinine reason."

I clench my jaw. We've had this argument many times

in the past. When we first married, I was still feeling the loss of my parents and not ready to lose the one thing I had left from them. I'd already had to give up the home I lived in with them. At first I told him when we had children I'd hyphenate it. Since we didn't have children, I decided to keep my name as it was.

Liam looks at my hand, and sneers. "Ditched the ring already? Are you cheating on me, Wren?"

My hands clench, my nails digging into my palms, the bite of pain helping me to keep from lashing out in return. It's what he wants, for me to fight with him. It's the only way we've been able to communicate for almost a year.

"Liam, this session is not about placing blame," the doctor chastises him.

He turns his ire toward his therapist. "You don't think the disintegration of my marriage is one of the reasons I had to escape with drugs and alcohol?"

I press my nails harder and feel a little wetness coat my fingers, probably blood. I imagine all sorts of scenarios where I tell him exactly what I've been doing with his father. How his dad is the best sex I've ever had in my life. I bite my tongue to keep from saying anything, and my mouth fills with a coppery tang of blood. Telling him would feel good for a moment, but the destruction of Griffin's relationship with his son isn't worth my momentary satisfaction.

Answering Liam, I say, "Whatever I'm doing, and whomever I'm doing it with, is none of your goddamn business. You lost that right when you knocked up my best friend. For months I tried to talk to you, to work on our marriage. You left me alone. To this day you have no idea all the shit that happened during the nights you told me you were working late. And, you know what, it's pointless to rehash everything now. I'm glad you're here getting the help you need. I do hope you find peace and happiness. There's a child you have to think about now, and this petty bullshit between the two of us means nothing in light of that. He or she will need you whole." I stand from my chair and pull my purse up onto my shoulder. "What is clear to me is that my presence is not going to help you get better. The opposite in fact. I think we only bring out the worst in each other."

"Wren, please wait," he calls after me. "I'm sorry, okay? You know I say things when I'm frustrated. I know I've fucked up. I need you right now. I can't do this without you."

I turn my wrist over. "You've never even asked me about this," I say and hold it up for him to see.

He scratches his head. "You cut yourself cooking. Right? I mean, it makes sense, you're a horrible cook."

"Hardly," I laugh, a tortured broken sound. "No, I took a broken shard from a mirror and sliced it myself. You never noticed I was gone for several days when I went to the hospital and ended up on a psychiatric hold. No one noticed, actually. I made it through all of that alone. You can do this. You've got your dad, Charlie, and Au—" I stumble over saying her name, and clear my throat. "Audrey. You've got a lot of people cheering you on. You won't miss me, you never did."

I continue to make my way to the door and try to escape to the truck. Before I make it out of the room, Griffin reaches out and grabs one of my hands. "Why are you bleeding?" he demands. He strokes his finger below one of the cuts I made with my nails and wipes away some blood.

I can see Liam eying us speculatively, and I yank away my hand. "I'm fine."

"C'mon, Wren," Liam begs. "Don't go. I was there for

you when your parents died, can't you be here for me now?"

"You mean when you gave up your scholarship to stay with me?" I ask.

He looks over at his dad. "You told her?"

Griffin opens his hands. "I didn't realize you'd ever told her that bullshit. Of course I told her."

Liam's lip curls. "The two of you have gotten very cozy."

Dr. Taylor takes his glasses off, and leans forward. "Are you wanting to stay married to Wren? Because, in my experience, focusing on who is to blame is not the way to go about saving a marriage."

Liam looks surprised by the question. "Of course."

"Why?" I blurt out.

"Because you're my wife," he replies, like that is enough of an explanation.

I shake my head. "Not good enough."

"What do you mean, *not good enough*? You are my wife."

"Maybe on paper, but you haven't been my husband for a long time now. Not since you decided to start screwing someone I thought was my friend."

"You keep bringing that up, and yeah, I fucked up, but a man has needs Wren. It was just sex. We don't need to end our marriage over something that didn't mean anything," Liam pushes.

I shrug. "I don't know if that's true or not. Audrey certainly seems to think you were wanting to leave me. Her friends seem to think you've been trying to leave me for years. And, just to clarify something, I don't give a flying fuck if you were emotionally invested or not. The moment you stuck your cock in another woman, you ended our marriage. For once I'm glad we didn't have kids."

"Not this again," he groans. "Your tune changed pretty damn fast. I thought all you wanted was a baby."

"I still want to be a mother you obtuse jackass, I just don't want to have a baby with you. So no, my tune hasn't changed. I'm glad we didn't because it means getting a divorce is fairly simple in our case. Your affair isn't the only thing you weren't emotionally invested in. Our marriage was the other. You don't love me."

Griffin tips his head to the door, recognizing I've had enough. I know he's telling me he'll see me in the truck. I am only a few steps from the door this time, but Liam grabs my wrist before I make it past him. "Yes I do," he insists.

I yank my arm out of his hand. "Then stop, because your love hurts," I say and finally flee before he has the chance to say anything else. Whether or not he stays and completes the program is out of my hands. I can't make him want to get help, just like I couldn't make him love me.

31

Griffin

The moment the door closes behind Wren I wheel around to face Liam. "I don't know if this is my fault. Maybe I failed to teach you how you're supposed to behave in a relationship. Or maybe this is because of the drugs, but the way you've been treating her is disappointing."

Liam rolls his eyes. "You're one to talk. Since mom left you've treated women like toys. You think I don't know about your revolving door of playmates? There's never just one either. You're going to judge me for getting a little on the side? Fuck you, old man."

"The difference is, I never make a commitment to the women I'm seeing. They know what to expect, and I'm not the only one they're seeing either. Also, I never cheated on your mother. I take marriage vows seriously, I thought you did too."

I eye the door, and wonder how much longer until I can leave here without making Liam suspicious. What I really need to do is chase down Wren before she tries to walk from the facility. Honestly, I can see her walking down the dirt road with no plan on how she's going to make it back to Harriston, three hours away. I should have handed her the keys, but as upset as she was, I couldn't be sure she wouldn't leave me here. She's always trying to run away from me.

Dr. Taylor stands and straightens his lab coat. He's fairly useless if you ask me. What therapeutic value is there in standing by and letting abuse happen without addressing it on the spot? I'm not sure what I expected, but I know I've less hope in Liam's chances of recovery now than I did a few days ago.

"Well, that was a productive session," the doctor says as he subtly moves between me and my son.

"In what fucking world was that productive?" I snap. "Were you watching something else? You stood by and let him verbally and emotionally abuse his wife. What kind of therapy is this if he's being a total prick and you aren't correcting that behavior?"

"Now, Mr. Hale, we don't assign judgments like that to interactions during therapy," Dr. Taylor chastises me.

I cock my eyebrow and wait for him to tell me he's joking. I'm not sure if the man has much of a sense of humor though. When he doesn't speak up, I force my temper not to boil over. "I've never been to therapy before, so maybe this is just how it's done, but in my experience when someone is acting like an asshole you call them on it. Especially if what they are saying or doing is hurting someone they are supposed to love."

Before I walk out the door I turn to Liam. "You made that girl family when you married her. I know she and I haven't always got on well, but family means something to me. If you aren't going to look after her, then I will since she has no one left."

"Are you sure that's your only reason?" Liam asks.

"What other reason would there be?" My heart pounds as I will him not to examine me too closely. Obviously, I've done a shit job hiding my feelings for her.

Liam shrugs. "She's beautiful and slightly broken. The perfect toy for you. I've gone out with you and Charlie enough to recognize your type."

My body shakes, and I hope he sees it as rage, but in truth it's that mixed with fear. "What type is that, son?"

"The type who will do anything you say, submit to you completely, and let you use them until you're bored and ready to move on to the next one," he answers without hesitation.

I grab the doorknob. "I can promise you that I'd never use Wren like a toy for my own pleasure to be thrown away when I was done with her."

Before I can accidentally say anything too revealing, I hurry out after Wren. What I said to him was as close to the truth I could give him. Wren isn't a distraction or some kind of amusement to me. She'd be my forever if she hadn't already promised to be his.

The entire way through the building I keep my eyes open to see if she's waiting for me, but she's not in the waiting room or in the lobby. By the time I make it to my truck I'm swearing under my breath. I don't immediately see her, which makes me think she really did make a break for it.

Stomping over to my truck, I yank open the door. It groans, protesting my harsh treatment.

"If you're not careful it's going to fall off," I hear Wren say, but I can't see her.

"Are you hiding from me?" I ask when I still don't see her.

She stands up from a bed of bushes, ferns, and flowers.

"Not from you. I wasn't sure if he would chase after me. I should have known he wouldn't, he runs from me not toward me. Now I just look stupid hiding in the bushes like some kind of freak."

"Do you want him to?" I ask.

The look on her face lets me know she's confused. "Do I want him to do what?"

I grab her elbow and drag her back to the truck. "Let's talk on the road," I say as I lift her into the truck.

Being trapped in a single cab for three hours while discussing whether the woman I'm falling for is still in love with my son isn't my idea of a good time, but there are some subjects that you can't ignore.

The engine growls as I turn the key. She waits a few minutes until she asks me again. "Griff, what do you think I want Liam to do?"

Risking looking away from the road for a moment, I face her. "Did you want Liam to come after you?"

She looks down at her hands. I don't want to let her run from me, even emotionally. Ironically, here we are talking about my son, but I'm always the one chasing her. I tip her chin back up with my finger. Her eyes widen to large circles, and she screams, "Griffin look out!"

I turn and look out the windshield again and see a large refrigerated truck coming straight at us. I jerk the wheel to the right and drive us onto the shoulder of the road. It's narrow, barely wide enough to let the truck go past.

Wren holds her breath while the truck rocks and shakes from the force of the wind as the truck passes by within millimeters. Once it's past us, I get back on the road until I find a wide spot on the shoulder and pull over again.

Wren trembles violently. I unbuckle her seatbelt and

pull her onto my lap. Wrapping my arms around her, I rock her back and forth until she stops shaking.

She clings to me, both of her hands fisted in my shirt. "I'm sorry for distracting you," she says very quietly.

"This isn't your fault. The road is too narrow, and that truck was going way too fast. But that doesn't excuse the fact I was distracted and wasn't paying attention."

Her green eyes find mine. "I didn't want Liam to chase after me, but I also didn't want to be the woman married to a man who wouldn't chase after her. That probably doesn't make any sense."

I frame her face with my hands, tucking her hair behind her ears. "Not to me, but I seem to do nothing but chase after you."

The corner of her mouth lifts for a second then lowers back down. "Too bad I'm not married to you."

Instant pain lances my chest. "Yeah," I kiss her softly, "it is."

Her hands are still shaking when they clutch my shirt and pull my mouth back to hers. There's something more in this kiss, it feels like she is desperate to feel something other than what she's feeling. In the past I never cared if a woman used me to escape, but I do with Wren. When she's with me, I want her completely. Mind, body, and soul.

Even worse that she's probably using me to feel better over what Liam said during therapy. My son treated her like shit. There's no denying that, but I refuse to be the balm to soothe the sting. Gently I push her back.

"No, Wren. I can't let you use me to take away the hurt he left behind."

A deep line forms between her eyes. "What?" Her eyes open wide. "You think this is about Liam?" She shakes her head emphatically. "I wouldn't do that. I wasn't even thinking about him."

Even upset I can't help but comfort her, and I rub my hands up and down her arms. "You're shaking. Look, I get it, that was a shit show, and it's only natural it threw you. But, while I want to be there for you, comfort you through almost everything, I can't be the one you turn to for this."

Wren takes a deep breath and manages to settle herself a little. "Griffin, my parents died in a car crash. I promise you, this has nothing to do with Liam. So, do you have an objection to comforting me after a near death experience?"

"Absolutely none," I say, and pull her toward me.

Her hands drop down to my belt buckle and start to undo it. I grab her hands. "Hold up, we don't have to rush. Let me get you ready for me so I don't tear you apart."

"I'm ready. God, I'm ready. I wish I'd worn a skirt."

I growl. "No you fucking should not have. He doesn't need mixed signals. You're mine, and I'm not going to share you."

Popping the button on her jeans, I yank down her pants. "Let me see that sweet pussy and judge for myself if you're ready for my cock."

The cab of the truck is too small for me to get down and taste her properly, so I'll have to let my fingers be the judge if she's wet enough for me. I trail my fingers across the center of her panties and groan. "Oh, baby bird, you're soaked. You are ready for me."

Sitting back, I put my arms on the back of the seat. "Okay, you wanted to ride me, right?"

Her eyes fall down to my zipper. "More than anything."

I grab her chin and make her eyes meet mine. "I think you need to feel in charge. To make you feel safe, am I right?"

"Yes," she whispers.

I put my hand back on the top of the seat. "Then take control."

Wren doesn't waste time pulling down my zipper and I lift my hips to pull my jeans down. Once my cock is free, she pulls her underwear off and straddles me. Although it goes against my natural instincts, I make a mental note to let her take over more often.

It takes effort not to pull her down on my cock while she rocks against my length, coating me in her wetness. My fingers dig into the upholstery while hers clutch my hair. Her tongue plunges in my mouth the way I ache to take her body.

She drops one of her hands, works it in between us, and begins to stroke my cock. I groan in her mouth and it sets her off. Her grip tightens holding me on the edge of pleasure and pain as she lines me up with her opening. I expect her to slowly lower herself on my cock, but as usual my girl surprises me and drops down in one hard thrust. She builds a fast rhythm and pulls her shirt over her head.

My head rolls back on the seat, and I shout. "Fuuuuck. Slow down," I beg. "I'm going to come too fast."

I need to make this good for her, but she doesn't let up so I can. Her thighs squeeze my legs, and I can feel her inner walls clench around my cock while she bounces on my lap. The tendons in my neck strain as I try not to blow inside of her hot cunt before she comes.

"Touch yourself," I demand. "Stroke your clit while you ride my cock. I need to feel you come before I fill you." I'm dying to touch her myself, but I told her she had control, and I'm trying hard to keep that promise.

Even though she's directing this show, Wren is naturally submissive. She follows my direction without question. Of course, she might be doing it because her body needs the release.

The scene in front of me is the most deliciously erotic thing I've ever witnessed. Wren's head is tossed back, her pale hair falls down her back and brushes the tops of my thighs. Her small, perky breasts bounce with her movements. Her hand rubs vigorously on her clit. I'm torn between watching her bring herself closer to orgasm and watching my dick move in and out of her pussy.

I feel the seat compress under my fingers, and I'm forced to think about the engine rebuild I'm working on back at the shop to hold on a little longer. Wren slows her movements, and I nearly shout in frustration. "Why are you stopping?"

"Where did you go?" She taps the side of my head. "In here."

I grunt. "I was thinking about rebuilding an engine. Baby bird, I'm about to blow inside of you, and I'd really like you to come with me."

Wren leans forward and licks the side of my neck before biting me just enough to make my pulse race. "Then why are you holding back?"

"Wrong thing to say if you don't want me to take over," I warn.

She rocks her hips, making me clench my teeth. "Why wouldn't I want you to take over?"

My hands twitch. I'm losing the battle to control myself. "Because I don't want you to feel powerless."

"When you touch me, all the ways you touch me, I feel safe and—" she cuts herself off.

Loved, she feels loved. She won't say it and neither will I. Speaking it will only make it harder when she has to leave. Since we can't speak the words, I'll have to tell her the only way I still can.

I wrap my arms around her and move her body on top of mine. I lift my hips every time I pull her down on my cock. I'm gasping into her mouth, and all logical thought escapes my head.

Wren's eyes glaze over and her mouth falls open, a long sexy moan slipping free of her mouth. Her pussy clenches tight around my cock, and I can't hold back any longer. Her nails dig into my shoulders, and I explode, coming in hot jets as I hold myself still deep inside of her.

32

Wren

"Have a seat and quit fussing over me," Dolores insists.

I ignore her demand for a minute and continue to take stock of her cabinets, making a grocery list for things that she's running low on. "Not likely. I don't have anyone else to fuss over, as you put it, so hush and let me take care of you."

"When you put it that way dear," she pulls a folded piece of paper from the pocket of her apron, "these are the errands I've been meaning to run."

Rolling my eyes, I take a seat across from her at the table and accept the cup of coffee she pushes my way. "Take a muffin dear and talk to me for a bit. I want to hear how things are going with that beefcake you're shacking up with."

"Dolores!" I narrow my eyes at her. "Was there even a pest problem?"

She raises one frail shoulder. "There could have been. Honestly, a house as old as this one, treating it was likely necessary."

"You manipulated me," I accuse.

Dolores laughs. "It was for your own good. The two of you are too damn stubborn, and someone needed to give you a little push to give this thing between you a chance."

I sigh. "It's impossible though. Long term it will never work out."

She shakes her head, her iron colored curls bounce with the movement. "It's only impossible if you accept it. The only thing you can't overcome is death. Everything else is just details."

"The possibility of losing his son is more than a detail. I can't be the cause of Liam hating him."

She pats my hand. "Liam also has a choice in this. He can rise above and do what's best for everyone. He had a shot with you, and he blew it."

"Yeah well, it doesn't matter. We aren't going to tell him about it. When Liam comes home, Griffin and I are done."

"Then what are you going to do?" she asks.

"I'm going to leave. There won't be anything left here for me. My marriage is over, my parents are gone, and my former best friend is having my husband's baby. It's best for me to move somewhere else and start over."

She tuts at me. "Just like that, huh? You're going to throw in the towel and give up without a fight?"

I shrug. "Maybe I'm tired of fighting."

"I know dear, but wouldn't you rather fight and keep something worth having instead of taking the easy way out?"

"Nothing about what I have to do is easy, but it's what's best for Griffin. That's what love means, right? I need to choose him, even if his first instinct is to choose Liam."

"No, honey, you need to choose you. Whoever or whatever makes you happy, choose that," she advises.

"Isn't that selfish?" I ask.

Dolores gives me a knowing smile. "Not at all. It's self care. You can't be there for others if you're empty inside."

I grab the list from the table. "On that note, I'm going to go run your errands, because the emptiest thing here are your cabinets. It's a public service to keep you from going out on your bike again."

"I only went to the pharmacy," she argues.

"You *tried* to go to the pharmacy. I heard that you hit a rock and nearly took out the Johnson's mailbox."

"Psh. What is it my granddaughter says? I'm a grown-ass woman. I've made it eighty-two years, I don't need you fussin' over me like I'm a small child."

"I can come back here. I don't like you being all alone in this big house," I say.

"Now you sound like my son. I'm fine, dear. You don't have to worry anyway, your stud muffin took away my bike. He says he needs to fix it, but I think he's just keeping it from me," she grumbles.

"That sounds like something he'd do. For now, call if you need a ride. You know I'll come over and take you," I tell her.

"And you know you've always got a home here. For now I want you to stay with Griffin. Maybe everything will work out."

I pull my keys out of the pocket of my hoodie. "I think you're more optimistic than I am. I'll be back soon."

I WAIT in line at the pharmacy to pick up Dolores's meds. A couple people are in front of me, so I play on my phone while I'm waiting for my turn. A familiar voice makes me look up.

"Is there a generic?" I see Audrey negotiating with old Mr. Phelps.

"I'm sorry, Audrey, these are the only brands I carry in the store," he informs her.

The person behind her starts to get irritated. "Are you getting them or not? Some of us have places to be."

She looks back and sees me trying to make myself invisible.

"I'll have to come back," she mumbles, and sets the large bottle down.

For a second I feel sympathy for her, but then I remember it's my husband's baby she's carrying. She moves out of line, but I'm not lucky enough to avoid talking to her. Audrey stops next to me. "Have you talked to him?"

My jaw clenches. "Are you seriously asking me if I've talked to *my* husband?"

Her hand falls to her bump. "Look, I know you're pissed at me. You're not my favorite person either, but my baby is innocent in this, and Liam *is* the father."

I scoff. "What did I ever do to you?" The question has been nagging me since I found out she was the one Liam was having an affair with.

"Oh come on, you knew I was into Liam back in high school. I thought I'd just wait the two of you out and I'd get my chance. I didn't think you'd marry him. You were supposed to leave this town, Wren. Why didn't you leave?"

"The why's don't matter. The only thing that does is that I didn't, and you decided to go after my husband. I don't blame you for the affair. He was married to me, not you, but I do blame you for ruining our friendship."

Audrey rolls her eyes, and starts to turn her body away. "What friendship? I stayed close to you for him."

I shake my head. "All that time we spent alone together, what did that get you?"

She idly rubs her swollen stomach. "We always talked about Liam."

"So that's it, we talked about my husband, and you kept hanging out with me?" I ask in disbelief.

She shrugs. "You married young. Those are the kinds of marriages that usually end in divorce."

"Wow, my husband is more fucking stupid than I thought." My lips twitch, and I have to fight a hysterical laugh from breaking free.

Audrey has a guilty look on her face, and she cradles her belly. My mouth falls open. "You got pregnant on purpose."

This time I do laugh. "He told you he wouldn't leave me, so you thought you could force him to."

"We belong together. He'll love this baby, and we'll be a family, like it always should have been," she says with a dreamy look on her face.

"Good luck with that," I say dismissively. Part of me wants to cling to my anger. It fills the void inside of me that wants to suffocate everything around me. That feeling is cold and so, so empty. My anger feels alive.

But, I realize I don't really need the anger. From the moment I let Griffin lead me into the storage closet I've been losing little bits of it. Liam is my past. A part of my youth I outgrew. If it wasn't his cheating, it would have been something else that came between us. We couldn't even agree on starting a family.

Audrey notices every person around us is staring. If they weren't actively gossiping, they will be. This time it won't be only about me. Judging by the looks on their faces, now they had a villain for their story. I know Audrey sees the same thing because her head drops down and she rushes out of the store.

Ignoring all the people still staring at me, I move forward in the line. "Hi, Mr. Phelps. I need the medications for Mrs. Howell."

"Sure thing. How are you?" There's a prying quality to his question, and I know he's fishing for more information.

"I know you just heard all of that." I wave my arms around gesturing emphatically at all the eavesdroppers. "Everyone in here did. I also know that you like being the center of town news, but I'd really appreciate it if you didn't actively try and spread my pain for the amusement of all the bored old biddies in Harriston."

His mouth gapes open. "I wouldn't. Of course—"

I hold up my hand. "Just the meds, please."

He hands me the bag and I shove the cash at him. I hold my head high and stroll with confidence I don't feel out the door.

33

Griffin

Keeping myself busy while Wren is out running errands is exhausting. There are a lot of things I've neglected taking care of the last few weeks while I've been spending time with her. Just knowing how short our time together will be makes me want to treasure every second I get.

I worked on the gutters for a couple hours, winterized my garden beds, and she still hasn't come back. I'm running out of projects, and not being busy is giving me too much time to think. Like, how many projects am I going to need to keep me busy when she's out of my life forever?

The loud rumble of a truck disturbs the silence of my quiet street. I stop my last project of the day, organizing my tools in the garage, to see who's mechanical beast needs a tune up. A truck that is more rust than metal turns the corner and comes to a stop in the driveway.

When I see the driver I groan. "What the fuck are you doing here, Liam?" I ask when he exits the truck.

"Nice to see you too, dad," he snaps back at me.

"You're supposed to be in rehab. Your counselor made

it sound like you were going to be there for at least the full thirty days," I explain.

He shrugs, flippantly ignoring my concern. "I've dried out, the rest of the program is just a bunch of foo-foo bullshit."

"That *foo-foo bullshit*, as you call it, is what helps you stay dried out. Who's truck are you even driving?" I ask.

He waves away my question. "My roommate checked himself into the facility and drove himself there."

"And he just let you take his truck? Liam, please tell me you didn't steal it," I beg.

Liam rolls his eyes, and if I didn't know he was twenty-four I'd have assumed he was a teenager. "C'mon dad, you know me. I'm not a thief."

I stare at him, wondering how he has the audacity to say that after everything he's done. "I thought I knew you, but you've done many things recently that make me wonder if I ever really did."

"This has been a lovely heart-to-heart, *father*, but I only came to get my car. Then, I need to go find Wren and make her listen to me."

"Good to see you have your priorities straight, car then wife," I reply sarcastically.

"Whatever, save your judgment. Where is my car? I went by my apartment and it's not there. It wasn't at the garage either," he says, looking around.

"That's because I sold it," I say, and wait for him to explode.

"I'm going to need you to repeat that," he says in a deceptively soft voice.

"I. Sold. Your. Car. Where do you think the money for rehab came from? You practically ruined my business with your creative billing and skimming money from the over-inflated profits. Wren doesn't have access to any of your accounts, and you took out thousands of dollars in her name without getting her approval. So, yeah, I fucking sold your car."

The vein in the side of his head starts to bulge. "Get it back. You had no right to sell my car. Your name wasn't even on the title."

"No, Wren's was. I can't believe you had her spend the rest of her parents' insurance money to get you a fucking car." I've been dying to confront him about this since she told me how he got the car.

Liam shakes his head. "She wouldn't do that."

I raise an eyebrow. "It's amazing what betrayal will do to a relationship."

His eyes narrow. "The two of you seemed really cozy at that therapy session. Makes me wonder what else has changed since I've been gone."

My fingers start tapping against my thigh. Wren could be home any minute, and I want Liam gone before she pulls in the driveway. Not because I care if he finds out, not right now at least, but because I don't want her to have to deal with him. I want to text her to stay away, but I don't see how I can do that with him scrutinizing me so closely.

"If you have something to say, spit it out." What we're doing might seem wrong, but it's not even close to the bullshit he's pulled.

Wren's car has a little rattle I've been meaning to check out for a few days. It should be in perfect fucking condition considering the man she married works in a shop, but like most things concerning her, Liam didn't pay a damn bit of attention.

I close my eyes when I hear the first hint of her car struggling down the road. She pulls up on the other side of my truck, a spot where she can't see us.

She starts talking to me before she comes around the

side of the car where she can see us. "I'm so freaking tired. Dolores had me running all over town. I've really got to find a way to block that doomsday preppers show from her tv. I swear she's stocked up for the apocalypse now."

"I did grab some stuff for us from the grocery store when she had me there buying dry goods in bulk. Dolores gave me a recipe and swears even I can't ruin this."

That countdown timer hanging above our heads is blaring now. We're out of time and it's racing towards an explosion. "Wren," I choke on her name, "Liam is here."

She steps around my truck, and immediately comes to stand next to me. I know it's unconscious, but it's a clear signal something has changed between us if she's turning to me for protection.

Her hands are clasped in front of her, almost like she's praying. "What are you doing out of rehab?"

Liam's entire demeanor changes. I'm getting another glimpse at the man she's been dealing with for far too long now, and I realize she's terrified. Without thinking I put my arm around her and tuck her into my side.

The corner of his lip curls up in a sneer. "I wouldn't give it to you, so you decided to give my dad a try, did you?"

She buries her face into my ribs, and clutches my shirt in her fists. I feel her take a couple of deep breaths before she lets go and steps back. Her shoulders roll back, and I watch her become a different woman. This version of her is a warrior. I'm proud, but sad because she shouldn't have to be this brave with her own husband.

"You're disgusting as usual. Why are you here?" There's almost no emotion in her green eyes. They're still beautiful, but cold and lifeless like polished sea glass.

Liam holds his arms out wide. "Me? Why am I at my own father's house? The better question is why are you?"

Wren's mouth opens and closes. She turns her face up to me, and I know she's only holding back out of respect for me.

"Son," I say to get his attention. "You need to leave."

Wren sucks in a breath, and Liam laughs. "This is rich. You shuttle me off to rehab so you could what? Play house with my wife?"

She's shaking her head. Her fists are clenched tight at her sides, and she's practically vibrating with fury. "I'm not your wife. Not really."

He lunges forward and grabs her arm before I even see him move. For a couple seconds I'm frozen in shock. I don't know why his behavior keeps surprising me, but every time, he acts contrary to the man I raised him to be.

"For months you've been begging for my attention. Throwing yourself at me every time I came around. Aren't you still thirsty for my cock? Come home with me and we can spend the rest of the day making up."

"It's too late for that. Let me go." Wren's heels dig into the ground as she tries to wrestle her arm out of his grip.

Finally, I snap out of it and grab his wrist, squeezing it until he lets her go. The momentum causes her to stumble backwards, but I'm too slow to grab her. She falls and catches most of her weight on her hands and rear, right into the rocks of my driveway.

I rush to her without delay. Gently, I turn over her hands and wince seeing her palms torn up with rocks embedded into her skin. "Oh, baby bird," I sigh and try and wipe some rocks away.

Liam charges me, knocking me down, and forcing Wren to crawl backwards on her injured hands.

He's on me before she's even safely away. Liam swings his fists wildly, barely clipping the edge of my jaw. "You're fucking my wife, aren't you? What, are there not enough sluts in town for you to get your dick wet?"

I don't reply to him, because I won't talk about Wren in the same way he is. My silence pisses him off even more and he lands a better hit to my gut, knocking the air out of my lungs.

"Fucking say something," he screams and punches me in the face, splitting my lip. The mouth fills with the taste of copper.

I put my hands up to prevent another blow to my face, but don't otherwise try to defend myself. "Stop," I say as calmly as I can. "Liam, it's not what you're thinking."

He lowers his arms, but his posture is still rigid. "It's not? Okay, then. Tell me you're not sleeping with my wife."

I close my eyes, although one of them is helping me along by trying to swell shut. "I can't," I whisper.

His hands clench in his hair as he screams at the sky, "God fucking dammit!"

I flinch. As much as I love her, hurting him was the one thing I didn't want to do. More than my need for her. Hell, I wanted to protect him more than my need to breathe.

I know this is the wrong thing to say, and the wrong time to say it, but he deserves to know I didn't risk everything for a quick fuck. "I love her," I admit.

Liam throws his hands up. "Fuck both of you! You can forget about rehab, I'm not going back. What point is there being sober when this is the shit I get to face?"

He spins on his heel and climbs back into his borrowed truck. His tires spin rocks back at us, one hits Wren on her forehead near her hairline. He's oblivious to the trauma he leaves, as usual.

Neither of us speak or move until the rumble of his truck can't be heard anymore. I turn to help her up, but she won't let me. I can see blood smeared all over her hands, and rocks dug into her skin.

She's shaking, but she won't let me get close to her. I'm torn. I need to go after Liam before he drinks himself into a coma, or worse. Finding pills in this town won't be hard, and he likely is already on the phone with his dealer. No idea where he'll get the cash for it, but my son seems to be very resourceful when it suits him.

Wren whimpers quietly, catching my attention again. There's a trickle of blood running down her face, and dripping into her eye. "Let's get you inside and see to your injuries."

She scoffs. "My injuries? Half your face is purple and your eye is swelling shut."

"What did you expect me to do, hit him back?" I sound angry, but it's at myself and this fucking situation.

She winces, and then her expression goes back to neutral. "Anything other than stand there and let him beat you like you deserved it." Her words are hot, but her tone is flat. She's losing the fight to see this through.

"I did!" I shout, the hurt and frustration is too much.

Wren nods, like she knew that's how I felt. "Why do you think you deserved that?" She points her finger at my split lip, which only starts to sting now that she calls attention to it.

"Because even though he didn't treat you the way you deserved, I knew he still loved you."

She shakes her head, making more blood drip from the cut on her forehead. "I might be young, and I know I have a lot to learn, but I've seen love before. What my parents had, that was love."

I look at my truck, wondering if it would be wrong for me to continue this discussion later so I can go and make sure he won't end up in a puddle of his own vomit.

Wren follows the direction of my gaze. "Go on. I know you want to go after him."

"I want to talk to you," I tell her. I might be prioritizing taking care of him right now, but she's still important to me. I need her to know that, to believe it.

"He's your priority," she says. Her voice sounds resigned.

When I come back I'll tell her that I'm not ready to end this between us. The worst has already happened. He's not going to get angrier at me. Somehow we can work through this. What I know for certain is, I was wrong to think I could walk away from her.

"We'll talk," I say, and pull my keys from my pocket.

It isn't until I make it to the bar that I realize she never agreed to wait for me to come back.

34

Wren

A sob bursts free the moment Griffin's truck leaves the driveway. I can't be selfish anymore. Not that it matters, push did come to shove, and Griffin went running after Liam. This tangled web needs to be cut, before it strangles me.

I give myself a minute to be sorry for myself, and then I force myself to move. Once Griffin comes back it will be too late. I'll look into his dark brown eyes, and all the resolve I have right now to do what needs to be done will evaporate. Sometimes we don't want the things we need. I want Griffin, but I need to step out on my own.

I've never done that. Lived on my own. Thanks to Liam's manipulations, I missed out on that important right of passage. I can't make things right for Griffin, but I can start to right some wrongs in my own life.

My eyes sting with unshed tears, but I can't stop right now. "Hi Patches," I greet my cat. "We're going to go on a little trip."

Once she's in her carrier, I race around trying to grab my things. I never really packed much to come over here, since I had only planned to be away a few days while the fictional pests were handled. One duffle bag, not even full, holds every sign I was ever in this house.

There's a notepad on the refrigerator. I don't want to pen a long torturous goodbye, but I did hear Griffin say he loved me, and I can't leave him without saying it back. Quickly I jot down the last words he'll ever get from me, because once I leave Harriston, I'm never coming back.

> *Griffin,*
>
> *Thank you seems like an odd thing for me to write. For a long time you were a giant asshole, but I understand why now. I don't think anyone will ever love me again the way you do. Even though I only heard you say it once, I'll treasure it forever. Even if it only lasted a few weeks, I can say I have been loved completely and beyond reason. Know that I love you too, even though it changes nothing. You will always be Liam's father, and he needs you more.*
>
> *Wren*

A single tear slips down my cheek and splashes on the page, blurring the last part of my name, but I leave it. I still have a couple of stops to make, and then I'm gone.

The first stop is to say goodbye to Dolores. I call Bess on the way, and ask her to meet me at the house. Griffin lives on the other side of town, so by the time I pull up, both women are waiting for me on the porch.

The smile on Bess's face falls the moment I step out of

the car. "You're leaving." It's not a question. In the short time I've known her she's been able to read me better than Audrey ever could.

I nod, and the tears I've fought so hard start to fall in earnest. Dolores clucks at us, and ushers both of us inside. Immediately she starts tending to my hands.

There's quite a bit of blood smeared on my hands and arms since I didn't clean out the rocks, then added insult to the injury by forcing my tortured flesh to grip a steering wheel. I try not to wince as she uses tweezers to pick out the tiny bits embedded in my skin.

"You really should go to the hospital and have these looked at," she chides.

I shake my head. "I want to get on the road. I can't, I can't—" my sobbing makes it hard to speak.

Dolores nods. "You can't face him again?"

I nod. "I'll ruin them if I stay."

She places her fragile looking hand on my arm, and squeezes. Talk about looks being deceiving. Here I am worried about her being on her own, but she's faced more trials than I have, and she's more than capable of caring for herself. Still, I worry about her.

"Bess here lives in a shoe box," I blurt out.

Dolores's face brightens. She knows I won't be talked into staying, and she's always happiest when she's part of a scheme.

"Just so happens I've got a cute little cottage come free," she directs to Bess.

Turning to me, she says, "I can watch Patches for you for a while, until you land on your feet."

I smile at her. I hadn't quite figured out how I was going to travel with a cat. I'm not sure where I'll even stay. "Are you sure?"

"I don't want you to go," Bess inserts.

I hug her. "I don't want to, but I need to."

She nods. "Yeah, I guess I can see that. But just so you know, I'm going to make sure he doesn't get to drink at the bar. And if Donovan serves him, I won't be servicing him."

Dolores winks at her. "I like you. You've got a lot of fire in your blood."

"You're not half bad either, granny D," Bess replies.

"We're going to get along smashing," Dolores says, probably so I won't worry about either of them. It does make me feel better knowing that my two favorite people, or I guess I should say two of my favorite people, will be looked after.

"Will you check on him?" I whisper. Dolores knows who I'm talking about.

She sets about wrapping my scraped hands in gauze and looks up to answer me. "I've been looking after that boy for most of his life. I won't stop now. I'm sorry you're both going to be hurting over the actions of another. I love his son too, but that doesn't mean I have to like him."

"Where will you go?" Bess asks.

I shrug. "For now, I think I'll see if my aunt Hattie wants company. She's down in Florida. Not that I think Griffin will come looking for me, but I don't want to be easy to find. I'll crumble too easily if I don't have some space to grow a backbone."

"Call when you stop tonight?" Bess asks.

Nodding, I stand up from the table. "I promise. I'm going to drive as far as I can tonight."

Dolores rises to her minuscule height and gives me a hug. "Now, whether there's a tenant in my cottage or not. This is your home. Whenever you're ready you come straight back here, I've got plenty of rooms in this big ole house that I don't use."

Her hand cups my cheek, and I can't fight the new

waves of tears that spill down my face. "Hush now," she whispers. "This is only a bump in the road. There's still amazing things ahead of you. Times like these are meant to show you how special the good days really are."

"I'm going to miss you," I choke out.

"Worry not little one. Don't you know how much we old people love Florida? If you stay down there I might just be heading straight for you," she jokes.

Bess hops in place. "Ooh! Road trip. I get to pick the music."

"Only if you are going to play some Black Sabbath. I'm not down with that pop garbage my grandkids listen to," Dolores grumbles.

Bess looks at me to see if Dolores is joking. I shake my head. "She's a total metal head."

She blinks. "I really freaking love you granny D."

"I'll teach you all my ways, Rainbow Brite," Dolores responds.

I shake my head at both of them. I really should have introduced them sooner. Now I won't get to see the damage they're going to unleash on this sleepy town.

There's solace in knowing neither of them will be alone. Unlike me, but some things can't be helped.

IT'S two hours before Griffin starts calling my phone. Two hours he spent looking for and possibly dealing with Liam without a thought about me. I feel bad for thinking about it like that. Liam is his son, and of course he has to be his priority. That doesn't mean I have to choose to be in a relationship where my needs always come after the person who hurt me the most.

My gas light comes on around the state line, so I pull

off and fill up. Griffin wouldn't let me give him the money from the sale of Liam's car, which Charlie finally managed to unload a few days ago. The bank is in the process of disputing the charges Liam took out in my name. But, to be safe, I made sure to put that amount away so I wouldn't be tempted to spend it.

That leaves me with a little less than ten grand to get set up somewhere new. Bess said she'd deposit my last check for me, so perhaps a bit more once that happens. Calling Hattie was awkward. We really don't know each other well. She's a lot younger than my mom, only about ten years older than me. But, we're the only family the other has, and she immediately offered me her spare room until I could get back on my feet.

I hang up the gas pump, and my phone starts ringing for the fifth time in the last hour. By now Griffin has found my letter, and knows I'm gone. He could have even checked in with Dolores and Bess and heard from them I'd left as well.

Not a single missed call is from Liam. I don't want to hear from him, but it confirms what I believed for a while now. He was with me because I was convenient. Liam doesn't like to be alone. And, he won't be. Audrey will overlook all of his faults, his callous words, and innate selfishness. She'll have the family she's longed for. I wonder when it will occur to Liam that she tampered with her birth control.

A memory from the past bubbled to the surface during the long boring stretch of highway through the southern Midwest. It was from when we were still in high school, and I was staying over at Audrey's house. This was before my life changed with the death of my parents. Audrey's mom, Mona, was lecturing her about a boy she was dating.

I remember how uncomfortable I was because I

thought I was about to overhear the same talk my mother gave me every time Liam came to pick me up. "I'd rather you wait to have sex, but if you choose to do it, make sure and use protection every time," she'd tell me.

That was not the advice Mona gave to Audrey. "Aud, that boy comes from money. If you don't get a ring on your finger by graduation, you're going to have to go off to college and find a boy with a future. But that can cost a lot of money, darling, so if you need to miss a pill or two, make sure that boy stays with you."

I never asked her about it. I knew her mother was a social climber, and really wanted nothing outside of our hometown, but I never dreamed that Audrey would stoop to such tactics. I guess she's a lot more like her mother than she ever wanted to be. Now Liam will pay the price for his stupidity, and so will an innocent child. I don't envy it with the two of them for parents.

The miles, memories, and events of the day start to wear on me. My eyes are drooping, and I know it's time to stop for the night. It's close to midnight, and my cell phone died around the fifteenth call from Griffin. I find a *Motolodge*, and pull into the sketchy parking lot.

The rooms, thankfully, turn out to be cleaner than I expected, and the price won't hurt my bank account too much. If I hadn't promised to let Bess and Dolores know when I stopped for the night I wouldn't bother turning my phone back on.

Text after text from Griffin pops up on my phone.

> Where are you?
>
> We need to talk.
>
> Bess said you left town. Why didn't you wait to talk to me?

> I can explain.
>
> Baby bird, please let me know you're okay at least.

The last one hurts. I would want to know he was okay, and that's the only reason I reply to him.

> I'm still breathing. I can't come back. It hurts too much. Just let me be. Please.

The three dots pop up on screen, disappear, then pop up again.

> If it's what you need, I'll try.

A sob escapes my mouth. I'm so fucking sick of crying. I promise myself this will be the last time I will cry over anyone named Hale ever again.

Tears stream down my face at how easily he gave in. I asked him to, but stupidly I wanted him to put up a little bit of a fight.

> Goodbye Griffin.

I shut off my phone again after sending Bess a text letting her know I stopped for the night, then roll over and soak my pillow one last time.

35

Griffin

"Wren isn't working tonight," Bess tells me the moment I stroll through the door of Donovan's bar.

"I know, she's back at my place." I take a deep breath. "Have you seen Liam?"

Bess might have a name better suited to a prized cow, but she looks like a mischievous pixie, and a very brightly colored one at that. Her large turquoise eyes open wide at the mention of my son, and her hot pink painted lips pop open in a wide "O" as she shakes her head at my question.

Donovan steps up next to his Technicolor punk girlfriend, and drops his arm around her shoulders. "Why would we have seen Liam? Isn't he in treatment?"

I shake my head. "He made a surprise visit to my house a little while ago."

"But, Wren was there," Bess says, still in shock.

I nod. "Let's just say it didn't go over well, and he drove off. I need to find him."

"How is Wren?" Bess asks.

My instincts scream at me that I should be focusing on her more, but Liam needed me right now. "Shaken. The sooner I sort Liam out, the faster I can get to her and make sure she's okay."

Bess's phone starts to ring, and she runs off to the office to take her call, leaving me alone with Donovan. "What do you want me to do if Liam comes in? Do I toss him out?" he asks me.

"No. Stall him if you can and call me," I reply.

Bess hurries back into the bar, unties her apron, and slings a messenger bag over her head to cross her body. "I'm heading over to talk to Wren."

Donovan crosses his arms. "You are, huh?"

She mimics his posture and the two try and stare each other down. "Fine," he relents, "but you're doing something for me in return."

She winks at him. "Oh, you can bet your fine ass on that."

A moment later she's racing out the door. I blink. "I bet life with her isn't dull."

Donovan smiles, and I envy him how open and easy their relationship seems. "She certainly makes it interesting."

He moves down the counter and serves a few of the regular customers. Men who used to run around with my father, and spend most of their old age camped out at the end of this bar pickling their livers like I imagine my father would be doing if he were still alive.

"Sad, isn't it," Donovan comments when he returns to me. "When I opened this place I thought it would be a constant party. It can be, but it can also be one of the most depressing jobs. Here I get a first row seat to watch men drink away their paychecks, and men like Liam throw away their marriages."

I clear my throat. "I'm well acquainted with this view. I

grew up with it, and unfortunately, I think I passed it on to my son."

"If he shows up here I can refuse to serve him," Donovan offers.

"That won't do any good. He'll find it somewhere, but I won't know about it if he goes somewhere else." I look at my phone and realize I've been here for awhile, which means he likely already went somewhere else. Grabbing a cocktail napkin, I scribble down my phone number. "Call me if you see him."

Donovan nods and puts the napkin in his pocket.

HARRISTON ISN'T a tourist destination by any stretch of the imagination, but the part of town I am driving through to search for Liam makes the normal neighborhoods look like a resort. Even though I've lived here most of my life, there are parts of this town I rarely see. Parts I make a point to avoid is more like it.

Picking up my phone I make a call to enlist some help. "Charlie, it's me," I say when he picks up.

"Griff, what's up?"

"Liam showed up at the house. Right before Wren came home."

"Shit," he swears.

"Can you help me look for him? He took off right after and I can't find him," I beg for help.

"Where are you?"

I exhale. "My old neighborhood."

"Shit," he curses again. "Remind me later to tell you this was going to blow up in your face."

I touch my swollen cheek. "Believe me, I'm well aware of that."

Across the street is my old trailer. I'm not even sure why it's still here in the park. All of the windows are busted and there's tarp over part of the roof. It's unlivable, but it would probably cost more to remove it than the space is worth. There are many others just like it, like there always has been.

The stain of this place isn't something you can wash away. Foolishly, I thought I left all of this behind when I moved out. I was wrong. All I did was pass everything down to my son. I'd failed to prepare him for the risks involved with the genetics he inherited. Melinda's family also had a history of alcoholism and drug addiction. Maybe Liam never stood a chance.

Charlie pulls up alongside my truck and kills the engine. He gets out and climbs into the cab of my truck. "Why are you here, Griff? There's no reason he'd come here."

My hands squeeze the steering wheel. "I don't know." My voice is quiet, almost inaudible. I clear my throat. "I don't know where to look for drugs. When I didn't find him at the bar, I drove around, and just sort of found myself here."

Charlie flicks on the dome light and takes a few minutes to study my face. "What are you going to do when you find him? By the looks of you, your last conversation wasn't very friendly."

I glare at him. "I didn't hit him back, so you can stop looking at me like that."

Charlie's eyebrows shoot up. "I'd hope not. You look like shit. He might be eighteen years younger than you, but he's not taken great care of himself. You've got a good forty pounds of muscle on him. Did you even defend yourself?"

Gingerly, I touch my busted lip. "Not really."

"I know you've got a guilty conscience over your relationship with Wren, but letting him beat on you is not the way to manage it."

I scoff, splitting my lip open again. "You think that's why I feel guilty?"

He nods. "Why else?"

My chest constricts, and for a second a sense of impending doom comes over me. "Do you think that's what Wren thinks too?"

Charlie gives me a pitying look. "How could she not?"

"Fuck," I shout and punch the dashboard.

"That was stupid, but at least I know you can still hit," Charlie quips.

"I left her at my house thinking I feel guilty about being with her. Liam said some horrible things to her, and then grabbed her. I intervened, but she fell and got hurt. And—" I stop to take a breath.

"Let me guess," Charlie interrupts, "your reaction clued him in on your affair with Wren."

My head swings his direction. "It wasn't an affair. They were separated."

Charlie puts his hands up in surrender. "You're splitting hairs, my friend. I doubt Liam cares about the distinction."

"At this moment I don't give a fuck what he thinks. You shouldn't either," I snap.

"Then what are you doing? You're worried about Wren, but here you are on the wrong end of memory lane chasing after the one person you seem to want to be the farthest from."

"You were right when you said I was doing this out of guilt, just wrong about what I feel guilty for." I look at the trailer across the drive. "My parents weren't always losers, you know. In high school my dad was a quarterback, popular, and my mom was the head cheerleader. They weren't great students though. They partied a lot. Eventually everyone they knew, most of them at least, grew up and moved on from that scene. Not them though."

I take a deep breath and exhale slowly. "When Liam was born I had to grow up fast. He needed me, and I wanted to give him a better life than I had."

Memories dig their barbed hooks into my mind and refuse to let me go. "When my parents had me, they were also young, but unlike me they clung to their youth. Eventually the booze led to pills. I never knew any other side to them. I promised myself it would be different for my son. What I didn't expect was that no matter what I did, he would end up just like them. So, yeah, I fucking feel guilty. I might not have given him the drugs, but I gave him the genetics."

"Griff, you can't blame yourself for this. You're a good father. Sometimes kids disappoint you. But, you're not going to find him in the past."

I clear my throat. "Any suggestions?"

"I'll swing by the girlfriend's house. Can you think of any other places he'd go to think or be alone?" He asks.

"Just one," I reply. It's a long shot, but there might be one place he'd go to think. One place that started this entire mess in the first place.

CHARLIE AND I SPLIT UP, and I point my truck toward the riverfront. Under the streetlight, sits Liam's borrowed truck. The tailgate is down, and he sits on the edge with his feet dangling and a bottle hanging from his hand. He lists to the right as he brings it up to his mouth, manages to straighten back up, and takes a long drink.

I pull up next to him, and he offers me the bottle as I stroll over. I wave it away.

He points to the spot closer to the water. "This is where it all fell apart." Again, he tips the bottle back.

I keep my mouth shut and let him keep talking. "She was never supposed to find out. Audrey was only supposed to be a diversion."

"You're not supposed to need a diversion from your wife," I speak softly.

He looks up, his eyes are unfocused and a bit red. "How would you know? You and my mom never made it this long. Are you really trying to tell me that you never got bored? You didn't want something on the side to have some variety?"

I shook my head. "I never once cheated on your mother. It was over a year after she left before I touched another woman. I won't lie to you and tell you I was in love with her, but I respected her as my wife. She didn't file for divorce for a few months after she left, and then it was a few more months until we reached a settlement."

Liam hiccups and wobbles where he's sitting. "Excuse me for not being a saint like you. Oh wait, saints don't fuck their daughters-in-law."

My fists clench. "I know it's hard for you to accept that Wren and I have formed a connection, but that doesn't mean I'm going to stand by and let you keep talking about her like that."

He looks at me with anger bordering on hatred. "She's my wife. If I want to call her a father-fucking whore, I'm going to do that."

Once again the urge to bury my fist in his face rises. It's just another way my son and I are different. The idea of actually hurting him is abhorrent to me. "You want to be pissed off? Then be pissed at me. I'm the one who owed you loyalty," I assert.

His eyebrows shoot up. "She's my wife. I think that should get me some fucking loyalty!"

I shake my head. "You think so? Let me see if I understand this." I start ticking off his offenses on my fingers. "You tricked her into declining a full ride scholarship to stay here with you. Then you block her access to bank accounts so you can take out lines of credit she didn't know about. I'm guessing you also didn't want her to see how much money you were spending on booze, pills and other women. Still, she loved you so much she continued to give you every paycheck she earned to deposit, and even spent the rest of her parents' insurance money to let you buy a fancy car while she continued to drive a piece of shit."

His nostrils flare and a vein bulges at his temple. "A car she fucking sold the moment my back was turned."

I shrug. "It was in her name. She needed it to pay off the credit you took out in her name. Which you will work to pay her back for because she never should have bought you that car. You're really fucking lucky that she left it up to me whether or not to press charges for fraud."

Liam stares at me without saying a word, so I keep going. "That sounds like a lot of fucking loyalty, but how did you reward her? You fucked her best friend and knocked her up. And before you turn on me about what I owed you, don't forget that I've dedicated my life to you. I was the one who took care of you when you were sick, went to all your games, and helped you with your homework. I taught you a trade and gave you a job. More than that I was building a business with you for you to take over one day, and you stole from me."

"Tell me son—" I'm breathing heavily through my

nose, trying hard to keep a rein on the little bit of control I've got, "what did either of us really owe you?"

"You're my dad," he says gruffly.

"And I'll always be your dad, but you're going to be a dad yourself, and it's time you start acting like it."

Liam suddenly jumps down from the tailgate and hurls the empty bottle towards a nearby tree. "I don't want that. I've never wanted kids, at least not now."

"Wanted or not, you've got one coming," I remark.

"I don't know if I can forgive you," he changes the subject.

"Then I guess I'm going to have to live with that. It'll be hard, but I know I can't live without her. Can you say the same?" I ask him.

He doesn't answer me right now, and maybe he never will. One thing is clear from this talk, there was a lot more broken between my son and I than me falling in love with Wren. He might never forgive me, that's true, but I know I'll resent him if I give her up for his sake.

A giant weight falls off my shoulders, and I know what I need to do. I grab my phone and call Charlie. "He's at the riverfront park drunk off his ass. I can't help him, he's too angry, and frankly so am I. Can you—"

"You don't even need to finish that question. I'll go handle him. I assume you're going to go make things right with Wren?" Charlie asks me.

"I can't live without her," I admit. It feels good to say that out loud.

"Then go get her. Forget everything I said before. If you need her go," he urges me.

I speed the whole way home, and rush inside the house.

"Wren? Are you here?" There's no answer.

That anxious feeling is back, but I have no reason to

think she didn't just meet Bess somewhere. Even so, I go through every room of my house. One thing becomes apparent during my search, there's no sign of her. Not just in the sense that she's not here, but because all of her things are gone.

That sinking feeling intensifies as I make my way back to the kitchen. I'd walked right past a note stuck to the fridge with a magnet. My hands shake as I take it down and read her words. The last line seems to blur, but I realize that's my eyes filling with tears I'd never admit to. So I read it again.

Know that I love you too, even though it changes nothing. You will always be Liam's father, and he needs you more.

"That might be true, but I need you," I say to the empty room. This can't be the end. I refuse to accept that. Hoping to have a missed call from her I dig my phone out of my pocket.

The only calls on it are the ones I've made to Charlie.

I know she's gone. It's what I've been telling her she needed to do when Liam came home. That doesn't stop me from starting to text her. Message after message and she doesn't respond.

Sitting here waiting and praying she'll reply is going to drive me nuts. There's one person I know spoke to her before she left. For the second time I make my way back to Donovan's Bar.

Bess stops me before I make it through the door. She puts her hands on my chest and pushes me out the door. Or I should say she applies pressure I interpret to be her trying to push me out the doorway. I help her out and move back outside, because I really just want to talk to her.

"I figured you'd show up here. Wren said she left you a letter."

Deciding to cut right to the chase, I ask her, "Where did she go?"

She's shaking her head before I even finish asking the question. "I don't know. She just said she was heading out of town and she'd let Dolores and I know when she stops for the night. I'll be honest, I didn't ask her for exactly this reason. She thinks you're going to be happy once she's gone. I figured you'd pull your head out of your ass and realize you can't live without her."

"I wish you'd have told me," I grumble under my breath.

Bess shoots me a look that practically screams she thinks I'm an idiot. "You knew. The tendency both of you have to lie to yourselves is mind boggling."

"I need her back," I tell Bess.

She nods. "I know. I do too."

"How are we supposed to get her back if we don't know where she went?"

Bess rolls her eyes. "This might be a foreign concept to you, but there's this thing called patience. Try finding some. She's going to call me, and I'm going to work my magic. When I see an opening, I'm going to try and lure her back. You need to be ready with some romance novel-worthy groveling."

"And how do I do that?" At this point I'm willing to try anything.

"Ask Dolores. She's got all the classics. And by classics, I mean Nora Roberts."

"Well, I was planning to see her after I talked to you."

"Tell granny D I said I'll see her later. And, Griffin—" she calls out to me as I start to turn away, "try and have some faith. She loves you and won't be able to stay away either."

36

Wren

After a rough night's sleep at the *Motolodge*, I get back on the road. Since I left late yesterday, I have all day today and part of tomorrow left to drive before I make it to my Aunt Hattie's house. That's a lot of time with my own thoughts.

Not that I can hear myself thinking over the rattle coming from under the hood of my car. I rub the dashboard and try to sweet talk it into continuing to work. Five years married to a mechanic and here I am driving around in a car on the verge of possibly exploding, and I don't have the first clue how to check what might be wrong with it.

I know enough about cars to know that when the needle moves into the red end on the temperature gauge that something is wrong. Well, that and all the sensors lighting up with engine warnings, and all sorts of other hieroglyphics. Around noon, I pull off the road hoping my car will somehow, miraculously, work right after I scarf down whatever passes for food at the gas station. I mean, it's essentially unplugging it, right? It worked with my ancient computer at the insurance office.

Thankfully, I manage to find a large traveler center so maybe my dining options will hopefully be better than a greasy fried burrito or a stale donut. I waste as much time as I can stomach. Somehow I let myself believe it just needs some time to reset.

"Please let it be long enough," I pray on my way out to my car.

Smoke trickles out of the edges of the hood. I might not know much about cars, but I know they're not supposed to smoke. I unlock the car, reach under the dash on the driver's side and pop the hood. That trickle of smoke becomes a plume. I start to reach for the cap where most of the smoke is coming from, when a callused hand latches on to my wrist.

"Don't grab that," he yells.

I pull my hand back. "I need to make it to Florida."

"Then you better get a bus ticket or start walking, because this thing isn't going to leave the parking lot," he says.

A laugh bursts free. I can't hold it back. All of the stress, the sadness, the fucking unfairness of my entire goddamn life sends me into the hysterical kind of laughter that earns you a padded room and a special jacket.

I straighten up and wipe the tears from my face. I'm not sure if they're sad tears, or from laughing. "Of course not. That would be too easy. Any idea what's wrong with it?"

I'm not sure how knowing will change anything, clearly whatever it is would need to be fixed. That means I'd either need to stay here and wait for it, or come back and get it. Neither option appeals to me. The only way I'm going to be able to move on and put all of this behind me is if I cut all ties to Harriston, except for Dolores, Bess, and Donovan. The car is just a vestige of my old life, and it's kind of poetic that it chooses to go up in flames.

The helpful stranger waits by the open hood for several minutes without saying anything. My last question just hangs between us. After he's apparently waited long enough that he thinks it's safe, he pulls a rag from his back pocket, screws off a cap, and grunts. I wonder if communicating like a caveman is a common trait of mechanics. Oddly, it makes me miss Griffin more.

I shake off the errant thought, and focus on what the stranger is doing. He looks at a few more things and then straightens up and steps away from the engine. "I'd have to check it over more, but my guess is your radiator is cracked. Depends on how long you've been driving around with it like that, but you may have engine damage."

"How much would it cost to fix it?" I ask. Even though part of me wants to just get rid of the car, my practical side knows that I don't have new car money.

He shrugs. "Could be a few hundred, could be over a thousand. I won't know until I get some more time with it."

"I'm sorry—" he extends his hand, "—I'm Gerald. I own the only auto shop here in town. I'd be happy to look it over for you. It's not going to be fast though. I've got three cars ahead of this one."

Using a scrap of paper from my purse, I write down my phone number. "My name is Wren. Sorry, I know an old receipt isn't the best method of record keeping."

He shrugs. "My desk is pretty much covered in client information written on old receipts, grocery lists, and if I'm lucky sticky notes."

"Of course it is," I grumble.

He ignores what he must think is a really random

comment. "I can tow your car to my shop, and we'll get it in as soon as we can. I warn you, it's probably going to be at least two or three days just to get it in the bay. And then, who knows what I'm going to find or how long it's going to take to fix."

I take a deep breath. It's going to be expensive to fix, I know it. Even if it's just the radiator, there's his labor, parts, and of course either hotel fees while he's fixing it, or a return bus ticket to come back and get it. My fingers twitch, and I have to stop myself from grabbing my cellphone to call Griffin. It only took a few weeks for my first instinct to become turning to him to save me.

"Take a look at it and call me," I say.

"There's a bus stop here at the travel center. You can go online and buy tickets. I'm not sure what the schedule is, but there's several that come through every day," he lets me know.

I grab my bags out of the car and move over to a picnic table on the side of the building to use my phone to buy tickets. I groan when I see the schedule. I'm in luck, there's a bus heading to Florida, but it doesn't leave until late this evening.

Shooting off a text to my aunt, I let her know about the delay in my arrival. Now I just have to come up with what I'm going to do with myself for the next several hours while I wait for the bus to take me the rest of the way.

The long wait for the bus is nowhere near as bad as riding on it for over a day. The bus is new enough, and since I'm not tall, leg room isn't a problem, but the space seems to shrink the longer I sit on the bus. We stop occasionally to refuel and for bathroom breaks. It's how I manage to survive this trip. I tell myself I only need to make it four hours before I'll get another chance to be able to get off and stretch my legs. In some ways though, it only makes it harder, feeling the freedom to move, only to have to confine myself back into my small section.

None of that compares to the smell. Even at only half full, the ripe scent of body odor starts to fill the bus after hour twelve. It makes me self conscious so I use every bathroom break to bathe myself in the sink. Unfortunately, no matter how many gas station baths I take, the smell still isn't coming from me, so nothing I do makes the stench go away.

My phone battery dips about five hours into the trip, and I am forced to turn it off so I can contact my aunt when we stop in Tampa. Then we still have a half hour drive to her condo in Clearwater.

Every time I close my eyes I imagine Griffin's face when he finds my letter. He sent me text messages, but I still haven't been able to bring myself to read them. I'm afraid. Either he's going to agree that me leaving was a good idea, or he's going to be begging me to come back. I'm not sure which possibility scares me more. But, if he's going to run off every time Liam throws a tantrum I can't go back. I've already been in a relationship where Liam always came first. I can't, won't, do it again.

Still, I miss him. Our time together was short, and I lie to myself saying I'll move past it. I know in my gut I won't. Home was a place of love. It was where my parents were always there for me to run to with any problem, knowing they'd somehow be able to fix it. We weren't rich, but I didn't care. Problems didn't penetrate the walls of our house. It didn't matter that I couldn't always have the things I wanted, because I always had what I needed.

Until that day. That awful day when a knock on the door cracked that foundation and popped that bubble of safety that had encased me my whole life. I continued to live in our house for another year, but it stopped being a home the moment I was told my parents had died in an accident. There was no one to blame. They weren't hit by a drunk driver. They didn't swerve to miss hitting a deer. Hell, it wasn't even icy out. My father wasn't speeding.

It rained. That was it. That was the event that ended my childhood. The water on the road was deeper than it looked, and their car hydroplaned. It spun and since he couldn't get enough traction to stop, he couldn't keep the car on the road. There was enough of a slope that the car flipped several times, and that was the end of our family. It took seconds for me to go from having everything I needed, to being completely alone.

I'd felt alone in my marriage too. Being lonely when you aren't actually alone is one of the most desolate feelings I've ever experienced. It's brought me some of my lowest lows in life. I've learned I'd rather be alone, than ever fake my way through a relationship ever again. The problem was when I married Liam I wasn't whole. I'd offered up only half of myself, because I'd had the other part of myself locked behind a mountain of grief. When that grief started to heal and I had more to give, I realized he was okay with only some of me. In return he only offered me the same. It wasn't enough in the end.

When Griffin wrapped his arms around me, I felt it again. That peace that comes when you know you're home. I fought it because I knew I'd only lose it again. I thought I prepared myself, but that was another lie. Just like when I told myself I was able to keep my heart out of it. Every part of me belongs to Griffin Hale, and I'm afraid it always will.

I'M WRECKED when we finally arrive at my aunt's house. The whole way down here I pictured her old apartment. A small one bedroom with a pull out couch. I was prepared to be happy with that, instead I'm pleased to learn she recently moved from her small one bedroom apartment to a nice two bedroom condo a few blocks from the beach. Of course it means she works a lot at a hospital in Tampa, but she seems happy with her life. I envy her that.

It's late when I get in, but she gives me a quick tour of her place. My favorite part of the tour is when I learn I'll have my own room, not camping out on her couch like I anticipated. The moment my head hits the pillow I'm out. That doesn't explain what keeps me there for the next two weeks. Fighting the darkness that looms in my mind takes energy I can't find. So I stop trying and let it swallow me whole.

A LIGHT TAPPING at my bedroom door wakes me up. Hattie waits for a minute, but I can't muster the energy to even answer her. There's so much I'm holding back from her.

She opens the door and comes and sits on the side of my bed. For a minute she looks like my mother, and my breath catches.

Despite all the time I've spent in bed, I don't feel like I've truly slept. Perhaps that's why I say, "Is it ever hard looking in the mirror? I wonder what she'd look like now, because in my memory she looks just like you."

Hattie's hand goes up to cover her mouth, then she nods, and puts her hand back in her lap. "For me it's hard when something big happens. When I graduated from college and got my job at the hospital, I wanted to call her and celebrate. And for the record—" she reaches out and tucks some of my hair behind my ear, "to me, you look exactly like I remember her when I was a teenager."

My mouth twitches. That's the closest I've come to smiling since I left Harriston. Tears spill down my face. "I miss her so much."

Hattie wipes her cheeks. "Me too, sweetie."

"Why aren't we closer?" I ask her. For the life of me I can't think of why.

She looks down at her hands. "I was young and selfish when your parents got married and there always seemed to be more time to catch up. I always seemed to be too busy with things that seem so stupid now. I regret it because not only did I miss that time watching you grow up, but I also missed that time with my big sister. Your mom was so much larger than life to me when I was growing up. I took for granted that she'd always be there when I was ready. And then she was gone. You needed me then, and I wasn't what you needed."

"What do you mean? You came to live with me so I could finish high school with my friends. You gave up your life here," I argue.

"I was assuaging my own guilt. I'd let my sister down so many times, the least I could do was go and look after you. But, I didn't even do that right. I felt so sorry for myself because I'd lost my big sister, that I didn't really see your grief. You dealt with it alone, and never once did you throw it in my face. I saw you getting closer to Liam during that time, and I felt relieved because he was looking after you when I didn't."

"Don't beat yourself up. I leaned on him then. We did the best we could at the time," I try and comfort her.

"You haven't told me what happened, or why you needed to come here all of a sudden. The last I really knew anything Liam was everything to you, and suddenly you're leaving him. You've barely eaten, or even left this room for two weeks. What happened?"

"I don't know. Life I guess." I take a deep breath. "He was cheating on me."

Hattie nods. "If there's one thing I understand, it's heartbreak. You're worrying me though, because you've been shut up in here for two weeks now. Eventually you have to get on with your life. If it hurts this bad though, I've got to ask, are you sure you made the right choice? What about marriage counseling?"

I turn away from her and stare at the ceiling. "There was no other choice. He was having an affair with my best friend."

Hattie gasps. "Oh, I'm so sorry. That's pretty bad. I can see why you wouldn't be able to get past that."

"Yeah, well I figured it out because she's showing."

Her mouth falls open. "No," she denies.

I shrug. "Yeah, she's pregnant. About five months I think."

"God, Wren. I'm so sorry I haven't been around. No wonder you've locked yourself in here. But, honey, you can't stop living. Especially considering how he's treated you. Have you ever heard that living well is the best revenge? You need to get up and show Liam you don't need him."

Something about the idea of getting revenge strikes me as funny. I try hard to keep from laughing, but fail miserably. Through laughter, I say, "I don't think that's necessary. Have you been talking to Dolores? You both give the same advice."

She purses her lips. "Mrs. Howell? I think a lot of people have been offered her advice at one point or another. Not everyone is smart enough to take it in.

Anyway, have you heard about your car?" she asks, changing the subject.

I welcome an end to the discussion of my marriage. "There's engine damage. It's more expensive to fix than it's worth, so I sold it to the mechanic I met at the gas station."

"What are you going to do without a car?"

I shrug. "I guess I'll get another one. I would like to find a job first."

Hattie nods. "I can help with that. My friend, Patrick, owns a pub a few blocks away. I asked him if he had any openings, and as it turns out, he needs a waitress during the day. I know the tips aren't as great as they might be at night, but he pays a decent hourly wage. If you're not interested it's no problem. Just let me know either way."

"Can I walk to it?" I ask.

"Yeah, if you didn't want to get another car right away, you'd be able to walk. If that's what you're asking."

"I want to save as much money as I can. I'm thinking I'd like to finish my degree."

Hattie smiles at me. "I think that sounds wonderful. What are you thinking of studying."

I pick at the comforter. I'd told Liam about this before, and he laughed at me. I swallow. "I'd like to get a business degree. Maybe get my MBA."

She cocks her head to the side. "Why did you fidget when you told me? It's like you think there's something weird about becoming a business woman."

I shrug. "Liam used to tell me I was reaching too high. Harriston didn't have a lot of use for a business degree, let alone a graduate degree."

Her mouth pulls into a tight line. "Have you thought about moving ahead with your divorce?"

"I have been trying hard not to think about anything."

"I can see that," she mutters. "Look, I know you want

to leave everything about your life in Harriston in the past. I know the last six months of your marriage was bad, but it sounds like you were overlooking a lot of shit long before that."

I lick my lips. "Can you help me with getting a divorce?"

Hattie grabs my hand. "There's a guy who's been trying to get me to go out with him for a while who happens to be a lawyer. I'll give him a call, but I thought you already filed?"

I shake my head. "Liam didn't sign the papers, and now I'm not there to see that he does. But, I don't want you to spend time with a guy you aren't interested in just to help me out."

She winks at me. "Who says I'm not interested? Sometimes it's good to see how far they'll go before going out with them. He's suffered enough."

37

Griffin

"When was the last time you shaved?" I look up and see Dolores shuffling her way into my kitchen.

"How did you get into my house?" I grumble.

Her eyes flick up to mine, and one eyebrow raises. It must be a superpower how she can give me as much hell as Charlie does, but with a look instead of a string of profanities. In one hand she holds up a planter and in the other hand my spare key.

"You've got a green thumb, boy, but you can't decorate to save your life. There was one thing on your porch, of course you hid a key there. Plus I know how paranoid you are about leaving a key after Liam locked himself out in middle school and spent the entire afternoon sitting in the rain waiting for you to get home because the neighbors weren't home."

She sets her large fake leather bag down on the table. "Now, do you want to grumble at me about anything else?"

I shake my head. "No, ma'am."

She nods, sending her gray curls bouncing around her head. "You look like crap."

"Thank you so much, Dolores. You say the sweetest things."

"Humph," she grunts. "I'm not here to butter you up. No siree, I'm here to give you a swift kick in the patootie. Now get off your rear, hop in the shower, and at least trim back the bush attempting to take over your face."

"What's the point?" I grumble.

"How do you expect to get Wren back if all you are doing is sitting on your rear pining for her?"

My jaw clenches so tight the muscle pops over the joint. "How am I supposed to get her back if I don't know where she is?"

She waves her hand as if what I'm saying is insignificant. "She'll be back. I've been watching old episodes of Matlock trying to get ideas."

"All episodes of Matlock are old, Dolores."

"Either way. That Andy Griffith found someone through the license plate. Haven't you tried calling in some favors to see if they could track down her car?"

I shake my head. "Who do you think I know that I can call in those kinds of favors? I own an auto shop."

"Don't you know cops or something?"

"Why, because they drive cars?" I ask. "Dolores, this is a small town, and I barely know who the sheriff is."

"Well, I thought it was a good idea. There has to be something we can do. She didn't just vanish into thin air."

My shoulders slump. I actually had been waiting for her to come over, but I thought she'd be coming to me with news, not looking for it. "She hasn't called you then?"

Dolores reaches out and pats my hand. "Not yet, but she will. Have you talked to Bess?"

I shake my head. I haven't done much of anything in the last couple of weeks. Liam and I haven't spoken since the day he found out about Wren and me. Charlie has handled the office tasks. I can't seem to force myself to step foot in there. I see Wren everywhere in there since she took that space over. The only thing I've managed to do in the last couple weeks is drag myself into the shop. Thankfully, she didn't spend much time there.

It's different here at home though. I find myself lingering in the living room. Even though she took home her things, there's still a lingering scent of the cleaner she used. The way she rearranged the furniture reminds me she was here. She tried to erase herself from my life, but I refuse to let her go. Even the goodbye letter she wrote me is never far away.

The front door opens and closes. "Why doesn't everyone just make themselves at home?" I grumble.

"Don't mind if I do," Charlie says as he joins us in the kitchen.

"Did Dolores tell you about how she wanted to search for Wren's car?" He's trying not to laugh, but he respects Dolores too much to offend her by laughing at her.

"It worked for Ben Matlock," she mutters.

Charlie schools his features and talks to Dolores. "Well, I've got bad news for you. The best we could do would be to look up part numbers for her car. As far as finding it, I'm afraid I don't have that kind of power."

"How did you learn how to do all of that in a few weeks when not long ago you acted like you didn't even know how to turn the damn computer on?" I ask him.

Charlie shrugs. "You've been really preoccupied, and I might have had the kid teach me how to use it."

He looks like he remembers something he needs to do. "Look, I just wanted to stop in and give you this." He drops a takeout bag from a local burger joint. "I just remembered that I forgot to order parts for that sedan we just got in. I need to go back to the shop and see if I can find a bumper and quarter panel. You know the one you made me work on alone because it's the same as Wren's?"

I grunt. We both know that's why I passed the car off to him even though I also made him do all the record keeping and invoicing for the last few weeks. I don't see what good he's doing by bringing it up.

"Make the kid help you. Since Liam doesn't seem interested in coming back to work we're going to need Julio to step up. He's going to classes to get certified, so he's serious about staying," I say.

This makes Charlie stop. "Would you let him come back?"

"If he agrees to random drug screenings and he's never allowed near the invoices, computer, or money," I say.

Charlie bobs his head. "Interesting. I'll see what I can do. Lord knows with a kid on the way he's going to need to start earning money."

I walk him to the door and go back to Dolores. "You know that Bess moved into the guest house, don't you?" she asks me.

"I heard that," I reply, trying to drag her to her point.

"I'm going to go home and see if she's heard from our girl. I'll let you know if she has."

Dolores holds up my key and sets it on the table by the door. "Get one of those electronic door knobs with the codes. Hiding a key isn't safe anymore." Having issued her final lecture, she's out the door.

STAYING in my house feeling sorry for myself isn't getting me anywhere. I want to believe Dolores, and that I'm going to convince Wren to come back, and if I do, she can't come home to find a sad sack mountain man sitting and waiting for her. I force myself to get off my ass, and trim back my beard to the stubble Wren prefers.

I need action, something to do. Waiting around for her to choose to come back hasn't worked in almost three weeks, and I don't have the patience to let her come to me. After the way I ran off after Liam, she might not ever do that. Right now she's probably somewhere believing that she isn't the most important person in my life. I need to correct that misunderstanding, then I need to spank her ass for thinking she was allowed to run away from me.

First I need to get her back, which means I need to find out where she's run off to. I'm not a cop, so I can't run some kind of trace on her finances or her phone. Unfortunately, there aren't many people in her life, and all the ones who are live in this town.

Until I think of how to find her, I need to get other parts of my life back in order. Starting with my business. Hiding from the things I need to take care of isn't helping, but it will ruin all the hard work Wren put in to save my shop.

I enter the shop, and mentally prepare myself to go into my office. Charlie is seated at my desk, gaping at something on the computer. Worried that he might have crashed the accounting software Wren installed, I hurry around the desk to see what he's done.

"This is that parts supplier in Oakville down by the state line." He points at the screen. "I found the parts I need, but look at the picture."

I get closer, and look over his shoulder. "Fuck yeah," I shout.

"Is that her car? Are you sure?" Charlie asks.

"How often did I take it so she'd be forced to ride home with me during those few weeks?" I ask him. It's a rhetorical question, because I had done it nearly every day.

"Trust me, I memorized her plate number, not to mention it has our oil change reminder stuck in the top corner of the windshield."

I grab the phone, and start dialing the number listed on the website. "Gerald's Autobody, Gerald speaking."

"Hey, I'm calling from Hale Automotive in Harriston. You've got a gold sedan listed on your website. It looks like my daughter-in-law's car, and I was wondering if you can tell me if you saw her," I say.

"Uhm, I'm not sure I'm comfortable with that," he hesitates.

"So you did see her. Listen, I know she was upset when she left here. My son said some horrible things to her, but seeing her car come up while I'm looking for parts is worrying me," I try and settle his apprehension.

"I guess, I don't really know much. Wren, right?" he asks.

My heart pounds, and I try and control the hope that I might figure out where she went.

"I met her at the Travel Center when I stopped her from screwing off her radiator cap with her bare hands."

I groan. "That sounds like her. Did she happen to mention where she was going?"

"Shouldn't you know that?" I can hear the suspicion in his question.

"I should, but—" I take a deep breath. "Look, I'm going to level with you. My son has a drug problem, and he said some really hurtful things. I went off after him, when I should have stayed and made sure she was okay. When I came back she'd left. I really need to make sure she's okay."

He sighs. "Florida. She said she was heading there. I suggested she take a bus and there was one that left that night for Tampa."

"You've been an enormous help," I tell him and hang up the phone.

I pull my keys out of my pocket. "I'm going to go home and pack."

Charlie goes the other way around the desk and stands in front of the door. "It's late. You are not leaving and heading to Florida tonight."

"I can go for a few hours, and then I'll stop at a motel. Even if I ride all day tomorrow I won't make it there until late at night," I argue.

"You don't even know where you're going," he says.

"Hattie lives in Clearwater. I helped Liam send some stuff to her there when they closed up Wren's childhood home."

"People move. Isn't her aunt like a nurse or something? There's no way she's still living in the same place she was in when she was back in school," Charlie asserts.

"How do you know so much about Wren's family?"

"This is a small town, Griff. Not only that, but there aren't a lot of people who can boast doing better than having a job at one of the three factories in town. You are one of the most successful people in town since you own your own business."

"I'd say the owners of the factories are more successful," I dismiss.

He rolls his eyes. "Those are national corporations. The owners don't live in this town. They exploit it for labor, but other than some low paying jobs, they don't contribute very much here."

I toss up my hands. "Okay, if you know so much about her, where does her aunt live?"

He shrugs and I swear I could punch him in the face. "Chill out bro. I don't know where *Hattie* lives, but I do know she's got a few friends from school she keeps in touch with. Let me make some calls. I'll get you an address."

I jingle my keys. "Text them to me. I'm not waiting anymore to bring her home."

"You're a stubborn asshole. Fine, you be safe and don't drive drowsy."

I nod. "Sorry to leave you alone with the shop."

He waves me away. "Yeah, yeah. I should buy this business from you since I seem to be the one running it."

I point at him. "That might not be such a bad idea."

He narrows his eyes. "What are you thinking?"

"Just that actions speak louder than words. Bess told me I needed to do some romance novel worthy groveling, and you just gave me an idea."

As I exit the building Charlie shouts after me, "You know it's terrifying when you get an idea."

38

Wren

"I thought I might find you out here," Patrick says as he drops down on the bench next to me.

Lifting my hair off my neck, I wipe it free of sweat. "Sorry. My head started swimming. I got too hot or something."

"It's pretty slow today. Take the time you need. I'd tell you to go home, but—"

"I'm fine," I argue before he can insist I go home. "It was just a little stomach bug. Really, I'm fine."

He exhales. "When a woman says fine, especially more than once, it usually means the opposite."

The door to the kitchen opens, carrying with it the smell of the day's special, corned beef hash. Nausea hits me instantly, and I jump off the bench and vomit into the bushes along the privacy fence.

Patrick covers his mouth, gagging. "That's it. Go home. Better yet, go to the doctor."

Hattie's friend or not, no boss is going to want to keep an employee who takes time off a few days after starting a job.

"Don't give me that look," he chides. "I'm not firing you, but I really do want you to go to the doctor."

I nod, and the movement sends a wave of dizziness washing over me and I wobble on my feet. Patrick jumps up and catches me as I faint.

When I open my eyes, I'm laying on the ground with my purse under my head. I blink, and try to sit up. Patrick puts his hand on my shoulder and guides me to lay back down.

"Don't try to get up. I called Hattie. She's off today, so she'll be here any minute."

"What happened?" I ask, still feeling a bit groggy.

"You fainted. And before you ask, you've only been out about a minute. Just long enough for me to lay you down and prop up your head."

"Wren, are you okay?" I can hear the panic in Hattie's voice as she comes around the side of the building.

"I'm fine," I assure her, but my voice sounds weak.

Her eyes narrow. "You are not fine, and you are going to the doctor. You've been feeling sick all week."

"It's just a bug," I grumble.

She holds out her hand and helps me onto my feet. "You know, I think we can go home. I thought your marriage has been rocky for six months, but— Never mind. Let's go."

"You're not making any sense," I grumble.

"Then ignore me. I think you fainted because you're a little dehydrated. I've got Gatorade in the fridge at home."

Hattie helps me to the car and gets me settled on the couch. She sets a large red sports drink next to me and the remote. "Veg out here for a bit." She hikes her purse up on her shoulder. "I'm going to go run an errand real quick."

I'm dozing off when she returns. She looks at the

empty bottle, and hands me a paper bag. "I hope you need to pee."

My forehead scrunches together in confusion. "That's an odd thing to say," I mutter. It becomes really clear when I pull out a cardboard box containing two pregnancy tests.

Hattie crouches down in front of me. "Is it possible?"

I nod. I can't believe it never occurred to me. I get up to hurry in the bathroom.

My hands shake as I open the box. There's tape on the end and I accidentally rip it straight down the middle, making me drop one of the tests. "Shit," I mutter to myself and pick it up.

"Everything okay in there?"

"My hands won't stop shaking, and I ripped the box."

Hattie cracks open the door. "Take a deep breath. We'll deal with whatever it says, but knowledge is power. It's easy, just open the package, take the cap off and pee on it. But, catch it mid-stream."

"Right, okay." Seems simple enough. Amazing that something so innocuous can alter the entire course of my life. Well, I guess it only confirms that my life will never be the same.

When I'm done, I set it on the sink, wash my hands, and go back to the living room. "Can you set a timer?"

I zone out, trying not to think about what will happen if it's positive. Griffin already had his life turned upside down by an accidental pregnancy. He's trying to fix things with Liam. Mostly, I'm afraid of what will happen if he has to choose between Liam and my baby.

Hattie rubs my arm. "I know the timing of this is bad. He's got another child on the way, but you are his wife."

"I still want a divorce," I insist.

"You're not a resident yet, and if you are pregnant, they're going to make you wait until after the baby is born.

Did you get any answers about whether or not the papers you filed back in Harriston were sent to the court?" she asks.

I drop down on the couch, and put my head in my hands. "I don't know how to do any of this."

She sits next to me and rubs my back. "There's no rush. We don't even know what the test is going to say." She chuckles. "Hell, you could already be divorced. Call that lawyer you used first. Burying your head in the sand won't make these problems go away."

Bile rises up in my throat, and I swallow hard to force it back down. "I'm pregnant. The test is just for confirmation. I don't know why I hadn't thought about it, but now that you forced me to think of it, I just know."

The timer goes off. I take a deep breath and stand up. Slowly, I make my way into the bathroom and look down at the test. I'm not surprised to see it say, "Pregnant," clear as can be.

I sit down on the floor of the bathroom and let my new reality sink in. It's terrifying. I never imagined I'd be doing this alone, but despite the less than ideal circumstances, I'm happy.

A smile spreads across my face, and I put my hands on my still flat stomach. "I've wanted you for so long," I whisper.

"Was it negative?" Hattie asks.

"Why do you think that?" I ask and drop the test in my purse. I don't know why, but I feel the need to keep it for a while.

She shrugs. "You look happy."

I can't stop the smile that spreads across my face. "I am happy, because I'm pregnant. I've wanted a baby for a long time. Even though I'll be raising him or her alone, I very much wanted a baby."

Hattie nods. "Well, then I'll be the best great aunt ever." She looks away from me and I see her try and sneakily wipe away a single tear. "Much better than I was to you," she says in a rough whisper.

I hold out my hand, and she takes it. "No more looking back. This is a happy day. Our family is getting bigger again."

Another tear slips down her face, but she smiles at me. "I really like that."

She grabs her phone, and pulls up a number. "What are you doing?" I ask.

"It's time I agreed to go out with Clark, that lawyer friend. If you can be brave and face being a single mom, maybe it's time I stop protecting myself from being hurt by getting close to someone again."

———

AFTER HATTIE MADE her phone call to Clark, whom I've been calling "Mystery Man" in my head, he, of course, jumped at the chance to spend time with her. I'm thrilled, because from the moment we learned I'm pregnant, she's been hovering. Honestly, I'm the one about to become a mother, but she definitely wins the title of mother hen.

Without her overbearing hovering, I can breathe and start to think about what I'm going to do. I haven't figured out how to tell her about Griffin. Before today it didn't seem like something I had to do. I mean, it's over, so what if she thinks I'm heartbroken about the end of my marriage. What does it help to tell her I'm actually upset about leaving my father-in-law behind?

The Gatorade helps the dizziness, and my nausea is gone, for now. I decide a walk down to the beach will help me think some things through. The smell of the ocean hits me long before I can see the gulf. It's only about a half a mile walk from her condo. The white sand looks so pristine. In a couple months this beach will be filled with tourists seeking sun and surf. Right now there's only a few people lazily strolling down the sugar white beach.

I thought ahead to grab a towel, and I spread it out on a spot further down away from the people out today. Taking my shoes off, I bury my toes in the sand. It's still winter, and even though spring is showing signs of getting closer, the sand is still cool on my feet.

Watching the surf roll up onto the beach somehow makes my problems feel smaller. It may be hard to figure out right now, but I just need to let some things happen as they're supposed to.

Before my thoughts can become too philosophical, my phone rings. I pull it out of the tote bag I grabbed to come down here. My phone is tucked next to a packet of crackers and a bottle of water.

"I Kissed a Girl," by Katie Perry plays, and I roll my eyes. "Bess, did you change my ringtone?"

She cackles in delight. "It's just a suggestion, Wrenagade."

"You're a menace," I tease.

"Uh," she starts and my stomach drops. It's one syllable, and yet it sounds so ominous.

"Why am I scared all of a sudden?"

I hear her breathe in, and now I'm really worried if she needs a calming breath before whatever she needs to tell me. "Bess, did something happen to Dolores?"

"No, oh, no. I'm sorry, I'm being a drama queen. This might be good news, I don't know."

I force my jaw to unclench. "If it's not a big deal how about you spit it out, so I don't end up prematurely on high blood pressure medication?"

"I'm at work, and Charlie came in," she begins.

"That's hardly news, Bess. It's Wednesday, the college girls are there tonight."

Charlie is nearly as attractive as Griffin. It's not fair really. Those young co-eds don't stand a chance.

"Right, well, that might be what brought him in, but I overheard him talking to Donovan. Griffin left last night."

Now it's my turn to take a deep breath. I want to know of course, but I need to cut this off. He's either chasing after Liam, or god forbid at that club with a new distraction. I had hoped he'd be a little sad, but maybe I won't tell him about the baby. As soon as the thought enters my head I dismiss it. He's a great father, and I know I can't keep this from him, but I can get my feet underneath me first. He deserves to be a part of the baby's life, but he doesn't have to be involved with my pregnancy.

"I can't hear about him," I insist.

"Too damn bad, girlie."

"Why? This is my pregnancy, and I can deal with it however is best for me," I seethe. Damn pregnancy hormones. I've been irritable a lot the last week or so, but I thought I was grieving or something.

"Your what now?" I could hear a pin drop on her end of the phone. She doesn't even sound like she's breathing now.

"Uhm, yeah, so it just occurred to me that you totally didn't know that since I only figured it out this morning, which means that is not your reason for telling me about Griffin. But, I just can't keep track of him. He let me go. Hell, he insisted for weeks that when Liam got out of rehab this is what I needed to do, and so I did. I'm gone."

"Okay, preggers, zip your lip for a sec, 'kay? Griffin is on his way to Florida. I only have a minute before Donovan finds me hiding in the storage closet and it won't be as much fun as when you go in here, feel me? I take it he doesn't know?"

"Why would Donovan know about the baby?"

"Girl, did you shove cotton between your ears today? Griffin, does he know that his bun is in your oven?"

"This is how it happens, isn't it. I'm already dumber. I'm a dumb blonde now."

I hear a click and check to see if she hung up on me. "What was that?" I ask when I see the call is still connected.

"I can't snap in your face, so I snapped into the phone. You've got a serious case of mommy brain. Drink lots of water and take a nap. You're going to need your wits about you, because he. Is. Coming. Charlie was asking some of the women about your aunt. One of them I guess is a friend of hers, and she was only too happy to tell Charlie all about where she lives and stuff. Your aunt needs better friends, he coulda been a psycho."

I shake my head. "Only in Harriston can you find out a person's personal business over a beer or in line at the drugstore," I grumble.

"Yeah, but remember, I overheard what Griffin is doing the same way, and am able to warn you, so don't knock it right now."

"Do you know when he's going to be here?" I ask.

"I'm sorry. It depends on how long he stopped for last night."

"He left last night!" I screech.

I stand and try and wipe the sand off my feet. Then I start shoving everything in my bag. "Bess, I've got to go. I went down to the beach, and I guess I need to go back to the condo before Hattie comes back and try and do damage control."

Bess groans. "You didn't tell her about Griffin, did you?"

"No, she, uh, thinks this is Liam's baby," I rush out.

"I know I didn't hear you let your aunt think you're having the baby of a cheating thief."

I scoff. "What was I supposed to say. 'Don't worry, Aunt Hattie. It's not Liam's baby, it's his dad's."

Bess giggles, and it grows into laughing so hard she gasps as she tries to speak. "You're having your husband's brother or sister."

Maybe it's the hormones, or the absurdity of my situation, but I find that so funny I snort. I laugh so hard I nearly pee myself. "Shit, I almost peed, and I can't even say the baby is sitting on my bladder yet. I've been downing Gatorade and water for the last few hours because I'm a little dehydrated."

It takes less time to get back to the condo as it did to walk to the beach, but I still wasn't fast enough. A familiar truck is parked in front of her place, and Hattie is most definitely back.

"Shit," I whisper into the phone. "He's here, and Hattie is yelling at him."

"Sorry I didn't find out earlier. Text me later and let me know how it goes." The line goes dead and I hurry to the front door.

"What the hell do you think you're doing here, Hale? So your son is such a chicken shit that he knocks up my niece and lets his daddy come fix things for him?"

She slaps her hand over her mouth, and her eyes open to anime character proportions. "Uhm, forget that. He doesn't know, because. Shit. Why are you here?"

It's like he can feel me close by. Instead of answering her his head swings my direction. He walks with a purpose straight for me. My legs refuse to listen to my silent begging for them to run. When he gets next to me, he grabs my arm and drags me to his truck.

"We need to talk, baby bird, now."

"Wren!" Hattie screams for me.

I wave to her as he drags me to his truck. "It's okay, Hattie," I shout so she can hear me.

"Get in the goddamn truck, Wren," Griffin grits out.

"Yes, daddy," I sass, and do as he says.

39

Griffin

My fingers clench the steering wheel the entire way to the hotel. Thankfully, Charlie took it upon himself to book me somewhere to stay when I left late the day before. He knew I'd head straight for Wren.

When I can breathe without feeling like fire is exiting my nostrils, I look at her. "Were you going to tell me?"

She turns her head toward the window. "I don't know," she whispers.

"Wrong answer," I seethe.

I'm so angry, at her, at Liam, at goddamn life. The fact she didn't immediately call me the moment she found out ticks me off. No, the fact she left in the first place has my blood boiling.

The hotel is close to her aunt's house. I force myself to slow down and not jostle her around too much. She might be pissing me off, but she's precious to me, even more so now. Then a dark voice whispers in my head, *"Are you sure it's yours?"*

I drag her into the lobby, and point at one of the chairs in the sitting area. "Sit your ass down while I check in. If you try and leave, I swear to God I will hunt your ass down, and you're not going to like it."

Her eyes flare wide, but for once she doesn't argue with me. I quickly check in and get my key cards from the front desk. Then I'm back, dragging her toward the elevator. She wisely doesn't say anything. My temper is being held by a thread, and I don't need an audience when I confront her.

There's a couple walking down the hallway when we get in front of my door. I grab the back of her neck to let her know I won't tolerate her trying to make a scene to leave. She strolls in ahead of me, some of the fire coming back to her.

She whirls on me the moment we're closed inside together. "Listen here, asshole. I've had a long fucking day and I'm not about to put up with your bullshit."

I laugh. "You've had a long day? I've had a long fucking three weeks. You just left."

"I did what you told me to do. I really didn't think you wanted me to stay the way you ran after Liam like that."

"He's my son!"

Her hands drop to her stomach, and she takes a step back from me. My words were careless, but we still need to get one thing cleared up. "Are you sure it's mine?"

She flinches, but doesn't answer me.

"Is that why you weren't sure you were going to tell me? When was the last time you were with Liam?" Even asking the question makes me sick.

"Fuck you! Is that why you dragged me down here? Do you want an excuse to get out of this? I'll give you one right now. You are off the hook. I will take care of this baby by myself. You want to know who's it is? It's mine!"

That thread holding me back, it snaps. I'm across the room before I even think about moving, and she's pinned against the wall by my much larger body. I tip her face up to look at me instead of my chest as she's determined to do. "Answer me."

Her hands push against my chest, and I laugh at her feeble attempt to move me. I might as well be a mountain compared to her. She gives up and sags against me.

"You need to move. Please, I'm going to be sick," she begs.

I step back and she runs into the bathroom. She barely gets the lid up on the toilet when she starts retching. Even irritated, I'm not heartless. I squat down next to her, and hold her hair back. She whimpers when she's done and leans against me.

There's no fight in her now. She lets me help her up. I have a spare toothbrush in the bag I brought with me and I hand it to her. When she's done removing the after effects of morning sickness from her mouth, I guide her to lay down on the bed. I sit next to her, and I watch a single tear slip down her face. "It's yours. There's no way it could be anyone else's. I haven't been with Liam in over six months."

"I'm sorry, I shouldn't have asked you that." Now, my anger is directed only at myself.

She takes a deep breath. "I know we started wrong. Maybe everything about us was wrong." Her hand moves back to cradle her flat stomach. "But I'm not sorry. I mean what I said. I won't make you choose. Liam needs you, I understand that. I'll be everything this one needs."

"You're coming home with me," I say. I can tell her I want her back, that she never should have left, but she's not wanting to hear me right now. It's going to take time to win her back.

"Griffin, I did what you asked. Just because I'm pregnant doesn't mean I need to come back. What are you even doing here? You couldn't have known about the baby before you left. I just found out today."

"Baby bird, I was coming to get you. Or at least I was coming to beg you to come back if I had to, but if you think I'm leaving you here knowing you're carrying my baby, you don't know me very well."

"I won't fight you, but only because this is too much to thrust on Hattie."

I tuck her hair behind her ear. "I'll take it for now, but I will be getting you back."

She doesn't answer, which in itself is an answer. She thinks we're too broken. I'll prove to her I can be what she needs. That I'm all she'll ever need. The time for me to coast through life is over. It's time I start taking what I want. For the first time what I want is exactly what my family needs.

"Sleep now," I tell her.

Her eyes drift closed and I cover her with the spare blanket.

I move into the living room portion of the room. Charlie somehow managed to snag me a king suite. It's probably not fancy by many people's standards, but for me this is luxury.

Wren's breathing slows, and I know she's fallen deeply asleep. My poor girl is really going to have a tough time with morning sickness. I hate that I can't take the pain and discomfort for her, but she won't deal with it alone.

Once I know I won't wake her, I grab my cellphone to let Charlie know I made it safely.

"Did you find her?" he asks.

"Yeah, I'm bringing her home."

"Just like that? Are you sure that's best? Liam is a fucking wreck," he advises.

"Well not everything is about him. Not anymore," I mumble.

"I know you need her, but maybe you two should be apart for a while. I'm not saying break up with her, but maybe do long distance for a while so we can get his stupid ass back in rehab."

"She's pregnant, Charlie. I'm bringing my family home. He's a grown man. He fucked up, and she's not suffering for that anymore. My baby isn't going to be without me because he blew up his life."

"Fuck," he sighs.

"How serious were you about buying me out?" I ask. I've been thinking about this since he brought it up.

"It was a joke, Griff. You've got a kid on the way. Now is not the time to do anything rash."

"I've got a plan. I'll fill you in when I get back," I tell him.

"When will that be?"

I poke my head back in the bedroom. "Maybe tomorrow. I'm not sure how long it will take to get back either. She seems to have really bad morning sickness."

"I hope you know what you're doing. Liam is going to blow a gasket," he comments.

I exhale, but Charlie starts speaking before I can lay into him. "I'm not saying you should cater to him. But it sounds like she's dealing with enough right now. Liam could add stress she doesn't need."

"She needs me. I just need to convince her of that first," I grumble.

"Uh oh. So she didn't welcome you back with open arms then?"

"I was a bit of a dick," I admit.

"You?" he laughs. "Totally shocked. How out of character."

"Yeah, yeah. Yuk it up asshole. I asked her if she was sure it was mine."

"I see, you are a dumbass. Dude, even I know she hasn't slept with him in months. Haven't you ever eavesdropped when he did actually answer her calls? You don't go out much, so I'm not surprised you didn't know he was stepping out, but damn."

"I'm coming to realize I've screwed up a lot lately," I admit.

"It'll all work out. Just take the time you need. I've got things covered here," he says.

"Thanks, Charlie. I owe you."

———

WREN WAKES AFTER A COUPLE HOURS. She covers her mouth with her hand. "Can you take me back home?"

"You are home," I tell her. "Wherever I am is your home now."

"I think that's my decision," she argues.

I put my hand on her stomach. "Not anymore. I already told you, I came here to get you back. If you think I'm going to let you go now, you haven't been paying attention to who I am."

She turns her face away from me. "I don't want to be with you just because I'm pregnant."

"You think I don't want you?"

"I think you told me a dozen times I had to go. I knew you would worry, but I figured I was making it easier on you," she says, refusing to look at me.

I pull my shirt off and get out of my jeans.

"What are you doing?" she asks.

"You ran from me, again. I think you need to be reminded where you belong and who you belong to."

She scrambles off the bed and tries to get around me. I lunge for her and hold her against me, her back to my chest. My hand moves to cover her throat. "It turns me on when you run from me. I will claim you over and over again until you understand who you belong to."

Wren whimpers. I slide my hand past the waist of her jeans. I groan when my fingers slide through her slit and find her wet.

"You were going to deny me this pussy? What were you going to do when the hormones take over and you're so horny you hurt? Would you have let someone else touch what's mine?" I growl in her ear.

She shakes her head as much as my hand on her throat will allow.

"Right answer, baby bird." I drag her back to the bed and strip her naked.

I pull a length of silk rope from my bag. "Bess told me I needed to read romance novels to perfect my groveling."

"You suck at groveling," she mutters.

"Well, I learned something else from what I read. I'm just not going to let you leave. I'm going to tie your ass up and fuck you into submission. You are mine, and I'm done with this bullshit idea of you leaving."

She snorts. "It was your bullshit idea."

"You didn't give me a chance to evolve."

"This is you evolved?" she asks.

"No, I'm afraid I'm just as much a caveman as I ever was. Actually, I'm probably worse now. There's something about finding out your woman is carrying your child that makes a man like me want to beat his chest with pride. Now it's time for you to accept that you. Are. Mine."

Her chin lifts defiantly. I know she's pregnant, and that should caution me, but I can't hold back. She can take me as I am. I'll never hurt her, not more than she'll enjoy at least.

When I go to grab her hands she starts to fight me again. A smile stretches across my face. I enjoy her fire. Crave it even. I flip her onto her stomach. Grabbing the cord with one hand, I have her wrists locked behind her back with the other. Quickly, I bind her wrists together.

Once she's secure, I pull her until her feet are on the floor, and her torso rests on the bed. I slap her ass, and she gasps. "You ran from daddy, and bad girls get punished."

She doesn't respond, so I slap the other cheek. "Let me hear you say it, baby bird."

"Yes daddy," she mumbles.

"I don't believe you mean it," I say and land a slap on her pussy.

She's trying to hold back, but between our weeks of separation and the hormones coursing through her body, a wanton moan escapes.

I drag my cock through her swollen pussy lips coating my cock in her wetness. She squirms, subconsciously trying to get more of my cock. "You ready to be my good little slut? Who do you belong to?"

"You, daddy," she says on a breathy moan.

"Yes you fucking do," I say through clenched teeth.

I am torturing myself while trying to tease her. It's been too long since I felt her inner walls squeezing my dick. I can't wait any longer. One hard thrust and I'm buried deep inside heaven.

My fingers dig into her hips. I can't be sure, but they feel a little wider. I can't wait for her to swell with my child. Just thinking about it makes me harder than I've ever been in my life. "Do you feel that?" I ask her.

"You think I only want you because you're pregnant? I'm hard as a fucking rock."

I slam my hips forward, rocking her up the bed. "Does this feel like I'm just here out of guilt?"

"No," she whispers.

I spank her lush ass again. With my dick buried in her I feel the vibration of the impact roll down my shaft causing us both to groan. "I do love that you're carrying my child. That I am the man who planted my seed in your womb. I'm really looking forward to servicing every need you have. Anytime you want my cock, it's yours. Only yours."

My words elicit a spasm of her inner walls. She starts moaning, and I push her higher and higher. Our bodies slap together as she starts pushing back with every thrust. When she starts to come, I fuck her harder.

"It's too much," she begs.

I prop myself up with one hand on the mattress so I can reach her clit. I strum the nub relentlessly, and she tries to squirm out of my touch. "You'll fucking take it," I growl.

Her cunt tries to strangle my cock, and I power through, fighting the urge to come myself. She comes so hard I feel her release gush, soaking my cock. Still I don't let up. I take her until the lightning shooting down my spine pulls my balls up tight, spreading a delicious fire through my body. I roar when I finally come.

Wren lays limp on the bed when I roll off of her. By the time I untie her hands she's blinking her eyes. "You made me pass out," she accuses.

I smile, and drag her up the bed to lay on top of me. Stroking her back, I tell her, "That's not the last time I'll do it either. I told you, I'm going to fuck you into submission."

"You're going to fuck me into a coma," she grumbles.

"Whatever keeps you from leaving," I admit. "Love and war, baby bird. Anything goes, and have no doubt I'm fighting to keep you."

40

Wren

There are several missed calls and a dozen texts from Hattie when I finally manage to clear my head from the sex fog Griffin seems determined to keep me under. Damn my hormones for helping him. I want to be mad at him, but my traitorous body is making it freaking hard.

Maybe I don't actually want to be mad at him, but I can't accept a life where my needs come after Liam. I know that's unfair. Liam is his son, and I know my little peanut will always come first to me, but I've already lived that life. Even more importantly, my child will not come after my asshole ex husband. Or, soon to be ex husband. I need to check on that. After Hattie told me about not being able to get divorced in Florida, since I'm pregnant, I told her I'd had divorce papers drawn up weeks ago. She asked me if they were filed, and I wasn't sure. I know Liam didn't sign them, but I had. So before I do anything, I've got to call my dad's friend and find out where I left that process. Maybe I can just file those.

I open my texts first, and it's a series of demands to get my ass back to the house to talk to her. Then some pleading, and finally she admits she's worried about me. It feels weird to have someone actually worry about me. It's been so long since I've felt like there was someone in my corner, and now there's a small crowd gathering. It warms me from the inside knowing my child would have more than me looking out for them.

Griffin rolls his bulky body to spoon me. His arm wraps around my waist, and he pulls me snugly against him as his lips drop to the spot where my neck and shoulder. "Are you hungry?"

His attention is bringing up a craving alright, but my stomach takes the opportunity to grumble like an angry bear waking up from hibernation. Totally not ladylike at all.

He chuckles, and I find myself melting in his arms. "We need to feed you and our little one."

I am able to turn in his arms so we're face to face. "You're not angry?"

His forehead scrunches. "Why would I be angry?"

I shrug. "We weren't trying to have a baby."

He kisses me sweetly, and my heart thumps hard against my ribs. I'm not used to sweet Griffin. Demanding, grouchy, asshole Griffin, yes, but sweet is throwing me for a loop.

"We weren't exactly trying to prevent it either," he says.

I blink several times. "You thought it was possible? I was on the pill."

"I was fucking you bare every chance I got. I saw the pills in your stuff. They're the kind that you have to take exactly at the same time every day or they might not work."

My mouth falls open. "I don't know what to say."

He smirks. It's a bad boy grin, not that anything about Griffin Hale is boyish. "How about thank you?"

"Thank you?" I ask incredulously.

"You're welcome."

I can see he's fighting not to laugh, but that doesn't stop me from slapping his chest. Not that it hurt him. Does a boulder feel pain when you hit it? "You did not just tell me to thank you for knocking me up."

"You wanted a baby. I gave you one. I think a thank you is the least you could say. Don't worry about it, you'll get it right next time."

"Next time?" I sputter.

His hands drop down to my ass, and he pulls me against his erection. It feels like Griffin has a breeding kink. The thought sends a wave of arousal I really do not need when I'm trying to be irritated with him.

Griffin rolls me to my back and presses his hard body into mine. A needy whimper escapes. My mind and body really need to communicate better to get on the same page.

"How many kids do you think we're going to have?" I ask, but my voice is breathy, and even I no longer believe I'm annoyed.

He hums into my neck as he nips the sensitive skin below my ear. "That's the great thing about having a young wife. You could give me three or four of them still."

I feel like I've been doused in ice water. We still haven't talked about how we were going to handle anything, and he has us married. Doubt creeps back in. Before I left he kept insisting I had to leave, because of what Liam and the town would think. Now that he knows I'm carrying our baby, suddenly all of that is no longer a concern. Not only that, but he has us getting married? I'm getting dizzy trying to keep up with the drastic shift in our status. We've never even really called this a relationship. We were fucking, and now we're getting married?

I shove at his chest. "I think I should get a divorce before we get too far ahead of ourselves."

He lets me up, astutely realizing my teasing mood is gone. His hands are out in front of him like he's trying to soothe a raging monster. "I know things are still messy, but we will work everything out."

I'm breathing hard through my nose, while I'm shoving my legs back inside of my jeans. "I'm hungry, and if I don't go and talk to Hattie she's going to call the National Guard. Let's just deal with this later."

Cautiously, he puts his hands on my shoulders. "No more running. You can be mad, worried, scared, whatever you feel, but you have to be here with me."

A single bob of my head is all I can manage, because the truth is the desire to run is strong. The problem with running is that the moment you stop everything you're running from catches up to you.

HATTIE IS FRANTICALLY PEERING out the curtains when we pull up to the house. The moment we are out of his truck she flies out the front door. She's far from her usual well put-together self. Instant guilt hits me.

"Is your phone broken? You of all people should know to reply to a message!" She's completely beside herself, and I know why. The guilt I was feeling intensifies. Unanswered messages, not being able to get my mom or dad on the phone, yeah, I remember why that would worry her.

She grabs my hands by my wrists and I flinch. "You will never make me worry like that again, do you hear me?"

I nod, and pray she lets go. Instead her fingers find the scars on my left wrist. With her medical training she doesn't even ask what they are, she knows. She takes a shaky breath, then swallows. Her eyes slowly fix on mine, and I can see the tears she's fighting to hang onto. "From now on, I'll be here for you. I don't want you to ever feel this alone again."

Griffin drops his arm around my shoulders and pulls me to his side. "She won't."

I groan, realizing he just told her the news I'd planned to ease her into without saying a word.

Her eyes widen and focus on his possessive display. "Wren?" she asks.

"Can we go inside and talk?" I ask.

Hattie's eyes narrow on Griffin. "You sick sonofabitch. I know she's not a child, but she is younger than yours. I might have been gone from Harriston for a long time now, but even I've heard rumors about the things you like." She points at me. "Hasn't she been through enough? I'm guessing she didn't run out of town in the middle of the night because of your son, did she?"

"Hattie," I interrupt. "It was more like late afternoon."

"You shush," she snaps.

My back goes straight. "Stop laying into him. Griffin didn't run me off. I left so he didn't have to choose between Liam and me."

Griffin is looking at me weird. There's no scowl pulling down his brow, or naughty smirk curving his mouth. This look is tender, and it's kinda freaking me out. Griffin is not a tender man.

"I know the age difference is freaking you out," he starts.

"That and the fact you're her father-in-law," Hattie interjects.

His mouth quirks. Probably at the reminder that daddy is literally part of what he is or at least was to me. My hand falls to my stomach, now he's daddy for another reason. His chest vibrates with silent laughter and he bends down to kiss my temple.

Then he becomes more serious, and refocuses on Hattie. "I know we started out wrong, but I could no more have avoided falling in love with her than I could stop breathing. I need her, and I promise I'll work my ass off to give her the world."

For a second nothing else filters into my brain. Everything stops. Hell, the world could be standing still and I wouldn't notice. Then in an instant everything snaps back into place. I slap him on the chest several times. Each slap punctuating my words. "Why do you keep saying you love me to other people instead of me?"

He holds my hands still on his chest. I fight the urge to pet him. I'm not even sure that is hormone related. Griffin has a very amazing body. "Stop with the violence, baby bird, I like it too much."

Hattie groans. "You really are a dirty freak," she mumbles.

"So dirty," I agree without thinking, and this time I do rub my hands on his muscles.

That effectively breaks the tension as Hattie bursts out laughing so hard she's gasping for breath. "Oh my god. Okay, I'm done fighting this. I mean he is pretty hot."

"He's also standing right here," Griffin grumbles.

I beam up at him. "There's my sexy grouch. You were being too nice and it was freaking me out."

Hattie rolls her eyes. "Yeah, I get it. This is the real deal. I'm guessing you came to get your stuff?" she asks me.

"Griffin wants me to go home with him," I tell her.

Her expression turns serious again. "Is that what you want?" she asks.

I look at Griffin, and for once he's not trying to push me into a decision. "I want us to be a family," I say mostly to him.

"We will be," he promises.

IT TAKES us a couple of days to get back into town. During the drive Charlie calls and lets Griffin know that Liam has agreed to come back to the shop to work. I can tell that Griffin is relieved to know that Liam will have a job, but also nervous to go and work with him again. I silently promise myself that I will do what I can to make it so they can still have a relationship with each other.

The first thing I know is that I can't go back to work at Hale Automotive. Which only leaves me one alternative. I'm not sure what Griffin is going to think about it. Actually, I'm quite sure he's going to hate it, but I know that Donovan will give me my job back.

Griffin is anxious to check in at the shop the morning after we get back because he said he fell behind on a lot of work while I was in Florida and he wanted to give Charlie a break. It's a bit of a relief to have some time to myself. I wanted his attention, and I certainly got it. Now he's watching what I eat, how much water I drink, and staring at my belly like it's going to grow before his eyes.

Part of him is still worried I'm going to take off again. I know that if I would have stayed we could have talked things out, but I'm not sure that would have been enough to convince me he could find a balance between our relationship and his relationship with Liam. Worse, I'm not sure I would have believed that he wasn't just trying to make things work because I'm pregnant. Him coming all the way to Florida to come and get me back, without knowing about the baby, even I can't deny he chose me this time. Now I have to choose him.

First step is to get my job back so I'm not a burden to him. I enter the bar and go and sit in front of Donovan. "Hey Wrenegade," he greets me.

"Hi, do you have a second to talk?" I ask him.

"Sure, do you want something to drink?" he asks.

Bess strolls past and mutters, "Dumbass."

His eyes go wide. "Of soda! I'm not trying to serve a pregnant woman booze."

Behind me a chair screeches across the floor and topples over. "Pregnant?" I hear a voice slur. "At least I know this one isn't mine."

I turn around and find Liam struggling to stand up. My head snaps back to Donovan. "How much has he had to drink?"

"You're not my mom," Liam says and hiccups. "Not yet at least." He laughs at his own joke.

He stumbles over and gets close enough I can smell the alcohol wafting off his breath. "This one's not mine." Liam continues to laugh. "The funny thing is you're actually my wife."

"Not anymore," I mumble.

His eyes narrow, and he stabs his finger into the bar top. "I didn't sign those papers."

I got a call from Dolores while we were driving. She went through the mail I'd received in my absence. One of my letters was from my attorney. "But I did. I didn't realize that your signature wasn't necessary. It just made it take longer."

"So we're divorced?"

I shrug. "Looks like it."

He smirks, and it looks nothing like when his dad does it. Griffin's grin sets my body alive, Liam's makes me feel like I need a shower. He leans closer into my personal space. "Maybe we can act out some of my naughty stepmother fantasies."

The door slams open, and in walks a pissed off Griffin. "Get the fuck away from her."

"Maybe I should have told you that. Never thought I had to ask you to keep your hands off my wife."

"She's not your wife anymore. You left her. I love you son, but I'm not going to join you in your misery. I love her too, and I'm going to marry her."

"This is bullshit," he sneers and pushes away from the bar.

"What's bullshit is you're going to be a father, and you're here drunk in the middle of the day. Blame me, blame Wren, but look in a fucking mirror and own your shit. Your kid doesn't deserve this. I know, I lived it."

Griffin reaches out to me, and I take his hand. When we're outside he leans down and says in my ear, "You're not going back to work at the bar."

"I've got to work," I insist.

"I know, baby bird, but I need you to give me some time. I've got a surprise for you."

A smile spreads across my face. He's already surprised me more than I ever anticipated, because for the first time, he chose me.

41

Griffin

"Wake up, baby bird." Gently shaking her shoulder I manage to rouse Wren from a deep sleep.

Her green eyes slowly open to look up at me. There's a weight that has lifted from her since we left the bar yesterday. I should have figured my shit out earlier, and it's going to take a long time for me to forgive myself for ever making her doubt me. Maybe even longer for lying to myself that I could ever let her go.

I thought it was for the best. She could live without me, find a man her own age, explore the world, not be held down by the years between us. Even worse, I'd pushed her away because of a lie I told myself. If she was gone, Liam and I could go back to normal, and I wouldn't lose my son.

Then she left, and I couldn't even look at him. I was so worried he'd resent me for falling in love with her, I didn't stop and think how I'd feel about him. Everything he'd done over the last year compounded. He stole from me, lied to me, and nearly destroyed my business. Wren was gone, I was a mess, and Liam and I weren't any better. The truth slapped me in the face the night I chose to chase after him rather than take care of Wren.

Liam and I weren't okay, and it had nothing to do with my relationship with Wren. Worse, I sacrificed my happiness and hers for the benefit of someone who, I realized, didn't give a shit about anyone but themself. Yes, many would see our relationship as taboo. She should have been off limits, and everyone in town was already talking about us.

"Coffee," she croaks, bringing me out of my head.

I shake my head. "No can do, little momma. Coffee is bad for the baby."

She scowls at me, and I'm so damn happy to have her back I smile at her bad mood.

"You're annoyingly happy this morning. Where's the dark cloud that's usually hanging over your head?" she grumbles.

I drop a kiss on her forehead. "Don't you know? That cloud didn't stand a chance against your sunshine."

She pouts. "I don't know how sunny I'm going to be without coffee."

My hand slips under the covers to rest on her stomach. "It's amazing what you can sacrifice for your child."

Her mouth curves into a frown. "Then shouldn't I still be in Florida? Liam—"

I put my hand over her mouth stopping her from finishing her sentence. "As much as I love him, you are the one thing I can't give up for him. A person can't live without a heart, and you're mine."

Her lips move under my hand, and even though I suspect she's going to argue with me, I let her speak. "You told my aunt and Liam you love me, but you've never said it to me."

The list of things I have to make up to her is long.

"Love is such a weak word. I need one that encompasses what you are to me. I'm not great at words. Hell, even you've said I speak more in grunts. Bess told me I needed to grovel, but I'm not good at that either. My language is made up of actions. But, I need you to know, I do love you. More than anything. I'd like to show you what I mean by that if you'll take a ride with me?"

Her eyes are wide and trusting. I don't deserve it, but I'm going to make sure it isn't misplaced. I need to prove to her that her heart is safe with me.

"WHY ARE WE AT THE SHOP?" she asks. There's a hint of panic in her voice, and I realize it's because the bay doors are open, and Liam is staring back at us.

He looks rough, bags are under his eyes, and he's clearly suffering from a hangover. His jaw is clenched like mine does when I'm angry, but he doesn't storm away. Charlie moves to stand next to him, and puts a hand on his shoulder. He gives me a nod, and I know he's got my back if Liam should get out of control.

"Get out with me?" I ask her.

There's a wariness in her eyes that makes me angry. I raised the man who put that look on her face, and it feels like as much my failure as Liam's. I can't keep blaming myself for his mistakes though.

"I can wait in the car," she offers.

Slipping my hand in hers, I give it a squeeze. "He's never going to be out of your life, and I know that's unfair. You are divorced, and without kids. Most people in your situation could walk away and never think about their ex again. Hell, I have a kid with mine, and I still haven't seen her in over twenty years. I know it's a lot to ask, but we're never going to get past this if we don't try."

"For you, I'll try," she whispers.

I get out of my truck, and run around the other side to help her down. She laughs at my sudden surge in protectiveness. "If you had a smaller truck I could do this myself. I could probably figure out how to jump down."

"And risk you falling and hurting the peanut? No way. I doubt you'll let me wrap you in bubble wrap, so you should probably prepare yourself for a lot of hovering. If getting a lower truck means I don't get an excuse to touch you, I'll just end up lifting this one."

Taking her hand, I lead her into the bay. She tries to pull her hand free, but I hold firm. The time for us to make ourselves smaller to appease others is over, or it will be over soon. My actions will prove to her that I'm not ashamed to be with her.

Liam sees our hands clasped and scowls, but Charlie squeezes his shoulder before he can throw any insults our way. I didn't bring Wren here for round two anyway. We're here to see Charlie.

"You called and said you made a decision about my offer," I remind him.

He smirks at me. "First I've got to congratulate our little mom-to-be." Charlie demonstrates his death wish by wrapping his arms around her and spinning her around.

She laughs, then groans, and I'm ready to take his head off. He sees the look on my face, and instantly sets her down. Then he sees the look on her face and winces. Liam grabs the back of his neck, looking uncomfortable. Then he strolls into my office and comes back with a chair.

Wren's face is the definition of shock, but she takes a seat. I'm still glaring at Charlie. "Morning sickness, dumbfuck."

"I'm so sorry," he apologizes. "Can I get you water? I can run out and grab you some crackers?"

I grunt, after all it is the language I'm most fluent in. Picking up her bag from the ground I pull out a bottle of water. "I can take care of my woman."

Liam's jaw ticks, but he doesn't say anything and he doesn't walk away. Wren doesn't notice. Her eyes are glued to mine, and her smile is blinding.

Charlie clears his throat, and I realize I was lost staring at her beautiful face. An activity I plan to do for the rest of my life.

He reaches inside his coveralls and pulls out a check. I reach for it and he pulls it back. "I want my name added to the sign."

My lip twitches. Wren starts to giggle.

"What's so funny?" Charlie asks confused.

Liam groans. "First or last name?"

"Last name. Why is that so funny?" he asks as the three of us start laughing in earnest.

"It's just that your name is Charles Storm," Wren points out, with tears caused by laughing, running down her face.

Charlie crosses his arms. "I'm aware of what my name is."

"Hale and Storm Automotive, uncle Charlie," Liam adds.

Charlie's eyes widen, and then he too starts laughing. "Well, shit. That's the first time I put them together and heard it out loud."

I smile. No one is screaming, and we were even able to laugh at Charlie. There's hope still. Everything isn't fixed right now, but maybe someday it will be.

"I like it. It's a bit cheesy, but no one will forget us." And I wouldn't forget to hope.

I reach my hand out to Charlie and he shakes it. "Welcome to the business, partner."

Liam nods his head at me, silently telling me he approves of the decision. There was a time he was supposed to be my partner in this business, but Charlie has more than earned it. Besides, I've got plans with his buy-in.

"Okay, baby bird, we've got places to be," I tell her and drag her back to the truck.

The drive to Centralia is long, but that's why I woke her up early. She has no idea what I'm up to, but she remains silent as we drive past the university she should have attended.

I pull up to a vacant building in the industrial part of town. A realtor stands out front with the keys. Wren waits in the truck as I sign my papers and take the keys.

When I come to grab her, I decide to answer the questions bouncing around in her head. I reach under the seat and pull out a fat envelope to Central Valley University. I already know it's an acceptance and full-ride to attend starting the next term.

Her eyes light up, and then her hand flutters over her stomach. She sets the envelope on the seat next to her. "It was a lovely dream once."

"It's a lovely reality now," I insist.

She shakes her head. "I can't. We've got the baby coming, and for some reason you have a building."

"You're going to college."

Her chin lifts and I brace myself for a dose of her stubbornness. "I don't want to put the baby in daycare."

"Come on, I want to show you something." I lift her down from the truck and unlock the front door.

The building I picked has all the necessary features, and some extras. The previous owners decided to retire, so the lifts and large equipment they agreed to sell with the building. There's a small office off the main business office that the owners' kids used to hang out after school when they were young.

I flip on the lights and lead her into the room. "This room has some sound proofing because the previous owners had kids and they hung out here after school. They said the noise was too much for them to do their homework, so they fixed it. I'm going to turn it into a nursery for the peanut. We'll have to hire someone who can help keep an eye on the little one, but I'll be here to keep an eye on them."

Wren sighs and looks up at me. "You've got it all figured out, don't you?"

"I don't know if we're painting it blue or pink, but otherwise—"

She licks her lips. "Green. Even if this one is a girl, you said you wanted three or four. Can't have you painting it every couple years."

I drop down to one knee, and put my hands on her hips. Wren gulps, and I figure she knows what I'm up to, even before the words are out of my mouth.

She shakes her head, and my heart stops for a beat. "Here? You can't—We're not christening the whole shop."

I hold my breath, sensing our wires are crossed. "What do you think I'm trying to do?"

Her face turns red. "You're trying to, uhm, go down on me?"

Laughter bursts from me for the second time today. I reach into my pocket and pull out a ring. It's simple, a classic cut emerald set in white gold. "I can get you a diamond if you prefer, but this matches your eyes when you're about to come. It's become my favorite color. And now that you bring it up, I know how I can see it again and make you say yes."

Before she has a chance to answer, I slip the ring on her finger, and flip up her skirt. Her lace underwear are already wet, and I bury my nose against the fabric. I'll never get tired of how fast she heats up for me. One sharp tug shreds the dainty fabric, and I bury my face in her needy cunt. She tastes like sunshine and happiness. Her groans fill the space, and this has already become my favorite room in the building.

My cock is angrily pressing against my zipper, and I decide not to punish him. Lifting her up, I press her against the door, and free my aching hard on. Her legs wrap around me, and I bury myself in one hard thrust. Eventually I'll have to take it easier on her, but not today.

"Let me hear your answer," I demand and nip at her throat.

"God yes," she groans.

My hand covers her throat, and I force her to look at me. "Wrong man, baby bird."

"Yes, daddy," she sighs.

"I love you, Wren. Forever."

Those words, and probably all of the pregnancy hormones have her drenching my cock in minutes. I wrench two powerful orgasms out of her before I come inside of her, buried deep, just like I did from the first time. Each time wishing I could keep her with me forever.

"I love you too. Forever," she promises me in return.

We started off wrong, but nothing in my life has ever felt more right. Drawn together by hurt and betrayal, but I wouldn't change a thing. In that darkness I found my heart. Turns out I wasn't incapable of love, I was just waiting for Wren.

Epilogue 1
WREN

A lot can change in a year.

If someone had told me I'd be standing here rocking my little girl, married to my soul mate, I'd have laughed.

It's been a whole year since that wretched night when I caught Liam and my former best friend in the back of his car.

I never could have predicted that night would send me running into the arms of the one man I thought hated me more than anyone else. The one man who has become the center of my world, and given me everything I've ever wanted.

"Are you ready Mrs. Hale?" Griffin asks me.

I blink to clear the fog of lust that came over me. Griffin in a suit is second only to seeing all those delicious muscles without a stitch of clothing.

"Are you okay?" he asks confused.

I nod my head. He holds out his hands. "Give me my little princess. She wants her daddy."

"I want her daddy too," I mumble.

He flashes me a smirk. "Oh, you'll be getting plenty

from me later, wife." He uses his free hand to swat my ass. "How else am I going to knock you up again?"

I clear my throat. "About that." Digging through my purse I pull out a pregnancy test.

He whoops, and our daughter cracks open one green eye. She's a carbon copy of me, and I hope this next little one will look just like their daddy.

"Shh, Parker, daddy's got you," he croons when it looks like she's going to start wailing.

As she always does when he's holding her, she settles down. His arms are our safe place, and I count my blessings to be taking this journey with him.

Her name is another gift from my thoughtful husband. I confided in him why I never changed my last name. I didn't want to lose the last connection I had to my parents, but Griffin wouldn't stand for me not taking his name. Instead he asked me if we could name our peanut Parker. Now my parents will still be honored every day, and the three of us will share the same name.

He cradles her with one arm effortlessly, and wraps his other one around me. He kisses me on the side of the head. "I love you, baby bird. Thank you for our family."

I start to choke up, until he continues talking. "I'm still going to fuck you like a slut later tonight," he whispers in my ear.

Rolling my eyes, I playfully swat him in the chest. "You're awful."

His hand drops down and he squeezes my ass. "You love it. And I love knocking you up. Can't get out of practice, we need at least one more."

I've accused him of joking in the past, but he probably is already planning when he can get me pregnant again after this one. Turns out my husband has a bit of a breeding kink along with all of his other kinks. And he's right, I love every moment in his dominant embrace.

Parker sighs and stares up at her daddy. It's her favorite thing to do. She's only a few months old, but she already shows more awareness than the books say she's supposed to. Griffin says she's going to be a genius like her mom. I'm far from being a genius, but with his help I am graduating in one more semester. It helps that she was born during the summer so I didn't miss any classes.

I've picked up my role as office manager for both locations. It's a lot of work, but I get to spend my entire day with my family. I couldn't have dreamed for a better job, or a better life for that matter.

"Are you ready to go see your brother?" he asks Parker.

I smile at him. It took months for Liam to come around, but it turns out the thing he feared most, becoming a father, was the best thing to ever happen to him. He would slay dragons for his daughter, and I know he'll keep fighting his demons for her too.

Audrey took off shortly after their daughter was born, leaving Liam to take care of little Natalie on his own. He finally took his sobriety seriously, and is now a dedicated father. He stepped up and works with Charlie at the first shop. Without his mother, or Natalie's in the picture, Liam found himself turning to the one person who's always been there for him. Griffin helped show him how to change diapers, get her through her first fever, and how to enjoy the chaos.

Tonight we're celebrating Liam's six months of sobriety. He hadn't wanted to make a big deal out of it, but Griffin insisted. "Learn from my mistakes son. Don't put yourself last. You have to be strong and proud to be a single father. You've come a long way, and it hasn't been easy. Learn to celebrate yourself too."

It's a small gathering at Griffin's old house, that Liam is renting from his dad. Actually, he's buying it from him directly. I'm glad he'll be surrounded by reminders of his childhood. I can't imagine a better example to follow than Griffin's on how to be a good father.

Liam joins me at the small buffet we've set up for our friends. He smiles at me without anger or resentment. "How are you doing?"

"Really good. How's Natalie?"

He smirks at me. "She's great. She's been asking about her grandma Wren."

I roll my eyes. "She doesn't even talk yet, ass."

He flips the chip in his hands. Then his look becomes serious. "I'm sorry for how I treated you. I know I fucked up when I lost you, but I'm happy to see you smile. The two of you are good together. It's strange, not going to lie, and I'm never going to call you mom, but—"

"Please don't. That would be too weird," I rush out.

He gives me the side eye. "Not as weird as hearing you call my dad, *daddy*."

Embarrassment heats my cheeks as I remember the day Griffin swore we had enough time for a quickie before Charlie and Liam came with the moving truck. "You were not supposed to walk in on that."

"Lucky for everyone I was already in therapy. I'll send my dad the bill for the hours dedicated to that lovely experience. Joking aside, I want you to know you didn't do anything wrong. I left you alone for too long." His eyes drop to my wrist, and I can see him fighting his emotions. "I'm so damn sorry."

I put my hand on his arm. "I forgive you. I never thought I would, but if you hadn't done that, I'd never be where I am now. And I can't imagine my life without him."

"Without who?" Griffin asks, and drops his arm around my shoulders.

Liam shakes his head, a grin pulling at his mouth. "Calm down caveman. I'm not flirting with your woman."

Griffin grunts. Things are better between them, but Griffin is still a jealous and possessive beast.

"I'm just making amends. I've owed Wren an apology for a long time. You too, dad. Thank you for not giving up on me."

"Being a parent is the hardest job you'll ever do, but it's worth it. I love you son, but stay away from my wife."

"She was my wife first," Liam says. I know he's joking. They seem to relish teasing each other about our odd triangle. I could live without it, but our past is what it is. We can't change it, and I wouldn't. Laughing is a much better alternative to yelling, so I'll live with it.

I loved Liam once, but now I know it was young love. It was never meant to last, and we were just too stubborn to see that when we were teenagers. But, it brought Griffin into my life, so I'd go through all the bumps again to be where I am.

"Yeah, well I'm the one who is giving her babies," Griffin grumbles, and then smiles.

Liam's eyes widen, and I know we're going to be okay when his face lights up. "Really? Again?"

Griffin smiles and nods.

"Can I have a brother this time, mom?" Liam teases me.

I slap him on the arm. "The two of you are too much."

Charlie saunters over with Natalie in his arms. "This little one is a chick magnet. She's even better than you were, Liam."

"Stop using my daughter to pick up chicks," Liam chides, but there's no heat in his words.

He takes Natalie from him. Charlie just reaches out for Parker. "You'll help uncle Charlie meet women, won't you, angel?"

"C'mon, Liam. Let me introduce you to the new Kindergarten teacher. She loves babies, and she's got kind of a naughty librarian vibe."

"I thought you were interested in Wren's aunt?" Liam asks, confused.

Charlie winks at me before turning back to Liam. "Oh, I am. I don't want you to be a grouchy old bastard like your dad was for so long. We need to get you a woman. This little angel is going to go say hi to aunt Hattie and help uncle Charlie make that shit official."

The two of them stroll off, scheming as usual. I groan when they're out of earshot. "That's what we need, more tangled webs in this family."

Griffin grabs my hand. "C'mon, we have time for a quickie while he's got Parker."

"That's what you said about the day we moved into our new house," I groan.

He smirks at me, his eyes glittering with amusement. "And yet you're still following me."

"Haven't you figured out by now? I'll follow you anywhere," I promise him.

His eyes heat. "Good, so follow me into the woods, baby bird. Daddy needs some attention."

Just as I said that day in the storage closet, the day that sealed my fate, "Yes, daddy."

Griffin hums in approval. "Good girl."

Epilogue 2
GRIFFIN

"Don't you think a bouncy house was a bit much?" Wren asks me.

I grimace. "If you think that was too much, then you're really going to lose your shit over the pony."

Her eyes widen. "A pony? You rented a pony?"

I shrug. "Rent, buy. Semantics."

"You bought her a pony?" she shrieks.

"My little princess is ten today. How many times is that going to happen?" Yes, I spoil my baby girl rotten. There were so many things I couldn't do for Liam when he was little, and I love spoiling them, so I do.

Wren's business acumen has Hale and Storm Automotive doing better than we ever imagined. Julio took over the Harriston location and runs it with his high school best friend, and now husband. They got married a couple years ago, and adopted a little boy.

Centralia is a more urban location, and with it comes a different clientele. Turns out there's a lot of demand to customize cars. So much so that Charlie and Liam moved their families here and we're all back together again.

Wren even expanded our lobby to a full scale coffee shop, and now we are never short on business. College students come in for anything from oil changes to custom wraps. Last week I turned a truck pink and glittery. I hated every minute of it, but the reigning rodeo queen loved her new rig. All that new business, along with the merchandise line Wren developed, means my princess gets a pony.

"What about when the boys turn ten?" There's a hint of fear in her voice.

"Dirt bikes." I nod. My boys won't be missing out.

Our nine-year-old twins run past us, and I manage to scoop up Clark before he gets away. "Hey little man, where's the fire?"

"Liam is home!" he shouts, as his little legs continue trying to run in the air.

"Lemme down dad! Logan is going to get to hold the baby first."

I thought raising one son was hard. My twin boys are holy terrors, and I love every minute.

I put him on his feet and he races off to see his big brother come over with his wife and their new baby, Griffin.

That kindergarten teacher, Claudia, that Charlie insisted Liam meet, really did love babies. After dating for two years, they got married and had another little girl a year-and-a-half later. This one is their only son, and all the kids love to take turns holding him. Audrey never came back, and eventually signed away her parental rights so Claudia could adopt Natalie.

Our old patterns are broken after all. My grandchildren will grow up in a house with two parents, and Liam no longer looks at Wren like losing her was his greatest mistake. Thank fuck for that. Being jealous of my son got old long before she was mine, I don't handle it well now that she is. I guess I am a bit of a caveman after all.

Charlie is no longer the most infamous bachelor around. He set his sights on Hattie and now he no longer has to satisfy his parental longings by taking my kids. Although he still relishes being their favorite uncle. The best part is he no longer gives me shit for preferring to stay home with my wife.

Natalie and Parker walk through the party holding hands with Morgan and Anna, Charlie and Hattie's girls. Natalie is a few months older than Parker, and I may have made sure there were two ponies in the stable between our houses. Wren will get over it as long as I am the one who cleans out the stalls.

Liam and Claudia live on one side of our house and Charlie and Hattie have the one on the other side. Since most of the kids are only a few years apart, they spend a lot of time running back and forth.

The boys run past again, this time they're joined by Bess and Donovan's son, Jack. He's a year younger than them, but the three of them are thick as thieves. With Wren's help Donovan expanded his business to a new location up here as well, and now we're surrounded by family, both those by blood and by choice.

Life is fucking fantastic. Wren and I were both lonely people longing for family, and now we've got a full house. The sound of kids running and playing is the best sound in the world.

"Isn't it grand?" Dolores strolls in with her cane. At ninety-three she's slowed down a little, but the cane is the only visible concession she's given to aging. Her kids finally convinced her to sell her big house, after she fell one day while Bess was working. She discovered the retirement village here in Centralia is actually a fun place to be. I swear she's got a more active social life than the rest of us.

"Hello, Dolores," I say and bend down to kiss her wrinkled cheek.

She pats me on the face. "Aren't you glad that old house had pests?"

I laugh. "You're the only pest I know of in that old place."

She harrumphs. "I'm old, I've earned the right to meddle. Besides, how else was I going to get more grand babies?"

"Hey, it's granny D!" Bess shouts.

"Looks like you adopted all the ones your kids didn't give you," I point out.

Dolores nods. Proud of herself, as she should be.

"Hello Rainbow Brite. How are all my grand babies?"

Hearing her voice all the children swarm her, and each of them calls her granny D like aunt Bess.

Wren rushes over and gets wrapped in a fierce hug. Dolores is freakishly strong for an old woman. Probably because she's taken over our yard so she could still have her flowers.

"There's my beautiful girl," Dolores says to her.

"I got some more flowers from the nursery the other day," Wren tells her, and they stroll off to plan even more gardens.

I look around at all the people gathered in our backyard. Once we were all just existing. Wren struggling with Liam's coldness, Dolores mourning the husband she lost too soon, Charlie trying to find happiness in the bed of every woman he met, Bess looking for a best friend to accept her brightness without trying to dim her shine, and me damned to want the one woman I shouldn't. Piece by piece we came together all because of the woman who owns my heart. She still doesn't fully grasp how important she is to all of us, but I try to show her every day. Not once has the darkness come back into her eyes, and I'll spend the rest of my life making sure it never does again.

It's an exhausting and wonderful day, but damn am I glad when everyone goes home and all the kids are in bed. I love being with our family, but my favorite moments are still the ones I get to spend alone with my baby bird.

Wren joins me on the back porch after the chaos of putting three kids to bed is over. She sighs and looks wistfully at the fireflies lighting up the sky.

I brush her hair, once again a sandy blonde, behind her ear. "What's on your mind, baby bird?"

She smiles, there's some nostalgia and a little sadness in it. "How fast it all goes. They were all babies a minute ago, and now they're these little people with their own hopes and dreams."

"To be fair, Logan wants to be a superhero, so we've still got time with them as little ones," I comfort her.

"I know, I just miss having babies," she sighs.

She swore we were done after finding out about the twins. I respected her decision, but I hoped maybe she'd change her mind. She's only thirty-four, plenty young to have another baby if she wanted. I certainly love giving them to her.

"If you want another one, I'm game," I tell her.

"You've already got four. How many do you need?"

I smirk at her. "How many are you willing to give me?"

"You're kidding, right?" But she's breathless, definitely considering it.

"You know how much I like being called daddy," I whisper to her.

Her hand goes to her throat, and I can't wait to replace it with mine.

"Run, baby bird. I'm in the mood to catch you."

She doesn't wait to be told twice. At least now when she runs from me it's only for fun, and I don't hesitate to chase after her. Never again will she go without me being right behind her.

Life, parenthood, and all the responsibilities of life haven't slowed us down. I love my children to the moon, but my baby bird is still my sun, the center of my existence.

I catch her like I always do, and though she loves hearing me tell her how much I love her, she understands I'm a man of action more than words. When I catch her I show her with my entire being that I'll love and worship her forever.

For once, two wrongs made everything right.

Acknowledgments

Hemingway is often quoted as having said, "There is nothing to writing. All you do is sit down at a typewriter and bleed." The instruments we use to write has changed since his time, but the sentiment is much the same.

Each time I write a book I spill a lot of my heart and personal trauma inside. Some people might dismiss romance, but for me this book is a lot more than a steamy taboo romance. This was a way to exorcise demons I've let live in my head for far too long.

Not all abuse leads to bruises. Some wounds are only found deep in your soul. While this is a work of fiction, I know what it's like to live through an emotionally abusive marriage. If you are experiencing any of the things Wren did in Two Wrongs, know that it is not your fault, and there is help.

First if you suspect a loved one, or even yourself needs help for substance abuse please reach out. In the United States you can call the SAMHSA National Helpline at 1-800-662-4357 to find resources in your area. If you are thinking of hurting yourself please call the National Suicide Hotline at 988.

I wouldn't be where I am today without my family and friends. My mother is always my rock, thank you for supporting me no matter what I choose to do, and agreeing not to read my books.

Fawn Sanchez, the best friend I could have ever asked

for. Who knew that awful English class would lead to twenty plus years of friendship?

My son, Luke, who will never read this, thank you for inspiring me to be better. For you I will always strive to move mountains.

My brother Tommy and sister Catalina, thank you both for always entertaining my crazy ideas and being my partners in crime.

To Renee Ericson for having the ability to read my mind and give me the most beautiful covers. Here's to ten more years!

All my author friends who are always around to help me out of a plot hole or give me a shoulder. Especially Debbie McQueen aka Duckie Mack. Thank you for always having my back and cheering me on.

Thanks to my ARC team for always being eager for my newest release and to Carrillo's Crew for keeping me entertained.

Brooke Black aka Brooke_and_Books, thank you for encouraging me when I told you what I was working on, and for spreading the word about this book. Also, just thank you for your endless support of the book community.

Thanks to my team: Lydia Harbaugh, Lori Rivera and Linnea Valle for keeping me on task, and helping me when I have imposter syndrome.

And finally thanks to Tracy Black and Tammy Manning for being the best alpha readers I could hope for.

About the Author

Kimberly Carrillo is a storyteller from the Pacific Northwest, currently living in a small town with her teenage son and a house full of pets. The author of the romantic suspense Destroy Series, and other books, Kimberly writes tales of beautiful, messy love. When she isn't reading or out supporting her son at sports events she can be found moving a cat off her keyboard so she can help the heroine find the love that she deserves.

Playlist

- Lose Somebody by OneRepublic and Kygo
- Break My Baby by Kaleo
- Breakeven by The Script
- Let's Hurt Tonight by OneRepublic
- The Mess I Made by Parachute
- Flowers by Miley Cyrus
- Hey Jealousy by Gin Blossoms
- Happier Than Ever by Billie Eilish
- I'm Not The Only One by Sam Smith
- Hold My Hand by The Fray
- Rescue Me by OneRepublic
- Love Don't Die by The Fray

Also by Kimberly Carrillo

Thank you for reading. Please take a moment to leave a review/rating on the platform of your choice (Amazon, Goodreads, or Bookbub). That is the greatest support an author can hope for.

Destroy Series (Available on KU)

Self Destruct

Destroy Me

Destroy You

Stand Alone Novels

Hunting Butterflies

Two Wrongs

Business and Pleasure Series (Available on KU)

Beck and Call

The Acquisition

The Merger

Pretty Monsters Trilogy (Available on KU)

Pretty Monsters

Perfect Sin

Peaceful Chaos

Want to receive bonus content? Join my newsletter to see Pretty Monsters' Sin and Raven's Wedding from Sin's POV:

Pretty Monsters Bonus Scene

Made in the USA
Coppell, TX
25 May 2023